BöDER
the GIANT

T.J.C.

BALBOA.
PRESS

A DIVISION OF HAY HOUSE

Balboa Press books may be ordered through booksellers or by contacting:

Balboa Press
A Division of Hay House
1663 Liberty Drive
Bloomington, IN 47403
www.balboapress.com.au
1 (877) 407-4847

Because of the dynamic nature of the Internet, any web addresses or links contained in this book may have changed since publication and may no longer be valid. The views expressed in this work are solely those of the author and do not necessarily reflect the views of the publisher, and the publisher hereby disclaims any responsibility for them.

The author of this book does not dispense medical advice or prescribe the use of any technique as a form of treatment for physical, emotional, or medical problems without the advice of a physician, either directly or indirectly. The intent of the author is only to offer information of a general nature to help you in your quest for emotional and spiritual well-being. In the event you use any of the information in this book for yourself, which is your constitutional right, the author and the publisher assume no responsibility for your actions.

Print information available on the last page.

ISBN: 978-1-5043-0100-8 (sc)
ISBN: 978-1-5043-0101-5 (e)

Balboa Press rev. date: 02/02/2016

DEDICATION

First of all I would like to dedicate every single story I ever write about 'Böder the giant' to Jamilla my daughter. She is the primary inspiration for helping me take this character from out of her bedtime stories and placing him into the first of many books about this fascinating giant.

(Also my mom – but I gotta say that!)

Chapter One

EARLICH

I remember, quite distinctly, the very first time that my master and I heard about Böder --- the giant. We were on our maiden business journey sailing against the current up the mighty river Dund towards Katra, (*the city of islands*) some three weeks travel by boat from Candare. The reason for this trip, as I recall, was that my employer, Tor Jellick – 'Master Merchant' and trading authority for the house of Conagger -- was to meet up with some fellow merchants in Katra. Through this meeting Tor Jellick was hoping to build up his trade contacts in the south.

After hearing the initial story about this most fascinating character, Tor Jellick gave me specific instructions to begin keeping a diligent record of all that was to be said, all that was experienced, and all that we saw in the future concerning Böder – 'the giant'.

The following accounts then are the comprehensive adventures, stories and personal encounters both Jellick and I have had with Böder, as accumulated, told and directed by Jellick and recorded by your humble servant -- Earlich prima scribe from the house of Gordesh and cleric to my Tor Jellick.

JELLICK

My record of Böder began in the year 286 according to the birth of Tordan (*king*) Frahq:

It was in the season of our summer as known in the land of M'Lenn-Fida. The crops were fully ripened and the harvesting had just begun. We had been aboard a large river boat called the *Riverrock*, for nearly thirteen days, bound for the city of Katra. The strong south easterly winds originating at the base of the Scintaire and Sehold Mountains had come rushing untroubled across the flat pasturelands of the southern provinces of Entarim. These warm winds had filled our sails almost from the moment we had pushed off.

It was mid-morning upon the Dund River; the sun was shining through a dappling of bushy white clouds in an otherwise clear blue sky. I was on the port (*left hand*) side of the *Riverrock* watching the far river bank passing slowly by. Since first light, it had been covered with a dark green hedge of dense wild under brush broken up by the occasional tall bush or overhanging tree. Above the river border lay a low greenish-blue smear of distant mountains. As I looked out across the sluggish brown water, I noticed what looked to me to be a large secondary river entering the Dund. As I watched the two rivers merge with mild interest, I heard Captain Stemm (*a tall, strong Ottarman*) yell out, "All hands stand alert! Eddron, (*who is Captain Stemm's cousin and first mate*) steer the vessel toward the closer shore!"

This I saw immediately was away from the new river. I was a bit concerned about this action and as the captain was standing close by, I asked him why he was steering us clear of this new river.

"That's not a new river, good, Jellick", he replied. "That's the Dund coming back on itself after going around the Black Island!"

"But that's a huge river island!" I exclaimed, half to myself, and stared in amazement at the enormous land mass looming up towards us. "So tell me captain, why are we avoiding the waters meeting?" I asked, thinking it might be because of turbulent waters or some other river related hazard.

"Oh we aren't avoiding the waters meeting. We are sailing wide of the Black Island because that is where Böder lives."

At these words of foreboding, I looked with renewed interest at the island as the vastness of the island slowly became apparent. We drew level with the dark shoreline of the Black Island and I could see that it stretched away into the distance. I looked up the length of the far section of the river but a bend in the Dund prevented me from seeing just how long the island really was. I pondered this for a moment and then I turned to Captain Stemm and asked.

"What is this Böder that you would steer us wide to avoid him like this, Captain Stemm?"

"I take it you have never heard of Böder then?" Captain Stemm asked, looking closely at me. My puzzled expression must have been enough for the Captain because he continued without my prompting.

"Böder is a ten meter tall giant. He is horrible to behold with a mean disposition a formidable appetite and an unquenchable thirst. For instance he has been known to eat a whole field of corn or grain and then gone on to rip cattle and other stock apart, eating them raw whilst they are still struggling in their death throes. After this base feasting he has gone on to consume several full vats of either wine or beer or whatever is at hand and all this, it has been told, has occurred in just one of his times of gorging!

"The stories surrounding Böder have told us that after years of putting up with his gorging and rampaging on their lands, several farming communities decided to end Böders marauding permanently. They banded together -- and led by a manimal who went by the name of 'Jack the giant killer' -- they conspired to track him down and deal with this overlarge pest. When this angry mob finally confronted him, Böder, spurred on by anger and irritation responded with violent force! He fought the mob like a vicious creature -- you know, a 'trapped in a corner kind of wild animal'. In the ensuing fight, at least thirty manimals were injured and four were killed, before Böder, bloodied and bruised, was finally subdued and bound.

"There was a brief counsel between the elders and governors from the represented communities. At first the mob were calling out for the death of Böder, but their leader Jack, surprisingly enough, came out in support of this giant and recommended leniency from them all. The elders took a little time before, after some wise and some say sensible counsel; they decided that Böder should be banished from the mainland forever. With this decision made, Jack was nominated to take Böder across the river and condemn him to live the remainder of his life on that island alone!"

"Why didn't they just kill him and be done with him?" I asked.

"That's a good question, but one I am unable to answer for I too have asked that question on a number of occasions. However, as I was not present at the meeting and the sources of my story have never filled me in with an adequate answer, I remain like you - ignorant of such details!"

"So why did they put him on this island then?" I persisted.

"All I know is they wanted to exile Böder permanently without killing him. But they wanted to send him to a place where they knew he would never be able to return from. Now it is well known that Böder was -- and still is -- deathly afraid of water. As a result of this fear of water this rocky island was found to be ideal for the purpose of holding Böder in exile. The waters of the Dund are both treacherous and deep and the shoreline is far enough away, so that even a giant of Böders strength and size is prevented from jumping or fording the river. Also, this island, as you can see, is large enough to support the needs of a single giant, and, even more importantly, it needs no guard or monitoring to ensure this overlarge creature remains in permanent exile. Thus the communities on both sides of the river are safe from Böder ever harassing them again!"

I pondered for a moment or two upon that statement -- 'the island was large enough to support the needs of a giant!' But then another thought came to me and took my questioning in a different direction.

"Why then, if this giant is frightened of water, are we steering as far from the island as we can? Are you frightened he might leap from the cliffs and try and take control of this vessel?"

"No I don't fear him trying to board us. But he has been known, on numerous occasions to bombard river craft with large stones and rocks from the tops of the cliffs. He hurls them at any and all vessels found passing too close to his island! Sometimes he wraps the rocks in dry vines and leaves and lights them on fire so that when they land on the boats they start fires and inflict great damage and injuries to those on board!"

As Captain Stemm finished his brief tale about the giant, he excused himself from my presence and went to take stock of some navigational matter, leaving me to my thoughts by the ships rail. I looked out again over the muddy river at the island with renewed interest as a trickle of sweaty fear made its way from the nape of my neck down the length of my spine and I shivered despite the warmth of the sun.

Despite being nearly two kilometers away, it suddenly seemed to be dark and foreboding. All the sides were steep cliffs like the walls of a fortress, which jutted tens of meters out and upwards above the surface of the river. The makeup of the island itself seemed to be of a dark rock, not unlike that of volcanic rock and ash. I began to ponder the origins of the island and decided from the mountainous terrain and the harsh shoreline that it must have, at one time, been an active volcano -- maybe even several volcanoes, judging from the three distinct peaks near the middle of the island. It took us over an hour to completely sail past the Black Island. This made its size enormous by any river island standard.

As the Black Island slowly diminished towards the horizon, I considered carefully all that I had heard, and I kept coming back to the perplexing fact that this all consuming giant should be found in so isolated a situation. And then a long forgotten thought made its way into my mind at that very moment and I realised with growing interest that we could very well become mutually beneficial to one another! I decided then and there, on that very boat, sailing against the current of the mighty river Dund towards the city of Katra, to find out as much as I could about this giant called Böder.

I called my scribe Earlich, *(a tall and handsome Weasalman of excellent education and good standing)*, over to me. I then instructed him to begin keeping a diligent record of all matters concerning Böder, "starting," I said, "with the conversation I have just had with, Stemm, captain and master of the *Riverrock!*"

At our next port of call, the large river village of Bernitz, I asked Stemm to allow me some time to spend in the village on the pretext of looking for some stock and merchandise as best suited my purpose. Then we, Earlich, Traxxa *(one of my most trusted guardsmen)* and I ventured into the village. At a small tavern I sat with them both and outlined to Traxxa exactly what I wanted from him whilst I continued on my journey to Katra.

"I want you to stay behind in this village and find out all that there is to know about this giant Böder -- his situation, his island, his exile, and the general feeling towards him by the people living locally and along the riverbank. Furthermore I want you to find out all that you can about the one they call Jack the giant killer! His real name for instance, where he came from, where he is today and what he is doing even now. But I'd like you to be discreet. Ask and enquire all you like, just do it tactfully and without drawing attention to yourself."

Traxxa nodded his head knowingly, but made no comment, he simply waited for further instructions!

"Finally -- and this is perhaps more important than anything else -- I want you to set up a way for me to meet with this Böder character. If the only way for me to do this is to travel to the Black Island then I will leave you to make the necessary arrangements. Is that understood, Traxxa??"

Seeing the nod and understanding in Traxxa's eyes, I placed a small pouch on the table, which he quickly secreted into the folds of his tunic without a second glance at it.

"Here is some slev (*the silver standard and main coinage of Durogg at the time*) to help you in your time here!" I said quietly. "I estimate, with the travel time along the river and the concluding of my business in Katra I should be back here in about two to three weeks. However, as we must allow for some unforeseen events I would like you to have everything ready for me in say, about a months' time. Is that clear?"

Again Traxxa nodded his head. However with a bit of prompting from me I had him go over, in his own words, all that he had to do whilst he remained on his own here in Bernitz. I nodded in satisfaction when he had finished at which point we stood up and grasped each others' wrist and shook them just the once. Upon releasing our mutual grip we turned and left the tavern together as one. Once outside, Earlich and I parted company from Traxxa. We made our way back down the streets of Bernitz towards the Dund where Captain Stemm had the *Riverrock* moored in patient preparation for continuing our journey to Katra.

EARLICH

When we were halfway down the street, I remember turning around to look back. I watched as Traxxa moved off easily and confidently in search of some suitable accommodation from which to begin his investigation into this giant called Böder.

CHAPTER TWO

EARLICH

The next time my Tor Jellick and I had anything more to do with Böder was two days short of four weeks after leaving Traxxa in Bernitz. Tor Jellick had successfully completed all his business dealings in Katra, and I noted that he was extremely pleased with himself and the way things had gone. We were still aboard the *Riverrock*, but this time Captain Stemm had us sailing much faster as we flowed with the Dund's current northwards. As we came around a bend in the nearly three-kilometer wide river we could on the distant horizon the dark shadowy peaks of the Black Island. Just then Captain Stemm spotted a slipstream breaking away from the main flow of the Dund on the port side and without hesitation he steered us into it. This slipstream took us towards an inlet which led directly towards a small bay. Tor Jellick and I were at the bow of the craft when this was taking place and we could see Traxxa waiting patiently for us on the dock along the foreshore.

Traxxa is a gaunt Wolfaman *(I believe from the Timber clan)* with a slight build but who is remarkably strong, with wiry, muscular arms and legs. In his flat sole breakaway boots he stands a little over two meters tall. His pale grey skin and deep sunk crystal blue/grey eyes, framed as it were, by his scraggly beard and his long, braided, tawny gold hair made him look almost anaemic and sick. But he is far from sick -- in fact he is fanatically healthy, extremely fast and very resourceful.

I personally have seen him a number of times meet with bigger and more violent adversaries than himself in battle and often times there has been more than one aggressor and on each occasion he has come out triumphantly with barely a scratch on himself. In point of fact, at each encounter, I have seen an unflinching, highly competent and efficient fighting warrior who has dealt with these problems of conflict with cold, calculating and often brutal efficiency. He seems to have a kind of fluid movement about him, like that of an experienced dancer so that whilst he is extremely fast, he is also well balanced and highly competent in handling most forms of weaponry. Moreover he is also an accomplished horseman and from what little I have seen of him upon the water, he appears to be equally capable of understanding and handling most watercraft.

In my brief talks with him, he informed me that he was originally from Frowash. However he had been banished from there due to some tribal feud or other. In any case he had been personally involved and this had somehow threatened the leadership of one of the larger regions. So he had been forced to flee with just the clothes on his back – which, as I see it, didn't amount to much. Frowash is one of the coldest of the far northern countries on the mainland of Durogg. So any of the countries south of the Sehold Mountains are always too warm for Traxxa, which explains, in part, why he continually seems to be dressed efficiently frugally, sometimes embarrassingly so.

But Tor Jellick doesn't seem to notice or mind at all and so I shouldn't either, really! And yet, on the other hand, Tor Jellick himself is a masterful dresser, combining silks with leather and lace and scarves with cottons and colours. He always looks so stylish and in control regardless of his apparel. In fact, now that I think about it, Tor Jellick makes whatever he is wearing look good!

Me; on the other hand, I attract dirt and filth like a magnet which tends to help me remain extremely conservative. I can be in a dirt free room and still come out with stains and shirt edge sweat and grime. Still, what can you expect from a scribe, for mink's sake? But I digress!

Getting back to Traxxa though. After proving himself again and again on his journey with us, he has become one of Tor Jellick's most trusted guardsman. As for me, despite his time with us and his proven abilities and loyalty, I still don't feel completely comfortable around Traxxa – but that's probably because he's made me realize just how inadequate I really am beside him.

And of course this is without him even trying and certainly not because he has seen me privately comparing myself to him.

(Deep sigh!)

JELLICK

Traxxa was waiting for us on the dock as the *Riverrock* pulled into the bay of Bernitz. After a brief exchange of reacquainting pleasantries, Traxxa turned and together with Earlich beside me, we followed him up the rock and dirt path which led towards the heart of the large river town. We returned to the small tavern where we had last sat and talked with him almost four weeks earlier. It had a comfortable, rustic look about it and was a short way down from the main town square. Once inside, Traxxa led us into an intimate room at the back where there was a large table laden with food and drink. It was only when we were seated and had begun eating that Traxxa told us of all that had occurred during his time alone.

"After you left, I made discreet enquiries as you directed about the giant at a number of places in and around Bernitz starting of course with this tavern!" Here he paused for a time as though considering carefully what exactly he wanted to say.

"Before I begin, do you know anything about the 'rule of the dragons' or the 'time of the giants'?" He asked quietly.

Earlich and I looked at each other and we acknowledged that we knew a little of the history concerning both dragons and giants. But realizing that I was unsure of what specifically he was drawing our attention to, I encouraged Traxxa to continue his tale.

"Well, as you may or may not know, when the dragons ruled the skies, during the early years of Frahqs' reign, this great tordan of the southern empire helped organize the petulant wizards to work with the wayward giants. Together they effectively destroyed all traces of the dragons known throughout the lands of Durogg and brought their rule to a close. The few remaining dragons that survived this onslaught, it is said, were last seen fleeing east beyond the Gloas Wastelands into and beyond the Dark Mountains. This, of course, is common knowledge concerning our history. However, what many people aren't aware of is that once the dragons were destroyed or banished and their rule had ended, it was the giants who began to take over and threatened to run riot without any authority to keep them in check.

But this time of the giants, was also short lived when a number of wizards and magic wielders banded together, and once more, under the guidance and leadership of Frahq -- bound up the giants' leaders and are credited with tricking the remaining giants into leaving Durogg as well. There was great confusion and uncertainty during this time as a temporary power vacuum began to form in the aftermath and a great chaos threatened to reign in its place throughout the central lands.

"This too ended swiftly when Frahq and his warrior Tors once again helped restore order and peace throughout Durogg. They did this by encouraging the Tordans and local Tors of influence, within the recognized lands and countries of Durogg, to re-establish their right to rule in their own lands.

"That however is another long and arduous story! But the point I wish to bring to your attention is this; despite being completely vanquished, there remained a few peaceful giants who were too tired, too old or simply refused to run away from the central lands. They did however recognize they were in great danger so those who remained behind quickly disappeared from view and chose to settle down in the wilds living in quiet seclusion dotted throughout the many lands of Durogg. The majority of these giants were allowed to live like this under strict terms and conditions which were monitored and controlled by the surrounding communities. The main conditions were that they weren't allowed to meet with each other or interfere adversely with the surrounding communities.

"I give you this brief history to help you understand how Böder fits into this picture. The story that I was told by the people of Bernitz is that, nearly twenty years ago, in a region to the north and east of here, a number of giants were found to be living closer to one another than the villagers and townspeople around about them would have liked. In effect they considered them to be a real threat. And the fears of the townsfolk were soon realized when some of these giants started to become unruly and unmanageable. A reward was made available to help subdue the few remaining marauding or troublesome giants that hadn't settled down completely. Then along came a young man, who, it is said, helped get rid of three cantankerous giants all by himself in one day and his reputation as a giant killer was established and he became known as Jack the Giant Killer!

"Continuing on from that time, about seven years ago, a number of local farming communities near here asked this very same Jack to come and help them get rid of a young adolescent giant who had suddenly become troublesome. That giant was of course Böder!"

"Troublesome, how do you mean troublesome?"

"Apparently he had been quiet and docile for a good while when something happened and, almost overnight, he changed dramatically. Some say that this change came about because he had reached puberty and was struggling to cope with the changes in his growing body. In any event, he decided to stand against the surrounding communities and began his rebellion by destroying fields, killing and eating animal stocks and draining the casks of both wine and ale from the private stores of farmers and inns and ale houses!"

"And how did they get Böder to go and live on the Black Island?"

"One day, it seems that Jack caught Böder after he had consumed a number of casks of ale in the yard of this town's main tavern in fact. Böder was sleeping off his huge drinking bout, and after consulting with the town elders, Jack was granted the permission he needed not to kill Böder but rather to exile him to the island!"

"But why didn't they just kill Böder and be done with him?"

"I had to ask that question a number of times before I got a satisfactory answer!"

"Which was?"

"Well apparently there is a prophecy -- or, at the very least a great fear, that one day some dragons might return to the central lands of Durogg. It is suspected that if they were to return and met with no real resistance they might very easily try and re-establish their time as Tors of these lands once more; especially as there would be no giants around willing to help defend the land or fight for the people and of course there are no magic wielders to maintain control over the giants!"

"What, so they wanted to imprison this giant, but not kill him, just in case the dragons returned - is that it?"

Traxxa nodded his head. "Pretty much!"

11

"Well I guess it makes sense to contain Böder and at the same time keep him out of their way!"

"Yes, I asked about this island prison, and apparently the young giant is unsure of water -- maybe even frightened of it. He either doesn't have the skill to build a boat or considers the river to be too fast or too deep for him to even try and get off the island without assistance. So he has been stuck out there for the last seven years now!"

There was a pause between myself and Traxxa before I asked the all important question.

"By what means, or rather, what do you believe is the best way to approach and get close to this formidable giant?

Traxxa thought for a moment and then continued.

"Well, I was told that Jack, with the help of all the villagers of course, put Böder into a boat whilst he was still sleeping off his alcohol induced condition and took him over to the Black Island. Eerily enough neither the boat nor Jack has ever returned. After a couple of months a small search party went over to the Black Island only to discover that Böder was stronger and angrier than ever. The search party was dismantled in a surprisingly quick and efficient manner and a number of the party were killed. Those who escaped with their lives had horrible stories to tell of Böder hunting them, stalking them and threatening to kill them with the supposed intention of eating them alive.

"I found, after further investigation, that many of the stories and supposed deeds of this giant's ferocity and propensity to kill have, as far as I can tell, not been entirely accurate. That is, whilst they haven't deliberately made things up or lied about him and his stories, they have, however, been exaggerated in a number of different ways in order to help keep Böder where he is and deter any would be sightseers from going out to try and meet with him on his island.

"Still, despite the search parties' harrowing experience upon the island, many hunters and adventurers seem not to care one way or the other whether there is a giant living on the island or not. It had been known for a long time, previous to Böder being banished there, that the boar and deer on the Black Island produced some of the best meat and hunting throughout all the known lands in the north of Durogg. Now however, since Böder has been on the island, the intensity of the hunt has increased with the added dimension, of being pursued by a fierce and angry giant. The risk, it is said, is that once Böder becomes aware there are hunters about, he quickly sets out to try and scare them or chase them from his island. And of course if that fails, he just continues hunting them down in order to capture or kill them and it has been told that on one or two rare occasions he has taken to eating them. Everyone I spoke to who has been out there to the Black Island, said the ultimate thrill of the hunt was the moment they realised that they themselves were being hunted by this giant. And yet every one of them also told me they would never do it again, for the risks were just too great.

"So I should just say at this point, all of the hunters said they knew of or had personally lost a member of their hunting party to the hands and mouth of this ferocious giant. And yet parties of hunters still venture over to the island a number of times each year just to hunt Böders deer. However, to limit the risk of being discovered and restrict the number of deaths it has been generally agreed upon that the groups of hunters who go on these Black Island hunts are to be small!"

"So what are you saying?" I asked warily! "That the best way to get taken to the island is to join one of these hunting parties?"

Traxxa nodded his head smiling

"This, I believe, is perhaps the only way to get anyone to take you across to the island without raising the town folk's suspicions as to your true intentions of meeting with Böder. Further to that, I have already taken the step of asking about how and when the next hunting trip is to take place. I was told, the next trip will take place within the next month. There are to be three boats and in each boat there is only enough room for a small party of some five hunters. Due to my proposed interest in the hunt on the island, I have been asked whether I would be interested in making up the numbers on one of the boats. If you want to do this, then it needs to be finalised quickly! But, I should warn you, the trip itself is very costly because of the risk to the boats and the men who are willing to take the hunting parties to the island.

I dismissed the subject of the cost with a wave of my hand, but it was the time I was really concerned about

"A month? Why is the wait so long?" I said a little crestfallen I must confess, as I could see money and opportunity being wasted in the waiting.

"Well, that month was two weeks ago, so now the wait is more like the next two weeks left!"

I considered this for a moment and decided it was worth the wait. After all, there were markets throughout all of Durogg so why not apply my skills and my craft to this large river town whilst I was here.

To conclude the matter decisively, Traxxa and I went straight away to arrange a position on one of the boats destined to go on the hunting trip to the island. We met with a wizened old Ottarman by the name of Frisha, who immediately told us with some pride that he and his boat made the journey to the Black Island at least twice a year. After a brief introduction and an outline of what was expected from each of us, a deal of sorts was agreed upon between the two of us.

Next, I was informed what it would cost to me if I wanted to be included in the hunting party on his boat. I told him I thought the price of inclusion was a bit too high just for the pleasure of hunting deer.

"It is not just for the sport of hunting the deer that you are paying for," replied Frisha evenly. "In fact, if the truth be known, the quality of the deer has deteriorated substantially since the giant has been out there. But this has only been commented on by the hunters during my most recent trips to the island anyway.

"No! The high price, such as it is, isn't even due to the potential risk to my boat or even to myself as its master, of which there is a very real danger. No - the main reason for the high payment is for me, allowing you, the privilege of being part of a once in a lifetime experience. And that is, of hunting game under the watchful eye of one of the most renowned hunters in all the lands of Durogg!"

At this I stopped to ponder this statement. At which point Frisha must have thought I was balking for a reduced fare to the island, as he spoke up quickly, in order to try and seal the deal.

"You must remember good Ser I am the only boatman at this time that has space available for you on his boat for this hunting trip. There will not be another trip to the island for at least another six months. Also you must realize that there are very few boatmen willing to risk their lives and their livelihood in order to take you to the Black Island. Come with me and I promise you two things, provided you make it through a night and a day of hunting on the island. First you will have the experience of a lifetime that has no equal! And second I will be there waiting to bring you back - should you survive that is!"

He smiled broadly as if he had just brought to our attention an amusing fact, one which we hadn't considered or even thought about before. He then waited patiently for us to digest this last bit of information and also allowed us the time to reach the only conclusion that his asking price was more than reasonable.

To be honest the money wasn't a problem at all, so I gave him what he was asking for and more but with a proviso and this was what I told him – "I want to hire your whole boat for just me and my man Traxxa." Here I pointed towards Traxxa. "And I will pay you for all five seats on your boat to and from the island. And in place of the other three hunters we will be bringing some supplies with us. Is that clear?"

At this point Frisha's smile broadened even more, if that was at all possible. I suspect this was because he quite honestly hadn't thought the merchant he had been talking to was actually prepared to go to the island in the first place. His hopes must have dropped as he thought for sure he was looking at an empty boat for the first time in years. Now, however, he had been given all the money up front, for a full boat which was always good even at the best of times. But more importantly than the money, he only had two passengers to worry about!

"Two things you should know though before you prepare to go." Said Frisha once the money was secured in the folds of his grubby tunic. He paused until we were looking at him. Sensing that what he was about to say was probably very important I focused my attention on the Ottarman but he continued to wait.

"We're waiting!" I said, feeling a little irritated at the drama being played out by this boatman.

"The first thing is, despite having no other passengers aboard there will only be room on the boat on the return trip for one kill per hunter, which is now just you and your man!"

Again there was an awkward pause. I bit my tongue and waited.

"The second thing to remember - and this is probably more important than my first point. No matter what happens you must not kill the giant. If you do, don't even bother thinking of getting off the island alive, because you will not. You will be hunted down and killed by all the towns folk of

Bernitz -- and probably by all the people of M'Lenn-Fida as well -- should they ever find out about your crime against our giant! In any case, if you do somehow kill Böder, by some unfortunate accident or other, then be warned - you will not find rest for the remainder of your days. Is that clear?"

To be frank I was a little taken aback by this last point I must admit and I looked closely into the eyes of this simple fisherman with a boat for hire. There was not one skerrick of mirth or con in his eyes and I saw that what he had just told me, he at any rate, believed strongly to be true.

Finally, I nodded my head as I accepted the last condition of our most interesting contract. At which we both stood up, extended our right arms and after grasping each other's wrist we shook them firmly once in accordance with the custom of sealing the deal.

It was only then that I was given a time and a place to meet with him from which we were to set off for the Black Island.

EARLICH

As we were walking away leaving Frisha sitting by the dock, I looked back casually and I saw him knit his brows together as a puzzling question seemed to be making its way across his face and into his thoughts. I suspect he was asking himself;

> '*What kind of stores was this strange customer wanting to take with him, on my boat, to the Black Island?*'

CHAPTER THREE

JELLICK

Traxxa, Earlich and I were once again back in the tavern, seated at the table laden with food and drink. Our transport to the Black Island had been successfully secured and I now had a little over a week to wait. During this time I planned to complete a number of smaller tasks which I had set myself to do in preparation for my meeting with the giant. In order for me to plan my next move more effectively, the first thing I needed to do was to glean all the information that had been gathered by Traxxa about both Böder and this fellow who was known as Jack the Giant Killer!

"So tell me Traxxa, what else have you found out about this giant?"

"I mentioned before that Böder ended up sleeping off a drunken stupor here in Bernitz after a month or two of terrorizing the surrounding communities. During his inebriated state the townsfolk asked this Jack fellow to help dispose of this slumbering beast."

I nodded my head, and reached for my glass of wine.

"Well my research on both Böder and Jack took me on a five-day horse ride north and west of here to a small stone walled village called Wurke near the Mirack River. Here I spent four days talking to the locals including visiting farmhouses and looking over the area, investigating Jack and Böder – for this is where both were born and raised!"

As he finished this last sentence, I cocked my head to one side, sat up and leaned forward in anticipation, realizing the importance of this information. Especially with regards to any future dealings with Böder.

Traxxa had paused sensing the change of tension in the air, so I encouraged him to continue.

"Well, in an overgrown forest, close to Wurke, Böder was said to have been born some twenty-two years ago to a giantess by the name of Sheralie. They lived on a farm under the same roof as a hard working farmer, a Bidoman *(half man half dog)* by the name of Jarck. Böder's mother, whilst physically impaired through an accident in her younger days, was both industrious and creative. They weren't very well off but neither were they to be considered poor. They lived comfortably with the little they had, and Sheralie knew how to make their modest little farm cottage into a lovely place for Jarck to retreat to at the end of a hard working day.

"Jarck and Sheralie weren't very young but they were popular with their neighbors' in the farming community and the town folk of Wurke. Though she couldn't walk Sheralie loved to get out in a cart converted into what was called a wheelchair. So it was that Jarck and Sheralie would drive their little horse and cart to visit the town when they travelled there to sell their produce on market days. I should also add that they shared the farm with Jarcks' son, from a previous relationship. His name is Jareck and he is said to be just three years older than Böder." Traxxa paused again as the significance of this last piece of information took root and understanding began to grow.

"So what you're saying," I said slowly, "is Jareck and Böder grew up as brothers?"

Traxxa nodded his head as his lips played with a smile.

"And this Jareck is also, quite possibly, Jack the giant killer of whom we have been told?" I asked with hands outstretched as though searching.

Traxxa nodded his head once more as he continued, "But it gets even more interesting! As these stories of the contented farmer, his wife and the brothers Böder and Jareck were told to me by the villagers of Wurke, something about what they were telling me struck me as a little odd and didn't quite make sense!"

"Odd? What do you mean by odd?"

"I can't explain it really, it just seemed too neat and tidy and clean."

I nodded my head trying to understand, "Continue!" I said.

"So I travelled throughout the countryside spending a lot of time with the local farmers and merchants and some of the older woodsmen and settlers in the more remote and wooded areas further out from Wurke. In time a fuller, more complete picture of events surrounding this strange family emerged!"

"Oh! And what did you find out?"

"It seems that, about twenty-four years ago there was a hard working giant farmer by the name of Driksad. He, and his young wife Sheralie, were trying to live a quiet farming life far from the village of Wurke in a more densely wooded area in the outer region. Anyway, to make this long story short, the local farming communities weren't very happy with this giant couple producing high quality crops from a land that was hard to tame. You could say there were elements of fear mixed in with jealousy in the hearts of the local farmers and the village folk. Tensions in the area were at an uneasy balance -- until it was discovered that this giant couple were expecting their first child. Now, it is well known that a giant couple can only ever produce two children at most in their lifetime. Still, this knowledge did little to put the minds of the surrounding communities at ease. Instead, it seemed to have altered the delicate balance of acceptance and tolerance in the minds of the local community and tipped it markedly towards fear, anger and antagonism.

"Tensions mounted slowly over the following year until it finally came to a head. This happened when word was received that two of Driksads' brothers had come to visit the giant's farmstead. It was presumed that they had come to help celebrate the birthday and coming of age for the first recognized giant boy born in the mainland of Durogg for well over three decades.

"As I mentioned to you earlier, communities throughout Durogg have had bans, for a long time now, on the congregating together of more than three or more giants. So the villagers and farmers around Wurke took the opportunity of the visiting brothers, as an excuse to try and force the issue and be rid of these giants from their region once and for all. I should also point out that the local farmers wanted the giants land because it was well tilled and maintained. So they had banded together and spread lies that these were bad giants meeting and plotting together, in which case they needed to be killed or driven from their land and sent either back into the mountains or at the very least out of M'Lenn-Fida. In fact, during my investigation, I found the only thing 'bad' about these giants was that they were peace loving farmers who had relatives visiting them for a short period of time.

"Anyway as it happened, one night a large group of vigilante farmers and settlers made their way quietly to Driksads' farm and surrounded it with the intention of driving Driksad and his family out of the area forever.

"They were led by Jarck, who had recently lost his wife in an accident which he claimed had been caused by the giants. Since then he had become something of a zealot in Wurke and an ardent campaigner for wanting the region to be free of these giants!"

"Hold on," I stopped him. "Jarcks' wife dying? Did the giants really have something to do with it? What did you find out about this claim?"

"I did enquire about this and apparently Driksad had come visiting Jarcks' farm on one occasion. By invitation I should add! Anyway he was there to help fell some trees and clear the land around the farmhouse. Then, as fate would have it, a mishap occurred and Jarcks' wife -- pregnant with their second child, were killed. This upset Jarck tremendously, obviously, and by then all he wanted was for the giants to be gone from the area!"

"Okay, I'm assuming that if Jarcks' unborn second child died, then the first child was Jareck? Yes?"

Traxxa nodded his head and took a sup of his wine.

"So the vigilante crowd had approached and surrounded the giant's farmhouse during the night. What happened next?"

"Well, remember now, this was a household of giants, this farmhouse would have been the equivalent of roughly four large barn houses -- built, we can assume, by the giants themselves. In any case, Jarck took the lead with a scythe and a torch in his hands and started it all by putting flames to the woodwork at the rear of the house. His intention, it seemed, was to burn down their house and thus frighten the giants into fleeing through the front door and head on down the trail where manimals waving weapons and screaming would encourage the giants to keep running away. But instead of fleeing through the front doorway Driksads two brothers smashed their way out of the house through the side wall and began chasing down those that had started the fires!"

"One of these people to be spotted and chased was Jarck. Jarck was older than most but he was also fit and nimble and exceedingly fleet of foot and he raced into a thick wood nearby. Driksads' older brother followed him recklessly into the dense trees spouting oaths of death and of killing and of eating. But, fortunately for Jarck, this giant got himself entangled and caught in amongst the thick branches and the dense trunks of the deeply rooted trees. Sensing the giant was having difficulty making his way through the thick wood, Jarck raced back toward the giant. Using the cover of darkness, and the trees with their limbs and thick foliage, he came up behind this twelve-meter giant and attacked him as he struggled in the dense wood. With tremendous effort and skill (*as that of a butcher and a farmer*), he sliced through each of the tendons at the back of the giants ankles using the large wheat scythe he had been carrying. At the first cut the giant howled in extreme anguish and whilst he tried to clasp at his painful right heel he was unable to reach down through the trees crowding around his waist and legs. The second tendon on the left foot was next and through sheer pain and the collapse of support in his feet, Driksads' eldest brother crumpled to his knees pulling trees and branches down around him. Dodging the falling limbs and branches and twigs Jarck -- more by luck than skill -- escaped completely unscathed. But now, thoroughly in the moment and full of the bloodlust of a fight, he rushed in between the giants bare legs (*as he was only wearing a pair of deerskin shorts*) and swept the scythe up once more and neatly sliced through the main artery of his left inside leg!

"There was another scream of unbridled pain as a huge river of blood spurted out and every which way. Jarck, completely covered in dark red blood and totally unrecognizable, began moving quickly and quietly through the trees of the forest looking for a way out. Before him lay tall dark cliffs which were the first of many large mountain foothills in the area.

"But it was Driksads' younger brother, who, upon hearing the screams of his older brother had come rushing heedlessly to his aid. He began thrashing the topmost branches of the thick forest above and around Jarck. This was done in pure angry frustration as he hoped desperately to frighten the fleet footed farmer out from under the trees and into the open field. Somehow it worked, for there were just too many branches and broken tree trunks crashing all around him. In any case, Jarck thought it would be much safer out in the open where other people in his vigilante group might assist him in helping to bring down Driksads' younger brother.

"But this didn't work out so well, for unbeknown to Jarck, when the giants had smashed their way out of the barn houses, the largely unarmed firelighters and torch bearers had scattered and run away in sheer terror. Thus they had been easy pickings for the younger giant and he had already torn two hapless farmers into pieces and was busily pursuing a third when he heard his older brother screaming in unholy pain. He turned and ran to where his hurting brother was still groping around trying to stop the bleeding and screaming in minking pain. Realizing that he had been attacked but not knowing the extent of the wounds, Driksads younger brother thought only of pursuing, capturing and killing the one who had dared to attack them and so he began to beat the tops of the forest. It was then that he saw Jarck race out from under the cover of the forest and into the open. With his blood covered scythe still gripped tightly in his hand, Jarck fled in terror towards a giant sized rope and wood swing bridge a little more than ten-meters away. The bridge was suspended high over a twenty-meter deep ravine.

"Jarck was a little over halfway across the bridge when he felt the planks and the ropes shuddering dangerously beneath his feet. He knew without looking behind him that the ropes supporting the bridge were being pulled out. Without a second thought he threw the scythe the remaining four-meters over the bridge and saw it land safely on the far bank. This allowed him the use of his hands and he fell to the floorboards and clung desperately to the wooden rungs of the bridge even as it dropped away beneath him. He swung down and forward with it smashing into the far side of the ravine. His fingers were caught between the rungs and the side of the ravine and he was in great pain but he held on grimly for his own life's sake.

"The younger brother screamed out a loud roar of unfiltered rage, the moment he realized that he was about to lose his prey instead of having him plummeting to the bottom of the ravine as he intended. Taking a quick look behind him, Jarck gasped for breath and with painful tears in his eyes which widened even more in terror as he saw the giant take a few large strides back away from the ravines edge. Jarck knew immediately that this giant was going to try and run and jump the cavernous drop and get him before he could escape into the forest on this side of the ravine. Forgetting his pain and that he was slightly winded from the drop of the bridge, Jarck scrambled up the rungs of the wooden bridge to reach the edge of the cliff. He was almost at the top when he heard the grunting of the giant as he finished his run up on the far side and Jarck knew that he had launched himself out over the ravine.

"Jarck felt the ground tremble as the ten-meter tall, solid young giant landed on the ravines edge not two-meters from him to his left. Jarck had not yet reached the safety of the top of the dirty bank and knew that he would never make it up at all, when suddenly he heard a loud gasp. Daring to look quickly to his left, he was just in time to see the edge of the ravines side break up and fall away and he watched in awe as the huge giant began slipping back over the edge and start to fall down into the ravine. But he didn't fall all the way in. The giant somehow managed to hold onto the crumbling bank and was even now scrabbling for a toehold. Jarck knew he had little time left before the giant would begin clawing his way up over the ravine's edge!

"Pushed on by sheer terror, Jarck pulled himself up and over the last few limply hanging rungs and stood for a moment or two on solid ground as he looked around for his scythe. Once he had got it, he turned quickly towards the giant. He gasped in fear as he saw its huge head begin to make its way up over the edge of the ravine. Without another thought, Jarck raced forward and swung the point of the scythe with all his might into the right eye of the giant. He then yanked it out almost as fast as it went in!

"The giant threw his head back and screamed in excruciating pain and grasped blindly at his eye with his right hand. But the scythe wasn't there it was sweeping out and up and away through the air. Jarck checked his movement. He watched as the screaming convulsing giant continued to try and stem the blood and pain emanating from his damaged eye. After quickly readjusting his feet he moved in once more to the edge of the ravine. With one vicious sweep of the deadly scythe he severed the bared jugular of the giant neatly as he held his head back howling in pain. Immediately the howling stopped and a loud gurgling, bubbling sound took its place. It was as if time itself stood still for Jarck as he watched the giants grip on the ravines edge gradually loosen and then, unbelievably, this huge, bleeding, partially blinded, giant tumbled back and down and disappeared into the depths of the black ravine.

"Unbeknown to Jarck, the giant landed heavily on his back shattering both his elbows and pelvis and fracturing his spine in five places and so he died slowly painfully in a crumbled bloody heap at the bottom of the ravine.

"Jarck dropped the bloodied weapon and fell to the ground landing on his hands and knees. He was emotionally exhausted and yet a feeling of triumphant exhilaration was coursing slowly through his body, trying to find a way out and express itself in action. He didn't remember how long he was down on all fours for, but a scuffling noise from over the edge of the ravine brought his mind back into sharp focus. He cautiously looked over and into the ravine but it was inky black and he could make out very little, but he thought he saw a shadowy figure trying to climb up the side of the ravine. The figure was a further few meters beyond where the giant he had just attacked had fallen. Fearing it was the same giant somehow miraculously, trying to make his way up from the bottom of the ravine despite its vicious wounds, Jarck looked quickly around desperate for something to chuck down on it. He saw a large boulder almost half as big as he was near the edge of the ravine just a little bit further on from where the climber in the ravine was. Taking his scythe in hand and after first establishing exactly where his intended victim was in the ravine, Jarck went behind the boulder and using the handle as a lever, he placed the blade of the scythe firmly underneath to use as a pivot. Jarck then pushed and shoved and levered the rock up to the edge of the ravine. A final check just to be sure he was in the right place, he then pushed with all his might and sent the boulder over the lip of the bank. Jarck staggered back and watched as it tumbled ever so slowly over and down into the inky darkness of the ravine below.

"He tried to follow it down, but once in the shadows he lost it and saw nothing. However, he did hear the satisfying crunch as the hard rock hit the hard head of a giant's skull followed immediately by a grunt of surprise and pain and then the sound of ground and rocks and the walls of the ravine collapsing and everything around him began falling away. Jarck leapt back as the bank he had been standing on followed the rock down into the dark abyss before him. A couple of seconds passed and then he heard the scream of a woman in pain emanating from the depths of the large black hole!"

Traxxa paused and I sensed this was for a change in the tempo.

"And what was the outcome of this story?" I asked quietly realizing that we were nearing its end.

"Well, the next morning the remains of the giant's farmhouse were found to be still smoldering. There were four dead and six injured farmers. Upon further investigation the three dead male giants were found. One had bled to death at the edge of the forest trapped and held up in a cruel position of kneeling in prayer by the branches, the thick undergrowth and the trees themselves. Another of the giants was found at the bottom of the ravine severely broken up, an eye gouged and his throat cut. Driksad was also found dead at the bottom of the ravine with one leg broken and his head staved in by a large rock. But the female giant Sheralie and the baby boy weren't found anywhere on the farm.

"It soon became obvious though that Jarck must have found Sheralie at the bottom of the ravine when he went down to check on the condition of the two giants that he believed he had killed or at the very least severely injured. Here he most probably found her after she also had fallen, possibly whilst following after her husband up the side of the ravine. In any case, both her legs were broken. But to his surprise and consternation he found the baby boy was completely unharmed and safe and still nestling in her arms.

"I was told by some of the older Bidowmen in the area the compassionate heart of the real Bidoman they knew as Jarck must have been moved at this point and he would probably have broken down. Some speculated why and how, but one Bidowman in particular told me, she thought Jarck took pity on this struggling, injured, giant woman with her son as he was reminded of his own wife and unborn child and it was because of this that he decided to rescue her. So, before anyone could come and finish off what he couldn't do, he went and fetched a cart and a horse and brought it into the ravine and after much effort transported the crippled giantess back to his own farm and nursed her back to an acceptable form of health. But her legs and had been damaged so much that they had to be amputated. Soon after this, Jarck and Sheralie made an agreement between themselves whereby she was given the run of the house and the farm and in return he enjoyed her companionship. In effect though he had made her his wife -- or at least was providing sanctuary for her -- and was raising her son as his own.

"Now, whether she ever knew the real role Jarck had played in the death of her husband and his two brothers, this I could never find out for sure. For some reason, best known to themselves, the communities around Wurke attributed the deaths to the legend of Jack the Giant Killer. Perhaps they were trying to deflect suspicion away from Jarck when the people realized that he had taken Sheralie into his protective care. Still, she must have had some inkling because some of the blood of those he had killed must have been on him -- that and the closeness of the name of the murderer. That's not to say he couldn't have washed the blood off himself before assisting Sheralie out from the bottom of the ravine, and people may have, out of respect for her, never retold the legendary story of Jack the Giant Killer in her presence.

Anyway, Sheralie died about thirteen years later when Böder was only 14 and within a year of her death Jarck too was dead. Some said they believed Böder might have taken revenge upon Jarck on behalf of his mother!"

"Why do you say that? Do you think Böder knew who really killed his father?"

"Well Jarck died suddenly and under very mysterious circumstances, but there's no proof that Böder had anything to do with this. Besides which, nobody was interested any way!"

"Why is that, I wonder?"

"Well, it turns out the locals were not overly fond of this new Jarck the giant lover -- especially when you consider what he was rumored to have done to Driksad when Böder was just a baby! It is one thing to drive a family of giants out of their home and steal their land, but quite another to kill off the father in order to gain a wife and a child!

"In any case, it is no small coincidence that Böder began his rebellious rampage throughout the communities of Wurke shortly after his mother and step father had died. When they were finally able to drive him off, Böder made his way slowly down here to Bernitz, causing chaos and destruction along the way and wherever he went. Once here in Bernitz he even outdid himself and became excessively drunk and totally uncontrollable. But before the locals could exact vengeance upon him, Jareck stepped in and offered the townsfolk an acceptable alternative to killing the young giant."

"Why here to Bernitz?" I asked a little intrigued.

"No-one knows for certain! But what I do know is that Jareck must have loved his much bigger, younger brother very much for he was prepared to do anything to protect him. He had obviously followed Böder in his cross country rampage and when the opportunity presented itself he had offered to take him into exile. Apparently he presented himself to the townsfolk of Bernitz as Jack the Giant Killer. This I assume was in honor of his fathers' infamous name but it also gave weight to his argument of exiling the young giant rather than killing him. And it obviously worked, for now Böder has been on the Black Island for just on seven years which would make him 22 by my reckoning and if Jack the Giant Killer or Jareck is only three years older than Böder then he would be about 25 years old!

"I only tell you this so that you have an idea of the age of the giant that you are endeavoring to meet up with. From this we can assume that his immaturity will give him courage and probably make him reckless operating out of emotion rather than thought. But he will also be energetic and possibly passionate about protecting himself and his brother and everything else that is on this island -- which he will no doubt consider to be his -- after all this time!"

At this Traxxa went quiet and drank deeply from his flagon of wine. Realizing that the story was at its close, I said quietly to Traxxa,

"Thanx for investigating Böder and Jareck for me and telling us their story. I would also tend to agree with your assessment of his disposition. Still, you have left me with a lot of things to consider and muse over. So come let us eat and drink and plan on how best to spend our time here in Bernitz while we wait for the hunt on the Black Island to begin!"

CHAPTER FOUR

JELLICK

Traxxa and I were in the last of the three low-slung dhows which skimmed silently over the surface of the darkened river. A large blanket of cloud moved slowly across the heavens to cover the sliver of the quarter moon diminishing the little light left in the night sky. The three tiller men cut quickly out and away from beneath the cover of the shadows of the river bank. Using the current of the Dund we made our way swiftly across the river to settle into the swirling eddy created by the Black Island. One by one, the sails came down as the three boats circled around the southern tip of the island. Once we entered the breakaway river that runs through the island, the soft slow splosh of the paddles came in to play propelling us slowly along with the current into the very heart of the island.

I had no fear of the sound of the paddles as I knew they would be lost in the soft sound of the rolling river and further absorbed by the dense foliage along the river bank. I nodded to Frisha who was quick to recognize my signal to hang back. Slowly we dropped back from the other boats as we made our way steadily towards the landing point on Böders Island. After nearly half an hour of paddling the two small river craft in front of us moved as one over to the river bank on the larger part of the island.

The two dhows beached on the soft sand of a little cove. Here ten hunters complete with bows and quills full of arrows and other hunting gear - alighted from the boats and moved quietly away vanishing quickly into the thick island bush. Once the hunters were clear of the boats, the owners with their two crew members pushed off and headed up the islands river back towards the main flow of the Dund.

Frisha landed in the soft sand as the others were pushing out and paddling off. With the others gone Traxxa and I alighted and the crew handed us the four large sacks of supplies that we had brought with us. We were about to step away from the boat when Traxxa stopped me. He undid the harness holding his sword and dagger and said to me "We'd best leave out weapons here so that we don't give this giant or is brother any cause to attack us!"

"What and carry no weapons -- even something for defence?" I asked curiously as I took off my short sword and removed the dagger I had hidden in my boot.

"You'll just have to trust my judgement," Said Traxxa evenly, as the hint of a grim smile played around the corners of his mouth.

"I hope you know what you're doing?" I nodded a little nervously as we dropped our weapons back into the boat. I looked up to see the perplexed face of Frisha as he began to give us his parting instructions.

"I'll be back here in 24 hours with the rest of the supplies which you have left with your man back in Bernitz. Good hunting and good luck!" And with that he and his two boys pushed off back into the river and paddled silently away disappearing in the gloom and the shadows of the night.

Taking two sacks each, Traxxa led me up into the bushes and away from the river. He went slowly and carefully, stopping every now and then to look around and smell the air as he sensed his way forward.

"The trick is to find out where they are living here on the island," Said Traxxa softly as I was just beginning to wonder what his strategy was. "And the quickest way to do this is to look for signs of their activity and follow it back to the source!"

He pointed to some crushed grass and bushes which looked to me like the imprint of a very large creature.

"I believe we have found the trail which would take the giant around the island this side of the river inspecting it and keeping an eye on his stock and the wildlife. Our best bet is to follow it back towards the centre of the island as it is there that I imagine he would set up his living quarters."

Intrigued I asked, "Why would he choose the centre of the island, instead of say, the highest point?"

"Well, considering he's a giant, height wouldn't be his main concern. He's also relatively young, which would make his pride the major factor in his life on the island. So, I reckon being in the middle of the island would make him feel like he is in control or perhaps in command, if you like, of his own little world!"

This seemed like a sensible assumption. So I fell into step just behind Traxxa as we followed the giant's tracks heading toward the islands centre.

After nearly two hours of walking we came across, what can only be described as, a large farmstead, suddenly and without warning. The sun was still an hour away from coming up and declaring a new day, but still, the soft gloom of pre-dawn was enough to have us fail to see what was in front of us even as we broke from the cover of the bushes and trees and began walking over it. We found ourselves standing on the very edge of the cleared area of a sizeable farm. Before us lay several fields of ripening crops.

Traxxa stopped and cautiously retraced his steps back under the cover of the islands trees. Here he carefully scanned the lay of the farm and expressed what I was feeling -- the astounding awe at the sheer size and layout of the homestead in front of us.

"Well, I don't know why we're so shocked. They *have* been here for some seven years and are from farming stock after all -- for mink sake," I said with a wry grin. Still I was annoyed with myself that I hadn't even begun to imagine exactly what I would see once I actually found where Böder lived. Mindful of this, I looked across the ploughed fields but saw nothing that even remotely looked like a house or a dwelling place.

"Can you see where the giant would be living?" I asked Traxxa quietly.

He didn't answer, just merely pointed to the far side of the clearing to what looked like a bunch of neatly stacked logs laid down in front of a towering dark wall of rock. This I saw was the base of the largest mountain on the island. Even as he pointed I saw a light come out from a hole in the log stack. This I realized was in fact a window and that life on Böders farm was beginning for the day.

Traxxa crouched down and leant against the base of a tree and asked,

"Now that we have found them, what would you like to do? Wait for an opportune moment, or, make ourselves known whilst they are still waking up?"

"You have a choice Traxxa." I said evenly. "You can either wait here for my signal or for when I return. Alternatively, if you receive neither, then wait for the cover of darkness whereupon you may return to Bernitz without me. Of course you could always help me to carry these bags and come with me to present ourselves to the island's host!"

At this, I began to walk purposefully across the fields towards the stack of logs. I didn't look back, but I felt and heard Traxxa following after me.

We came up to the stack of logs as more light threatened to spill out over the mountains in the east as the sun had started staking its claim for the day.

To the right of the large stack of logs, I saw a dirt ramp shored up by extremely wide and deep log steps leading down to what can only be described as the beginning of a very large cave. The opening was stopped up with ten roughly-hewn logs standing on their ends and which, judging by their appearance, was most probably a door. Behind these logs might very well live the giant we were looking for!

To the left of this large stack of logs I saw an indistinguishable number of much smaller caves. These too had logs for doors but these were stopped up on the outside by much smaller logs. These could either be storehouses for the crops or rooms for unwanted guests. I smiled silently at the irony and searched for a break in the logs wherein there might be an entrance or a door of sorts upon which we could bang upon and announce our presence.

Sensing my indecision, Traxxa whispered for me to look to the left. I saw just before the ramped steps leading down to the giants' door there was a cleverly-concealed break in the logs which was like a sheltered alcove. Here I saw the outlines of a door.

Taking my life in my hands I made my way cautiously over to the alcove. At its entrance and to my right, I saw just how deep the steps leading down to the giant's door was. At this point, I almost lost my nerve but decided - what indeed do I have to lose. And then I suddenly realized I was most probably -- almost certainly -- the first visitors they had ever had whilst living on this island. In which case -- if I was them, at the very least I would be curious to know who would want to visit me and what they wanted.

I moved into the alcove and there before me was a comfortable manimal sized door whereupon I put knuckle to wood and knocked three times.

One to gain their attention,

Two to let them know it's real,

And three to let them know it was not a mistake.

There was a moment's pause and then a deep set growl as though the heavens were about to declare a tremendous storm. This was followed by a muffled voice saying what sounded like,

"Quiet down, I'm just gonna go see who or what it is - yeah!"

Then a booming voice called out.

"And me!"

At the same time as the manimal-sized door was opening inwards, the door to the giants cave just to the right of us was being lifted up and pushed open with the effortless ease that could only be attributed to a creature with enormous amounts of strength.

Our whole attention was drawn to this amazing feat. But what took me by surprise and scared the minkle out of me was the presence of a huge face popping around the wall to look at us in the alcove. It was easily four times bigger than that of a normal manimal. And yet it was the unshaven face of a boyish young man in his early 20's. He had long flowing locks of sun-bleached gold which reached down over his shoulders. His eyes were hazel brown, with a prominent beauty spot on his right cheek. But what struck me the most of all was his lovely big grin of delight which made him look like a very happy large teenage boy.

"What do you want?" He spoke with such a deep imposing voice that it caused a shiver of fear, or delight, to race up and down my spine so quickly it made me want to go and relieve myself.

"How can I help you?" said a more normal voice behind me from the manimals doorway.

I dragged my eyes away from the imposing giants face and looked squarely into the handsome face of a swarthy well-tanned Bidoman (*half man - half big dog*).

"You must be Jareck?" I said and extended my arm in greeting.

"I am and who might you be?" answered Jareck mechanically accepting my arm by gripping my wrist and allowing me to grasp his and we shook as was the custom of greeting in M'Lenn-Fida at the time.

"My name is Jellick and this is Traxxa my companion and I was wondering if I might trouble you for some of your time and your hospitality?"

There was an awkward pause, so without waiting any longer I turned to greet the giant. "And you must be Böder, I have heard a lot about you and I am deeply honoured and pleased to finally meet up with you!"

At this, I stepped forward and extended my arm. The look of confusion and pleasure was almost too much for me and I had to do everything in my power to stop from laughing out loud. Instead I looked up and smiled with what I hoped would be a reassuring smile and not an intimidating grin. Böder looked quickly at Jareck for some reassurance and not receiving anything at all took it upon himself to spread his lips in the biggest smile that I had ever seen in my entire life. He then proffered me two fingers that were almost as big as my entire forearm, which I quickly grasped and shook them in greeting. Traxxa followed suit by grasping Böders fingers and then grasping Jarecks' wrist. I remember quite distinctly, that it was at this very moment the sun peaked over the island's mountains and the warmth and light of the day broke out all around us.

"Please won't you come inside?" offered Jareck and he stepped aside to allow us to enter.

The first thing I noticed as I stepped through the door into the house of Jareck and Böder was just how big the space was. We were seeing the beginnings of a huge cave beneath the mountain which was probably a silent volcano. Next I saw we were walking on the floor of a ledge which was about five meters up from the base floor of the cavern. This made us almost level with the chest of Böder as he came into the room after closing his door. It was brightly lit inside despite the walls of wood closing out the natural light from the entrance and the black walls of the mountain cave. I tracked the light back to its source and saw three of the largest light crystals that I had ever seen set high up into each of the three rock walls. There were a myriad of other much smaller crystals dotted around the cavern, though the majority of these were not lit up. They were, however, all set into the rock walls and I realized that they were all naturally set and not brought in from another source. On the far side of the cavern floor, behind Böder, was a very large fireplace with a small fire flickering quietly. I was intrigued despite myself as I watched the spiralling wisps of smoke descend up and into a widened hole in the wall which was acting as a natural chimney.

My eye continued to rove and I saw that all the furnishings were crude and very basic. Though they seemed to have served their purpose well and were durable to the extent that even a giant could use them all and not suffer from their use. Though I did notice there was a distinct lack in the more personal details. For instance the clothes these two were wearing were both minimal and roughly put together. And both their grooming habits left a lot to be desired.

It was only then that I realized I had drifted away from my host, so I quickly turned to him.

"I'm sorry, I was just admiring your home, you seem to have done a terrific job here on your own, so far!"

Again I saw the hint of pride sneak across the faces of both the Bidoman and the giant. "Do you mind if I look around for a bit?"

"By all means, you are a guest, would you like something to eat or to drink?"

"That would be great, thank-you, but first we have a few gifts for you!"

At this Traxxa stepped forward and presented the four sacks that he had been left holding.

"Ooooh!" Böder squealed with delight. "Gifts! Show me, show me, show me! What are they?"

The first two sacks were emptied. These contained five chickens and a cockerel in each. Both cockerels had their legs bound and wore blindfolds to stop them from being aggressive in the confines of the sacks. In the next sacks were two nanny goats with three kids as well as two bound and blindfolded young billy goats.

Böder was almost beside himself with delight.

"No-one has ever brought me a gift of chickens and goats before!" He cried. "Are they for eating?" He asked hesitatingly

"You can eat them if you want to," I said, "but I thought that you might like to look after them and have fresh eggs and goat's milk on a daily basis!"

As I said this I saw them both pause and give thought to that prospect, so I continued carefully.

"However you're welcome to do with them as you wish. That is the principle of a gift. They are now yours! Besides which, if you decide to eat these, I can always bring some more for you for breeding the next time I come back. That is if you wish for me to return?"

"Return?" said Jareck quietly with just the hint of menace, "what makes you think that you will be leaving, in order for you to return?"

"Let me ask you a question good Ser Jareck," I asked evenly overlooking the subtle threat, "do you have any eggs or milk here on the island?"

After a long pause, Jareck replied just as evenly.

"No, there is no milk on the island and no eggs that you could call us having on a regular basis.

"We raid the nests of native birds!" said Böder quickly but with a touch of sadness about him, "but that is terribly unsatisfying!"

"And that is why I will be leaving and returning, but only if you please," I said quietly. "I have brought you something you both could use – is that right?"

After another long pause it was Böder who replied,

"Yes, that's right Ser Jellick. You have brought us something we have not had for some seven years now! And I for one am delighted that you have done so!" And here he looked uncertainly at Jareck.

"And that is what I do, Ser Böder, I am a merchant and my pleasure is gained by obtaining for people the things they want, need or desire. Now, I am here to ask you both --," and here I looked deliberately at Jareck, "what do you want that you can't get here on this island of yours and will you allow me the privilege of serving you by bringing those things here to you?"

"But we have nothing to trade," said Jareck sadly as he realized almost suddenly with concern the balance and importance of this strange encounter.

"You let me worry about what you may or may not have that is good for trade Ser Jareck. For that is my skill!" I said smiling for the first time since being in their home.

I could almost visibly see Jareck going over in his mind all the many things that he and Böder had longed for over the past seven years. Finally, he looked closely at me and his face suddenly broke in relief as he smiled and he indicated with a wave of his hand that he wanted for us to sit with him at his table.

"I would like to invite you for a second time but with greater sincerity this time to break your fast with us. So come and eat and drink with us and we can talk about what we would like for you to get for us!" In half concern, half relief he turned to his much bigger step brother, "what do you think Böder?"

"Ooooh yes please," said the amiable giant who wandered over to the huge fireplace to retrieve what looked like a slab of cooked deer meat and some gourds of drink.

"And I would be delighted to accept your request!" I said smiling in relief as well.

So Traxxa and I followed Jareck over to the large table which stood near the lip of the ledge overlooking the large sprawling living quarters of my very first giant.

CHAPTER FIVE

JELLICK

We had barely finished our breakfast when Böder jumped up and proclaimed that he had to go and let some of the workers out from their prison cells so they too could have some breakfast and begin their working day.

"Before you go good Böder!" I said. "I think I should warn you that there are ten hunters on your island at this moment hunting the deer and boar in the forests!"

Böder paused for just a moment as the information sank in and then he thrust his huge arms out, put his head back and emitted a terrible roar as one who had just suffered a physical blow from some hidden weapon. His roar was tremendously long and loud and chilling and made even more terrible by the confines of the cavern. It could easily have sent fear into the hearts of even the sturdiest of warriors if they knew this terrible roar was intended for them.

Böder moved purposefully over to the far side of the cavern and picked up a huge tree branch that I hadn't noticed before. It had been trimmed down into one of the most fearsome club I had ever seen in all my days.

"Hold steady there Ser Böder," I called out standing up and moving away from the table. It was never my intention to intervene but rather to grab his attention if only for a moment. He noticed me and in mid stride he stopped and glared at me with darkened eyes and in such a way that my very being froze in absolute and total fear at what this giant was capable of doing. But the pause was just enough for me to get a quick word out.

"Rather than chase these hunters all over your island wasting your time, energy and effort, why don't we just go and meet up with them when they are preparing to leave with their kills in the boats that will be coming to pick them up? Then and there you can confront them about what they are doing!"

When I had finished, an interesting look passed over Böders' face, before the look of unsurpassed rage he had been wearing only a moment ago was replaced slowly with the smile of one who was now privy to some deep and dark secret. His darkened eyes returned to their original soft-brown colouring and somehow conveyed in a look that law and order in his life had been restored, which up till then had been chaotic and unjust for so long.

He looked down at the club in his hand and as casually as a normal manimal would throw his cloak onto a chair he tossed it effortlessly across the cavern where it landed with a loud clatter against the far wall. He then strode purposefully over to the large tree stump which had been his chair and dragged it back to where he had been sitting during our breakfast together. I could see he was about to say something but Jareck spoke up first.

"Why are you telling us only now about this hunting party, when you have known about them even before you knocked on our door early this morning?"

I too had returned to my place at the table and answered as calmly and as evenly as I could muster. "Because I knew there were other, far more important things for us to talk about before I let you know about the hunters."

"I reckon you came over with these hunters, didn't you?" asked Böder leaning forward.

"Yes we sailed with them, but I hired my own boat and ensured that no hunters were with us on our journey over here!"

"The only reason that you are alive at this point is that you have no weapons on you!" Said Böder softly, leaning his big hairy face up close to mine. "You do realise that don't you?"

I nodded weakly, not daring to open my mouth. In retrospect that soft voice of Böders was far more sinister and frightening than the roar he had emitted just moments before.

"So, Ser Jellick! It seems to me that you have come here with a plan concerning these hunters!" Put in Jareck. "Would you care to tell us what that is please?!"

"What I propose is this," I said when my fear had subsided enough to allow me to speak without quivering like a reed in the wind. "I saw as I approached your door earlier, the other doors with the logs jammed up against them to stop them from opening. I assume this is where you have imprisoned the hunters you have caught over the years who have come to your island to rob and steal from you – is this correct?"

"Yes it is and what of it?" said Böder leaning forward threateningly once more.

"My suggestion is that you free all of your prisoners and send them back home. We can take them down to the boats when they come in this evening and you can vent your anger against these hunters and thieves by roaring at them if you wish. Then in your mercy, you can allow them all to leave on the boats that have come for them!"

"And why would we want to do this?" Jareck asked with genuine interest in his voice.

"You will do this because you will be telling the lands around your island that you are changing and are no longer the fearsome and terrible giant that your legend speaks of!"

"But they are trespassing on my island, killing my deer and stealing them from me!" Böder protested with feeling and allowing his voice to rise in the process.

"Yes they are, aren't they?" I replied soothingly. "So you know, that when the hunters return to be picked up this evening they will have their kills with them – won't they?"

Jareck and then Böder nodded their heads but I also saw Böders huge knuckles whiten as he grasped the top of the ledge with feeling.

"Now, under normal circumstances to replenish your store room, you too would have to track and kill your own deer for food isn't that correct?"

Again they nodded their heads.

"Well instead of being upset about this, you simply thank them for killing the deer for you and take whatever you wish from them. In doing this you will have done three things without any effort on your part. The first thing is, you will have robbed them of the excitement of being hunted by the fearsome giant that they have come to this island for. Next, you will have robbed them of their kill, and finally you will have meat for the next couple of days or weeks and all without having to waste your time tracking your own deer across your island in order to stock up your larder!"

Böder and Jareck looked at one another in stunned amazement. Then Böder turned to look carefully at me as though he was trying to decide if he was receiving enough justice in this one event after being robbed by thieves and hunters for so long. And then the moment broke and he smiled once more and again I saw this lovely boyish grin of his that had captured my heart from the outset.

I saw out of the corner of my eye that Jareck too had turned to face me and was also looking long and hard at me. If I didn't know any better I would have sworn he was trying to gauge the measure of my character. After a long and awkward pause he finally spoke.

"Now Ser Jellick. What of you? Didn't you come across with these hunters? So don't you owe them some sort of allegiance or loyalty?"

"No good Jareck, not at all! My first allegiance is to my calling, which is that of a merchant. The idea that these hunters can presume to have the right to trespass on someone else's land and steal from them makes my passions rise to the extreme. One of the reasons for my wishing to be a part of this journey -- aside from meeting with you of course -- has been to try and help stop the hunters from coming here altogether. Now, one of the best ways that I believe this can be achieved is to try and dispel the legend of the 'big bad giant'. That is why I am asking you to consider freeing however many prisoners you have enslaved here on this island. Robbing them of their freedom is, I feel, just as bad -- if not worse -- than robbing you of your deer!"

For a moment I saw a shadow of anger flash across both Böder and Jareck's faces so I moved on quickly.

"For instance, take a closer look at your own situation! You may have lost some meat or even some stock over the many years you have been on this island. They have been taken from you -- or stolen if you prefer -- by the hunters who have come and gone. But now look at what some have had taken from them by you. In their case they have lost their homes, their families and their lives, not to mention what their wives and children might have lost. Where is their husband or father, brother, or even their servant, their worker or provider? Is that the kind of legacy you want to have attached to your names?"

There was a long audible pause after this.

"But do you know what these 'trespassers' have done?" asked Böder thoughtfully. "They have reduced my herds and have brought diseases to my island and over the years the quality of my deer has slowly gotten worse!"

"And so, with my help, we will replenish your deteriorating deer stock and together we will bring you a better style of living here on your island! But this will be done by your own hard work and not just from something you have inherited as part of the conditions of your exile!"

This caught them completely off guard. They paused with mouths opened ready with a quick reply. Then to my surprise I saw the anger in their eyes change to chagrin followed by a visible slump in shoulders and a closing of mouths as the wind was taken from the sails of their boats of injustice.

"And how do you hope to do this?" Jareck asked softly with just a hint of scepticism.

"Well I've already begun -- or have you forgotten so quickly?"

I saw a little flash of uncertainty whip across their faces as I continued. "Don't you now have the potential for milk and eggs on a daily basis?"

"Aaaaahhhh!" They both said as one, in understanding.

"And finally, as a sign of good faith, when the boats come to pick up the hunters tonight, my own boat will also arrive. However, it is not just coming to pick me up it will also be bringing some more supplies for you!"

"Supplies?!" Again they answered as one. It was amusing to see how these two oddly matched brothers could think and respond as one.

"Yes supplies." I continued. "Before I came here I tried to work out what you might like, want, or need after seven years away from the constant contact with others from the mainland. So I took it upon myself to gather some stores for you, which, if all goes well, you should have by tonight. That is, if you are still wanting them?"

"What kind of things?" Böder asked excitedly.

"Well let's see... I believe I've got at least five of the things you told me over breakfast that you wanted, being loaded onto my boat even as we speak!"

"Seriously?" said Jareck hardly daring to believe what he was being told.

"Yes, very seriously good Jareck. My man Earlich will be bringing some casks of wine and beer, some grain for sowing, and some implements for cooking and for eating and drinking out of."

"But we have no money! Or things of value that you might consider worthy of trade! Do we?"

"Well now that you mention it Jareck, there is one thing that you have that no-one else in all the lands of Durogg has and that is something that I desperately would like the services of!"

"Really! And what is that?" Asked Böder with the same level of interest and excitement he had shown before.

"You!" I said smiling at their confusion. "You have the services that only a giant can deliver, and, in return, I will help you replenish your island stock, revitalise your impressive farm, and offer you an ongoing agreement for the regular supply of other goods and stores. Most of all I am going to give you a goal and something to work for. But, before we begin, I think it might be best if you released your prisoners and give them that breakfast you told me about earlier. You might also consider giving them some good news and a measure of hope."

Böder looked quickly to Jareck for support and guidance.

"Yes Böder," Jareck said resignedly but nodding his head all the same. "Let them out and tell them we'll be setting them free and sending them home tonight!"

"Oooohh yeah! Alright!" Böder said with a flourish and without further prompting he stood up and bounced like a child out of the cavern!

We, Traxxa, Jareck and I watched with smiles on our faces as the biggest kid I had ever seen skipped out of our presence to set his prisoners free.

When he had gone I turned to Jareck and asked him about their time on the island and about the prisoners and how they had managed together.

"When we first came here – what, seven years ago now? -- we were pretty scared at being on our own, effectively cut off from the mainland. A month after we were here, they sent a search party out to our island -- probably to try and find out whether Böder had eaten me or something I suppose. Anyway Böder was very angry with them all by this time and he set about destroying one of the four boats that had come here to check on us. He then killed two and injured three of those in the party before I could call to get him to stop and calm him down. The rest of the frightened party sailed away with the bodies of their dead and wounded, screaming and shouting back to us their oaths and curses, coupled with threats of vengeance and retribution! But we never saw them or anyone else like them again.

"Seven years ago there was an abundance of boar and deer on this island -- like you wouldn't believe. At first we just ate what we could catch, without thought or concern for the next day. About five months into our exile we came across a terribly ill old Ottarman who had become stranded here. His name was Kael and he was a great fisherman. His boat had been wrecked in a storm and he had only just survived and was fortunate to find himself washed up on our shores. We nursed him back to relative health and while he recovered slowly, he watched us carefully and with interest. In his time with us, Kael saw how we were coping and made us realise with soft talk and gentle instruction that if we continued killing and eating the way we were doing, we would have no main meat in the future. In fact, by the time he came to us, we had already killed and eaten almost all the boar on the island and had less than half of the deer population left.

"So Kael helped us to understand how we could manage our island. He told us to build pens for the boar and domesticate them -- like pigs, only bigger. He said, by doing this, it would allow the deer to flourish without having to share the island with its aggressive neighbour. He then showed us how to fish and live off the island. And finally he helped us recognize what we were good at and to utilize our skills as farmers by clearing the land and looking for natural food and crops on the island and to begin replanting and cultivating them. Being from this area he showed us what to look for and how to begin our farm. Unfortunately Kael had been more seriously injured than we ever realised and he died within a month of his landing on our island. Böder and I were very upset about him dying because he had been a great help in getting us started and teaching us to live in a different way here on the island!

Then about six months after we had been exiled here, we heard some noises early one morning and discovered our first hunting party making their way through our island hunting and disturbing our herds of deer.

45

Anyway Böder went berserk! You should have seen him! I have known him since he was 2 years old but I have never seen him so angry and so out of control like this before. He destroyed both their boats and killed all the hunters except two of them in a ferocious melee of anger and rage. I knew that it was foolish, even perilous, to intervene, yet I had try and do something. I stepped in between him and the remaining two hunters and at the last moment Böder recognized who I was and he allowed his out of control anger to subside just long enough for me to persuade him to let them live.

"At this time we were still living in a couple of rough makeshift lean-tos on the edge of our fields. But we had accepted this as part of our time on the island up until that point. However, with two petrified hunters to imprison and look after, we quickly realised that we needed to be looking for a more permanent solution to our accommodation needs. It was then that one of the hunters told me about these natural caves that he knew about. He had come across them whilst on a previous hunting trip to the island long before we had been exiled out here.

"So we investigated them and realising they would suit our needs most adequately we made an effort to move in almost immediately. There was a bit of work to do such as make the opening to this cave bigger and to dig out a decent entrance to allow Böder better access. We discovered as we talked with our prisoners that one of them was a builder and the other was a stone mason. These skills were put to good use as we allowed them to help us fix up the caves and improve our accommodation. When our cavern and prisons were finished with, we let these two hunters leave the island by allowing them to build a makeshift raft for themselves and watched as they simply floated away down the river.

"Of course there were other hunting parties who made their way to our island. We tried to chase each one around and scare them off. Once or twice Böder would catch some of the hunters and if I didn't get to him quickly enough to declare them a prisoner, Böder in his anger and adventurous spirit would simply tear them apart or throw them off the cliffs to drown or float away in the river. Whenever we captured someone we would put them to use by having them work in our fields, or maintain our fishing nets or have them teach us some of the skills they might be proficient in. So far we've had a baker, some farmers and a smith. But mostly we would just let them work in the fields, build pens for our boar and the young deer, or tend to our accommodation. Then after a time we would let them go. Throughout the seven years on this island there has been four occasions when we have had to bury some of these thieves and intruders. One died from natural causes, whilst two died trying to escape and earned the wrath of Böder, whilst the last one lost his life making poor choices as he tried to escape and essentially killed himself."

"So how many prisoners do you have here at the moment?" I asked intrigued by the ingenuity and simplicity or their rehabilitation programme.

"There are five prisoners in the cells at the moment. But of those five there is one -- a Larcaman (*half man half large cat*) by the name of Barill -- who has been with us for nearly three years now. In fact, this is the longest time that we have ever held on to any one prisoner. The reality is though; he doesn't seem to want to leave us or the island. I think he has found that he is useful here and I can only guess that he mustn't have had much of a life back on the mainland. So despite the fact we have offered him his freedom many times, he simply doesn't wish to go. In fact we don't even have him locked up – he is free to roam the island whenever he wants. He is a great hunter and fisherman but has told us his skills and trade is that of a smith. But unfortunately without a forge, an anvil or the tools of his trade he has been unable to share these skills with us more fully.

"Hmm!" I said thoughtfully. "Now good Jareck, would you find this impertinent of me if I asked to be shown a bed of sorts where I might get a couple of hours sleep before we leave for the boats late this afternoon? You see I've only had four hours sleep since early last evening and I know we have a lot of things to do this afternoon and I'd like to be fully rested and alert doing them!"

"Yes surely, you can have my bed. I'm going to go and see how Böder is getting on. Besides it will give us time to talk. What about you Traxxa?"

"I'll be fine sleeping on the mat thanx Jareck", and with that he lay down where he had been standing and closed his eyes. In fact he was asleep even before I had reached Jareck's bed to find my own way to sleep and rest!

CHAPTER SIX

EARLICH

Early in the morning, before the sun had fully broken over the distant horizon, I was down on the docks of Bernitz to meet with Frisha. Here I learned how he had fared in dropping Tor Jellick and Traxxa off on the Black Island. His report was encouraging and was of a tremendous relief. As he went off to get some much needed rest, I began the task of rallying the servants that Jellick had allocated to me and throughout the day we loaded up Frisha's boat with the supplies that he had instructed me to acquire for him. By the time Frisha returned later that same day, we were all loaded up and I (*even I*) was ready to go out with him to the Black Island. Later that evening, I met with Tor Jellick on the sandy shore of the island's river and shortly thereafter I had some time to talk privately with him whereupon he told me of all that had transpired between him, Jareck, Böder and the thieving hunters.

JELLICK

I felt a strong calloused hand nudging me closer to the shore of consciousness and pulling me gently out from the waters of a deep sleep. After first acknowledging I had heard his call, I brushed away the irritating hand and lay quietly for a short time on the hard, *(though not completely uncomfortable)* bed. With my eyes still closed I tried desperately to remember where I was, what day it was and what was I supposed to be doing.

When I finally opened my crusty eyes I saw the rugged smile of Traxxa looking down upon me. I noticed the steaming mug of something smelling nice, in his hand being extended to me. And then I knew where I was and what was happening. I sat up quickly, accepted the mug and took a long draught of the soup in my hands. I swung my legs out over the edge of the bed and wriggled my feet into my boots. Then, after another sip from the mug, I stood up and walked thoughtfully across the cavern's ledge. It was then that I saw the front door was standing ajar. Without hesitating I changed direction and walked out into the glorious sunshine of an early afternoon in the middle of the Black Island.

I walked along a stone path through an overgrown front yard and over to a wooden fence. This was the front of the boar's pen. I was quietly pleased to see the chickens and roosters I had brought with me scattered around the yard beginning to peck it free of bugs and seeds.

I glanced over to where I had seen doors to the other caves earlier in the pre-dawn. All the doors had been removed and I could see quite clearly they were empty of life. I could tell they were being used as prison cells for the captured hunters as there was the look and stench of enslaved humanity about them. I also saw that a few of the caves were being used as store rooms.

I looked the other way and saw the rolling hills of lush cultivated fields extending all the way down to the large emerald blue lake nearly two kilometers away. It was surrounded by the dense dark green island jungle of tall trees, thick bushes and unkempt grasses and other plant life. The scene was completed by the purple haze of the mountains in the distance and the canopy of a cloudless blue sky above making the sight positively breathtaking.

I took a big slurpy sip of soup from the mug in my hand and just stood there admiring both the taste and the view oblivious to all else around me. I slumped down and sat against the corner post of the boar pen and drank in the serenity of the sluggish river curving its way round the smallest of the island's mountains becoming a frothy waterfall on the far side of the lake. I was mesmerised and suddenly, strangely content.

I heard but didn't acknowledge the sound of Traxxa moving up and standing quietly beside me. I sat there with my thoughts of nothing, simply enjoying the warmth and humidity of the sun and the islands late summer sounds. But slowly the stench of the boars and rotting vegetables in and around the pen began to eat into my senses and I knew that it was time to get up and begin what was left of the day.

I stood up, turned to Traxxa and told him what I thought we would be doing for the remainder of the day. As we talked, we walked away from the boar's pen back to our hosts' cavern. When I had finished I also told him that I intended to leave him here on the island to try and train Böder and possibly Jareck in the art of one on one combat.

"How do you feel about that?" I asked.

"I don't feel anything in particular," was Traxxa's response, "but can I ask what am I training them for?"

"I want them to be competent with a weapon that will hold up the fighting skills of a mountain troll."

"A mountain troll? You mean the one who has your personal treasures?!"

"Yes that mountain troll!"

"You do realize what you're asking me to do don't you? I mean it's common knowledge that some trolls have lived for hundreds maybe even a thousand years. And with that kind of knowledge and experience they will be very difficult to defeat!"

"I do understand all that, but hear what I have to say on the matter first. Now, I don't expect you to get Böder to such a level of fighting competency, in the short time that we have available to us, that he can actually kill the troll. If he does, well and good! However, I would be happy if you could instruct him in such a way that he might at least be able to hold him up just long enough in the dark of an early morning say and wrestle him into the light of day thereby letting the sun take care of the rest!"

"Ah I see what you mean! But you said time available what do you mean?"

"Well, with the closing of summer and the coming of fall and then winter which will bring with it the cold and the snow in the mountains, I reckon we've got about four months before he would have to wrestle with the troll. We would need to be there of course before the troll begins to think about going into hibernation! Then with half a month to travel there I reckon you will have about just under two months to train our giant friend. Do you think you can do that in the time available?"

"And if I can't?"

"Well, then we'd just have to wait till spring next year. But I'd rather get it done this year if we can! What do you think?"

"I guess it's possible. It will all depend on Böder of course and what skills he already possesses. But more importantly will Böder want to do this?"

"I have some other plans for him that might encourage him to take on the risk of fighting this troll. So I guess we'll just have to go and ask him!" Traxxa chuckled.

"Like you haven't given them enough to think about already and this is only their first day with you and it isn't even half over yet!"

We both smiled and went off to look for Böder and Jareck. We found them with their five captives erecting what looked like a rough looking fence between their fields and the shore of the lake.

"Good afternoon!" I greeted them warmly.

They turned and smiled and I knew that all was well between us.

"Are you well rested now?" Jareck asked.

"I am thanx. What are you erecting here? It looks like a fence of sorts. For what? To keep hunters out, goats and chickens in?

"We're not exactly sure!" Jareck said with feeling. "There seems to be a large creature of sorts in the water. And it can only have come here recently because we hadn't noticed it before yesterday."

"As you can see by the marks in the mud," said Böder pointing to some strange claw prints in the mud by the lakes shoreline, "it has come up on the bank and taken one of our boars which had most probably come down here to drink."

"Hmm!" I said thoughtfully as Traxxa and I began examining the marks in the mud. It was obvious something very big had come up out of the water and attacked something else, for there were deep scuffle marks in the soft mud along the lakes shore. Upon closer investigation I could see the cleft hooves of that of a boar, certainly not a deer, and came to the same conclusion as Jareck, that it had been taken back into the water.

"What do your hunters think?" I asked before giving my own opinion.

"Well Barill here --" said Jareck pointing to a compact and very solid looking Larcaman, "thinks it could be a crocodile. But the others reckon it is much bigger than the largest crock they have ever known or heard about! Why, what do you think?"

I turned to Traxxa who realised that he was expected to give an opinion of sorts so he began slowly and carefully.

"They are no tracks of a crocodile that I have ever seen. If you look here, there are only the markings of its feet in the mud. Now if it was a croc -- especially after taking its prey as big as that of a boar -- not only would it show signs of its prey being dragged through the mud, but we would also see the signs of its own body or at the very least its tail dragging in the mud also. You will also note that the creature seem to have a much greater stride than that of even the largest croc that I know of. With its size and stride I would say that this creature was moving very fast. This tells me, that it is both big and as comfortable on land as it is in water. From the little that I've seen, my guess is that you have a drazil in your lake - and that is not a good thing at all!"

"A drazil? What on Durogg is a drazil?" Asked Böder excitedly, perhaps thinking it might be some sort of interesting creature to apply his hunting skills to.

"A drazil, good Böder, is one of the most ferocious killing lizards that these lands know about. The smallest drazil is estimated at being about three times bigger than your biggest crocodile. It may not be quite as dangerous as a dragon in that it can't fly or breathe fire, but, it's still one of the most feared creatures in the water and on land just behind the leviath, which -- as you may or may not know -- is an extremely large two headed serpent. But the drazil likes to live in the dark caves of mountains and near large bodies of water where it can hunt and breed. If this is your first sign of this creature on your island then I can only imagine that it must have come up recently on the currents of the Dund and is probably even now looking for a place to establish as its own. So tell me, what do you know about the waters of this lake, how deep is it? How does it fill and empty itself and also more importantly how does it interact with the Dund flowing around the shores of your island?"

Böder and Jareck looked at one another for a moment or two and then directed their gaze at Barill, who simply shrugged his shoulders telling us, 'don't look at me'!

"Kael," Jareck spoke up finally, "the old Ottarman, who was washed up on our shores and showed us how to fish the island's river and lake. He drew our attention to the fact that despite however much the water from the river empties into it, the lake never seems to rise -- or go down for that matter. Whilst we never once thought to see how deep the lake really was, I do remember though, Kael pointing out to us where there was a slight show of turbulence in the lake by the rock wall. He told us that was probably where the water from the lake was escaping through tunnels under the mountain."

And here Jareck pointed to where the water of the lake met the sheer rock face of the largest of the volcanic mountains on the island. It was the same mountain where Böder and Jareck had made their home further up the hill opposite their farmlands.

"We assumed, but were never sure, that there must be a number of underground rivers flowing out from this lake under the mountain and perhaps emptying back into the Dund further north. But, as I say, we don't know for certain as we haven't dared to investigate further. Water is not something we enjoy being around other than to drink and bathe in as quickly as necessity dictates!"

"Well, if it's any consolation," said Traxxa slowly and deliberately, "these sticks in the mud will never stop a drazil if it wants to venture up the hills into your farmland and through your crops!"

With that there was a lapse in thoughtful silence by all those putting the posts in the mud. After a respectful time, I asked quietly

"Böder, can I take a moment of your time? I would like to ask you to consider a proposition that I wish to put before you!"

Böder roused himself from his quiet reverie, looked quickly to Jareck but realising it was his own decision to make, he replied, "surely good Jellick what is it that I can do for you?"

"I am leaving on the boat that is coming for me tonight, but not until after we have helped you unload the stores that I have arranged for you. Is that clear?" He nodded.

"I understand! But I sense there is more that you have planned for us! Is that correct?"

Whilst we were talking we had been walking away from the others, but I noticed that Jareck and Traxxa were just a few steps behind and following us. I didn't mind as they were both a part of my intentions regarding Böder and his island anyway.

"I wish to leave Traxxa here with you on the island for a couple of months in order to train you in the use of arms and fighting."

"And why would I want to learn these things?" Böder asked a little testily though slightly intrigued in spite of himself.

"I would like to prepare you and help provide you with the ability and skills needed to defend yourself against an opponent that may be stronger and more ferocious than yourself! What do you say to that?"

"Is this because of the drazil that has come to live in my lake?"

"No not necessarily. Though I don't suppose any more harm would come to you if you apply whatever you learn in order to get rid of this drazil. No, you see I wish to prepare you for a fight with a mountain troll. Do you remember you asked me earlier today about what there is of value on this island?" Böder nodded his head.

"And I said there was you! Well I wasn't jesting with you and I wasn't spilling words needlessly. I had a very precious family heirloom taken from me by a mountain troll earlier this year and I would like you, with your size and strength, to help me recover this personal treasure!"

At this point I could see that Jareck was making moves to interrupt. But I continued quickly in order to keep him out and maintain control of the conversation.

"If you help me, if you both help me," and here I turned to acknowledge Jareck, "then I will ensure, for the remainder of your days, that you need never have to be without some of the luxuries that you might have been missing in your time here on this island. What do you say to this?"

"But what makes you think that Böder needs training by your man?" Interjected Jareck unable to contain himself any longer.

"A good question Jareck, so let me ask Böder one in return. In your time on your rebellious quest across the lands of Durogg and on your island, have you ever encountered any adversary equal to you in strength or size and build as yourself?"

"No!" answered Böder whilst Jareck shook his head thoughtfully.

"And whilst you're still just a young man -- albeit a lot bigger than most -- isn't it true that you don't have any real experience in the art of fighting other than imposing your brute strength and size upon others that are considerably much smaller than yourself?"

Böder and Jareck nodded their heads in unison this time and the looks on their faces showed me they were both anticipating a more salient point.

"And now you have on your island, a creature which I did not design to be here, but is probably more than your equal. If for no other reason than to help you prepare to meet with the drazil in your lake I would leave Traxxa with you to train you in how to combat so formidable a creature!"

It was at this point that Traxxa spoke up.

"I should probably point out at this time, that it is well known that Drazils when moving to a new territory will usually travel in pairs! So to the best of my knowledge there might very well be two large flesh eating lizards living on your island at present. But more than this, they are most likely, at this very moment, preparing a nest beneath your mountain in which to breed. And this means of course that in a short while there may be a whole family of these creatures that you will have to deal with!"

After a short thoughtful pause, Jareck turned to me and said.

"So, Ser Jellick, where is this place where these hunters will be meeting up with the boats this evening?"

We were in place, hidden and waiting for the ten hunters to make their way to the rendezvous with their boats. The worst part about the waiting was that neither Jareck nor Böder had given me any sign of a commitment to come with me to try and help me recover my family's treasure from the troll. Nor had they even given me their blessing to allow Traxxa to remain and help train Böder in the art of fighting and weaponry. I was just beginning to resign myself to the fact that perhaps they weren't going to comply with my plans and that I might have to write my whole investment in them off as a complete loss when the hunters began to return.

Slowly, over the next quarter of an hour or so, they made their way, one by one, warily out from the dense under brush and placed their six kills on the sandy river bank. It was only when they had all arrived and were sitting by a small smokeless fire that Böder rose up out of the small ravine where he had been hiding. Together we approached the hunters with the confidence of owners who had got the drop on a load of poachers.

"You have a choice my friends", called out Jareck as he broke into their little clearing, "you can either pay five slev pieces for each deer you have killed or you can forfeit them back to me and my brother!"

The hunters rose as one and began preparing their weapons for a fight, but then Böder let out a ferocious blood chilling roar as I have never heard before and never wished to hear again. Six of the ten hunters froze in absolute fear, but four hunters took off in four different directions. Two ran too close to Böder who swatted one into a tree and the other he picked up with the ease of a man picking up a large domestic cat and threw him effortlessly back into the huddled men around the campfire.

One of the men ran directly at Jareck and was almost on him when he simply fell over unconscious from a smack on the head from Traxxa wielding a small branch in his hand. Even as the man was falling to the ground Traxxa turned and hurled the branch at the fourth man who was just about to vanish into the underbrush by the side of the river. He too fell down as the branch struck him on the shoulders and head. Traxxa walked casually over to him and picked up one of his legs then dragged him back to where the others were waiting in silent dread.

I noticed out of the corner of my eye that Jareck was watching Traxxa with undisguised interest. Perhaps he was in shock at the quick turn of events or perhaps even annoyed that Traxxa had interfered with his right to battle one of the fleeing hunters I don't know, nor did I particularly care, because there were things we needed to do before Frisha landed.

At about the same time as Böder had roared and the brief scurrying melee with the hunters had taken place, the boats arrived from out of the gloom of darkness and were just landing. And even now both boats were desperately trying to back paddle and get out of there without being set upon by the giant.

However, it was all too late, even as Böder finished hurling the hunter towards the others by the campfire he saw the boats landing and moved purposefully out towards the river. He was upon them in the shallows in two strides and grabbed the bows of each boat and hauled them up and out of the water as easily as a man would pull a canoe up onto the sandy shore. As he did this, the captains and the crews of both boats tumbled about bumping into one another falling to the deck whilst several fell out of the boats and into the water. Needless to say they were shaken and bruised when the boats were dropped to the shore, but none were seriously injured.

Only when all had been taken care of, which included accounting for each of the kills and only after slev had passed hands, were the two boats -- with their sullen loads of frightened hunters, returning captives and furtive fisher folk -- allowed to cast off. As they were paddling away from the sandy shore as fast as fear and adrenalin would allow, we noticed that in their enthusiasm to leave as quickly as they could they had left the majority of their hunting equipment behind. This included seven bows, and seven quivers nearly full of arrows, six hunting knives and two short swords.

It was just as they were disappearing around a bend in the river that Frisha and his boat pulled into the sandy bank. Meanwhile, Jareck, who had been talking in low, earnest tones with Böder, broke from his conspiring whispers and approached me a little sheepishly.

"Good Jellick," he began awkwardly. I gave him encouraging non verbals for him to continue, though I was silently fearful of hearing the worst.

"Well, Böder and I have been talking and after seeing how Traxxa took care of those two fleeing hunters with the calm, efficiency of a competent fighter, we have decided to accept your proposal to have Traxxa stay with us and teach us how to fight and defend ourselves!"

"That's great -- !" I started to say but he held up his hand.

"Böder and I would also like to help you recover this family jewel that you spoke of, even if it means going up against a mountain troll. We have in just this one day seen that there is a lot of life left in the living and you and your plans have shown us, even in just this short period of time that life can be interesting. So we will help you and listen to all that Traxxa might have to teach and show us -- if that is still alright with you?"

"Of course it is Jareck and thanx for your honesty and letting me know about your decision so quickly. I appreciate that very much, as many people will often 'umm' and 'arrgh' in order to gain a better result for themselves!"

Jareck seemed to be pleased with my response for he turned quickly to return to Böder to perhaps share with him what I had just told him.

Just then Frisha landed upon the sandy bank and Earlich was the first to jump ashore. He moved up quickly to greet me warmly and my two island hosts. After reacquainting myself with Frisha, I introduced him as the boat's captain along with his two sons to Jareck and Böder both of whom seemed to receive them well enough. Though it must be said the boatload of new island guests were a little awe struck at first by the size and comparative charm of their overlarge host -- but then it is not every day that you get to meet an eight meter tall giant especially one that smiles warmly at you. When all the welcoming pleasantries were complete, we as one began to unload the boat of all its stores.

Strangely enough, with each item that came off the boat, it felt like I too was being unloaded. By this simple act alone it seemed somehow to help me clear my own decks and so allow me to start preparing for the next step in my plans. But this feeling of emptying and replenishing always seemed to come at the conclusion of a satisfactory deal that I had orchestrated or played a part in. Nevertheless, it was just those few words from Jareck that had set my spirits soaring and I felt positive for the first time in nearly a year about the prospect of regaining my family's treasures from the troll.

One thing that amused me greatly though, was the way in which Jareck -- and particularly Böder -- were responding by 'oohing' and 'aahing' as each of the many stores that had been planned for them from the outset was being unloaded. I sensed though that it was much more than just the items they were receiving that excited them so much. I knew -- I just knew -- they were slowly being presented with the hope of full restoration of themselves after so many long years of being neglected and forgotten.

There were things I had gotten for them that I hadn't told them were coming, and yet, it was for these very items that seemed to matter so much more than even I could have imagined. Perhaps the two brothers hadn't even considered how much they needed or wanted them until they saw the items. For instance I watched in fascination as they caressed the axes and many of the other farming and domestic implements which they seemed to marvel at when they saw them being unloaded.

The last piece to come from the boat was the one thing that I wanted to present to Böder personally. It was something that I had found in my travels to Katra and had been very expensive indeed. It was the one item which, if Jareck hadn't confirmed they were going to go ahead with my plans, Böder would never have seen or heard about. So I made sure it was last and asked Earlich to help me get it out from the bottom of the boat. Then together, we presented a giant's sword in its sheath to a delighted young Böder who took it easily enough out of our struggling hands, and in stark contrast it immediately looked comfortable in his right hand.

He drew the sword from its sheath and swished it back once then twice just to get a proper feel for it smiling broadly all the while. He then looked down on me continuing to smile and nodded his head just the once. Despite the fact that there was little light other than the stars and quarter moon I believe I saw a tear trickle from his right eye which he quickly wiped away.

"I will see you in a month and a half," I said to Traxxa and moved to grasp his wrist in friendly departure. Here I also handed him his sword and short sword and throwing knife which had also come across with Earlich and Frisha. Traxxa responded like he had known all along that Jareck and Böder would agree to our plans in the end. Then I turned to Böder and thanked him for his hospitality and extended my arm for the customary parting of ways between friends.

Böder was delightfully happy and took to the custom of arm grasping and shaking three times with an enthusiasm and a grin that was as infectious as it was amusing. And finally I turned to Jareck who I noticed was standing to one side watching and studying me. This, I must say was a little unnerving, and now for some reason I suddenly felt a little unsure of myself, so I said carefully.

"I will leave you to take these stores up to your farm and I will see you when I return in about six weeks. Please look after Traxxa as you would an honoured guest if only for my sake -- and take everything he says regarding fighting and weaponry to heart for his words and ways will almost definitely benefit you both in the long run!"

"I will – th -- that is, we will look after him, good Ser Jellick and thank you for your gifts and the stores you have brought us!"

I extended my arm for the customary goodbye between friends, but he moved inside it and hugged me as a brother, and whispered in my ear.

"I am only just beginning to realize what an advantage it would be to have someone such as yourself meeting with Böder and me on a regular basis! I have seen how happy Böder is in just this short time with you and I just want to say thanx for coming to visit with us!"

With that we parted ways and I began to walk towards Frisha's boat when Traxxa touched my arm. I paused and looked at him.

"I have an idea on how to deal with the drazils, so when you come back can you bring me some poison that has the potential to kill a dozen horses?"

I nodded my head and turned back to follow Frisha to his boat. As I settled into my seat aboard the water craft, I smiled quietly to myself. Still it amazed me just how far ahead Traxxa was in planning and dealing with strategic issues and threats.

As we sailed back across the Dund I thought more and more about Jareck and his relationship with Böder. It was only then that it occurred to me what might be troubling Jareck and yet exciting him at the same time. He knew that their world was about to change and he wasn't completely sure he wanted it to head in the direction I was intending to take them or if indeed it was the right path to pursue.

Still little was I to know that their time with Traxxa was going to be more crucial than I could ever have imagined!

Chapter Seven

Earlich

Six weeks have passed from the time Tor Jellick and I left Böders Island until we returned. When we reached the island, Frisha's small fishing boat was laden down, alarmingly so, with more supplies including one of the largest anvils that I had ever seen along with hammers and other smiths tools for Barill. To help transport the supplies up to the farm house Tor Jellick also brought over a two wheeled barrow. Personally I don't know how Frisha managed to get all the supplies onto his little fishing boat let alone navigating it safely across to the island without it sinking. This in itself was a credit to the skill of this Ottarman and his understanding of the waters of the Dund. Needless to say all these new supplies continued to thrill our big giant friend no end.

We spent two days upon the island during which Traxxa told us of his time with Böder, Jareck and Barill. Traxxa is not a born story teller and it took all our efforts just to get him to tell us of all that had transpired. Where he lapsed into forgetfulness or missed some interesting points we recovered the information from the very eager assistance of either Böder or Jareck and occasionally even Barill contributed which of course helped maintain the story line.

Traxxa

Even with Böders strength and size, it still took us four trips to carry all the supplies Earlich and Frisha had brought over up from the river bank to the farm. We did one trip that first night and by way of a celebration at the prospect of a new lease of life on the island, Böder, Jareck and Barill wanted to sample one of the barrels of beer. With many years of sobriety between Böder and Jareck, it didn't take long before the idea of making another trip for the supplies vanished along with the beer.

Next morning -- or whenever we finally woke up -- after a lengthy breakfast, we made our way slowly back down to the river bank. We finished bringing up the remainder of the stores, including what the hunters had left behind, as the first hour of darkness began descending over the island. During these trips to and from the river bank, it was interesting to watch both Böder and Jareck as they carried the supplies. I noted their movements, their strengths, their levels of endurance and their application to the task at hand. I noted with mild interest their limitations and from this I began to formulate a strategy on how best to train Böder for the dangers that I thought he might encounter in the near future.

After the second trip up from the river bank, Barill made the suggestion that he would stay back at the farm and prepare one of the two deer that had been left behind by the hunters. Böder clapped his hands at the suggestion and danced a little jig, which made us all laugh. But we all agreed that this was an excellent idea and after encouraging Barill to look amongst the supplies to see what tools there were to help him prepare the venison, he began the task of preparing it and cooking it on an open fire. As we walked back towards the river I suddenly realised what a wonderful motivator the promise of a decent meal was for these two - especially for Böder.

That night as we settled down to take our fill of the barbequed deer, Barill offered to serve Böder a drink. We were all a bit curious about this sudden desire by Barill to serve our giant host when, with Jarecks help, he presented Böder with his own mug. He had taken the empty barrel of beer that we had finished off the night before and had placed a rudimentary handle onto it so now Böder had a mug that best suited his giant hand and over large mouth. Barill had taken a strong curving branch and had skilfully carved it into the shape of a handle. It was a simple enough gift, finished off by a skilled artisan using the tools that had only just been brought over to the island and yet, as Böder accepted it from its maker, a tear of joy trickled down his cheek.

It was these little things that helped me see the true character of this amiable giant. This, I believed, was the second time in as many days where he had been made to feel special, and he and Jareck both noticed it.

We put the stores into the storage caves and fixed up temporary doors that would still not be easy to get at without the strength and size of Böder. Barill indicated that he was happy to keep the cave that he had been using as his quarters. Apparently the fact he could have his freedom and leave the island whenever he wanted did not influence him into trying to change his living quarters. For the moment at least!

I decided to use one of the vacated caves as a place to call my own but only after I had cleaned it out as best I could. I declined to have the large wooden wall of a door put fast against the caves opening, but, with Böder's help, we placed it in such a way as to allow me movement in and out of the cave as I desired while keeping out the elements and the chill night air and possibly a Traxxa eating drazil.

It was my second night on Böders Island and everybody was settling down into a recognizable routine. Despite myself, I found that I was comfortably exhausted and collapsed early in the evening onto my roughly made bed in my cave like room expecting a good night's sleep.

Later that night, I was disturbed from my sleep by a loud scuffling noise outside the solid wooden wall of my cave. Instantly alert, I got up noiselessly from my bed and listened intently to the noises just outside my entrance. It sounded like some large creature was trying to find a way in and was scratching at the logs to try and make the entrance larger. I was suddenly very grateful to Böder for securing my door/wall firmly with the wooded post dug deep into the ground on the outside. Silently I reached for my swords and made my way cautiously to my caves entrance. The creature suddenly lost interest in my door and lumbered off snuffling and snorting as it went. Moments later there was a loud squeal and it was obvious by the sounds that one of our boars was being taken from its enclosure. I knew what was outside and I was reluctant to go out into the dark to meet with a hungry drazil which had only moments before been trying to get into my cave to get at me.

I looked out of my doorway but could only see shadows and the darkness of the night. I threw my swords in their sheaths over my shoulder and secured them with the harness straps. I then dropped to my hands.

As I did this my hands became paws and I padded out into the night air in the form of my animal self, that of a timber wolf. As I moved forward my eyes were adjusting to the night light. I picked up the intense stench of the large carnivorous lizard immediately and moved cautiously keeping to the shadows of the cliffs and caves, towards Böders cave.

I heard the sound of the drazil to my right moving quickly away from the pens and out towards the fields. There was a sound to my left and I stopped and looked. It was Barill in his large cat form just coming out of his cave. He stopped nervously and looked at me, acknowledged my presence and fell into step with me as we moved forward up to Böder and Jarecks' cavern. Barill was already changing back into his human form and was reaching up to knock on their door. I decided not to stop with him as I had spotted the drazil out in the middle of the field moving very fast down towards the lake. I felt it was more important to keep the drazil in my line of sight. There were no clear features in the darkness as clouds had all but obscured the moon and the starry sky but it was huge standing almost four meters at the shoulder. Its length was indiscernible but I could just make out the large male boar in its mouth and from the way that the drazil was carrying it, it was as though it was carrying one of its own young.

I heard Jareck opening his door and coming out of his lodgings behind me and then there came the almighty roar of Böder who had yet to open his door. At the sound of the giant, the drazil increased its speed and was entering the water of the lake even as Böder was coming out of his home.

I was happy enough just to have been able to watch, undetected, this magnificent reptile run down through the field, enter the water and vanish beneath the surface of the lake. But more than that, I was glad it hadn't dropped its prey and turned to meet with the roaring threat behind it. This told me a number of things. The first being, food was more important, at the moment, to the drazil than establishing its territory. The second thing I realised was by taking the boar meant that it was probably taking the food back to its nest -- otherwise it would have eaten it already.

Later on when the sun had come up, after checking out the extent of the damage done by the drazil, we found the wooden wall covering the storage cave had been moved and the carcass of the second deer left behind by the hunters had been taken. It had obviously been drawn to the smell of the dead deer got in and eaten it. To me this was astounding as it told me at once of the huge appetite this creature must have, but it also confirmed in my mind that the drazil had taken the boar back to its nest. This was done to either feed its mate or in preparation for the coming of its offspring. Either way it was not a good sign at all.

As I investigated the wooden wall of the store cave, I saw that it had been pulled open with great care. And yet when I talked with the others none of us could recall hearing any noises of this break in and theft. This disturbed me greatly because even I hadn't heard it until it had come snuffling around my own door. This told me that it was an exceedingly careful and a deviously cunning hunter.

I told the others over breakfast my thoughts and fears regarding the drazil. I also described it in as much detail as I had been able to see despite the darkness.

"It is about seventeen meters long and has six legs. There are two in front at the shoulder and four legs at the back. Its tail is about twelve meters long and though I couldn't see it clearly, I believe it would be a powerful creature and a deadly adversary. Its snout and teeth are about the same length as that of a six meter crocodile though it is not in direct proportion to this reptile!"

"What do you mean by that?" Böder asked a little confused.

"Well let's say the drazil is roughly three times bigger than a six meter croc, agreed?" They all nodded in agreement. "Then it stands to reason that -- if it was in direct proportion -- then the snout and jaws should be three times bigger as well!"

"But, you're saying it's not, it's only the same size as the six meter croc! I see what you mean now!"

"Yes that's good -- but don't misunderstand me, the jaws are much bigger and stronger than that of a croc even though the length of the snout and teeth are roughly the same!"

"How can you say that? After all you can't have had a good look at it and it was running away from you in the middle of the field -- and in the dark of the night as well?"

This time it was Jareck who was questioning me. Not with scepticism you understand! It was more like he was genuinely interested in knowing -- probably in order to try and assess the true extent of this new enemy.

"The first thing is the drazil didn't eat the entire carcass of the deer it took from the store cave. It left a little under a hind quarter but from this I could measure the bite and the teeth. Secondly the fact that it was carrying your full grown boar with the ease that it was tells us that its jaws and neck muscles must be incredibly large and strong. But more than that, when it heard Böders roar it increased its speed without a faltering in its step, which tells us it must have incredible strength and stamina as well!"

"I wish I had come out sooner," said Böder despondently, "I could have taken it on with this!" And he grabbed his new sword and swished it back and forth easily enough with just one hand. It was a very big sword for any one of us -- a bit rusty perhaps and probably needed to be cleaned and sharpened -- but in Böders huge hand it was like a short dagger. The way he handled it everyone could see that Böder already loved it and was just dying to put it to some use.

"Well I for one am very glad that you didn't come out to fight with the drazil last night -- sword or no sword!" I said evenly.

"But why not?" He said pouting just a little. "It took my boar and the deer! I could have taken that stupid drazil on!"

"There are a number of very good reasons why I'm glad you didn't try to take it on. First it is a huge killing creature which we know very little about. For instance, we don't know how quick it is, how it fights, what its strengths are or its weaknesses are -- if it has any, that is. But the most important thing of all was that it happened in the dark of night. So now Böder, what are your eyes like in the darkness?"

After a short pause his head dropped just a little

"Not very good I suppose. I'm very good at smelling things, but during the night, I would need a torch or a light crystal to help me see what I'm doing and where I'm going!"

"That's exactly what I mean. To take on a drazil and one we know very little about at this time, despite how big and strong you are, you will need to have every advantage in your favour -- and not being able to see as well as it can in the dark is definitely not to your advantage."

Böder to his credit nodded his head and said wisely, "I see what you mean. So what do we do now? I don't want this drazil coming up and stealing my stock and threatening me in my own house every night!"

"Well, I've been thinking about that very thing all night. In fact I've been thinking about how to deal with this drazil ever since I first heard about it. But first, before we begin to talk about taking on the drazil, we need to think of a way to stop it from coming up onto your farm. We have to let it know that this is your territory not the drazils -- agreed?"

They all agreed.

"So, it appears that this drazil has just eaten well -- at your expense Böder!" He smiled to let me know that he was with me.

"It's a reptile, and most reptiles have a slow digestion rate which means we have about two – three days in which to prepare a trap, before they come out looking for more food. Because next time they come it will be on our terms okay?"

Again they all agreed and even looked hopeful and with purpose. So we talked about the fence they had been trying to put up the other day and with tools in hand we made our way down to the lake shore to look at what could be done. With the prospect of proper tools to help cut down trees to make new posts and sharpening them into stakes, Böder, Jareck and Barill looked with renewed interest at the task in hand.

"What if the drazil comes back tonight and we aren't yet ready to deal with it?" asked Barill.

"A good question! Any thoughts?" I asked.

After a thoughtful pause it was Jareck who suggested we set up a fire trap just behind the fences in case the drazil began to test the fence and found it could just clamber over them. So with this in mind as Jareck and Böder went to cut down some more trees to use as posts, Barill and I dug a trench a meter wide and half a meter deep. It was the length of the field between the first outcrop of mountain rock at one end and thick and heavy bushland at the other end. Barill and I decided it was just too thick even for a drazil to bother trying to get through it. As we were digging and filling the trench in with dry grass and fire fodder, an idea came to me on how best to deal with the drazil and not have to meet with it in open battle, which if the truth be known I did not relish at all.

I left Barill to finish off and found Böder and Jareck felling trees further up the hilly slopes away from the lake. I got some strong vines and with Böders help we tied a couple of the logs up and tied the other end of the vines around each leg below the knee.

"What are we doing this for?" Böder asked interested yet mystified.

"Your training is beginning!" I said evenly. "The biggest weakness of all giants as everyone knows is your legs. So whenever you lift something heavy, or climb or exercise, I want you to think about how you can turn this into an exercise that will help strengthen your legs particularly below the knees. So now walk slowly dragging these logs using only the lower half of your legs. I've put bark around your shins so as not to damage your skin too much!"

Böder took a few steps dragging the logs behind him.

"How do they feel?"

"Alright!" replied Böder a little tentatively. "Awkward and uncomfortable but otherwise alright."

"Okay just go slowly until you've got your balance and know how each log feels and responds to your stride. Remember you're on a slope and the logs may roll so you need to be aware of the way they move. We're right behind you to help you in case there is any problem."

Böder began walking slowly back to his farm, whilst dragging the two small tree trunks behind him. As we walked behind the lumbering giant, I described to Jareck what I planned to do in order to tackle our drazil problem. He liked my ideas very much and so we discussed how we would set about making our trap.

It took us the best part of three days before all the wooden stakes had been driven into the ground with the help of a number of huge rocks and powered by Böders almost unquenchable strength. The stakes were placed in clusters atop of a small rise that separated the sand and muddy shoreline of the lake from the beginning of the ploughed fields of the farm. Behind the stake barriers was our fire holding ditch. In the middle of these barriers facing the lake I described to Böder, Jareck and Barill how I wanted our trap for the drazil to be done. They were all keen to set the trap up quickly. After talking with Barill about how he could help he designed and cut out a large spade from a slender tree trunk for Böder to use in digging out a large ditch in the middle of our barriers.

As he was digging the ditch the rest of us were trimming the stakes to sharp points. As we did this, Jareck said something that caught my attention.

"If this drazil is so cunning and careful, won't he mistrust the only opening in our barrier in front of the fields?"

"Well then why don't we put a door in the opening and make it think that we are trying to keep it from coming through, when in fact we want it to go in!"

'This was said by Barill who was working beside us. Both Jareck and I looked at him in amazement, this was such a good idea that we told him this! So we took one of the empty caverns large wooden doors and placed it in such a way that it filled the only gap there was between the clusters of sharpened stakes facing the lake. This job alone took us nearly all of one day as we had to roll it down the hill using tree trunks as rollers and set it up on some makeshift hinges attached to a large post. This allowed us to swing it open easily. We each made it a point from then on to pass through this door alone to find our way down to the lake or back up to the farm -- though it must be said we were all small enough to squeeze between the wooden stakes. All except Böder that is but he was only too happy to use the door as he just looked on it as one big game to try and fool the drazil.

During the third night, after the drazil had broken into the storeroom and taken both the deer and the boar, Barill heard the drazil snuffling around our barrier fence and scratching tentatively at the large wooden door. It was just after midnight and he was on watch and as he heard the first sounds of the creature he lit his torch and placed it over the fire pit. The dried grasses and fire fodder had been liberally laced with boar fat and oil. Immediately the ditch became ablaze and the fire raced across the front of the farm fields. As the fire got going, Barill put his lips against a bone hollowed horn and blew it raising the alarm. This had us all racing swiftly out of our beds and down to help him by the stake barriers in a little less than three minutes. The huge drazil in the meantime had been so startled by the sudden firelight that it had staggered back in confusion. Its fear had increased at the strange sound of the blaring of the horn. By the time we arrived to help Barill cope with the creature, it had retreated back into the lake and disappeared from sight. We were all very pleased that our makeshift fire fence had worked out so well, but we decided to stay with Barill and tend to the fire for the rest of the night.

Next morning, I worked out we were going to be finished digging out our trap by the end of the day. But we needed to be sure, so we reset the fire fence and Barill and Jareck went off to hunt for some fresh deer meat. Whilst they were gone, Böder and I continued digging the ditch come pit and eventually the trap behind the wooden door. For the first five meters or so I had Böder dig it just a little wider than what we had estimated to be the width of the drazil. This went on flat and straight as the farming fields rose up on either side to begin forming the sides of the pit. As Böder shovelled out the main dirt of the pit, I meanwhile used a mattock and chiselled out the dirt so that the edges of the pit dropped by half a meter.

"Why are you doing that?" asked Böder when he saw what I was up to.

"I don't want the creature to become comfortable as he walks into the pit. So the moment it walks in here it will find by the slight unevenness of the floor at the edges it a little uncomfortable and maybe try and move along a little quicker to pass it by."

"But won't it stop and try backing out of our trap the moment it finds it uncomfortable?" Asked Böder interested by all that was being done around him.

"Aaahhh! But you must remember why it's coming in here in the first place! Once past the small ditches on either side of it, the floor will become even once more and it will start to relax believing it has overcome the obstacles in front of it!"

Böder smiled at the thought and continued digging. It took him almost all of the day to finish digging out the pit so that in the end it went into the side of the hill for about twenty-two meters. In the last ten meters, the walls of the pit came in gradually so that by the end it would be a tight fit for the drazil and so providing it with no space to turn around or even to try and climb up and out of it. The sides of the pit ended up at almost eight meters high and had been shored up in strategic places so that the walls wouldn't collapse in on itself and so provide the reptile with the means of climbing out. To be safe though, we placed a number of clusters of sharpened stakes facing downwards along the tops of the walls and at the end of the pit to discourage the drazil from even thinking about trying to climb up and out of our pit-come-trap.

When Jareck and Barill returned late that afternoon, they had two deer carcasses with them. Slashing one of them open we took out its innards and placed it on the floor at the end of our pit/trap. With the door to the pit closed – though not secured, -- we went and put the rest of the deer on the fire and set about having a final meal before the battle for supremacy over Böder's Island had begun.

The drazil did not come by that night nor the next, though we were all camped out in the darkened corner of the field waiting for it. During the days I began instructing Böder in the handling of his sword. I showed him how to wield the blade whereupon he would try and imitate my movements. I showed him a number of different fighting stances and explained why, when and how they would be used. The next thing I showed him was how best to move his feet and other exercises that would help him in his meeting with the drazil in the pit. I asked him if he wanted to be the one to jump on the creature when it finally got caught in our trap.

"Do you think this is really the best way to deal with the drazil?" asked Böder during one of our training sessions.

"The drazil is a large, ferocious reptile. It is extremely strong, fast and dangerous. The claws alone are long and sharp and are quite capable of causing you great harm. Its four hind legs and lengthy tail give it the strength and capability of instant height with a very strong foundation from which to take on all adversaries known throughout all of Durogg, including giants and multiple attackers. To get some sort of perspective, you are what, just over eight meters tall? Well this drazil is nearly eighteen meters long and yet it stands at only four meters at the shoulder. However, if it was to stand on its hind legs it would measure well over eight meters and still be twice as strong, and equally ferocious and vicious. To top it off the Drazil is much faster and instinctively reactive and has much larger teeth than you. Put it this way Böder, you have never faced such a foe in your young life so we need to take these strengths away from it if we even hope to have any chance of defeating it. Besides I can't risk you fighting this drazil and getting yourself injured in any way! Don't you remember, Tor Jellick has instructed me to prepare you to go head to head with a mountain troll, not get yourself cut to ribbons by a large lizard!"

Despite my dire words of peril, Böder smiled at the way I had put it to him.

"But do you really think the drazil will just walk right into our trap?" He asked a little uncertainly.

"Absolutely! Without a doubt -- and when he does we just have to be prepared! So now get your arms up grasp your sword and thrust down, as I have shown you!"

As Böders practise continued, Barill and Jareck set about tending the farm which had been largely neglected over the last week or so. Jareck was still marvelling at the many stores, tools and equipment that he now had and he was anxious to use them just as much to see the results as to know and feel the comfort of their serviceability. He was enjoying himself immensely and so too was Barill who could only smile at his friends unexpected happiness.

We had placed all our left over scraps of the deer, skin and bones and offal into our pit along the floor. Thus on the third evening after the pit had been complete, just as the sun was setting I spotted the drazil emerging from the lake. It made its way straight up to the closed door and I signalled to the others to keep quiet as the snuffling by the drazil around the barriers and where the door began. We all held our collective breaths. And then we saw the door torn away from its fixed position like it was paper on bamboo sticks. We as one crouched and moved silently over to the top of the pit and peered down and into it. Böder was moving along with us but a little further back so as not to be seen by the drazil in the pit. I was pleasantly surprised to see, much as I had predicted, the creature moving quickly to pass the awkward ground at the beginning of the trap. With the floor returning to normal it had moved comfortably onwards but then almost immediately it found itself getting squeezed in by the sides of the pit as it moved forward. It paused for a moment before putting its snout into the air which it sniffed suspiciously. But with the stench of the rotting deer meat at the end of the trap calling strongly to its greater basic instincts, it threw caution to the wind and moved quickly up to it.

At the prearranged moment when the first mouthful of the deer meat was taken, Böder, after first determining where he would land, leapt over the edge of the trap and landed on top of the neck of the drazil. At the same time as his knees ploughed onto the back of the drazil's neck, his mighty arms -- which were in the air to maintain balance and hold his sword -- came crashing down. Thus at the very instant Böder landed on top of the drazil, his long rusty blade was entering the skull of the startled reptile. To everyone's surprise the drazil was dead and dropping to the floor before it had fully realized it was even under attack.

We all let out an almighty cry of triumph and danced a very untidy jig around the top of the pit. But the poor ecstatic Böder couldn't get himself out of the pit because when the drazil dropped down dead its body weight trapped the giants left leg against the side of the pit. So for the next 2 hours or so, sniggling and laughing at the predicament of our big friend, we helped dig him out of the drazils grave. Finally, when he was out, we helped Böder replace the door to the trap before we returned to the farmhouse to celebrate the kill with a feast of roast deer meat, fresh farm vegetables and a whole cask of beer.

For the next month or so, I had Böder out daily on a regular schedule of exercises and training, both physically and with his sword which he loved wielding. In all our time together, I noticed that more than anything else this young giant, had an insatiable quest for information and an almost overwhelming willingness to learn. Along with his huge stature he had an immense appetite for new things and new experiences. Many times Jareck and occasionally Barill would join in and provide the young giant with the support and encouragement that he probably needed. My primary concern though was to help build up the leg muscles and strengthen the young giants' shins as well as helping him with his balance, speed and endurance. These exercises included him running up against the current of the river coming into the island from the Dund at least once a day and walking or running two or three times a week up the steep sides of the mountains on the island.

In doing this, I found I inadvertently helped Böder to overcome some of his fear of water as he came to understand a little bit more about its movement and the feel of it around his legs and feet as he worked his way through it. But I could still see how much he hated the unseen nature that the deep water hid from him. So when I could, I encouraged him to put his head below the surface and paddle on his belly in the deeper parts of the river. Though I warned him against swimming in the islands large lake at the end of the farm. We hadn't noticed any activity or seen other signs of anymore drazils during the rest of our time on the island. But this didn't mean they were not around and that it was not a very real danger to any of us - especially in the greater depths of the islands lake.

As I spent time talking with Jareck and instructing Böder in running through the river, Jareck pointed out they had always had a problem with freshwater crocodiles particularly in the section of the river between the waterfall and the Dunds' entrance. Not only that, but the numbers had been increasing over the years and yet very few had ever ventured down into the lake in all the time they had been on the island. But now, especially since coming down to train with Böder, he had noticed there had been a significant drop in the number of crocodiles on the island.

He wondered aloud if this might not be a direct result of the drazils setting up their territory on the island.

I was silent as he talked about this, but I thought it was highly likely.

On a number of my training sessions with Böder, Jareck and sometimes Barill would also join us in our training exercises. Jareck had taken possession of the weapons left behind by the hunters and using their blades many time he would take up a sparring role with me. During this time I noticed that he too slowly came to understand and master the more basic principles of swordplay. But it was the bows and quivers full of arrows that captured his interest the most and often during our weapons time together, Jareck would move to one side and practice for hours perfecting his technique and shooting at fixed but lifeless targets.

And then one day, mid way through the sixth week of my time on the island with Böder, Jareck and Barill, there came a knock on the door. This, it turned out to be, was when you had returned to come and take us onto the next part of our adventure together!

CHAPTER EIGHT

JELLICK

After the six weeks were up, we arrived back in Bernitz and once more employed the services of Frisha and his boat. I'm not so sure that he was best pleased to see me. But we paid him well, and for this he made his services available to me again with a smile and the greeting of a friend. I had sent Earlich ahead of me to purchase all the supplies that I had in mind for Böder and Jareck. Most of these were what they wanted on their island based on our previous talks.

We left Bernitz early the next morning and after crossing the Dund uneventfully we arrived at the river which took us into the heart of Böders Island. We followed the course of the island river up to a major bend which then curved around the islands smallest mountain to a high waterfall which dropped down into the lake. It was at this bend which we judged the river to be at its closest point to Böders farm. After a half-hour walk we came across a barrier of spikes and a large barricaded door at the bottom of the farm facing the lake. We squeezed in between the clusters of spikes and made ourselves known to the hosts of the island and reacquainted ourselves with Traxxa. Over a healthy celebratory lunch which included Frisha and his two sons. We took a quick tour around the farm and we marvelled at all that Böder, Jareck and Barill had achieved since we had last been there. During the course of the day, Traxxa and the others gave us a more detailed account of all that had transpired.

The most important thing I wanted to find out though was Traxxa's assessment of Böders progress. Once we were away from the others, Traxxa told me the young giant was doing very well -- so much so that he felt that Böder was more than ready to meet with Trow - the troll in possession of my family's treasure. This was very encouraging so I talked with Traxxa about what our next move should be in order to begin our journey towards Trows Mountain.

Two days later, Barill left us by the boat waving and giving parting words of encouragement before he turned back towards the farm. He had told us that -- he was going to begin the task of laying poisoned bait around for the drazil. I smiled to myself at Traxxa's foresight. Barill also indicated to me privately that he was very excited to have received some of the supplies that we had brought over which were specifically for him. He then confided in me that whilst we were gone he was going to set up his smith's workshop, for which he thanked and embraced me out of sight of the others.

Böder reassured us he was happy to stay awake in the boat whilst crossing the Dund. So after packing the travelling gear into the boat's hold and reassuring Frisha that all would be well on the crossing we moved to leave.

Böder pushed Frisha's small fishing vessel to the head of the islands river. He tried a couple of times to get into the boat, but each time it had threatened to tip or simply submerge, such was his weight. I was considering the possibility of returning to Bernitz to try and hire the services of a much larger river craft, when Böder spoke up and said that he was willing to try and paddle across the Dund with us whilst hanging onto the boat as it went.

I looked across at Traxxa expectantly who just shrugged his shoulders.

"Did I forget to mention that I've been helping Böder to overcome his fear of water. As a result, I think I may have taught him how to swim. I don't know if that was a good idea or not! What do you think?"

I smiled briefly then looked quickly at Frisha.

"I believe it would be prudent if you kept this information from anyone on the mainland -- at least for the time being! Do you agree?"

Frisha looked at me like he had just eaten a mouthful of hot chillies but nodded his head in quiet agreement. His biggest fear, I realized soon enough was that the boat would capsize in the middle of the river with Böder hanging onto the side. But, to his credit, he said nothing and so we began the task of taking our giant friend off the island for the first time in seven years.

We entered the main flow of the river and the current took us quickly across to the mainlands river bank in as straight a line as was possible. Böder held on diligently with his right arm across the width of the small boat in an effort to maximise stability both for himself and for the small craft, whilst his left hand held onto the port side gunnels. He was also careful to keep his head above the water in order to listen carefully to any instructions either Frisha or Traxxa might try and give him such as the finer points of kicking or pushing the boat in a particular direction. Meanwhile, the rest of us sat on the far side of the boat to help counter the giant's weight. In this way we made good time and I was enthralled though I had feared the worst. In fact Böder indicated that he had thoroughly enjoyed the experience and wouldn't rule out trying to do it again if the need arises in our journey together.

We thanked Frisha emphatically for his help and promised him a healthy reward when next we returned to Bernitz. However we stopped short of telling him where we were headed and what we believed we would be bringing back with us after dealing with Trow. We then parted company watching as Frisha and his sons began sailing back up the river towards Bernitz. When they were gone we turned and made our way directly inland.

At our first opportunity, I purchased a number of horses to help us match the easy stride of our young giant friend. Our journey over the lands of M'Lenn-Fida towards the very edge of the mighty Taka Mountain range where Trows Mountain was, took us the better part of ten days. We moved as quickly and as silently as we could through the wilderness, bypassing towns and villages and avoiding as many of the trails and main roads as we could. At the few farmhouses and settlements which we came across, we sent Böder around with at least one of us for company to avoid being detected, whilst the others would go in and purchase regular supplies and other essentials for our trip.

On a number of occasions we came across fellow travellers, a number of farmers, as well as some hunters and trappers. But on each occasion either Traxxa -- who was riding as scout -- warned us of their presence or Böder was able to smell or see them well before he was in danger of being seen himself. In this way, to the best of our knowledge, he was always able to conceal himself or move quietly around those ahead of us thus and avoided detection.

The only real problem (*which we encountered almost immediately*) was the affect Böder was having on the birds and creatures of the forests. The silence caused by his presence was almost overwhelming and certainly noticeable -- so much so that anyone roaming through the forest at the same time as us wouldn't help but notice the eerie silence. We were discussing this around our campfire on the first evening of our journey together and were wondering how we could best counteract the impact Böder's presence was having on the wildlife. Strangely enough it was Earlich who made the suggestion that his bird imitations might just help persuade the birds of the forest to accept the giant no matter how imposing or threatening he might appear to them!

We were all a little bit sceptical of this suggestion. But as no-one else was able to come up with a better idea we decided to sleep on the matter. In the morning as we were making preparations to move on, we again noticed the stillness and quiet descend over the wood as Böder began ready himself and move about. Earlich had been standing by watching and waiting and when the silence prevailed he made a number of different bird calls, all sounding incredibly familiar and lifelike. To our astounding surprise the birds and creatures responded and the sounds of the forest returned to normal. Thus it was that whenever the quiet in the woods threatened to extend beyond a general lull, Earlich would make his bird calls, and on each occasion the forest would to call back.

Another incident which we needed to address also happened on the first day of travelling overland with Böder. Within the first four hours of our journey, Böder indicated that he was going to disappear into the bushes and quietly give back to nature what food and drink had given to him over the course of the last few days. Before he could disappear however, Traxxa called out to him, causing Böder to pause and wait, twitching anxiously. Traxxa went over to him and said something that only the young giant, upon lowering his head, could hear. Böder nodded his head in understanding and then moved off quickly yet silently for a little time by himself. When Traxxa returned to our huddled little group I asked him what it was that he had said to the young giant. To which Traxxa replied.

"The quickest way to tell people that a giant is in the area or has passed through, without actually seeing one, is by coming across some of his natural deposits."

"Aaahhh!" I replied in understanding. "So what did you tell him to do?"

"I told him to hide, bury or disperse his contributions back to nature in a way that no hunter or farmer would recognise it for what it was! In case they should, by chance, stumble across it in the woods!"

Here he smiled awkwardly at the base humour of what he was talking about. I helped him finish his awkward moment with a smile and the words

"Hide his giant turd!?"

"Exactly!" Responded Traxxa thankfully and his smile broadened considerably.

We all chuckled conspirationally at the thought of what Böder had to do to avoid being detected by the people in the area.

To be honest though, I don't know what we would have done had he been discovered! The idea of a giant trekking across M'Lenn-Fida with us was probably not one that would have endeared us to any of the local communities. Then again, if word had got out that he was there, we probably wouldn't have been able to control whatever reaction we might have received anyway. Luckily, these are all moot observations as we encountered no problems and had no incidents for which I needed to record.

On our journey we discovered a number of interesting facts about our large giant friend. The first and most potent was the strange things any meal with red in it did to his poor stomach (*and our even more violated noses*). We found this out firsthand when Böder shared a stew with red peppers in it with us. The effects upon him and us were almost catastrophic. It was only after this discovery that Jareck decided to tell us of the danger of serving Böder bloodied meat. He warned us of the consequences of such a meal, as recounted from his earliest recollections of their time together on their farm when they were much younger. He then proceeded to describe in superb, graphic, detail the smells and sounds that brought about the gagging of both he and his parents in the small constrains of the farmhouse. He continued with a passable imitation of the wondrous sounds made by the constant rumblings of Böders stomach which would follow for hours afterwards.

These and other stories from Jareck about Böder had us all rolling around laughing as he recounted the effects of unwittingly feeding him anything with red in it. This meant red vegetables -- particularly beans and berries, beets, and fruit such as red apples and blood grapes including their produce such as red cider or wine -- and now, as confirmed by the smell around the campfire, red peppers or capsicum.

One of the funniest moments on this occasion (*as I remember it*) was when Böder, having just finished his big bowl of stew with its spicy red peppers, whilst still sitting, leant over and away from the campfire to retrieve a couple of pieces of deadwood to feed the fire. He had his back to the fire and without giving any warning he just farted and the explosion of fire and flames from the giant's backside as the expanding gas made its way across the campfire had such devastating results. It singed all the hair on poor Earlich's head and narrowly missed consuming Traxxa completely who had just stepped back out of the flames path after placing a kettle of water near the fire.

"So much for him being less dangerous than the dragons!" said Traxxa with a straight face. At which Böder and Jareck burst out laughing. In fact we continued to recount this story of the great flame from Böder's backside for weeks thereafter. Unfortunately it didn't do too much for Earlich. It made him look like a half-sheared sheep with a ruddy, raw, flame swept complexion. Later, when his face wasn't so tender, we shaved the remaining hair off his face and head just so that he looked half decent - a little like a priest of Succoth (*a serpent worshipping cult*) - but otherwise normal.

Soon after, as we slowly recovered ourselves from Böders outburst, Böder and Jareck opened up and told us of the journey from their farm near Wurke to the island in the middle of the Dund.

Jareck began by recounting some of his earliest memories of Böder and the impact that the young giant had had on his own family life.

"I was only five when Böder was brought into our homestead on the farm. I don't remember many of the early days but as I grew up, I simply believed him to be my younger but bigger brother and loved him as such, even when he started to outgrow me -- which was almost right from the start.

I didn't resent Böder becoming a part of my life, in fact I thought it was great having a bigger brother. I remember being with him when he first began to walk and falling on top of me when he lost his balance. From then on he was always with me, from doing the chores to helping me ride the horses or climbing trees or just playing with him!"

"Were you treated well, when you were younger?" I asked Böder smiling.

"I only remember growing up believing that I had always been a part of Jarecks' family, so I think I was always treated well. Mind you, that's only because I don't have anything to compare it to. But if you're asking was I mistreated I would have to say no, if anything I think I was treated better than Jareck. I don't know if that was because Jareck was the oldest and should have known better or if my step-father was compensating for the part he had played in what had been done to my real father."

"Oh so you know what happened to your real father then?" I asked a little warily.

"I think I knew from an early age. On a couple of occasions I had heard my mother arguing with my step-father and it was largely to do with how we had come to be living with them on the farm."

"And how did your mother die?"

"My mother died of a disease associated with some complications from her crippled legs. She became sick and I wanted to take her to the healer in Wurke, but Jarck wouldn't let me take her to the town. So when she died a few days later I was really upset and I resented my step-father's interference in my wanting to look after my mother.

"Anyway, it was about six months after she died that my anger came bubbling out in an argument fuelled by a couple of flagons of wine with Jarck. It was in the middle of the night and Jarck and I were sitting in my room which was like a barn that had been added onto the farm house. Jareck was sleeping in his room and the argument with Jarck got so heated that I simply lost control. All the frustration of the last couple of months spewed forth during this argument with Jarck and I simply lost control and began to tear the barn down. It was during my destructive outburst that I somehow loosened a beam in the main building and it came down and fell into the hearth fire which, unbeknownst to me it set the rest of the house on fire. When I finally realized there was a fire in the house, my first thought was for Jareck. So I rushed out to rescue him and in the process I lost sight of Jarck. In any case I really didn't care what he was doing or where he was -- all I cared about, at that moment, was to make sure my sleeping brother was safe."

As he said this, Böders head went down and he looked a little sad. I had never seen Böder like this before and as I looked on in quiet speculation it was Jareck who spoke next.

"When it was all finished and we knew that my father had perished in the fire, I remember we sat beside the ruins of our farmhouse and sobbed together as brothers. Both of us cried because we saw there was an immediate loss of our childhood home. This of course was coupled with my tears of grief for the loss of my father and for Böder it was for the loss of his mother. But you see, we both hadn't realized, that he really hadn't expressed any grief for her at all, until then."

As he said this, I noticed he placed a hand on Böders arm as though to transfer comfort to him through just his touch.

"Did you know how Böders father had died?" I asked him gently.

"If I didn't know exactly what had happened, I knew roughly that my father had played a significant role. But I also believe that he had acted, in whichever way he had done, out of the deep despair and emotion that was caused by the loss of my mother in the accident with Böders real father!"

"So what happened next?" I asked totally caught up in their story.

"Well, we realised that our neighbours would blame Böder for the destruction of our farm regardless of how it was explained to them. Remember, he was a giant and the local community was still very wary of him especially when you consider how he became part of our family. So Böder took on the notion that the only option available for him was to leave -- and leave quickly!

I wanted to go with him, of course, but he left immediately, before I even had time to consider what I should do. Besides I still had to tidy up our affairs before I could get going -- for instance someone had to bury my father. So I stayed behind and gave a lame story about what had happened to Böder to all the neighbours who came in response to the fire. Anyway, when everything that I thought was important was done, I followed after Böder, but it was something like three days later!"

"So Böder, where did you go and what was your plan?" Traxxa asked.

Böder thought about it for a second or two,

"Sorry," he said, "It's not because I can't remember what I did," He said evenly, "I'm just trying to remember what I planned to do in the 1st place and the sequence of events that followed afterwards.

"I remember walking off on that first night and looking back and seeing the smouldering, flames finishing off the farm that I had known as my home for some fourteen years or so. It was then that I realized what had taken place. So I sat at the top of a small hill and cried by myself."

He paused and looked closely at those sitting around the campfire with him. When he saw that he was in a safe place with friends who weren't judging him, he continued slowly.

"I remember sitting there and thinking that I really should go back and help Jareck bury his father. But somehow I just couldn't bring myself to do it, so I got up around dawn and headed north. The reason I went north was I thought there would be less people and I just didn't want to deal with anyone at the time. I knew where the villages and communities were so I avoided them easily enough. About halfway through the day I got hungry and raided an orchard eating the fruit I could find and running away when I thought I had been discovered.

"When I came to the Mirack River a great feeling of despondency just kept washing over me and immobilising me. So I sat down and cried again because I felt I was being frustrated at every turn. I was tired and hungry. I had no home. I had just lost the only father I had ever known and this was probably caused by my own frustration and inability to face certain issues. I had run away from the only family I cared about instead of helping him to bury our father. And now I had come up against one of my biggest fears that of water and I didn't know how to overcome the fear or get across the river. I couldn't think any more, so I found myself a hollow and crawled into some thick brush and lay down and slept.

"During that first night I was awakened by a pack of dogs on a hunting trip with their masters. They had discovered me and began baying at my bush. They weren't hunting for me but I didn't know that, but I still had to get up and deal with them. I kicked out at the dogs which backed away and I picked up a log and battered my way past the hunters and their dogs. They had a kill which I took as part payment for disturbing me in my sleep. I had to move then, but I knew that I didn't want to follow the

Mirack because there were settlements all along the river. So I decided to head south and then east and I was determined not to stop for anything or anyone, anymore. If I came to a river I would find a way across it somehow, but I just knew I had to keep moving. My thoughts were for the Gloas Wastelands -- and possibly even the Dark Mountains -- because this is where I believed no-one would be there to bother me. The only thing is, I had no money and no food and not even a change of clothes, but I was going to do whatever it took to survive -- even if that meant stealing and taking without compromise. And that's what I decided then and there to do!

"On one occasion I ate nearly a whole field of corn I was just so hungry and another time I killed a cow, cooked it and ate it completely in three meals. But my biggest problem was I got a taste for beer. I remember on my journey south, I raided a couple of isolated country ale houses and taverns looking for food, but found instead a number of barrels of beer. Being thirsty I broke them open and drank both of them in one sitting. But then the taste for beer took over and I craved for nothing else. Eventually I arrived at this large river town by the Dund and after breaking into the main tavern there I drank three whole barrels of wine or beer or whatever. And when I woke up, I found I was on the Black Island with Jareck -- and that's roughly all I can remember!"

"Was it hard to follow after your brother?" I asked Jareck, sensing that their story wasn't quite complete.

"No, not really! He threw me for a day or so when he went north, but by the time I began tracking him down, like I said before, he had been gone for three days already. By this time he had decided to head south and to make it easier for me, I received information from some local hunters and then farmers who pointed me in the direction that my wayward brother was heading. But I found Böder was travelling quickly like he was determined to get somewhere and again it was only good fortune that kept me heading south a day or so behind him.

"I finally caught up with him in Bernitz and watched over him while he was still sleeping off the effects of the barrels of whatever he had been drinking. We were fortunate in three ways. First I had some money left over from the farm and was able to pay for the barrels that he had drunk. Next, I had the good luck born of a haggling farmer to begin bargaining with the elders of Bernitz for his life. I reminded them right from the get-go that the dragons might come back some day, and a community like theirs could always do with giant to help fight for them. I then pointed out that Böder was just a big rebellious youth and should at least be allowed one mistake despite the fact that he is a giant. I then told them that Böder was deathly afraid of water and did they know of any place that he could be exiled to. And to help seal the deal, I told them that I personally would take him there to ensure that he remained in exile!

"I guess I should point out at this time, that just before my bargaining with the elders, as I had been approaching the town of Bernitz I came across a party of hunters who were returning from a successful hunt on the Black Island. They were happily boasting to me where it was and just how good the hunting was there! So my introducing the subject of exiling Böder to an island was slightly planned in our favour!"

Here it was Jareck's turn to pause and grin sheepishly before continuing. It was also here that I began to see Jareck in a new light.

"But I personally believe that what clinched it for us was when by a stroke of intuition I gave them my word as, the son of Jack the Giant Killer, that I personally would monitor this giant! It was this, more than anything else I had said before that got them to respond positively. Apparently they had heard of Jack the Giant Killer and the respect that went with this name was enough to buy us the authority to have Böder sent over to the Black Island!

"And that's our story in a nutshell really. Not very inspiring I'm sure, but that's basically all there is to us. But what of you Tor Jellick? Why are we going to this mountain and why do you really want Böder to fight this troll for you?"

It was my turn to pause and think for a moment. But I decided that these people deserved to know my story and understand why I felt it was so important to track down this mountain troll as we were doing.

"Earlier this year, shortly after the mountain snows had finished melting, my caravan and I were travelling down from the southern provinces of Nyang. We were making our way down to the Mirack River where we were hoping to find some water transport to take us through the heart of M'Lenn Fida. We were returning to my home after a successful business trip in the coastal lands of Korgan.

"Anyway, we were camped near the foothills of a large mountain when six travelling outlanders, met up with my caravan. They had no proper invitation to join us and I wasn't aware of them until I had returned from a short hunting trip. I was informed they were fellow merchants and that a request had been made asking if we would allow them to travel down with us to the Mirack River. I was a little wary but agreed despite myself. Two nights later during a particularly bleak night of clouds, rain and wind, three of these outlanders entered my private quarters whilst we were all eating in the main tent. They ended up stealing a number of highly valuable items including a chest full of family heirlooms and some pouches full of treasure. These valuables were of tremendous personal value to me as they had been handed down to me by my father, who in turn had received them from his father and so on for some six generations.

When I learned of all that they had taken, I called some trusted guards to me including Traxxa and we set off after the thieves until we came to a bridge which led up into the wilds of a tall mountain. We tried to cross the bridge, but then we were confronted by this ugly little troll who gave us his name as Garog. He told us that we could only pass with the payment of a bridge tax. One of my bulkier guards thought that he would deal with this insolent troll by himself and attacked him outright with his sword drawn. The troll was exceptionally fast and ruthless and for a small troll he was incredibly strong. He ducked under the sword arm of my guard and picked him up, with the apparent ease of someone throwing a large raggedy doll away and then threw him from the bridge. As soon as he did this, I signalled to two of my archers who fired an arrow each towards Garog. At the same time Traxxa threw a dagger at the bridge troll but all these missiles had little or no effect at all upon the creature. In fact I believe they just bounced of his tough hide!"

At this, we all looked at Traxxa who nodded his head in agreement, saying.

"I saw my dagger and the arrows bounce off the thickened skin of the troll and he didn't even seem to notice that the weapons had actually hit him!"

"Anyway," I continued selfishly keeping my story going, "my guard fell into the icy mountain river below the bridge. He was instantly swept away with the forceful current and we lost sight of him. I sent some men after him along the river bank but he was never found. Garog then told us that the toll was now double of what he would normally have asked us to pay. I restrained the remainder of my guards as I feared more lives might be lost, so I paid him the toll he had asked for and continued the pursuit of the thieves up into the foothills of this mountain.

"We found the thieves -- or what was left of them -- on our second day on the slopes of the mountain. All were dead and dismembered and scattered about the place as though they had been cut up and what wasn't eaten was thrown away as waste. My own treasures and everything of value on the thieves had been taken from them. Shaken and confused, we returned to the bridge and when Garog reappeared for a second time to demand another toll, I asked him what was in the mountain that could have destroyed the thieves so completely and taken my family treasure.

"Whereupon Garog told us that Trow his Tor and master lived and ruled this mountain and he did not take kindly to people trespassing on his lands. He also told us the only reason the thieves had ended up dismembered and eaten was because they must have refused to pay the tribute asked of them. We asked who it was that could do such a violent thing like this to three highly skilled thieves and Garog laughed at us and said his master was a mountain troll and was about five times older, bigger and stronger than he was. So I paid Garog his toll a second time to cross his bridge and returned to my caravan. In the quiet of my private quarters I made a commitment to myself that someday I would return to that mountain and on that occasion I would regain my families treasure, come what may.

"And that's my story, do you have any thoughts?" I asked in general, but was really directing my question towards Böder who, I saw, seemed to understand this.

"I think," Böder replied very slowly, "I will have another drink of your fine ale Tor Jellick!"

And he smiled his boyish grin and we all laughed as we remembered the story he had told us earlier about him acquiring a taste for beer.

CHAPTER NINE

EARLICH

My time as the shorn sheep from Böders' fart fall out was relatively short lived. Fortunately my companions had mercy on me and shaved what remained of the hair on my head which helped make me look almost normal. Still if anyone comes near me with the intent to make fun or provide pity, I just go into my chanting priest of Succoth routine and I'm left well alone. It's going to be a long journey for me – I can tell!

(Sigh!)

JELLICK

On the third day of winding our way up into the mountains of Taka we came upon a fork in the trail. It was here that I recognized the most significant of landmarks for me. I knew from here that up around the bend was the bridge that I had been on the look-out for. Aware of the significance of this, Traxxa spoke up at this point and urged us all to proceed with caution and so we hid and tethered the horses and moved silently through the woods to look out over the bridge.

I said quietly "I believe, that should we attempt to cross the bridge then Garog will appear again. I also believe that once we have paid the toll and crossed the bridge, he will somehow get ahead of us and tell his master Trow that we were on our way up there to deal with him. If this is the case then Trow will either hide from us and we won't ever find him this side of the winter solstice, or with Garog beside him, he will attack us as he wishes. Remember, I have seen the bridge troll move and fight and if Trow truly is five times bigger and stronger than Garog, as Garog boasted to us he is, then he will be a very formidable foe indeed. Also do I need to say that this is Trows territory and there is no doubt that he would use his knowledge of these mountains to try and gain an advantage over us! So I think our first plan of attack is to get across this river without letting Garog know that we are even here!"

I had just finished speaking when Böder, interrupted me gruffly and told us to look down the trail. We followed the direction of his pointing finger and saw a beautiful young Bidowman walking slowly along the path that would have her pass just in front of our hiding place in less than a minute.

"Quickly Jareck," I said, "you are the most pleasant of all of us, go down and meet with this girl. Try not to frighten her and ask her if she would be so kind as to come over here so that we can talk with her. Perhaps she knows another way across this river that we don't!"

And so I watched as our farmer friend went down to the trail and waved a greeting to the young girl. She seemed a little nervous and perhaps uncertain at first, but he somehow reassured her through his manner and smile. We continued to watch as he implored her to come and meet with us beneath the trees which were hidden out of sight of the bridge.

She was a little hesitant at first but Jarecks' manner and charm must have convinced her, for she began to walk with him. I suspect that curiosity was the main driving force behind her willingness to accompany him, though I did notice that she was preparing herself to flee at the first sign of danger. This was both a good thing and to be expected from a young country girl.

When she approached, I stepped forward and greeted her warmly and thanked her for coming to meet with us. I then introduced our number one by one to her, first myself, then Earlich who stood self-consciously to one side. Traxxa made himself seen though he remained in the background. Finally I called out to Böder who introduced himself by stepping out from behind a huge oak tree. He knelt down quickly to minimize his height and placed his large branch for a club to one side as though suddenly aware of how fearsome it must look to the young girl. Needless to say, the sight of this eight meter tall giant in rough deerskin pants with his huge club beside him and the giant short sword stuck in his belt, got a surprised "Oooohh my!" out of the girl. But, by the same token, it was Böders boyish smile and cheerful greeting that seemed to charm and calm the girl both at the same time. She returned his wave and complemented his smile with one of her own.

In all my travels, from before and since then, this was for me, one of the most defining moments that I have ever known. And it set this young girl apart from everyone else I have ever met upon the road.

Her smile and acceptance of us all, particularly that of our giant friend Böder -- was done so quickly and with such innocence and naivety, that it truly was a most beautiful and magical moment. I will never forget how she had accepted all of us for who we were in just that simple sweet smile!

She then turned to us and said.

"My name is Kaira and the toad in my basket is called Ribbet!"

Whereupon, she presented her picnic basket to us so that we could all see inside. And there, sure enough, was the largest and also the ugliest looking toad I had ever seen in my entire life sitting quietly amongst a number of small cakes.

From that moment onwards, Kaira proved to be just a delightful young Bidowman. Her innocence and honesty was so refreshing that we felt compelled to tell her briefly why we were hiding amongst the trees to alleviate any sort of a dark shadow of a thought. But of course caution was our guide, so we told her only that we were watching for Garog and considering how best to deal with him. It was nearing the time for our midday meal, and as we were all hungry we asked her if she would like to share a meal with us and to tell us a little bit about herself. She was genuinely pleased to be asked to eat with us and to be given the chance to talk about herself. So, as we sat eating, she told us her story of how and why she was there walking along the path by herself.

KAIRA

"I live in a small mountain village called Tungston some three hours' walk from here, east towards the valley!" And here she pointed back down the trail past the junction to the left where our paths had met.

"Tungston lies nestled in a beautiful valley where grapes and grains and other crops are grown. It is a wine-making village and when my people aren't making wine then they are making beer, and if they aren't making beer, then they will be singing about making wine or beer and having yodelling contests.

"I live with my family in the heart of Tungston; well actually our house is just to one side of the main square of the village near the mountain river. I have two sisters and my father is a hard working carpenter. I did have a mother, which my father said died, but I know for a fact that she wasn't a very nice woman and has run away with a muck maker from a neighbouring village. So the joke around the village is that she has gone from the poverty that our family could offer her into the poverty that only a muck maker could give her.

"Be that as it may, my story is not about poverty, my mother, or even the yodelling contests. This story is about me, Princess Kaira – and I am the princess of a mountain field!"

Here she laughed a magical laugh that sounded a little like happy water splashing over the rocks and tumbling down to become a waterfall. I looked around at the faces in our group and was amazed to see the huge grinning face of Böder and even Traxxa was smiling at Kaira and the way she was telling her delightful story.

"I used to be princess of the barn and the hay but that will only be until the cows are to be fed in the wintertime!"

Again she laughed but only briefly this time.

"But now I am princess of the mountain meadow. Four mornings ago, before the first of our chickens had even begun to fart, my father came into my bedroom and woke me up very gently, as is his way, but this time he looked very worried indeed. He said quietly to me. "I have some bad news - Datyia (*she is my younger sister*) is terribly ill. Kaira, could you please go and gather some 'allium satium'.? This," he told me, "is a rare flower which you will find up in the mountain meadows and just might help to stave off the fever and possibly help her to recover. I've asked Shayla (*that is my older sister*) to stay at home and cook up some soup and look after Datyia while I go down through the valley to get the local healer who I know is visiting three valleys away. I should be back in about two days and hopefully with the healer in tow. Now you must promise not to go near

94

Datyia at all today because what she has might be passed on to you and I don't want you to get sick as well!"

"Then, before I could ask him what does an 'allium satium' look like, my father leaned over me and kissed me gently on the forehead and was off and out of my room and gone.

"Well, I got up and went and had a quick breakfast and asked Shayla what does an allium satium look like, and where do I go to get some. Shayla did her best to describe it to me as she has always been fascinated by plants and herbs and such and how they can help us. She also knows a lot more about the healing qualities of most plants than anyone I have ever known. Armed with this information I put together a small hamper of food and drink and set off to find some of this allium satium. As I made my way towards the mountain pathway I met a trio of older women from the village who smiled at me and said good morning. Feeling resigned to fulfilling the custom of our village, I went over to the old ladies and told them my tale of what was happening at our house, that Datyia was ill and was being looked after by Shayla and that my father had gone off to get the healer and would be back in two days' time.

"At this the women squealed with delight and made as though to rush off home and gather all their own ill ones together. For it is well known the coming of the healer is a good thing for the villagers, for it allows them to complain to someone who might actually help them get rid of their more prominent ailments -- or at the very least listen to them about their ills. But as they began to shuffle off, it suddenly occurred to me that Shayla hadn't actually told me where to find the plant I was looking for. So I pleaded with the old ones, to please tell me where I could find some allium satium!

"One of the oldest hags from out of this bunch of old women, *(and who looked like she had fallen out of the ugly tree and had hit every branch on the way down)* stopped, and turned back to look at me. I'm sure she sized me up and down the way people who mistrust others do before saying.

"Young girl head up towards the tall mountain", she said pointing westwards, *(well actually she croaked the words out she was so frail and her wizened old arm stalled half way up to the pointing position)*. "The flower of the allium satium grows in abundance in a huge meadow just on the other side of the Flook River."

"And placing a vein-crusted hand gently on my arm, she (*I can only assume it really was a she*) carefully described what the plant looked and smelt like and also how to pick it and carry it, and how to cook it and serve it and could I get some for her and possibly even for her four daughters as well. Anyway, after what seemed like an hour of listening to her, but was probably only a minute or two at best, I was finally able to sidle away from the old bat and ran like a heckilty-back (*a mountain chicken - known for its speed much like a road runner*) off towards the west road.

"The west road out of the village is a mere track. It is easy enough to follow but at times it is a bit steep and I would imagine in the wet or snow it might even be considered a bit dangerous, but other than that I had no troubles at all.

"Further on up this trail it branches off again." Kaira pointed ahead to where we could just see the junction where a smaller track broke away from the main trail and made its way down to the bridge.

"The main trail continues all the way around the mountain and follows the entire Tung Mountain range south to Gush if you wanted to go that far." She said boasting her local knowledge. "Whilst the other trail turns down towards a great stone bridge which crosses over the river Flook.

"As I approached the bridge that morning I saw that the river was clean and clear and was a bright blue, almost like a cloudless sky. But it was the bridge which scared me most of all, for it looked gloomy and dark as though it was clouded in a permanent shadow. I noticed a number of very large, old, gnarled and stunted trees huddling around the four brick and stone corner posts of the bridge. These trees each had big thick clawing branches with horrible dark greenish grey, razor like leaves which seemed to be hanging down and reaching desperately out over and hovering just above the bridge. It was as if they were trying to protect the bridge from ever receiving any sun or seeing the blue sky.

"I took all this in and, though it made me shiver a little bit, I made a determined effort and quickly approached the dark and gloomy bridge. When I was barely halfway across the bridge there came a loud roar of anger and a small, ugly thing leapt out from behind the pillars at the far end of the bridge. It was brandishing a short sharp dangerous looking blade and yelling in a deep raspy voice.

"I am Garog and I am master of this bridge. I built it, I look after it and I live under it. So if you wish to cross my bridge which I built and look after ---" And so on and so forth. But by then I had stopped listening to his rant as it was as boring as anything I'd ever heard. I only perked up and returned to what he was saying when he finished with... "I require a gift from you -- a trinket if you like, some gold if you've got it,…or…. perhaps…" Here he paused and looked long and hard at me. Slowly, he licked his lips.

"Perhaps I will let you cross over on my bridge, for just a kiss of your sweet lips!"

"Whilst he was staring at me, I in turn was looking at him, …err it, …err the thing. He was smaller than me, about half my height, but he was broad of shoulder and bulging of stomach so whilst he may have been shorter than me, he was nearly twice -- maybe even three times as big as I could ever be and at least twice as ugly as the old hag from my village. At the mention of 'kiss' and 'lips' I quickly focussed on his face and was horrified to see that Garogs' lips were green with a sort of brown fungus on his top lip. (*This really did bother me, as I feel he needed to have someone look at his lips and very quickly; maybe even have the application of some fire therapy administered to it!*)

"As he spoke, I saw gaps in his teeth and where there were no gaps there was blackness and chipped fangs. Following the line of the creatures gnarly nose up its face I could just see Garogs eyes which were set rather too close together and the pupils were as black as charcoal on sickly yellow irises. I also noticed that he held a permanent squint which seemed to bring his eyebrows down and together (*if he had any*). Instead, what I saw was just a dull green hardened lump making it look like he was forever frowning and which hung menacingly over his eyes so they always appeared to be in a permanent shadow. His forehead was spotted with what looked like stunted miniature mushrooms and his hair was grey and so straggly and sparse it was almost as if the hair itself had given up trying to grow and was saying; 'why do we even bother staying on this head at all!' His clothes looked and smelled like rags that had been weathered by a storm or water sewage. On top of that, he had an overwhelming odour about him like rotting fish.

"To stop myself from gagging and to muster up some fake courage, I spoke up loudly at this point.

"'I don't have anything to give to you by way of a toll, but all I really need to do is to go up into that meadow and come back.' I pointed to the clearing that I could just see, which was outside the line of the trees that were huddled around the bridge.

"'Well then, it's a kiss then,' said Garog and it began to pucker his salivating lips.

"'No I can't!' I cried desperately, '"Look! I just want to go over to that meadow for five minutes and then I'll be right back across your bridge and off down the road like you've never even seen me and I wasn't even here!"

"'That trinket round your neck will do then, if you don't want to give it to me then it's a kiss or go away!' said this ugly troll sternly.

"'What this,'" I said and I pulled out a fine link gold chain. It was long and thin and had a little golden teardrop clasp which held onto a small pearl. It had been hanging around my neck and hidden in the folds of my shawl but it must have glinted somehow because the creature had noticed it. But I protested anyway. "No I can't give this to you, it was given to me by my mother and I --'

"'Look little girl,' Garog said despairingly, "it's either a kiss, or the trinket, or get off my bridge! Khedd -- gimme a break!'"

"I thought of my sick sister and the fact that my mother had run away with the muck maker -- anyway! So I resigned myself and took the chain and pearl off from around my neck and threw it over to the troll. "Here take it, now, can I go?'

"Garog reached out a bloated grubby hand and caught the chain easily as it flew towards him. He looked at it briefly, smiled a horrible smile and said gruffly as he shuffled to one side. "You may pass!'

"Without waiting for a second invitation, I dashed across the remainder of the bridge, passed the ugly troll cautiously and then sprinted like a heckilty-back up into the meadow.

"'Now to find this blasted allium satium flower,'" I muttered to myself.

"'Over there by the large rocks at the edge of the meadow," came a voice at my feet. Looking down I saw what appeared to be an ugly toad. *(It must have been my ugly day; first the old lady then the troll and now a toad).*

"'Did you just speak?' I asked the toad rather stupidly. I mean, because if it hadn't, how was it going to answer me? To be fair, I really didn't expect to get any sort of an answer at all. But, I couldn't see another living creature around and for a frightful moment I thought Garog had followed me up into the meadow. As I stood watching it, I saw the mouth of the toad move and I heard a lovely smooth voice follow.'

"'Well, actually I did. Now if you want me to help you get this allium satium, pick me up and take me over to those rocks at the edge of the meadow and I'll show you where the flower is!'"

"So, without really thinking about it I picked up the toad, and headed off in the direction the toad had told me to go. As I trudged across the meadow I looked down at the toad and asked.

"'What is your name and how is it that you can speak?'"

"'My name is Ribbet, and some old beeatch of a weeatch turned me into this toad and threw me out of her cart and onto that bridge. Then, even before I had finished rolling, that malformed troll back there grabbed me and threw me over here and in doing so my leg got damaged when I landed. Now there is your allium satium, grab it and let's get out of here!"

"I saw the plant that had been described to me by both my sister and the old hag back at my village so I grabbed all that I could see and made my way back to the bridge. I was just about to step onto the bridge again when Garog jumped out from behind a bush by the bridge and said,'

"I am Garog and I am master of this bridge. I built it, I look after it and I live under it. So if you wish to cross my bridge which I built and look after and... so on and so forth *(again wots with the boring troll bit)*? Until finally, ...'then I require a gift from you -- a trinket if you like, some gold if you've got it ...or....in your case, I will let you cross over my bridge for just a kiss of your sweet lips!"

"'But I gave you my gold chain just a moment ago'", I cried out most indignantly -- I must say. 'Now let me pass over your blasted bridge this instance, for I don't have any gold and no more trinkets!'

"'Aahhh!" Said Garog with an evil smile, "that trinket you gave me allowed you to cross my bridge just the once. Now if you don't have any more trinkets, I think I shall take that kiss now!" And he stepped forward puckered up his gross green lips with its top lip fungus and after shutting his closely-set, beady-black, eyes, he moved his face up to meet mine.

"I was in a real bother this time and I could see there was no way out for me other than to turn and run away -- and I simply couldn't do that! So without really thinking I put poor Ribbets butt up in between myself and the pus-lined green lips, the dirty rotting teeth, smushed flat nose and the seeping eyes as Garogs face got closer and closer to me. All in all, the bottom line is, Garog inadvertently kissed Ribbet's bulbous green and brown butt!"

She paused as her infectious waterfall laugh cascaded from her lips once more. This time we all joined in with her and looked with a new kind of respect down at Ribbets butt. Perhaps we were half expecting to see if there were any lasting marks left on its tough hide made from the trolls kiss. Kaira took a sip of a drink and plopped a small morsel of food into her mouth before she continued.

"Now!" And here she whispered conspiratorially drawing us all in together just to hear her. She was a marvellous story teller I thought, as I strained along with the others to catch her every word of this most fascinating tale.

"I don't know if you know this, but many frogs and toads can secrete a highly toxic sweat like film all over their skin. This is in order to protect themselves from predators -- and in this case from trolls. It seems the sweat from Ribbet was more than enough to cause poor old, ugly, Garog to become immobile the moment his lips touched Ribbet's butt. Well to say the least I must have looked on in gawping astonishment as Garog became instantly like stone. But then I remembered, what I just told you about the characteristics of sweaty toads, that this had been told to me, *(probably by my sister Shayla if the truth be known. She's good with that kind of knowledge and stuff)*. So I can only presume, that Ribbet must be one of those toads!

And here Kaira, smiling broadly, presented Ribbet for all of us to see with his freshly bandaged leg and his bulbous green and brown bottom. It was as if by showing us his butt that this was all the evidence needed to verify his unique abilities. And then she continued with her story.

"I was about to run across the bridge there and then because I didn't know how long Ribbet's toxin would hold Garog in his trance, but then I remembered my necklace. I looked for it quickly going through all the uggh pockets and pouches about his person *(and here she shivered with disgust and made a delightfully squeamish like face at the memory)* but I couldn't find it! I didn't want to stay any longer than I had to, so as soon as I was done, I ran across the bridge and back down to Tungston with Ribbet and my large bunch of allium satium flowers!"

JELLICK

"So what are you doing back up here again today?" I asked her politely.

It intrigued me to watch Kaira as she talked with us. I noticed that she didn't stop to look at me to see whether there was any malice or ulterior motive in my question when I asked it. It was as though she was completely oblivious to the mood of her companions and seemed to take us all on face value. This childlike interaction with us was refreshing and yet somehow a little unnerving at the same time.

(Hmmm! I believe I will enjoy watching this innocent young companion of ours whilst she talks and stays with us)!

"Well, some of the allium satium helped my sister Datyia recover very quickly. I hadn't used it all and so I sold what was left of it to some of the other women in my village, in particular to the old hag who had told me where to find the plant in the first place! But the very next day after Datyia had fully recovered which was yesterday, Shayla came down with the very same illness that had afflicted Datyia And since my father had not yet returned home from his search for the healer in the other villages, I decided that I would take the journey up here again today and get some more allium satium!"

"What? And you think you can try and cross Garogs Bridge again by hoping that in wanting another kiss, the troll will be foolish enough to kiss Ribbets butt again is that it?" Jareck asked her a little sceptically. "Is that why you've bought the toad with you again, or did you find another trinket at home?"

His tone was a little harsh and we all looked at him a little incredulously. Even Böder showed some annoyance at the way his brother had talked to her just then. But Kaira didn't seem to mind his words at all, or take any kind of offence from them, for she continued along easily enough.

"No silly! That's why I made these small cakes. I scraped some of Ribbets sweat off him last night and added it to the cake mix before I put it into the oven. I was hoping to go up to Garog and offer him one of my cakes by way of me saying 'I'm sorry' to him for not kissing him properly the other day. I'm hoping that there will be enough toxins in the cake so that when he's eaten it, it will allow me the time to fetch some more allium satium from the meadow. Then once this is done, there may be some time left for me to look for my pendant and gold chain in his hole which is probably somewhere near the bridge."

As she finished off her plan, I looked at her with renewed admiration. As I did, I noticed the others in our party were also looking at her with a new kind of respect - even Jareck seemed to be impressed.

"So then, why have you brought Ribbet with you?" Traxxa asked the question gently, which, if the truth be known, we all wanted to know the answer.

"Because I wanted company for this journey, he talks to me and to be quite honest he keeps me amused. But more than that, he said he can show me where to find some more of the flowers I am looking for!"

And though we had yet to hear or even see for ourselves the wonderful abilities of this remarkable toad, I suspected there was something more to this young and beautiful Bidowman and her pet toad than we had at first imagined.

CHAPTER TEN

EARLICH

As we were considering how to cross the Flook River we were fortunate to meet up with a vibrant young mountain girl by the name of Kaira. There was something about this young Bidowman (*possibly of golden retriever stock*) that has captured each of our hearts from the moment we met up with her. She was to become such an integral part of our company that I thought it only fair to describe her more fully at this time.

She had a sweet angular face with a cute nose and bight intelligent brown eyes. Her shoulder length light brown hair complimented her light tan complexion. She was obviously from a rural mountain family but her clothes had all the characteristics of being well designed and exceedingly well made. She wore a light coloured blouse with short puffy sleeves and a full bodied brown leather skirt that ended just above the knees. She was also wearing a brown leather waistcoat (*or corset really*) that came from her waist and pushed up her small perky breasts which only seemed to accentuate her lovely feminine charms. She was also wearing tough leather boots fit for life in the mountains yet still had an elegance and charm about them.

The way she dressed and carried herself, told me that here was a practical country girl who was both comfortable and yet fashionable enough to be able to present herself well in whatever environment she found herself in. Despite all this she still had a peasant look about her, or, in the words of Jareck she had a 'pleasant look' about her.

She was carrying a picnic basket. In it was a small leather jacket a packed lunch a flagon of water and Ribbet (*her toad*) which sitting amongst some small cakes. She claims the toad can speak and that it has special powers, both of which are hard to believe.

However, if experience has taught me one thing it is this; the world is very strange so I must assume almost anything is possible. But furthermore if something I don't understand is spoken of through the honesty and innocence of a young girl then it is almost likely to be probable. I certainly cannot discount her stories, (*that is until she is proved to be either lying or it is the concoction of an ill or self-seeking mind*) so I believe I am willing to listen, watch and learn all that she might have to impart to us.

JELLICK

Once we had heard Kaira's story and how she planned to deal with Garog, we were all left a little speechless to be quite honest. There were a great many arguments for not letting her do this thing on her own and for storming the bridge and defeating Garog by force, though our knowledge of the trolls strength and speed made us think twice about doing this. Then of course what would we do if, when upon rushing the bridge with Böders strength and size and Traxxa's skill, Garog simply didn't appear at all? It would be like swinging a sword at an adversary who just wasn't there!

Kaira told us that the closest place where we could cross the Flook River safely was at least a good day's ride in either direction. Furthermore, it wouldn't serve to take us any closer to where Trow was thought to be dwelling. So it was decided that we needed to deal with Garog quickly, quietly and permanently before we could venture up into the mountain and continue looking for Trow.

Much to my chagrin we reluctantly let the young Bidowman leave the shelter of our hideaway and the security of our company to go down to meet the disgusting and potentially dangerous bridge troll on her own. Though to be fair to myself, there really wasn't much we could have done anyway, short of physically restraining her. She was a very determined young girl with her heart firmly set on searching for a flower and recovering her little necklace.

Jareck was quick to point out that it wasn't that unusual for someone to venture so far out of their comfort zone with the single objective of regaining a small treasure from a troll. His point was irritatingly received and I smiled at the comparison to my own quest.

We watched feeling helpless and wretched, as Kaira left us hiding in the shadows of the trees across from the bridge and stepped out onto the path. As she made her way down to Garogs Bridge I noticed both Traxxa and Böder had taken out their weapons and were readying themselves to rush to Kaira's aid the moment she appeared to be in any kind of danger.

In fearful silence, we watched as Garog jumped out in front of Kaira the moment she stepped onto the bridge. Though we couldn't hear him, we saw him gesticulating and we knew he was going through his routine of demanding a toll. He paused in mid-rant, arms in mid-swing and went quite still as Kaira began to take control of the conversation. His arms came down and he stepped forward tentatively as the young girl offered him her picnic basket with its cargo of small cakes inside. He took the basket roughly from her hands and reached in and pulled out one of the cakes. He sniffed at it carefully, not from suspicion, we found out later, but from the small pleasure one receives from smelling freshly baked cakes that had been specifically made for them. He savoured the moment and then hungrily he plopped the cake into his mouth and even before it had been crushed by his broken and gaping teeth he had grabbed a second cake and was in the process of shoving this in as well when he stopped moving altogether. We watched in stunned amazement as Garog froze, one hand grasping onto the handle of the basket the other clutching a cake halfway up to his mouth.

Traxxa was the first to move and was halfway to the bridge before we all rallied to our senses and broke from our trance to follow swiftly after the Wolfaman. But it was Böder who was the first to reach the bridge but then he halted and stood uncertainly by the bridge pillars. I looked at him and realised he was unsure about whether the bridge would take his weight or not.

"It's alright Böder", I said encouragingly. "Despite his ugliness and awkward form, bridge trolls are remarkably gifted at building some of the strongest and best bridges known throughout all the lands. Traxxa,"

I called out, "take Kaira with you and go look for Garogs lair and gather whatever you think is of value and bring it up to the bridge!"

He nodded but said nothing, he simply turned and smashed the hand of Garog which had been holding the basket with the flat blade of his sword. At which a couple of the troll's fingers broke allowing the basket to drop out of the clenched fist. Traxxa caught it before it hit the ground. He placed it to one side and then he and Kaira disappeared into the bushes by the far side of the bridge.

As we stood around Garog, each of us went through his pouch and the pockets of the shirt and vest the troll was wearing but could find nothing of value on him at all. We then tried to pick him up, but he was so heavy we were unable to move him at all. I grabbed at his dirty tunic to try and get a good grip on the troll but it tore and came away easily in my hands. It was then I saw the gold chain with a pearl pendant hanging around the troll's neck, hidden in the ugly folds of his rough leather like skin. I took it off Garog and slipped it into my pouch and turned to Böder. He was standing awkwardly by wanting to help but not sure what to do exactly.

"Böder, would you be so kind as to help us carry Garog up to the meadow where the early afternoon sun can do with him as only the sun can!"

Böder reached down as Earlich, Jareck and I each tried to pick up a piece of the troll and carry him off his bridge. But the weight of the frozen troll was alarmingly deceptive. Even with the incredible strength of Böder we could still only just pick him up. So there we were, three grown men and a giant staggering slowly, half dragging, half pushing and moving the big fat bridge troll as best we could towards the meadow. The moment the sun caught the head of Garog as it came out from beneath the shadows of the trees, the troll began to turn to stone. Suddenly the weight of the frozen body increased dramatically as the ugly green flesh was replaced by ugly green stone and before we could do anything he slipped from our grasp fell to the ground and rolled out into the sunlight. The rest of Garogs body slowly changed to stone and when it was done it just lay there like a statue that had fallen over. We were wondering what to do with this dead lump when, with a loud roar, Böder swung his tree trunk club up and smashed it down onto Garogs statue and it split into several pieces.

"What are you doing?" I called out loudly a little alarmed at the noise and the sudden ferocity of the gentle Böder I thought I knew.

"I have heard stories that trolls that have been turned to stone by the sunlight can be restored to their former self if human blood is poured over them. This I believe can be done by witches or people with knowledge of trolls. Once they have done this, whoever has poured the blood will be able to instruct and command the trolls at will and have full control over them. Can you imagine what kind of a servant someone could have if they knew of this? Besides he will be easier to throw away once he is in smaller pieces!"

I was not really sure whether this was true or not but his last point made a lot of sense. The last thing we wanted was for Trow to find Garogs stony body lying here in the meadow and realize that someone was on the hunt for him.

Böder lifted his club again and we stepped back to let him have the room he needed to smash it down onto the statue of Garog. He did this three more times and whilst his crude tree club was savagely pulped at one end, there before us were five pieces of the troll lying in the grass. We staggered with each small piece of the troll statue and threw them over the river embankment and watched them tumble and roll down into the clear icy flow of the Flook River.

It was as we were finishing this off that Traxxa and Kaira emerged with a number of small chests, trunks and bags. Upon inspection of each we found they were full of slev, glemm and toms *(the money of the land)* as well as trinkets and other valuables. After a quick inspection, I realised that none of these chests contained any of my own stolen treasures. But I'd already suspected this.

I turned to Kaira who was looking distraught and close to tears. I remembered immediately, with a pang of guilt, what I had taken from around Garogs neck. Quickly I brought the gold chain and pearl pendant from out of my pouch and handed it over to her. All I could do was to look on in helpless pleasure as this lovely young Bidowman squealed with delight and excitement at recovering her own small treasure. She took it gingerly from my proffered hand then leapt up into my arms and gave me a wonderfully big hug and a smattering of quick kisses on both my cheeks.

"I wish I had something to give to Kaira as well", said Böder wistfully and Jareck nodded his head in agreement and we all laughed at his innocent candour.

"So, now to find some allium satium", said Jareck who saw this as his opportunity to give something back to the girl as well.

After securing the chests, trunks and bags of slev, coins and treasure we hid it all in the bushes near to the bridge before making our way up into the meadow. I watched as Kaira took her basket and lifted it up. She moved her head close to it and it appeared as though she was mumbling into the basket. Immediately I realised she was attempting to talk to Ribbet who had been sitting quietly in the basket the whole time we had been tidying up Garog's affairs. She straightened up and pointed to a distant part of the meadow and said,

"Ribbet believes that we will find some more allium satium over in that part of the meadow."

Not wishing to dispute the wisdom of a toad, and found to be wanting, we followed after Kaira as she trudged through the tall grass of the meadow. As we did this, Traxxa and Jareck returned to gather our horses and bring them across to us.

Now that Kaira had her pendant and her basket was full of her noxious flowers we were at last ready to continue up into the mountain and go looking for Trow. At this point, we turned to say goodbye to our young Bidowman friend. However to my dismay, Kaira showed no sign of wanting to leave us even though I tried unsuccessfully to encourage her to return to her home in Tungston. But she was adamant that she was going to accompany us, for, as she put it, we were part of her adventure now and she wanted to see it through to a successful conclusion. I sought vainly for other arguments to support my cause until she exclaimed quite forcefully,

"I am going to go with you regardless of what you say and that is that! I helped you destroy Garog in order to get to Trow and I won't go home until I have seen that mountain troll destroyed as well or at the very least driven from off this mountain. Then when this is done I will help look for and try and recover all of the trinkets and the many treasures that have been stolen from us -- that is from me and others in my village and also from those in the surrounding areas -- over the many years!"

For the second time today I was at a loss for words because of this young girl. I turned to the others in our party for support and help in encouraging Kaira to return home. But none of them wanted to have anything to do with this decision to send her off home, instead they all suddenly had vital things to do and avoided looking me in the eye. I suspect they were actually enjoying having her with us and were all silently siding with the young Bidowman in their own way.

In truth I could see that she had a right -- probably even more than I -- to witness firsthand the destruction of Trow. As I thought about it she had been quite remarkable and appeared to be perfectly capable. After all, in the short time that we had met and known her, she had helped us cross Garog's Bridge, recovered his hoard of stolen treasures and assisted in taking care of the troublesome troll -- all in one go.

So I shrugged my shoulders and said, "You do realise that we could be up in these hills for many days don't you?"

"Yes! But I still want to come with you!"

"And what about your sick sister and all these allium satium's?"

"I'm sure that my father will be home by now along with the healer, so I believe she will be alright! Besides I'm told this plant endures and actually increases in potency once it has been harvested." She replied quite strongly.

Resigning myself to the stubbornness of the young Bidowman I decided to place some guidelines on our relationship. I thought at the very least I needed her to see right from the beginning this was not a child's game and that I was ultimately in charge of our little expedition. So I told her.

"You can come with us on one condition then, that you will do as I say when we meet up with the mountain troll." But then I undid all my stern fatherly input by finishing up lamely with, "will you agree to that at least?"

She nodded her head and smiled sweetly up at me. And for some unexplained reason we all smiled along with her.

During my talk with Kaira, Traxxa had moved silently away from our group leading his horse as he went. He moved slowly back and forth examining the border between the open meadow and the fringe of trees at the edge of the mountain forest. He disregarded the main trail that made its way from Garog's Bridge and heading off to go around the mountain. Instead he looked for the smallest sign of another way up into the mountain itself. He turned and called out to us and then moved into and through the wall of trees surrounding the meadow and disappeared.

"Time to go!" I called out and grabbing the reins of my own horse and a pack horse I led them up to the trees to follow after Traxxa. As we entered the first line of trees we saw a number of small, yet interesting, mounds of rocks. They were the colour of dusky emeralds with veins of grey and a touch of red in them. Earlich bent to touch and examine one asking at the same time.

"What are these?"

I turned to see what he was talking about and realising what it was, I laughed saying.

"They are snot rocks!"

"Snot rocks?" He said picking it up and examining it closely, his curiosity piqued.

"Yes when a troll wants to clean its nose he closes one nostril with his hand and snorts to expel the snot out through the other nostril. When normal snot lands on the ground it remains there and will disappear over time as does dust or dirt, but if the sun hits the snot of a troll, then this snot becomes hardened stone. So what you're holding is a snot rock from a troll. It's probably one of Garogs!"

We were all laughing by this time as Earlich, realising what he was holding, suddenly recoiled and dropped the snot rock as though it was a hot piece of dung. We sniggled and laughed all through the remainder of the day at the snot rock saga. Little did we know at the time, but Earlich would take years before he could even begin to rid himself of the tendrils of the tales about how he lost his hair in the fart fire and now his intimate fascination with snot rocks.

I moved up to walk with Traxxa as I wanted to talk to him about how he planned to handle Trow if and when we found him.

"First thing we need to do is draw him out of his lair and encourage him to come looking for us," said Traxxa. I discovered later that Traxxa had been thinking about how to deal with this troll for a long time now; in fact it had been from the first time I had spoken to him about my intentions to go and try to recover my treasure from Trow.

"And how do we do this?" asked Böder who was suddenly walking silently beside us, despite his size. Remarkably he had minimized his stride to keep pace with our own whilst still avoiding all the obstacles a forest can provide. I was impressed to see Böders curiosity being verbalised quickly, especially when it came to planning a strategy to meet with an enemy. But then, I remembered, he had spent the better part of six weeks training under Traxxa's instruction and guidance.

"Aahh Böder just the one I want to talk to," said Traxxa easily welcoming his large company into the conversation as we walked. "I am taking us back to the place where we found the thieves that had been ripped apart by Trow -- the ones who stole Jellick's treasure. This is the best place for us to start looking. Trow has obviously been there before and remember how easy it was for him to find those thieves on the one night that they were on his mountain. From there we give misinformation to the troll concerning the number of our company."

"How do you plan to do that?" asked Böder genuinely interested.

"We can do that easily enough by setting up a camp telling anyone who looks upon it that there is only one person -- a lone trapper or a single traveller for instance. The next thing we will do is leave one of our horses by a lit campfire. The fire will provide smoke and heat and the smell of the horse will encourage the troll to come forward. He will see the camp; hopefully he will eat the horse and wait for the return of the person to whom he thinks the camp belongs to with the devious intention of ambushing them!"

"Eat the horse?" I asked a little perturbed.

"Yes, eat the horse!" Traxxa replied matter-of-factly. "We can only assume that he may be hungry. Given the size and strength of Garog we must assume that Trow is bigger, stronger and possibly even faster. So to help reduce these attributes we feed our enemy and hope to slow him down."

"Slow him down? How do we slow him down?" Böder asked.

"First, he will have waited for this non-existent trapper to return. Second he will hopefully try and eat our horse, both of these things will take up his time. And finally have you ever tried to fight or do some work or exercise when you have a full belly?"

Both Böder and I looked at one another and smiled for here was the insight that showed us that Traxxa was truly a cunning master hunter.

It took us nearly three hours to get to the place where we had found the dead thieves earlier that year. I remembered the place because of some interesting rock formations and a little stream running around a shady glade. The perfect place for a camp and an ambush, I thought. The sun was just beginning to find the horizon and we knew that in less than an hour it would be dark. Traxxa and Jareck quickly set up the camp with a small tent some food and a half full cask of beer. They then tethered one of our pack horses near to the stream, whilst Böder and Kaira went to find some sticks and brush to get a small fire going. I warned Kaira that she was to stay close and never lose sight of Böder and encouraged Böder to remember that it was to be a camp for one man. Böder seemed pleased that he was working closely with the young Bidowman. I could see it in his face and smile.

Earlich and I took the other horses and our equipment and moved them well away from the rocks and upwind of the campsite. We then prepared a cold light meal from our supplies. After finishing their chores the others joined us. We ate in subdued whispers as the evening on the mountain suddenly grew darker and chillier as the sun left us with the cold blanket of a mountain night.

As we were halfway through our small repast Traxxa stood up and went over to whisper something to Kaira. She nodded her head and putting her food to one side she went silently over to Böder who was leaning back against a small dirt rise. We all watched her quietly as she climbed the small dirt mound and whispered carefully into Böder's ear. He seemed to be slightly amused after watching Kaira coming over to him in this way, but after hearing what she had to say he looked first at Traxxa and then back at Kaira for a moment before nodding his head in agreement. We all watched in amazement as Kaira then gathered the strands of unruly long hair on either side of Böder's head. She then carefully began to braid first one side and then the other. She then took both side braids around to the back of Böder's head and braided them together there. When she had finished and was moving back to her place around the small camp, we realised, quite suddenly, as though we had all come out of a trance that she had successfully tied Böder's hair down so that it was no longer flowing freely about his face. As Böder touched the sides of his head to know what the braids felt like, Traxxa spoke up quietly.

"Just so your hair doesn't interfere with your face or sight during the coming battle!"

We looked to Traxxa who was smiling quietly at the impact Kaira's hypnotic actions of braiding someone's hair had had upon the small company.

We reluctantly returned to our food and when we had all finished eating, Traxxa began to take control once more. He instructed Earlich and Kaira to stay with the horses and to keep them settled and quiet should the troll appear. He also told them to have the horses ready in the off chance that Trow discovered them or something went wrong in which case they were to ride off at a moment's notice. When he was satisfied with their preparations and were well hidden away, Traxxa took us up carefully and slowly towards the fake camp. At a good safe distance he made us settle down to wait. Once settled we strapped our weapons to our backs and took on our animal forms because our eyes operated were much better in the dark then.

Traxxa sat close to Böder as he settled down behind a large fallen pine tree and gave some last minute instructions. The one point I heard and which had the most impact upon me, though I am not a fighting manimal, was.

"In order to counter your difference in weight with that of Trow," Traxxa was saying quietly to Böder, "you need to concentrate on holding Trow up by going low and using your legs and shoulders to maintain balance, direction and force! Have you got that?"

Böder nodded his head as he closed his eyes to indicate he understood all that had been told him and he really didn't want to hear anymore. Traxxa seemed to sense this because he asked with genuine concern.

"How do you feel?"

"Ready to go!" Böder said through compressed lips but which turned quickly into a confident smile.

He then looked out towards the prepared campsite in silent anticipation his hand mindlessly clenching and unclenching around the haft of his sword.

Chapter Eleven

Jellick

We had only been waiting about half an hour when we sensed something was happening and though we stared intently out we saw nothing. Then our decoy horse whinnied softly as though disturbed and with all our senses on high alert, we smelt the distinct odour of the damp and rot of a troll before we saw him. We watched in silence as he moved cautiously around the entire campfire, and despite being about six and a half meters tall, this large creature made no sound that we could hear. I couldn't take my eyes off of him and it was a credit to his mountain lore that this Troll blended in so incredibly well with his surroundings that to us, even with our night eyes, he appeared only as a darker blotch of a shadow beneath the trees and the rocks around the campfire. We all breathed deep and silently to keep ourselves calm and in control of our heartbeats and fears as we waited and watched. The troll went around the camp once and then stopped at the rocks near where he had first appeared. He sat down with his back to the rocks presumably to wait for the occupying camper to return.

Traxxa whispered softly to Jareck and I,

"Take your time, but I want you two to move back up the mountain and with great care try and get behind the rocks where Trow is sitting. If he has a lair nearby I believe those rocks may be holding the key to its entrance. If Trow sees you, or you are discovered, do not try and meet with him -- just run back to us and have Böder deal with him is that clear?"

We both nodded that we understood. Still whispering Traxxa motioned us to move off.

"Now go and I warn you, don't make a sound, for I guarantee this troll will have very keen ears!" As he was speaking he looked around towards where he knew Trow to be sitting half expecting him to be perking up as though he had heard our whispers even from so far away.

We nodded once more and together we moved off keeping low and quiet until we were well away from the line of vision of the troll, who was still sitting silently, watching and waiting. By this time the half moon had come up, the few clouds had dissipated and the bright night stars began to stud the velvet black sky. All this certainly made it easier for Jareck and I to see ahead as we moved forward slowly carefully keeping one eye on our footing and the other eye on where we wanted to go, with the occasional glance back towards where we believed the waiting troll to be. We had lost sight of him almost at once as we went higher up the mountain, but we still moved carefully, not daring to step on a loose stone or a snapable twig. When we thought we had gone high enough we made our way straight across to where we imagined the high side of the rocks were -- the ones from which Trow had emerged! We came to a large rocky outcrop and began climbing them. Though not a great skill of mine I was still determined to climb the rock face as best I could. The ascent was not particularly difficult or high and once at the top we found we had come to a sort of rock ledge which was well above the rocks that we had been aiming for.

Whilst keeping low we peered over the ledge and found we were directly behind and well above Trow. Although he was sitting in the lee of the huge rock we could just see a horrible clump of long black hair tied up in an ugly pigtail at the back of his large head. He looked to be an old mountain troll for he seemed weather worn with darkened splotches about his shoulders and chest as though someone had tried to burn him but had failed. We couldn't see much of his face but I did notice that his ears were tattered and torn and there were slits in his face where his nose should have been. He was a lean mountain troll, with large powerful hands and well defined arms and legs betraying taut muscles and great strength. He wore no shoes or protection around his over large feet and had no clothing about his person other than a simple deerskin loin cloth around his waist.

Looking beyond Trow we had a wonderful view of all below us including our fake camp. I tried looking for Traxxa and Böder and was actually fearful of seeing them but they were too well hidden even for my badger's night eyes.

We had barely settled down to watch and wait from this vantage point, when Trow stood up carefully and went completely around our set-up camp once more. He went around in a much bigger circle than before and took a much greater length of time doing this. When he came back upon the pack horse we had left tethered near the camp he moved up slowly to the horse, making a clicking sound which seemed to soothe the fidgeting beast. When he was close enough to touch the horse, he put out his hand in a manner that suggested he was going to stroke it and then in a movement too fast to see, he smashed his fist into the horses head and the poor beast dropped to the ground instantly without ever moving again.

Over the next hour or so -- which took us into the early hours of the morning -- the troll skinned the horse, tore off its limbs and began to eat some of its raw flesh. Whilst chewing on the horse meat he picked up the two left legs of the beast and as easily as going for a stroll he made his way back up a rocky path between the boulders he had been sitting against and moved up to the rock face which was directly below us. We peered over our secure ledge which was some ten meters above the troll and watched as he put one of the horse legs down on the ground and then with his free hand he banged on a huge rock. A mere five heartbeats passed when to our amazement the rock moved out silently and we realized that we were looking down on the door to the troll's lair. Trow picked up the horse leg and handed them both to someone standing just inside the doorway whom we could not see. With the horse legs stowed in his cave, Trow moved off back to our camp to continue eating what remained of the horse carcass. But what kept our attention, more than watching Trow move about, was seeing the rock door to the troll's lair below us had been left open.

Trow sat down near the smouldering camp fire and put a few bits of wood on to keep it going and pulled off raw strips of meat with his bare hands to eat while he waited. He consumed the horse slowly as though he was enjoying this unexpected meal and didn't want to rush it at all, but all the while he was constantly on his guard and was continually looking around the camp, stopping occasionally to put his nose up as though sniffing the air or turning his head as though listening to the sounds of the woods around him. Whenever he did this there was the awful feeling that he had discovered the other horses or heard or smelt our friends hiding nearby.

With another leg in his huge hand and eating it as one would a chicken leg, Trow became curious and he went over to the small shelter we had set up around the campfire and started going through the things that were stored inside it. Here he found the cask of beer and in a moment Trow had ripped out the cork and consumed a large portion of the beer in just one long swig.

He finished eating our horse and discarded its bones in a heap near the skin. He then finished off the beer and tossed the empty cask away. Sitting silently for a short time as though enjoying the moment, Trow suddenly stood up and made his way over to a tree. We knew that he had gone there to relieve himself.

It was then that we saw Böder, sword in his right hand, galloping across the open ground with such speed we were barely able to keep up with him - - even from our vantage point high up on the rock ledge. When he was almost on top of the troll, Böder gave out a blood curdling roar and slashed out with his sword. He had been carrying the sword across his body so that as he swung it up towards the head of the troll his arms were going to be open wide as he hit the troll.

Instead of tensing at the roar behind him as most people would have, Trow dropped his knees and head down just a fraction both at the same time and turned towards the roar, dropping his loincloth as he did so. This instinctive reaction saved him as Böders blade passed harmlessly mere millimeters over the top of his head. As it passed over the troll the blade neatly cut through the base of the knotted ball and long pigtail which made up the sum total of Trows hair and sent it flying off into the middle of the clearing.

Böders flying body hit Trow with such force that the two of them smashed into the huge pine tree that the troll had been standing by and it snapped in two just below where they hit it at its base. The noise of this impact between giant, troll and tree must have been heard many kilometers away.

Even as I was watching the fight play out before me, I realized instantly that here were another of Traxxa's brilliant battle tactics. The beer would have dulled the troll's senses if only momentarily, and would have made him want to relieve himself soon thereafter. From this I remembered when one is urinating it can be seen as one of their weakest moments in their daily lives. They are open and vulnerable and during this brief state of pleasant relief they are also, if only slightly, distracted. So Traxxa had sent Böder to hit Trow hard when he was most vulnerable.

Over the next couple of moments we watched as troll, and giant and toppling tree rolled down and around in the open area of the mountain clearing. In his confusion and pain after Böder had slammed into him, it seemed Trow didn't know for certain what was really happening to him. As a result of this Böder was first on his feet and as Trow slowly began to respond and tried to get up, Böder hit him full in the face with the clenched fist holding his sword. But Trow simply rolled with the punch and put a little space between himself and his aggressor. From there, perhaps realizing he was in one of the greatest fights of his life, Trow finally reacted and began to exert the true measure of his strength and abilities. Anger fuelled his movements as he dodged another blow and he barrelled under the swinging sword and into the midriff of the giant -- and then the fight was on!

Trow delivered a number of rapid blows to Böders mid-riff and sword arm and Böder eventually had his sword knocked from out of his hand. From then on it looked like Böder was in real trouble. Trow was faster, stronger and much more compact whilst Böder though taller was slower and his fighting movements seemed to be more awkward and unsure. Trow was the masterful fighter and Böder the novice.

Just as we were losing heart as Trow began asserting himself in the struggle, we watched in awe as Traxxa rushed up behind Trow and began to attack the back of the troll's legs. Angered and irritated by this distraction the troll found his focus on the giant was broken and tried desperately to swipe at the constant irritation at his back. This seemed to encourage Böder and he pressed the troll even more. But then suddenly the whole dynamics of the fight changed dramatically and Trow began to fight differently. At first we thought it might be because of Traxxa's assistance in the battle but the troll looked to the sky and began to move purposefully away from Böder swiping desperately at Traxxa as he retreated. We knew immediately that he was making his way across the clearing below us and back towards his lair.

Sensing there might be another reason for the change in Trows focus; I quickly looked to the horizon and could just see a slim line of soft blue with a subtle reddish gold glow around its edges. I realised then that the break of dawn was less than half an hour away. Wonderful timing I thought, as I nudged Jareck back to our objective. Together we made our way down the rock face to try and secure the door to the lair before whoever was still inside decided to close it up with the coming of the sun.

We reached the rock floor after using a great length of rope which Traxxa had thoughtfully given to us and some useless mountaineering skills which we had developed all on our own. Once safely on the ground we made our way to the doorway and looked cautiously around the door. We saw nothing but a dark corridor with a number of light crystals glowing a far way down inside the cave. We stood there unsure of what to do next so I did what I do best -- I made a decision.

"You stay here and make sure no-one closes this door and I will go and help Traxxa!" Jareck looked slightly relieved that he didn't have to make this decision and simply nodded his head dumbly. We looked just inside the doorway and saw a small natural rock alcove.

"I'll hide in there then," whispered Jareck pointing to the alcove, "But don't delay -- I have no desire to meet the one who could so easily take the legs of a horse out of the hands of Trow!"

And with that Jareck stepped in toward the back of the alcove and made himself as small and invisible as he could, whilst I turned to go and find Traxxa.

I followed a wide walkway down and around the large rocks and almost ran into the back of the struggling Trow who was barely four meters from me. He was fighting desperately to escape the grasping, clutching hands of Böder. I had no time to determine features, as Trow moved closer and closer back towards me. I was alarmed at being so close to such a tall and grotesque a troll fighting so violently and so desperately with movements so fast and so strong against someone who I considered to be my friend.

I looked around helplessly back up the walkway towards the doorway and remembered how important it was to let Traxxa know where the entrance to Trows lair was. Then suddenly Traxxa was there in front of me. He came in behind the Troll and was continually stabbing at his legs, buttocks and lower back. I couldn't actually see him breaking the toughened skin of the troll but I knew he was doing just enough to interrupt the troll's focus and giving Böder the opportunity to take control of their fight.

It was then I saw that Böder's hands were empty. Of course -- I remembered seeing his sword being knocked from his hands. It must be lying somewhere out in the devastated clearing. I thought -- if I could just get the sword I may be able to hand it up to Böder and help our cause even more.

I went to make my way around the left hand side of the troll. I'm sure I was only a temporary distraction to Trow. He glanced down at me, but must have sensed I was no real threat to him for he quickly turned the other way to swipe at Traxxa with his right hand in an attempt to try and stop him and his annoying little sword attacking his defenceless ass cheeks. Despite Trows speed and turn, Traxxa stepped back ever so slightly to be just out of reach and slashed at the hand as it went by with his sword. It was in this moment that Böder grabbed Trows left hand and arm and pulled him down and around so quickly that Trow found it difficult just to remain on his feet. As Trow struggled to regain his balance, Böder quickly stepped up and around Trow so that now he was standing in between the mountain troll and the doorway to his lair. We all saw that it was just a matter of a few minutes for Böder to continue wrestling with the troll; holding him up the way he was doing before the sun would break free from the line of the horizon and stop Trow permanently.

I looked on in awe and forgot what I had set out to do as the tension mounted quickly. I noticed that Trow had also seen just how soon it was before the sun broke over the mountain peaks in the distance. For with a frenzy of punches and kicks and using all his squat bulk, Trow began pushing Böder up the walkway back towards his cave entrance. It was obvious he saw that his only hope lay in pushing forward quickly and gain the safety of his cave, even if it meant he had to push this stupid giant into his lair first. Once this was done then his strength and speed in the darkness would only increase and he could dispense with him as he wished.

Böder remembered Traxxa's words at this time and he went as low as he could and with his feet set firmly against the opened cave doorway he effectively held the much heavier troll at bay. And then the sun broke over the line of mountains along the eastern horizon and the first warm rays touched the head of Trow and he screamed a most deafeningly, horrible, scream which turned into a loud and frightful sounding howl. In his death throes Trow reached out desperately and grabbed onto the thickened hairs of Böders strong blonde beard with the desperation of a dying troll.

As suddenly as it started the screaming stopped and Trows head was all stone. Then slowly before our eyes wherever the sun touched Trows body it too slowly turned to stone. It reached his arms and then his hands and then in horror I looked on as the transformation to stone began to make its way into Böders beard which started to become like lightened stone. I screamed when I saw this, but before I could even think to warn Böder of what was happening, or do anything about it, Traxxa raced up the sides of the rock wall and pushing himself upwards and out he leapt high into the air and turning he brought his sword smashing down onto the dying hand of Trow. Immediately the troll's stone hand, Traxxa's sword and all of Böders beard exploded violently into a shower of dust, fine stone, and shards of steel. (*And that is why even today, Böder's face has the smooth skin of a very large baby and has never been able to grow any kind of beard or facial hair.*)

Once the grip holding Böder in check disappeared, he fell forward and dropped to his haunches in order to catch his breath and rest for a moment. He was as white as a ghost and appeared to be badly shaken and after several deep breaths we could see that he was thoroughly exhausted. After encountering such a fierce adversary and receiving such a battering, Böder was bleeding in many places and covered in bruises and scars. But to our incredible relief and great joy, he was very much alive!

EARLICH

Kaira and I had waited patiently, shivering slightly with the cold as the others looked out for Trow and dealt with him accordingly. When we heard the alarmingly loud crash as the two titans demolished the trees around the clearing, I thought that that was our cue to get atop our mounts and ride away. But Kaira wasn't having any of that. Before I could stop her she had raced off back to the fake campsite hoping to help in whatever way she could in the fight between Böder and Trow. I had to follow her of course as I couldn't let the young Bidowman go up there alone. We reached the clearing and I grabbed her and pulled her down and back into the bushes so that we could watch the fight without being seen or inadvertently becoming involved. I believed at the time that it was best if we let Böder handle Trow alone -- after all, that is what he had been training six weeks for. When Böder and Trow had disappeared around the large rocks on the far side of the clearing, Kaira and I emerged and made our way tentatively out to the campsite. Kaira saw Böders sword and went to retrieve it but it was much too big and heavy for her, so I offered to fetch it by myself and take it up to our giant friend. As I was dragging the sword as best I could away I looked back in amazement as Kaira finished folding up the remarkably well skinned hide of our horse. She then discovered the ball and pigtail of Trows hair lying in the middle of the clearing and picked this up as well.

"What are you doing?" I asked her sternly.

"This would make some very nice clothes or boots for someone." She replied, "We must not let the death of your horse go to waste!"

"And the trolls hair?" I asked in an unbelievable tone.

"Why this would make excellent thread to sew the horse hide up silly!" Kaira replied easily enough with a smile that would disarm a drazil.

Her answer staggered me and I was at a loss for words that even in the midst of danger, destruction and death she could still make sense and use of the things around her.

"Why don't you go back and fetch our horses then?" I said in quiet awe. "And when you get back we can begin to break this camp together!"

"Okay!" She replied easily enough, and skipped off to complete the task given to her.

As I watched her head off, I mused thoughtfully to myself about what a truly resourceful this young Kaira was proving to be.

JELLICK

As the morning sun destroyed Trow's life and ended the battle, we all came to a shuddering halt. During this pause for breath, we began to take stock of the situation which we now found ourselves in. There was a huge rock behind Trow which prevented Böder from pushing his statue out of the way and it was now completely blocking the doorway. His arms were up and in such a way that there was no way we could push him backwards or to one side. This was when we realised that Böder was unable to get out of the doorway into Trows lair.

Earlich at that very moment turned up with Böders dropped sword. He handed it over to Böder under the arm of Trow. Böder tried again and again to break up the hardened troll with his sword but because of the confines of the rock wall and the cave entrance he just couldn't get enough momentum in his swing to affect any kind of damage on the solid stone statue. But even if he could have hacked off the stone arms there still was no room for Böder to get past this exceedingly heavy rock troll.

In dismay we looked towards the entrance to Trows lair. The huge rock behind Trow effectively blocked out the sun at the doorway during the daylight hours. Furthermore, the only room for the sun to impact the doorstep was exactly where Trow now stood, frozen in time and precisely at the moment the sun first breached the distant mountain peaks.

"With the coming up of the sun in the morning, why then didn't he have something to block out its rays from ever reaching this spot?" I asked no-one in particular as I looked thoughtfully towards the horizon where I could see the bright warm sun climbing steadily into the morning sky.

"He did." Traxxa said quietly beside me. "Until very recently there was a huge tree over there, which did just that." and he pointed to where the tall pine tree had been. "Fortunately for us though, it was taken out at the onset of the battle, when Böder tackled Trow at the very moment he began to relieve himself!"

And here we all smiled at the memory of that first encounter.

"So then," I said, "as there is nothing more for us to do out here, let us go and explore Trows lair and see if there is a second exit which might allow Böder to get out. Earlich!" I called out, "gather the horses and wait nearby in case we need you!"

Earlich nodded and left, whilst Böder hefted the sword in his hand and turned to go down into the caves which made up Trows lair. Remembering at the last moment that there was probably somebody with great strength waiting for us, I moved to tell Böder this, just as Jareck stood up and made himself known. This caused me to pause for a moment and that's when a terrible scream startled all of us at once. A huge thing rushed up at us from out of the darkness with the obvious intent of attacking our giant friend. Böder had taken the lead and was bent slightly forward in order to enter the long rocky hallway. Inadvertently he had his sword out in front of him pointing naturally towards the darkness. At the sound of the scream he tensed and held his ground when whatever was rushing up at him simply ran into the sword and pierced its own heart with its own impetus. Stunned we looked down at the collapsing creature at Böders feet. And there by the half-light of the open rock door we saw the form of a very rare, very dead, female mountain troll!

"That would explain who took the two horse legs from Trow when he dropped them off here earlier," I said a little relieved. "So come, let us see what other surprises this lair has for us!"

Böder crawled awkwardly over the dead female troll in the tight confines of the corridor at the caves entrance. He then took the lead again with his drawn sword as ever pointed before him. He had to walk hunched over slightly as he made his was slowly down the corridor towards the light crystals ahead as the tunnel had been made with great skill to accommodate Trows height.

I couldn't help but notice, as I clambered over the foul smelling dead female troll that she was covered in remarkably well fashioned deerskins. This intrigued me greatly.

When we reached the first of the light crystals, we found the long corridor broke out into a large untouched rocky cavern. Though it smelled strongly of troll it was however clean and well maintained. I looked back up the corridor we had just come down and noticed the stone floor was smooth as though polished and the walls and ceiling showed signs of being extremely well crafted and cared for.

I returned my attention back to where we were and saw that Böder was able to stand upright and he did so in quiet relief. He stretched his back and arms out in the space and sighed to himself with a deep satisfied smile on his lips. He sat down limply and told us he needed to rest for a moment or two before continuing. This we all agreed was probably a good idea for all of us.

CHAPTER TWELVE

EARLICH

Whilst the others explored the caves of the now dead Trow, Kaira and I brought up the horses and took over the fake camp. We kept the fire going and thought about cooking up a warm repast which the others might appreciate when they came up out of the cold dark rocky lair. It was then I noticed the remains of the dead horse and thought, 'waste not…'!

So Kaira and I began making preparations for a hot cooked meal!

JELLICK

From the large main cavern, the lair we discovered consisted of a vast complex of caves and rocky rooms all linked together by extremely well-crafted troll modified tunnels and corridors. For the remainder of the morning we explored every nook and cranny of which we found a surprising number of clean and tidy rooms. From these we brought to the main cavern everything and anything we could find which we thought might be of value. When Trows lair was completely ransacked, we saw before us a great number of trunks and chests filled to overflowing with a huge pile of treasures, including clothes, trinkets and a vast amount of slev and glemm and other valuable coins and items including maps and diaries, scrolls and parchments.

Shortly after we began our search we came upon a small troll. He was very young and appeared amiable enough which, from the outset, we sensed that he posed no real threat to us. Because of this we made an effort to communicate with him in order to make him feel safe and did all we could to reassure him that we in return meant him no harm. Once he realized that we were trying to be friendly, he told us in his gruff troll voice that his name was Bartrow. Then in an obvious effort to endear us to himself he began to open up some cleverly concealed doors which led us into more hidden rooms and corridors which in turn revealed even more chests and trunks of treasure and trinkets and heaps of other valuable items.

At this time I asked Jareck to go back up to the main door into the lair and bring Earlich and Kaira down to help us explore and retrieve as much of the treasure that we could find. When they came down into the trolls cavern they came bearing the burden of a cooked meal and some flagons of drink. This was an unexpected pleasure and everyone rallied to grab some sustenance. We even invited Bartrow to join with us which he did with much gratitude in his manner and voice. I watched him carefully as he sat with us and ate and he seemed to like the food we offered him. Well he didn't throw it away or vomit it up so I can only guess that our food was alright for him.

Shortly after our repast, Bartrow opened up a concealed door which led him into a large room full of neatly stacked and well-maintained weapons and tools. At this, Böder became absolutely ecstatic and danced for joy such was his delight as many of these appeared to have been fashioned to fit the hands of a giant. He called out excitedly for us all to come and look at his room of giant prizes. Jareck and Kaira were the first to respond to Böders call and when he saw it, Jareck took for himself a wonderfully fashioned bow with a matching quiver full of quills and also a lethal looking, leather-handled double-headed axe.

Again I kept noticing just how well kept and stored everything in the armoury was. It was as though Trow had had a deep appreciation for the workmanship and crafting of all the different kinds of weapons that he had either stolen, killed for, or possibly even forged himself. There were a number of very interesting pieces of armour and weapons specifically made for those of a bigger-than-normal size, including some vicious-looking shin guards, all of which I noted with a smile. Böder thought they were wonderful and he quickly claimed these as his own. Though to be fair we wouldn't have argued with him over any one of them as they were much too big for us to use. But the most prized weapon which he took ownership of at once was a large mace (*a long shafted handle at the end of which was a vicious looking steel ball with spikes sticking of it*).

"This will do very nicely to replace the branch I've been using as a club!" he declared triumphantly, when he had our undivided attention.

When Traxxa entered the room he took a few seconds to soak up the full extent of the small armoury and smiled grimly before moving slowly around looking closely at all there was. Occasionally he would pause and touch an article or examine a blade or the handicraft of a handle more intensely than the others. He seemed to be particularly drawn to a double sheath and harness set which would allow him to carry two blades at once on his back at all times without interfering with his movement or stride. (*These would be ideal for when he took on his animal form. This had always been the downside of manimals taking on their animal forms in battle as they are unable to use or handle any of the conventional human weapons*). He picked up the double sheath harness and then went about looking for some blades that would fit nicely inside them.

He eventually selected five slightly curved blades and set them apart. He looked carefully at each blade, held them in his hand and closed his eyes to feel their weight without interference from his other senses. Finally he chose two of them and after a few practise strokes with each he placed them into their sheaths and put the harness over his shoulders to see how the harness fitted. At his call, I went over to him and helped adjust the harness so that it fit him how he liked it to be. When he was satisfied he dropped to his hands and turned immediately into his timber wolf form. He padded around the armoury a few times as we all watched intrigued by his attention to all the details of these weapons. He stood on his hind legs and returned back to his human form. He then turned to face Böder who had been watching him transfixed.

"Do you mind if I take these blades and the harness to replace my broken sword?"

Böder seemed only too pleased to be able to give something back to Traxxa and said smiling warmly.

"Of course you may have it, and you don't have to ask me for anything in these caves as I consider that we are all part owners of the wealth and wonders hidden down here!"

Traxxa nodded his head in acknowledgement and looked around the armoury once more and moved purposefully towards the exit when he saw a toughened leather pouch hanging on a hook just inside the doorway. Intrigued he took the pouch down and examined its contents. Perhaps it was his stillness that caused all of us in the room to pause again and watch him carefully. Upon my question about what he held, he dipped his hand into the pouch and brought out what looked like a five pointed steel throwing star. Whilst we had never seen anything like it at all, we quickly lost interest in it as they weren't big or formidable enough in comparison to many of the other pieces of weaponry in the room. As each of us turned away to continue our own forms of foraging, I couldn't help but notice that Traxxa was totally mesmerized by the stars in this pouch. Then suddenly, as if he had made up his mind, he let the star he was holding slip back into the leather pouch and turning to Böder once more.

"Do you mind if I also keep these?"

Böder just smiled and nodded his head and waved his hand as though to say of course and stop bothering to ask me. So, hefting the pouch of stars once more in his hand as though weighing them in the balance, Traxxa turned and made his way out of the armoury slipping the pouch into the folds of his tunic as he went. At that very moment I saw a most thoughtful expression on Traxxa's face. It was one I had never seen him wear before in all the time I had known him.

Whilst I saw nothing in the armoury that I wanted for myself, later Earlich and I estimated together what the room was worth and it was a most considerable sum indeed, in any of the larger markets throughout Durogg. So with Böder and Jareck's help we began to empty the armoury. As we worked throughout the day I was trying to figure out just how we were going to take everything we were finding here in the caves and transport it all down off the mountain.

Shortly after emptying the armoury I found, to my great delight, the chests and all my very precious family heirlooms and personal treasures. I paused for a moment in quiet relief before calling Böder over to me whereupon I expressed my deep personal gratitude for all that he had done for me. Here I showed him exactly what it was that he had helped me to regain. I should point out at this time, I may have been a little emotional as I didn't quite realise until then just how much these items truly meant to me.

"All this treasure is yours and Jarecks', Böder!" I said magnanimously, "for I have got what I came for --", indicating the chests at my feet, "and for this I want to thank-you very much. All I ask is that you allow Jareck, Earlich and Traxxa to choose from this treasure what they want by way of a payment for their help and services!"

To which Böder in his boyishly simple manner smiled

"With all this before us let them take what they want -- but don't forget to include Kaira and her wishes as well!" He said almost apologetically, waving his hands wide.

"And to this request I will agree!" I said smiling. "But now let's work out how to get this great mound of treasure out of this cave, off this mountain and back to your island!"

With a little prompting and imploring to find another way out of this labyrinthine maze of caves, tunnels and rooms, Bartrow took us down what appeared to be a shortened, empty walkway. As we reached the extent of the dead end, Bartrow climbed up a cleverly hidden set of steps in the staggered rock wall to his right. When he was about three meters off the cave floor he reached his hand into a large nook. After fiddling about for a moment or two, there came a loud click from the rock wall in front of us and it became a door which cracked open to reveal a secondary exit from the caves.

Bartrow hurriedly climbed back down and stepped away from the rocky door as we were able, with Böders help, to pull it open. We then moved cautiously through it and found ourselves outside on a wide ledge of rock. There to my utter amazement I realized it was the end of the day as the sun was barely half an hour away from setting. Yet, in my mind, the day had barely passed at all. Regretfully, I realized that we were going to need to stay the night in or around Trow's caves. I looked around for points of reference and quickly worked out that we were about 500 meters back along the rocky outcrop, from where the first entrance was. More importantly, we found nearby, a number of carts, two with four wheels and five others with two wheels standing idly by in various stages of disrepair and decay. They were obviously the spoils taken from hapless sojourners who had been caught by Trow as they travelled through his mountain territory.

We decided to spend the night in the camp we had already set up in the little glade, and arrangements were made to get things under way. The legs of the horse that Trow had killed the night before were found in the lair and we offered these to Bartrow as part of his evening meal, whilst we ate our fill from our own provisions. During our time around the fire that night, I turned to the young troll.

"Bartrow," I said as gently as I could. "Forgive us for imposing upon your life here so quickly and simply believing we could take what we wanted and forgetting that this, until recently, was your home. Do you mind telling us what your relationship with Trow was like?"

Bartrow looked at me carefully seeming, as it were, to try and read me with his beady black eyes, assessing me in his own way. After an awkward moment which threatened to extend into a lengthy silence, he suddenly opened his mouth and began telling us his story in his gruff troll manner.

"During the last warm months, my mar and dar brought me through the distant mountains." He pointed west and southwards. "They told me they were looking for a new home. One night my dar met with Trow and his mate. They told us we were welcome to stay in the mountains nearby. But it was a lie and we were tricked. One night, shortly after we began living in a cave two nights walk from here, Trow came by and made my mar and dar dead. He did this quickly and violently. He then smashed the cave in and buried my mar and dar forever in rocks and dirt. He took me and all they had with them out into the open in order to take everything back to his caves. I have been with them since then and I have hated being with them. So I am very happy inside now they are dead like my mar and dar. It is for this reason alone that I didn't attack you when you first entered my caves. And it is also for killing Trow and his mate that I want to give you my thanx. And it is also why I like you and want you to be my friends!"

As he finished his disjointed and rough account of how he had come to be living in the lair with Trow and his mate, Bartrow then made a startling statement.

"But, I don't know if staying in these caves is good for me or not. What do you want to tell me? The only thing I want is for my parent's things to be left with me?"

This we all agreed was without question entirely appropriate.

As we turned to talk quietly amongst ourselves about what we had just been told, we inadvertently took our attention away from Bartrow.

Suddenly Kaira screamed out.

"Noooo!!!

Startled, we all jerked back to face the young troll just in time to see that he had found the basket with Ribbet and the small cakes in it. But it was too late, for he had already placed two of the cakes into his mouth and now he sat beside us, frozen in time. There was nothing for us to do but laugh.

"At least we won't have to watch out for this young troll tonight, fearful lest he attacks us in our sleep!" Traxxa said matter-of-factly and with that he grabbed his blanket and curled up near to where the frozen troll was sitting and fell promptly asleep. We all realized how right he was and after Böder put on a few more logs on the fire to keep it going throughout the night we all decided to follow Traxxa's example and were all soon sound asleep before the fire.

We all slept very well indeed that night. Traxxa was the first awake and seeing Bartrow still in his frozen state he went and got the horse hide and covered him over so that none of the sun was able to get at him. Then with Böders help we watched as they dragged him into the shade of some bushes and trees by the edge of the clearing.

After a quick morning breakfast, Böder and Jareck agreed to take on the task of trying to rebuild some of the wagons we had found the night before. They took the horses around to the side entrance, to see if they could fit some of them up to the wagons. Whilst they did this, Traxxa, Earlich, Kaira and I made our way towards the main entrance to start moving all the treasures up from the lair to begin loading them onto the wagons.

At the main entrance I saw that the rock statue of Trow had been completely destroyed. When I questioned Earlich about this he told me that upon a suggestion from Kaira early yesterday morning he had climbed up the rock wall to the ledge where Jareck and I had hidden during the first night on the mountain. Then with a little manoeuvring, he had pushed a large, heavy boulder off the ledge above Trows statue which Kaira had seen from the campsite. With great precision the boulder had landed on the stone troll and completely demolished both boulder and statue. At this point I recalled Böders warning about how the stone statues of trolls might be brought back to life and into servitude through witchcraft, so this endeavour was a very pleasant surprise indeed as it saved us time and energy trying to figure out how to break up the troll's statue.

It took us nearly all day to complete the ransacking of Trows caves and it was only then that we realized we had loaded up all three of the carts that Jareck and Böder had managed to salvage. Earlich did a quick count and told me there were twenty-eight various sized chests of treasure and clothes and a large number of loose weapons and tools. After the carts were fully loaded we moved down to the clearing to pack the final pieces of our supplies and camp onto the carts. It was here that it occurred to me that we really hadn't talked about what was to be done with Bartrow?

I made mention of this to the others and we turned as one to look towards where Bartrow was still sleeping beneath the horse skin under the bushes.

"Do you think we should ask him if he wants to come with us?" I asked.

"Look at him!" Kaira said, *(which was impossible of course because of where he was at the time, but we understood what she meant by this).* "Can't you see that he is just a young troll probably only 10 years of age *(this was a wild guess, as the age of most trolls are very hard to determine, but we could see that he was very young as far as trolls go)* and he is both worried and frightened for his life? We need to make some hard decisions for him and help him -- after all he has helped us ever since we first broke into Trows lair!"

Feeling thoroughly chastised, we all stopped and looked again towards the bushes where Bartrow was sleeping. I turned to the others, who were looking as guilty as I was feeling. Everyone was all for taking on the troll without any further questions and I was also in agreement with them. So turning to Kaira I told her.

You're right we will take him with us! But you must ensure Bartrow remains completely covered at all times under the horse skin as we travel -- as his life depends upon it!"

Kaira squealed with delight, threw herself upon me and gave me a big kiss on both my cheeks again. She dropped down and went over to the bushes and made every effort to comfort and care for the still sleeping, stunned troll.

"Böder!" I said. "Would you please assist Kaira in making sure that Bartrow remains safe from the sun and well hidden amongst the treasures on the cart!"

Böder just smiled his lovely boyish smile and nodded his head and followed Kaira over to Bartrow.

As we were making ready to leave I took Earlich and Jareck back through Trows lair with me. Together we retrieved as many of the light crystals dotted around the caves and walkways that we could find, get to, remove and carry.

"These are the last of Trows wondrous treasures", I said to the others, smiling as I began turning the light crystals off one by one by passing my hand over them. I then placed them carefully into some large sacks and onto the carts.

Traxxa came over to me at this time and asked me to accompany him. He took me to the bottom edge of the clearing then had me turn back to face the three carts each with their small mountains of treasure and our horses all hitched up to them and all ready to go.

"Do you remember our hike up here the other day?" He asked casually.

"Yes! What about it?" I replied feeling exhausted just thinking about the steep climb and rugged terrain we had covered following what we thought was Garog's trail up to his master's lair.

"Well do you see our three carts! Do you think they could have come, the same way we did, up from the meadow?"

I thought about this and decided there was no way..

"What are you suggesting?" I asked him hopefully

"Well, based on the number of carts we saw by the secondary entrance into Trows lair, I believe there must be a trail ideal for carts not far from here. That is how I think Trow has captured so many of them!"

"Let me guess," I said smiling slightly, "You've looked around and you've found the trail. Am I right?"

"You are! And it is behind us and just beyond those rows of bushes at the edge of this clearing. In fact you can see where the wheels of some of the carts at least have come up through the hedge. After all, this is a nice place to make a camp!"

135

Now that he had pointed it out to me I could quite clearly see what he was talking about. So with this insight we led the horses with their carts down through the hedge and came immediately upon a well-established trail.

Our trip back down the mountain became relatively easy once we started along the trail. As we travelled down towards the meadow, Traxxa pointed out to me at least three other trails which branched away from the one we were on but they all looked overgrown and ill-used. At each point he drew my attention to the fact that the trail we were following appeared to be well used and maintained. I began to wonder what it was he was trying to tell me. So I asked him outright.

"What about these other trails Traxxa? What are you thinking?"

"Well!" He said slowly, "If I was travelling through these mountains and knew or even heard about Trow I certainly wouldn't be following a trail that led right past his lair – would you?"

I shook my head slowly trying to follow his line of thought.

"And yet, of all the trails we have seen, this trail appears to be the most well-used and best-kept. This tells me at a glance that more people must be using this trail more than the others, so by deductive reasoning this must be the safest of all the trails, and yet in reality it isn't! Do you agree?"

I nodded my head slowly as I began to see where he was taking me.

"Exactly," he said triumphantly. "My feeling is that Trow himself has been keeping this trail well-kept, cleared and maintained in order to deceive any wayward wanderers into believing that this is the easiest and best way around this mountain."

"Right past his own front door!" I answered as understanding filtered in to my tired old brain. But as the full implications of what he was saying hit me I couldn't help but admire the clever ingenuity of the dead troll and his devilish intentions. He had made it easier for the innocent travellers to choose the better trail which he had designed, probably even built himself -- then kept it cleared in order to make it easier for him to ambush them.

"Yes it is a very clever yet simple trap indeed!" Traxxa said smiling grimly. "That is, of course if this is one of Trows ploys to bring his food and their treasures to himself without having to track them down and follow them all over his mountain!"

I nodded in agreement and for the rest of the journey down to the meadow I thought with sadness about the number of hapless victims the troll had lured to their deaths because of a well maintained trap.

Though the trip down the mountain was much longer and tiring it was largely uneventful.

It was late afternoon of our third day on the mountain when we finally reached the field where Kaira had found Ribbet and had picked the allium satium. Böder crouched down suddenly amongst the trees and told us there was a huge crowd milling around the bridge, formerly controlled by Garog and waiting along the far edge of the field. As we paused in the shadows of the wooded fringe, Kaira came forward and recognized them immediately. She turned to me and said.

"They are my kinsfolk from Tungston!"

Then without hesitation she stepped boldly out from under the cover of the trees and called out to us *(which included Böder)*, that we were to step out as well and not to hide or be fearful of those in the field before us.

We learned soon enough they had all come up at the behest of Terron, Kaira's father, to help him find out what had happened to his daughter. He feared that she had been taken by Garog -- or even worse by Trow himself. What surprised me most though was that almost the entire village had come up and were willing to risk their lives to try and rescue her from the trolls. This gesture alone by the villagers told me a great deal about Kaira, who she was and what she meant to her family, friends and her community.

Initially all the villagers were a little overwhelmed and fearful at the sight of Böder, walking slowly across the field just behind Kaira towards them, but this was soon eclipsed by their excitement and relief at seeing Kaira safe and unhurt. Their feelings of relief soon turned to amazement and then thorough delight and ecstatic happiness when they learned that both the bridge and the dreaded mountain trolls were dead and all largely due to the mighty hands of the giant who was standing silently before them.

To help reassure her would be rescuers, Kaira, with Jarecks' help, went and retrieved the hidden treasure that had been taken from Garogs hole as Böder and the rest of us pulled the three carts out from the wood and into the middle of the meadow. From here Kaira proudly showed her family and fellow villagers all the treasures that had been liberated from Trows lair. In the end, at Böders insistence, the villagers were encouraged to look for and retrieve their own treasures. Whatever had been taken from them was available and ready to be returned to them plus much more.

As it was getting late, we decided to make camp in the field and take our time talking and mixing with the village folk of Tungston. Once we made our intentions known, a group of elders offered to escort those who wanted to return, back to their homes in the village now that they knew Kaira was safe. The men returned at length with a great supply of food and drink and tents to help accommodate the people who had decided to remain in the meadow with us.

During our first night in the meadow with Kaira's family, friends and those from her village, we listened to a great number and varied tales of how the trolls had terrorized, harassed and plundered their village and the surrounding communities for so many, many decades.

As the night progressed and through the telling of the tales and stories there was a palpable feeling of relief and joy by these simple villagers. Even as each in turn spoke around the large campfires, the slow realization of what had truly been done to the three terrorizing trolls began to sink in. These sombre tales of terror and pain changed into expressions of relief and joy and this in turn slowly became gaiety and laughter accompanied by festive feelings. Then it became a time of music, dancing, songs and a wonderful time of feasting and drinking and a thoroughly delightful form of celebration which lasted well into the night and early the next morning.

We didn't know it at this time of course but this day of revealing the death of the trolls became an annual day of remembrance. Songs and poems were written and fabulous stories told and retold about the events of this day. Festivities and celebrations, feasts and drinking throughout the entire mountain communities were also held on this day each year for many decades afterwards. Such was the effect that our friend had had upon these people it became known throughout the region as 'Böders Day'!

CHAPTER THIRTEEN

JELLICK

Word of Böder's -- or rather, 'the giant's' -- victory and the demise of the trolls quickly spread. Before noon the next day there were people from all of the surrounding villages and communities coming up to meet with us and admire the giant -- from a respectful distance of course! Many tales were spun which told of what the trolls had done to this person or that group and then they would go on to describe in great detail what the trolls had taken from them.

Where we could, we looked for and helped individuals, families and communities to look for their treasures, trinkets and heirlooms in order to return it to them. All were so grateful just to have their prized possessions returned to them in much the same way as I had been. Some gave small rewards as they saw fit, though we asked for nothing. It soon became apparent though that many people had just come up to see the treasures being returned and looked with awe upon the ones who had despatched the trolls. In the end it took five full days for all the villagers and people from all about to come and reclaim their possessions.

At first the villagers and others from the local communities had come requesting the return of their treasures with fear and scepticism in their hearts. But this soon changed to respect and admiration as slowly word spread of the mighty contest that had taken place between Böder and Trow. The story was told and retold of how the courageous giant had triumphed over both the male and female mountain trolls after a great and lengthy battle. They also heard how he had battered Garog into many pieces after being cleverly tricked by the very brave and crafty Kaira. From these stories of conquest and victory and the recovering of their stolen treasure it soon became apparent that a change in attitude towards Böder the Giant had taken place.

During this time, upon my instructions, we kept Bartrow well out of sight of everyone who came calling on us. I did this for fear that some people, unreasonably, might want to inflict some sort of justice or further acts of vengeance upon Trow by killing the troll who was called Son of Trow. He hid and slept in Garog's burrow during the day and played about the meadow and explored the local forests during the night. After all he was believed to be barely ten and he needed his exercise and time to have fun. On these occasions, Böder would often go with him to keep him company and to ensure that no harm came to him. This gesture towards the young troll presented me with another interesting side to Böder that I hadn't seen before.

On our second evening in the meadow we were sitting around the campfire. Kaira, as always, had the basket wherein Ribbet stayed, beside her. At one stage she was distracted from our mealtime conversation and bent over towards Ribbet. It seemed apparent to us that she was attempting to talk with him once more. Privately I suspected that her claim that she was able to communicate with the toad might be some sort of childish hope or dream that this young Bidowman hadn't grown out of. After all hadn't she said she was the princess of a field or some other such thing? But then again, perhaps she truly believed he was really a cursed prince, or some other such childhood fantasy.

When she had finished with her pet toad, Kaira looked up and talked with us though she seemed to be addressing me in particular about continuing her journey with us. To which I responded not unkindly.

"Why do you wish to travel with us any further? Your family is here and waiting for you to return with them. Also your life is with your people here in the mountains."

Kaira looked quickly towards Ribbet once more before returning her gaze to me before replying evenly enough.

"Ribbet wants me to take him down to meet with the witch who changed him into this toad. He told me just now that if I were able to meet with her personally then there's every chance that she would restore Ribbet back to his original form!"

At first, I was very reluctant to have her accompany us. But still, I looked around at the others in our group to try and gauge their reaction to Kaira's request to stay and travel back with us towards Böders Island.

Sensing resistance from her request at this point, Kaira leant over her basket and listened for a moment before turning back to us and said.

"Ribbet tells me the evil witch who goes by the name of Zharlla was the one who cast the spell on him. He also says and that if we head directly east we should catch up to her around the city of Regil-Ter, which is, as you know, the capital city of M'Lenn Fida!"

"And how does he know this," I asked her, deciding to play along and humour her. The others were listening but were not contributing to the conversation. I suspected that whilst they liked Kaira very much they too hadn't heard Ribbet speak and were like me, just a little bit sceptical of this 'talking' toad.

Kaira answered, pretending not to notice my attempt to humour her.

"Ribbet tells me Zharlla heads south for the city of Katra and the warmth of the countries around the Tamanette Sea each year about this time. On her annual pilgrimage south, Zharlla usually stops for the Late Autumn Festival held in Regil-Ter. Here Zharlla will spend up to a month enjoying the festivities, present her troupe of carnival performers and ply her skills as a witch, you know telling fortunes, selling potions and antidotes and casting spells for people!"

"But we have no time for this!" I exclaimed in exasperation. "If people learn of Böder travelling throughout the countryside with us, we could meet with a great deal of trouble, despite what he's done for the people around this mountain. People are still very wary and incredibly fearful of giants, especially ones who travel freely throughout their lands!"

It was at this point that Ribbet spoke up and to our utter amazement we all heard him speak clearly and understood all that he said.

"You might wish to know that in Zharlla's caravan of entertainers there is a captive that I believe will be of great interest to you!"

"Oh! And what 'interest to us' is that Ribbet?" I asked, despite myself as I half expected the toad to lapse back into his quiet servitude once more.

"They have a young giantess by the name of Xalarlla *(pronounced Shalarlla)* being held captive by that evil weeeatch Zharlla! I know this because up till recently I too was part of her performing troupe. I fell out with that weeeatch over some trivial matter which I don't wish to recount to you. But I do know that Xalarlla was being treated very badly by Zharlla that she lives in chains and is regularly forced to perform feats of strength and power to amuse the simple townsfolk. However, I also know that in Regil-Ter -- at the Late Autumn Festival -- the Judicial Games will take place and the chances are that Xalarlla will be pitted to fight in the arena. She has been in these games before, so I implore you, if not for myself, at least give some thought for the giantess. She is a beautiful woman with a wondrous heart who has been abused and taken advantage of from her earliest days and I would imagine, with all your many treasures you would be more than able to buy her freedom from this weeeatch. And in return for this gift to Böder from me, all I would ask in return is a small stipend from out of Böders treasure to help pay for the antidote to alter my condition. And with Kaira intervening on my behalf I'm sure that Zharlla will succumb to her charms -- as we all have -- and will accede to have me changed back to my original form!"

Böder's ears had perked up the moment Ribbet had mentioned 'young giantess', for they were hungry for the chance of hearing about other giants and his heart was more than responsive to their troubles. But it was the plight of this Xalarlla - the giantess', that had captured Böders heart immediately and more or less determined what we were about to do next.

We, on the other hand, were still all dumbfounded -- not by the words, but by the fact that Ribbet had actually spoken and we had all heard him. Only afterwards did the subject matter seep out and we began to measure what Ribbet had said and how much this would affect each of us.

But still, we could not escape the fact, Kaira wanted to be a part of our plans to venture to Regil-Ter. I looked around at the others and knew instantly they were all very happy to have Kaira travel with us as Ribbets carer -- after all he had been living in her basket for well over a week now!

So in the end, I told Kaira we would allow her some time for her to travel down to her home in Tungston and say good bye to her father and sisters and pack herself a travelling bag. She also told us that she would like to gather the needles and sewing things which were the tools of her trade; for we had learned that she was a struggling seamstress.

Jareck took a pack horse and went with her on the journey to her home village just to ensure that she got there and back safely and help her to carry her travelling bag. I'm sure she would have been alright on her own, but Jareck insisted on accompanying her, such was his growing feelings for this young Bidowman.

From the outset, Earlich and I dealt with the continuous number of passing villagers and claimants helping them to reclaim their stolen treasures and trinkets. During our time in the meadow, Traxxa began practising daily with the throwing stars -- sometimes for hours on end. It appeared he was teaching himself how to use this new and exciting weapon which he wished to master as quickly as possible. Something else I saw -- which intrigued me even more than the throwing stars – was Traxxa would often take out both his swords at once and began the slow process of learning to wield them together in unison. This was a skill I'd never seen him use before and I thought this was a most interesting development in this gifted warrior.

I was also pleased to see him take Böder aside and begin to talk to him about what he might expect should he become involved with any sort of games in the arena. From then on Traxxa began instructing Böder on how to use his mace effectively. As well as this he encouraged him to become familiar with all the weapons we had taken from the armoury including showing Böder how to handle and throw many of the weapons such as the spears as though they were darts and the swords as though they were daggers at targets and trees. Whilst a lot of the spears he gave him were far too small for his huge hands, still Böder persevered and Traxxa showed him how to adapt his size and use this to his advantage. In the course of this training many blades were broken or simply disappeared never to be found again with the overzealous throwing by the young giant. In this, I saw the master instructing the pupil even as he himself was learning to handle a new weapon.

Still many of their training sessions took place during the evening whilst under the cover of darkness -- mainly because Bartrow was showing a keen interest in these exercises and wanted to be a part of the training process as well. Traxxa willingly took the young troll under his instructive wing teaching the young troll how to handle many of these weapons *(though I never actually saw him claim or carry a weapon of his own)*. Bartrow was quick and eager to learn and Traxxa was a competent and patient teacher. Whilst their training nights started in this field they continued on throughout our journey as we travelled down towards Regil-Ter.

For accuracy and speed, Traxxa encouraged both his students to simply throw rocks or lumps of wood in quick succession at moving targets, such as at a deer or birds and even the occasional, highly elusive boar. Most would miss but many times we had a meal obtained from a stone hurled by Böder or Bartrow during their practise time.

Bartrow had by now become comfortable with us as his new friends. One day he indicated to Traxxa that he wanted to go back to collect the chests which held all that was left of the memory of his parents. He told us that he had hidden them especially for himself deep in the bowels of Trows lair. So on one of the evenings when Kaira was down in the village packing her bags and saying her good-byes, Traxxa, Böder and Bartrow went back up to Trows cave. They took some light crystals with them as they were going to search for more weapons that Böder and Bartrow could use to practise with as well as reclaim Bartrow's chests.

TRAXXA

We approached the main entrance to Trows lair and clambered over the shattered stone statue of Trow. We tried to move some of the larger lumps of the troll but they were just too heavy -- and besides where were we going to move them to and for why? The door was still open and we moved what we could of Trow which allowed us just enough space to clamber through. At one point Böder found himself getting stuck so he stood back and pulverised what was left of some of the larger pieces of Trow with his mace. The reduced rubble allowed him to move past and into the corridor leading down into what had become the dead troll's caves.

As we stepped silently into the leading tunnel, each of us noticed, almost at once, there was a distinct new odour about the place. Bartrow made the comment that he had smelt this new scent before but only on some very rare occasions and only in the deepest recesses of the caves. As we made our way down to the main cavern the second thing we noticed was that Trows dead mate was no longer lying in the middle of the corridor. Despite myself this unnerved me greatly. What kind of creature could take the very heavy body of a dead female troll -- which had been at least five meters tall -- out of the corridor and somehow remove it completely? By the light of the crystals we could see the smear of dark red troll blood. It started from where we knew she had fallen when she had died and which now led down to the main hall. We looked at one another and decided as one and without words of any kind to continue our quest to retrieve Bartrows' chest and get out of the caves as quickly as possible. I doused our small light crystal and we moved forward cautiously.

There was light in the large main cavern ahead, but this we knew came from some large light crystals in the centre of the halls ceiling which we had not been able to retrieve when we left. The new smell we had noticed when we first entered the caves grew stronger as we made our way down to the opening into the main cavern. By the light of the overhead crystals we had a clear view of all that was in the large cavern. Carefully we looked around but could see nothing moving, though we saw the dead female troll. She was lying in the middle of the vast cavern and she appeared to be half eaten. That is to say she was missing her limbs; or rather, the flesh on her limbs were completely gone and all that was left were the bones. They appeared to have been picked clean, but in a macabre twist, they had been left still attached to the main body. It was as though whoever had eaten the limbs hadn't even bothered to remove them. This above all else in the caves disturbed me the most. Upon closer inspection I saw that the clothes covering the troll had been interfered with and it appeared that the creature or creatures that had eaten her arms and legs had made attempts to get to the softer flesh of her torso and organs beneath the chest bones. But, fortunately for us, there were no other signs of her assailants anywhere in the huge cavern.

After ensuring all was clear in the hall we followed quickly after Bartrow who led us silently across the rocky cave to one of the side corridors. Both Bartrow and Böder had realized quickly enough that there was a very real and dangerous presence in the caves now and as such they spoke no words nor did they make any sounds as we continued after the young troll who led us deeper and deeper into the bowels of the lair.

After what seemed like an agonizingly long time, we finally arrived at a small room. By now Böder was almost doubled over such was the reduced height of the ceiling in these endless corridors and walkways. In any case, Bartrow was quick when he came to the hiding place of his few treasures. He removed the stones covering the hole where they had been stored and picked them up and made to move off labouring slightly under their weight. Böder offered to help him carry the couple of chests that comprised his few possessions. When they had been distributed between the two of them, they turned together and we began to make our way cautiously and ever alert back towards the main hall.

Once more, at the opening into the main hall, we paused and scoured the large cavern to make sure there was nothing waiting for us to emerge from the depths. Behind us from the dark depths of the corridor we had just come up through I heard the quietest of a clicking or a chittering sound, like that of a squirrel or some other small rodent. I knew both Böder and Bartrow had heard it as well and as I looked up at the young troll, I thought I saw, for the first time since I had known him, a small measure of real fear in his eyes. And then I knew what it was that was behind us. It had been the smell, the eating of the limbs, even the ability to move an incredibly heavy troll out of the corridor away from the lairs entrance which caused me to remember what we were about to encounter.

They were known to me as grontics. They are a small rodent like creature that looks a bit like a rat but are much bigger than most domestic cats. They are known to walk on two legs and are ferocious carnivores and scavengers. Most grontics live in the very depths of caves usually beneath the mountains and are known to scavenge off the larger creatures such as trolls, drazils and other large carnivores. It quickly dawned on me that, the moment the trolls were no longer living in the caves the grontics had come forward to claim it as their own. But there had to be a large number to have been able to physically drag the dead female troll down to where she now lay in the middle of the main hall. They were obviously intent on eating her here at their leisure. They must have been disturbed by our returning to the caves, but something told me they would not remain scared of us for very long.

I turned to Bartrow and Böder and implored them both to run, for to even contemplate fighting so vast a number of them in these caves would be madness and futile. Whilst they would only be as big as the largest domestic cat they would be more voracious, cunning and tenacious than a frenzied pack of wild dogs but in much greater number and it would be like trying to fight a swarm of ants which means that conventional weapons would be of no value and have little or no effect. And so we ran!

We headed towards the main entrance corridor and moved as fast as we could! As we entered the corridor I looked back across the large cavern where sure enough coming out of every other tunnel and corridor entering the large cavern came great swarms of the short, brown haired, rodent like creatures known as grontics. They were running on two legs -- occasionally using all fours to try and gain maximum speed and making straight towards us. They were chittering and chattering in their frenzied screaming way with blood lust in their eyes and a determined hunger in their grinning multi-fanged mouths.

Without another thought, I turned and ran as fast as I could, following hard on the heels of my two large friends. Despite carrying the heavy chests of Bartrows memories and his large mace as well as being confined by the low ceiling, Böder made the best progress of us up the long corridor. Bartrow despite his awkward appearance also made good speed. But it was the sight of so many of the vicious little creatures that spurred me on with the greatest urgency still, I was the last of us to make it through the doorway and out into the cold night mountain air.

I could hear the first of the grontics snapping closely at my heels as I came through the door and darted quickly out of the way as I saw both Böder and Bartrow ready with rocks in their hands waiting for me to break free. Their hands were full of the smaller pieces of the destroyed statue of Trow. As I dived out of the way the giant and the troll hurled the rocks and stones back through the doorway to scatter the fast moving grontics. Immediately there was the crunching sound as broken bits of stone troll ploughed through the mass of furry little grontics. We could hear the breaking of bones of these ferocious little creatures as well as the sound of fragments tearing through their flesh and smashing into their bodies. No sooner were the first bits of statue thrown than both giant and troll picked up more lumps of rock and threw them through the doorway with as much speed and regularity as their strength and stamina allowed. I also reached down and grabbed what I could, hurling stones and rocks and bits of statue until such a time as we heard the chittering and the snarling of the damaged grontics receding back down the corridor. No doubt they were convinced they had successfully chased the intruders out of their newly acquired territory.

When we couldn't hear them anymore, Böder, Bartrow and I cleared the area as best we could in order to push the door leading into the lair closed. It required all of our combined strength and determination to eventually close the large rock door. Even as the troll's door closed completely we heard the satisfying click as the intricate locking system (*that trolls are famous for*) firmly secured the opening. We knew then that no-one who didn't know about the secrets of this door would ever be able to find it, let alone open it ever again.

"Well that means the grontics will have to find another way out of these caves, which I'm sure they will." I said trying to bring a bit of levity back into our spirits. "But, in the meantime, I think we should warn the local townsfolk that there is a new threat living in these mountains, now that the trolls have gone. No doubt Trow and his mate helped keep the grontics from dominating these mountain caverns, but now it is their turn to rule the dark places beneath this mountain!"

JELLICK

When Traxxa, Böder and Bartrow returned they told us in detail of their encounter with the grontics. I had heard about these creatures, but more in myth and legend form and usually used to scare little children rather than having them actually living in the dark recesses of caves beneath the mountains.

Nevertheless, our friends were safe and Bartrow was careful to place his most valued items on the cart himself after instructing us never to allow anyone to touch it, or open them.

We assured him that we would honour his wishes. Bartrow smiled awkwardly and then went towards Garogs burrow to sleep and be on his own.

When Kaira returned from her visit to her home, we were still in the meadow and yet the number of people visiting us daily had not eased. With every encounter we began to warn the people who came to us that there were grontics in the depths of this mountain and there was every reason to be wary of them especially during the night. Grontics much like trolls hated the light of day, *(though of course they were not known to turn to stone),* but still they were aggressive territorial scavengers who would not venture very far from their mountain, but would defend it if they felt they were being attacked or threatened.

We would like to have stayed on longer to accommodate all the people in the local communities by returning to them all that Trow had taken from them. However, the words of Ribbet returned to our ears about where Zharlla would be and for how long, so we decided that it was time for us to move on!

We broke camp the very next morning. We said goodbye to the friends and acquaintances we had met and made. Just as we were getting ready to leave the field in the mountain we watched by the side as Kaira said goodbye to Terron and her two sisters. As this well wishing and embracing was taking place, Böder approached the small group apologised for interrupting as he knelt down and with our help he presented the third smallest cart, along with a pack horse and gave it to Terron. One look in the cart and Terron slipped to his knees he was so overwhelmed with gratitude and emotion. We all rallied around to support him and after looking in the cart we knew instantly why he had fallen down so, for we saw a single large treasure chest full to overflowing.

"This," Böder said a little uncomfortably, "is for you and your family for all your help."

At this point Terron played the social game and refused the tremendously generous gift by saying. "But this is way too much for us; after all we didn't really do much by way of helping you! Please Böder, I can't take this treasure!"

"But I insist Terron," responded Böder awkwardly. "This is just a small token of my appreciation for you and your family. And after all, you're not taking it; I'm giving it to you!"

"And I appreciate this gift from you Böder, I really do! But I truly didn't do anything to warrant such a generous gift from you and as such I simply can't accept it."

As Terron was playing this game of refusal with our friend, I watched Böder carefully and could see that he was actually enjoying the interaction with this simple village Bidoman. In light of this play, I could see how this very generous gift, in the eyes of those close by, had actually doubled, perhaps even tripled in value, by this clever social game of refusal. And then Böder, to his credit, extended the play by giving Terron a reason for receiving the cart and treasure by including Kaira as part of the reasoning behind the gift.

"Consider this then as a gift from me to you to help compensate you and your family for the loss of your daughter to the whims of an adventure!" And then he sealed the deal by getting Terron to respond positively by asking. "I hope you don't mind this little gift for the price of your daughters' companionship?"

And here, realizing it would defeat the game if he continued to refuse; Terron accepted the gift and replied warmly.

"No. Not at all Böder! Thank-you very much!" And he extended his hand and arm and warmly grasped the two fingers the large giant had offered by way of an embrace. "I will always remember you and your loyal friends; I know that you will look after Kaira for me, no matter where you take her or what adventures she follows you into!"

Terron then turned to include us in his positive response and embraced each of us in turn smiling and weeping as he went in an emotional show of appreciation and celebration at the receipt of this sudden, overwhelming fortune.

About a year or so, later on, as I was travelling through the area, I returned to Tungston. I was fortunate to meet up with Terron again and I became a welcomed guest in his house. During this visit we swapped stories of our adventures and fortunes. He then recounted, with tears in his eyes, the sudden fortune given to him by Böder. This, he told me, had made him the richest and one of the most respected Bidoman throughout all of the mountainous regions.

The first thing he did upon receiving Böder's gift, was to seek out the local healer and arranged for him to receive a monthly stipend in order for him to take Shayla on as an apprentice. He then began teaching her all that she needed to know about the art of healing and the manufacturing and administration of medicines and healing potions.

The second thing he did was to purchase a comfortable house, a shop and a warehouse. He transformed the warehouse into a large carpenter's workshop. Next, with all the tools, apprentices and staff he needed, and along with Datyia working beside him, they began making themselves known as the number one carpenter and furniture maker in all the area.

I have returned many times to Tungston over the following years and I always been able to call in on Terron and his family. They have always welcomed me as a friend and treated me and my entourage with the greatest show of respect and hospitality. During these many visits I have been able to keep him informed on what had been happening with Kaira, Jareck and of course Böder.

From out of our friendship, I have been able to build up a working relationship with Terron as well. As a merchant I was able to supply him with fabrics, tools, dyes and information pertinent to his trade. On top of this, I have also purchased many of his marvellous furniture creations and helped to sell them on for him. By doing this I have been instrumental in helping him make his name known to many of the larger markets throughout the land.

Terron is a quiet, industrious Bidoman and is greatly respected throughout the community and loved very much by his family and friends. It is because of Böder and Kaira that I have been fortunate enough to have met up with and interacted so completely with this wonderfully creative, yet simple and down to earth Bidoman.

In many respects, this is a fine example of the kind of by-product that has resulted from my friendship with Böder the giant and my seeing firsthand the impact he has had on those around him.

CHAPTER FOURTEEN

EARLICH

I was really looking forward to visiting the city of Regil-Ter again. I have been to Regil-Ter on a number of occasions and I must say it is one of the most beautiful cities in Durogg that I have seen thus far. It is both the capital and the largest city of M'Lenn-Fida and is situated on the Mirack River near where it merges with the Dund River. Regil-Ter is built on, in front of, and around a thick natural stone dam which has created a very large and very deep natural lake on the Mirack River. To avoid the city flooding during certain times of the rainy and melting seasons, a number of sluices have been built along both sides of the lake. These can be opened at any time to allow the excess water to run down through manimal made canals and channels to flow around the city providing a number of water services to the surrounding farms and local agricultural lands.

Regil-Ter is rumoured to have once been called the 'Regal Terraces' as the founding fathers designed the original city structure to extend across the top of the dam through the use of walkways, bridges and terraces. It is also known by its other name, the 'City of Waterfalls'. This is because the water from the lake breaks over the stone dam in fifteen different places creating a series of beautiful waterfalls, pools and rivulets all the way down the open side of the dam. The waterfalls eventually drop all of twenty-five meters before creating a number of large streams which run around the cities ten main islands at the base of the dam. Once passed the islands, the many streams reform to become the Mirack River once more. From then on it flows unhindered for roughly five and a half kilometers before joining up with the Dund River.

The ten islands, which make up the main body of Regil-Ter, are all joined together by three major, multi-arched stone bridges which connect them to both the north and south banks of the Mirack River. The biggest island, in the middle of the river, holds a large number of government buildings, the largest stadium or arena in M'Lenn-Fida and a huge number of hotels, brothels, drinking houses and opium dens. It is also where the two main markets of produce and fish are located. The stadium on this large island is where the country's Judicial Games are usually held, and it can reportedly fit crowds of over 50,000 people. Then there are the terraces along the top of the dam, which allows a much larger audience to look down and enjoy the shows and entertainment that are held in the stadium.

The Late Autumn Festival, which Ribbet told us the witch Zharlla would be attending, is essentially when the people of Regil-Ter open the city's gates to all the producers, farmers, herders and growers within their country and the surrounding lands in order to throw a huge street party or festival. This festival takes place during the entire tenth month of the calendar year to celebrate the blessings of the harvest. It is just like turning the city into a huge marketplace or a very large country fair in the city. Farmers and growers come to Regil-Ter to present the surplus from their summer produce, and abundance of their stock and to have some fun and enjoy the plentiful sideshows, parades, street markets and performers in the process. They come in from all over M'Lenn-Fida and from as far away as Entarim, Nyang and Jeion to the north and from Gru-Nish-Dan in the south.

Craftsmen, merchants, smiths, street performers and other skilled artisans from all over also come to the city of Regil-Ter to help in the celebrations and try to make lots of money from the influx of people who are in a market mood. Thus they all help to turn the Late Autumn Festival into one of the largest agricultural markets in all of the north of Durogg.

Tor Jellick and I have known about this festival for a long time, as all merchants of any standing in the north would have done. After talking to Jareck and Böder about it, they told me they too had heard about the Late Autumn Festival but had never actually gone to one. I guess now is as good a time as ever for them to find out about it in person!

However, the biggest problem I can see us facing in Regil-Ter will be meeting up with this witch, Zharlla. Now that we have actually heard Ribbet speak, we must assume, if his word is true (*and there is very little reason why it shouldn't be so*) then Zharlla will be, to us, a very powerful and possibly a most challenging adversary. As such, we will probably need to be very wary of her and watch out for her at all times as we seek to bargain with her.

So the first thing, as far as I can see, is to find Zharlla from amongst the many revellers, merchants, street performers and the great number of people the festival will have attracted.

The second thing is to try and get her to change Ribbet back to his original form -- for his and Kaira's sake.

And the third objective for coming to Regil-Ter will be to find out if this giantess Xalarlla is, as Ribbet says, being held in captivity and subjected to the cruelty he has outlined to us in great detail. Whether this information is true or not, we are to try and secure her freedom through whatever means possible. Once this has been achieved -- assuming of course that it can be done -- then we, or rather Böder, will offer her an alternative life with him on his island. In fact he has already expressed his desire to do such a thing.

But of course all this has to be done without letting anyone know that there is a troll killing giant, a baby troll, a magically enchanted toad and two carts belonging to our giant friend, filled with a treasure of unimaginable wealth and all camped near to the city.

Hmmm! It seems that life around Böder just gets more and more interesting as our days in association with him continues!

JELLICK

The news of our departure from the meadow on the mountain above Tungston attracted a huge waving crowd who'd come to and see us off. As we were readying ourselves to leave, the ladies of Tungston came over to us as a group and presented Böder with a large gift of thanx. Like a little boy on his name day, he quickly unravelled the present. We all stared in amazement as the gift became twenty-one different weather-proof doonas all stitched masterfully together to create a huge colourful quilt. It was reinforced and bordered beautifully by strips of tanned leather. We realized instantly of course that Böder now had protection from the elements in the form of a blanket or even a tent. It was indeed a most wonderful and practical gift. I looked at Kaira and I think somehow she had had a large hand in the making of this thoughtful gesture from the women folk of Tungston. Needless to say Böder was almost overcome with emotion by the workmanship, love and care that had been shown and sewn into this beautiful present of appreciation. He kept smiling and thanking everyone and anyone over and over for his new blanket.

Shortly after this the emotional goodbyes -- between Kaira and her family, and the villagers of Tungston and the surrounding communities -- began. Then Böder with his blanket draped over his shoulder like a great tordan, led the two remaining horse-drawn carts and our small band across the late Garog's Bridge and we left the mountain meadow behind us for good.

* * *

Our intention was to journey east then meet up with and follow the Mirack River down towards Regil-Ter. I noted with particular interest, in just the short time we had made ourselves known to the mountain communities, Böder's three cartloads of treasure had been reduced by just over a third. There were now only nineteen chests of treasure (*which did not include mine and Bartrow's chests containing our own personal items*) as well as all of Böder's tools and the remaining weapons (*those that were not lost in the woods or broken by their target practise*).

On our journey eastwards, whenever free time allowed, Traxxa practised using both his swords at once. He also continued to instruct both Böder and Bartrow in the art of handling all kinds of weapons. He gave specific time to further develop his and Böder's throwing skills with stars, spears and whatever else the pair of them could handle. Bartrow continued to enjoy roaming the countryside by night-- many with Böder, other times with Traxxa and sometimes with them both. Kaira also kept herself busy by making a number of clothes for both Böder and Bartrow. These included a comfortable pair of large boots for Böder made of horse leather. Aside from this, our trip was fairly uneventful apart from the fact that we had a rather interesting discussion about whether we should go visit Jareck and Böder's old farm. But in the end we all decided against this venture and travelled very wide of it.

Finally we reached the outskirts of Regil-Ter just a few days after the Late Autumn Festival had officially begun. We moved slowly around to the south side of the city and made our camp in a well hidden glade about a two hours ride from the large capital city of M'Lenn-Fida.

To Bartrow's credit, on this first night of running free around the glade and exploring the surrounding woods with Böder, he found a well concealed cave near to where our camp was. This turned out to be an ideal place for Bartrow to sleep in and hide from the sun during the day. We were also able to push one of the carts filled to overflowing with the giant-sized tools and the remainder of Böders treasure in with Bartrow. I decided to inform him that he could have the job of protecting and guarding these things. He seemed genuinely excited and proud to be placed in charge of looking after Böder's treasure like that. He told me much later, he thought that was such a wonderful thing I had done, asking him to do this. And he was smiling so broadly when he told me this, I was fearful for a moment that his little ugly troll face would split in two.

The next day, we secured the camp the best way we knew how by leaving Böder and Bartrow to guard it. Then together with Traxxa, Jareck, Earlich, and Kaira carrying a carefully wrapped up Ribbet, we rode into Regil-Ter to begin looking for Zharlla.

Regil-Ter is not a particularly big city, as far as cities in Durogg go, but it has so many different levels and areas with so many things happening all at the same time so the city appears to be much larger than it really was. In fact, the city was awash with colour from flags, pennants, banners and kites. There were also caravans, circuses, carnivals and tents with all sorts of entertainment on both banks of the Mirack River and camped all around the lake. Then of course, each of the Islands had their own activities happening on them all the time with market stalls, street performers, musicians and various other shows, sights and contests all contributing to the festival atmosphere. Finally, there was the largest island with its produce and fish markets and the stadium which had its own special programs planned for the Late Autumn Festival. This, we soon discovered was to become the centrepiece of all the celebrations for the city of Regil-Ter.

But we had to start somewhere, so we began searching for Zharlla on the south bank of the river for the simple reason that this was where we first came into contact with Regil-Ter. We also worked on the principle that if Zharlla was going to travel south, as Ribbet had said she would at the festival's close, then this is where she would most logically set up her circus troupe. We stabled our horses in a farm which was about a ten-minute walk from the outskirts of the market city and made our way in with a throng of morning people. We had been looking for barely half an hour before Ribbet called our attention (*by speaking to Kaira once more*) to the colours that he said were those of Zharlla's.

Being a merchant, the idea of bargaining with Zharlla came naturally to me. I left Traxxa and Jareck out of our initial meeting with Zharlla as I wanted to reveal as few of our group to her as I could. I entered the area under her colours and after enquiring about where she was, we were shown a flamboyant, brightly painted caravan. I knocked at the door and it was opened to reveal the pock marked face of an overweight, middle-aged Vixawman (*half woman half fox*) with large sparkling glemm earrings. Whilst she wore bright makeup on her cheeks around her eyes and on her lips, these could not hide the fact that age was not treating her kindly. Her natural colouring and hair was matted and dirty and her clothes, once bright and cheerful, were now old and faded and she was permanently covered by a shawl. But despite this, I still noticed the many slev and glemm necklaces full of charms and pendants hanging from around her dull red neck. When she presented her hands in the traditional female gesture of greeting, I could see they were still strong and firm but were also dirty and calloused from working close with the earth (*this was the sure sign of a very powerful witch*). All her fingers were covered in either glemm or slev rings, and there were an unknown number of gaudy bangles and bracelets around her wrists and ankles. I got the impression that whilst she no longer cared about her own personal appearance and hygiene; she was nonetheless still bound up in the external cosmetics which might explain the wearing of so much jewellery. (*But it was definitely not my place to make any comment aloud to this effect*).

Standing at the base of the stairs attached to the rear of her caravan, I introduced myself and Kaira. When she saw we weren't a threat, she came out and sat down on the top step and invited us to talk as we wanted. It was a little awkward talking to her like this but I stayed with it. I started off by asking about her health and enquiring in the polite way, as was the custom of the first meeting by strangers, about how she was coping and enjoying her life. I also gave her a compliment letting her know that we believed she was a great and powerful witch whose abilities and skills were widely spoken of, and telling her we were very privileged to be meeting with her. When the preliminaries and niceties of a first encounter had been established, I decided not to waste any more of her time so I asked her directly how it was that she had been able to cast a spell that had changed Ribbet into a toad. But I did this through complimenting her and believe I inferred no disdain in my words or expression.

To our confused amusement, she didn't seem to know who we were talking about at first. That is until Kaira brought Ribbet out of his basket and presented him to her. Here Zharlla expelled a wicked, cackling, snigger which sounded like it was just a little short of an unpleasant laugh.

She then told us contemptuously. "His name is not Ribbet but 'Ribard'! He was my own personal bard until I caught him stealing from me!"

Ribard at this point tried desperately to interrupt, but I silenced him with a wave of my hand saying.

"You've had more than enough time to tell us your story! Its Zharlla's turn now and she can tell us whatever she wants and we will be the judge of what we wish to believe!"

I noticed as I did this that Zharlla was looking out at me from under her very dark eyelashes with a little respect and a sort of half amused smile which played gently around the edges of her wrinkled and weathered lips.

"I caught him thieving some of my more valuable oils and ointments," she said quietly, softening her voice considerably. "As this had not been the first time he had done this to me, I fed him a special potion in his evening broth which turned him into the creature you now hold before me. And I'd be careful with your hands dearie," she said to Kaira, "the oils off his body are a potent sleeping draught!"

"Yes, we know this!" I said. "Now tell me, what will it take for you to transform him back into his original form?"

"Hmmm what have you got?" She asked slyly.

"Are you saying that you can change him back and are willing to do this but you wish to haggle over price?" I asked politely, "Is that what I'm hearing?"

"Just before I took the time to transform this toad into a real toad, I knew for certain that he had been looking through my personal collection of parchments. In particular he was poring over a very valuable, very rare scroll of mine. From the time I threw him out until even now, I have not been able to find it. Does anyone know anything about this?" At this point she looked directly at Ribard.

"Well, what do you have to say about this Ribard?" I asked, sensing the truth in her accusation.

"If this scroll is returned to you undamaged, will you change me back? Is that it?" Ribard asked suddenly, taking my style of response unto himself.

"That's what I'm saying! Well, that and the cost for the ingredients for both potions plus a small amount for my time and inconvenience. Let's say half a hundred weight of slev!"

I looked at Kaira and she looked at Ribard. He whispered something whereupon she leaned closer to hear what he was saying.

When it looked like he had finished speaking to her, she stood up and said to Zharlla. "There is a loose panel above the back wheel on the right-hand side of your caravan. The scroll is hidden behind this."

At a nod from Zharlla a nearby servant girl quickly left and returned a few minutes later with a rolled-up parchment bound in a colourful blue string. Zharlla took it, unfurled it and looked closely over both sides of it. Then, as if satisfied, she nodded her head.

"Come by tomorrow morning about this time with your payment and I will have the potion ready for the toad. Once you have it, you can decide whether to change him or not! That's up to you. However, the moment I hand this potion over to you I don't ever want to see him again -- is that clear?" And again she looked directly at Ribard as she said this.

After first checking with Kaira I accepted her terms and we left.

"Why didn't you ask about Xalarlla the giantess?" Kaira asked the moment we were out of earshot of Zharlla's caravan.

"First things first!" I said comfortingly. "We get Ribard," and here I had to smile, "changed and then we approach her with another request -- our

160

next deal if you like! Well; we're here in Regil-Ter would you like to look around at the markets of the Late Autumn Festival and check out the many attractions this beautiful city has to offer?"

"Yes I'd like to do that!" Kaira said, suddenly full of girlish charm and excitement, clapping her hands and dancing around for a moment or two.

At this, I smiled quietly to myself. When we caught up with the others, Traxxa, Jareck, Earlich, Kaira and I spent the rest of the day enjoying ourselves by walking all over the islands of Regil-Ter. We crossed a great number of the bridges and climbed the stairs up to some of the many beautiful and grand terraces that made up the many unique features of Regil-Ter. We looked around soaking up the atmosphere of the festival, the markets, the street performers and the many other activities the city had to offer us.

At one point in our tour of the city, after watching some exceptional fireworks fired off over the islands, Traxxa excused himself from our presence and told me that he would meet us at the stadium in about two hours. I watched him head off towards where the fireworks had been set off and wondered idly what he was thinking about and what he was planning to do next.

As we wandered down one of the many crowded avenues with their stalls and street performers, I was drawn to a poster of which there were many. This one in particular informed us that the Judicial Games would commence in three days' time. More than that though, one of the main features about these games this year was the big event which was featuring a female giantess by the name of Xalarlla. I stood and pondered this for a moment or two before joining up with our small company.

We reached the stadium and I was really impressed by its size. But more than its size I was amazed at the large number of people milling all around. Just as I was beginning to wonder how on Durogg I was ever going to find Traxxa in amongst the crowd, Traxxa stepped forward from out of an alcove, smiling warmly at us. He was carrying an exceptionally large backpack over his shoulder and had a sly confidential look about him that I rarely ever saw in him. It was like he had a huge surprise for us but knew that now was not the time to show us. Furthermore he knew it was going to frustrate the minkle out of all of us as we would each try to work out what the surprise was until he revealed it to us. But he refused to divulge what he had in his backpack whilst we were in Regil-Ter and kept smiling secretively about it all the while.

I resigned myself to letting him have his little secret and told him briefly of the poster I had seen. He nodded, as if to say he, too, had seen a similar poster. We moved with the crowd until we were before the archways that led into the concourse beneath the massive seating of the stadium.

Parts of the stadium were opened to the general public, though of course, the arena and many of the stalls were empty. I was frustrated with Traxxa as he seemed to take an inordinate amount of time just looking and taking in as many of the features of the stadium and all around it as he could. He gave careful consideration to such things as the many gates, the archways, the perimeter concourse and even the lanes that surrounded the stadium.

Later on, as the afternoon was drew to a close, we made our way slowly towards the south bank of the Mirack. As we walked, I took Traxxa aside and talked softly with him.

"Traxxa - what are you thinking about the arena?"

"There are a number of interesting options available to us, but I would need to investigate a little further as well as talk about it some more. Why? What are you thinking?"

"I was thinking that I need to watch over Zharlla. Are you up to hanging around Zharlla's caravan for me tonight to see if you can find anything more about this giantess. I saw on the poster back there that she is to be the main attraction in these Judicial Games. Try and find out as much about these games as you can, but don't let Zharlla or any from her troupe hear of your investigation into this matter. We'll go back to the camp and get this half a hundred weight of slev that this witch has asked for. Try and find a place to stay overnight, but be careful there is something not quite right about these games! In any case, we should be back here tomorrow as per her instructions, so look out for us and we'll catch up with you then, is that clear?"

He nodded in understanding and then carefully extended the backpack he had been carrying out to me and asked, "Can you take this back to the camp for me. But I advise you to take great care of it; don't drop it or bounce it around too much, for your own safety's sake!"

With these words ringing in my ears, I took it gingerly from out of his hand and assured him that I would look after it for him. But I couldn't help myself, so finally I asked. "Why the great care? What's in the bag?"

"Do you remember the fireworks we saw earlier?" He asked

I nodded my head, but I felt there was a lot more to come.

"Well I tracked down the man who set the fireworks off and I was rewarded with an insight into the use one might gain from setting off our own fireworks. In any case he sold me some samples and told me to return with some more slev and we would talk some more. So I want to ask, when you return tomorrow would you bring me a bag full of slev so that I can purchase some more of his time and the results of his interesting work and materials."

Infuriatingly, my curiosity was peaked without the reward of really knowing. But I also knew somehow that Traxxa had given me all the information that he would for the moment. But still, I had something for him and so I handed him a small pouch of slev and glemm which I always seemed to have about my person.

"Will this do?"

He smiled knowingly and nodded his head.

"That will do nicely and might also afford me the luxury of getting myself a room for the night!"

"If there's one to be found!" I replied a little matter-of-factly!

"There's that too!"

He responded slowly realizing the truth in what I had just told him. He nodded his head grimly.

"Still, until tomorrow then!"

At which he turned and made his way off through the surging, flowing evening crowd.

As I watched him leave us, I had a gut feeling that he was somehow comfortable at being alone in this busy market town. After all he hadn't walked off with shoulders slumped as though banished from our presence or anything like that. Quite the opposite in fact - if the truth be told! He seemed to have a slight spring in the few sure confident steps he had taken before disappearing from my view. Only as I turned back towards the others, who were waiting patiently for me, did I realise, with a start, that Traxxa really hadn't had a day off, *(so to speak)* in well over nine months -- nearly a year. Perhaps he was content to have a day *(or a night)* away from all of us just to do what he liked after all?

This I concluded would be sound reasoning in understanding where Traxxa might be, at this time. In any case it was not worth my worrying about, or even giving it any undue thought. So I turned my attention to focussing on the problems ahead of me. The bag Traxxa had given me was still in my hand. I hefted it once to test its weight and was reminded instantly of Traxxa's warning for to me to be gentle with it. So, from then until we got it back to the camp, I was. Still this didn't stop me from wondering what was in the bag and what was Traxxa thinking about and planning to do next?

Before leaving the city completely we took the opportunity to buy up some supplies for the camp and a full cooked carcass of beef for a feast that night which would satisfy both Bartrow and Böders huge appetites.

That night we all ate well, though throughout our feast I found my thoughts drifted off occasionally to wonder idly how Traxxa was faring and what devious activities he was planning or possibly even getting up to.

Still this didn't stop me from sleeping soundly that night!

Chapter Fifteen

Earlich

We have met with Zharlla -- and I gotta say she scares the minkle out of me!

Jellick

We woke refreshed and after a huge breakfast Jareck, Earlich, Kaira *(still carrying Ribard in her basket)* and I, with the slev strapped to the supply horse, made our way back to see Zharlla.

When she finally made time to meet with us, the first thing she did was to demand the bag of slev as though it had been hers from the outset. When she was satisfied that we had given her the correct quantity, she gave us a small bag filled with some foul smelling grey powder.

"Feed as much of this to the toad as he will eat!" She said. "The more he eats the better and quicker will be the results. Allow a full day and a night for this to change him back to his original self!"

At receiving this powder, Kaira thanked the witch profusely and made to move away. I had been watching Zharlla carefully during our small transaction and it was only when Kaira thanked her that I sensed Zharlla's feeling toward us change slightly. This was an interesting shift in attitude and yet it had come about from a simple gesture of thanks from this lovely Bidowman. Under a half bowed head I continued to watch carefully as Zharlla studied our young friend more intently than before as we moved away from her caravan. When the caravan and all associated with it were out of sight we made our way carefully once more to the tavern nearby and sitting at an open table we ate and drank our fill. Just when I thought we were going to have to make a special trip back into the city to look for Traxxa, he turned up suddenly as though from out of nowhere to be with our group once more. He had with him another large sack, similar to the one he had given me the night before. Needless to say I was both relieved and glad to see my old friend safe and well.

As we sat eating and drinking, Traxxa told us of his night roaming the streets of Regil-Ter and watching over Zharlla and her troupe of performers. But first he gave us a bit of a background into the kind of conditions the city would be presenting to us at this time!

TRAXXA

"During the celebratory month of the Late Autumn Festival it stands to reason that other, more unsavoury people will also make their way to Regil-Ter. They will be prostitutes, thieves, pickpockets, con-men and gangs with evil intent. They come in from all over the north of Durogg to try and take advantage of the huge number of the innocent visitors. These consist largely of farmers and country folk as well as the inter-city punters and the over abundant supply of expectant marks this huge festival attracts.

As a result of these nefarious groups of people, the mayor and the councilmen of Regil-Ter usually ask for help from the surrounding cities of M'Lenn-Fida to bolster their own patrols, militia and law keepers. This just means there are a much larger number of armed guards and soldiers than would otherwise be on duty here in the city. They are here to help keep the peace and maintain a semblance of order by patrolling the streets and watching over the festival, the markets and the celebrations which are scheduled to take place every day of this month.

Bottom line though is that any unsavoury characters that are caught at this time during these festivities are to be recruited to fight in the arena and so become part of the Judicial Games.

Furthermore any prisoner from anywhere in M'Lenn-Fida can volunteer to be a part of these games. They know that if they can beat the judge they are scheduled to fight against then they can go free. They will be exiled from M'Lenn-Fida forever or until the time of their prison sentence runs out but essentially they are free to go. And that is how the games operate. Once a year during this festival all known prisoners are given the opportunity to gain their freedom if they agree to fight in the games. Now, if Xarlalla is to be a judge, she will have to fight some of these chosen criminals in order to dispense justice and so create a spectacle for the crowds. If that is the case then it stands to reason she is most likely being held somewhere in or around the stadium.

I went over to the stadium and looked around as much as I could without making too much of a nuisance of myself. Once there I believe I found some interesting options available to us. These options, which I will go into in greater detail back at our camp, may afford us the luxury of helping to prepare Böder if he is destined to do battle in the arena.

I nodded my head as Traxxa said this, but that was only because we had already talked about some of these options on our journey down to Regil-Ter anyway.

Of Zharlla and her troupe I saw very little movement of either of them. Suffice it to say, Zharlla never left her caravan, nor did she have any visitors. Though I did see her just the once standing at the top of the steps to her caravan. But that was only briefly and then she went back inside when her servant girl brought her food and drink. She then remained inside her caravan for the remainder of the night as best that I could see.

"And another package – I see?" I asked politely

Traxxa just smiled.

"I think it is time we made our way back to camp. I have things to do and discuss with you in the quiet of our camp!"

JELLICK

I recounted to Traxxa, on our ride back to the camp, what had transpired between us and Zharlla. This I'm sure gave him some more things to think about.

First thing back at the camp was to give the entire potion to Ribard in three bouts of feeding him and then we simply sat around waiting for the change.

Ribard changed slowly but was fully himself by lunchtime the next day. Kaira was horrified to realise that he wasn't the handsome prince her imagination and his luxuriant voice had somehow led her to believe. Instead the creature with the deep resonant and soothing voice was really a loathsome, unattractive middle aged Lizarman, (*half man half lizard*). But in this case, Ribard was more lizard than man with no hair and the skin color of tainted green, as though he was sickly all over. His eyes were yellow with black slits across them whilst his hands and feet had more claws about them than fingers or toes. Furthermore, his tongue, which was split, showed us the true nature of this manimal, for it implied that his kind spoke two ways at once (or in other words, he was a teller of truths, half-truths and lies) which, in some cases, even he couldn't discern what was truth and what were lies.

Unfortunately for us we couldn't really comfort Kaira with any good news about Lizarmen. This was because, whilst they were one of the most unusual manimals in Durogg, we knew very little about them. What we did know though, was, they were known to be carriers of diseases and parasites and had been largely responsible for several outbreaks of plagues. So collectively we decided to keep this information from Kaira who was already showing signs of being greatly upset. Perhaps she already knew these things about the lizard part in Ribard's character.

In any case, each of us somehow sensed the deep disappointment in Kaira and rallied to support her in her time of being 'let down' in this way.

Böder to his credit was the first to act and gave the Lizarman a small chest filled with slev and glemm.

"This," he said "is the least I can do by way of a payment for the help you have given to Kaira in finding the flower for her sick sister! Consider this as a thanx from all of us as well for the help you gave to us in causing Garog to sleep which allowed us to deal with him and cross the bridge without a contest!"

We all agreed by nodding and smiling grimly as we silently acknowledged in our own way the help he had given to each of us as being part of our group.

With a lingering touch of hands between him and Kaira, (*which the young Bidowman clearly seemed uneasy about*) Ribard then saluted each of us before turning to make his way slowly out of the camp area. His leg, which we had largely forgotten about, had healed by this time, mainly due to the constant attention Kaira had given him whilst looking after him and changing his bandage regularly. Still, we could all see that he had a slight limp which was clearly going to be a factor in his movement for a long time to come.

Seeing this, I thought it only fair to help him further and so I called out to him that he could take one of the pack horses for himself. He turned to me with a word and a sign of thanx and I could see that he was genuinely pleased to accept the offer. He untethered one of the pack horses and made his way over to the cave where Bartrow was sleeping and called out to him to give him a brief farewell. This in itself, I thought, was most interesting indeed. Without a word from me, Traxxa shadowed the Lizarman for a little while until he was absolutely certain that he had gone from our camp altogether. During Ribards departure, I saw Jareck and Böder conferring quietly to one another a little way off from everyone else. More interesting developments I shouldn't wonder I thought to myself.

Shortly after this, Böder came over and sat close to me. I could see that he wanted to talk. Perhaps he wanted to pick up from where he and Jareck had left off in their quiet discussion moments before. When I thought it was appropriate I turned to Böder and asked him gently.

"Is everything alright with you Böder?"

He looked at me carefully through pitiful dark brown eyes that were on the verge of watering up with tears. In that moment I realised his boyish good looks were dampened by this aura of sadness that hung around him. I waited until he was ready to talk and then he spoke.

"Jellick, I don't understand what is happening. There is a dull greyness in my spirit seeing Ribard go off in the manner that he did. To me, it's like there is a sudden loss to our group. I mean obviously there is." Here he paused in order to regain his composure before speaking again. "But to me it's like someone has died and we can't get them back. I mean, I know we've lost Ribbet, but it was Ribard who ultimately left us. Isn't that right?"

I didn't answer immediately allowing a suitable time to pass before saying, as gently as I thought appropriate.

"That's right Böder, he left us. But I suspect it was because he no longer felt he was part of our group. Yet, despite these new feelings of yours Böder, I think I understand exactly what you must be going through right now. However I'd like to point out to you my friend there has always been something about Ribard's character that didn't allow any of us, except for Kaira perhaps, to warm to him the way we would have liked to in a potential friend. However, I think in many ways we had all tolerated his presence solely because of Kaira. For myself, I'm happy to see him go. But this sadness I sense you are feeling, has probably been brought about by your identifying yourself with Kaira's sadness!"

There was another long pause as Böder pondered this and then he finally said.

"You know I think you're right Tor Jellick. I think I'm sad because I feel Kaira's sadness. Jellick; is this a good or a bad thing?"

I smiled warmly and touched his hand which was near to me.

"Böder, you are a marvel and a great friend to Kaira and that is what matters at this time!"

He smiled back and I could see the young giant returning to normal right in front of me. The most extraordinary thing that I noticed at this time was his eyes lost their darkness and they became hazel green. It was then that I remembered that whenever Böder was happy or there was a lighter background around him or if he was amongst the green of the trees and bushes his eyes took on a green hue. And yet when he was angry or sad or with a dark background behind him then his eyes were brown and even dark like the first time I had met with him in the cavern on his island. I found this to be a most interesting phenomenon about my young giant friend.

That evening, as we talked quietly around the campfire, with both Bartrow and Böder sitting close by, we discussed the potential problems we might encounter in trying to free Xalarlla from her obligation to the Judicial Games. Nothing in principle was agreed upon, though I believe I understood a great deal more about what each of us was wanting for the giantess we had yet to meet.

The next day Traxxa, Jareck, Kaira, Earlich and I made the trek back to Regil-Ter to talk with Zharlla about Xalarlla the giantess.

Zharlla seemed genuinely pleased to see Kaira and me once more (*at least that's the first impression I got from her upon our – what, now third meeting*). So taking the initiative, right after the customary greetings, I got straight to the point and began bargaining for Xalarlla's freedom.

"What do you want for the giantess Xalarlla that is part of your troupe?"

"Now what do you know about me having a giantess?" She asked cannily. "What has that slimy toad of a Ribard been talking to you about me? Or is it that your giant wants her freed so that she can satisfy his own needs and not yours?"

I wondered how she knew about Böder, but decided to say nothing and believed she saw nothing in my face that told her otherwise. Either way, I'm sure that I will find out eventually.

"How is it that Xalarlla has been put down as the main event in the Judicial Games?" I asked.

"My 'giantess' was taken from me by the town officials when I first arrived in Regil-Ter for the festival. It turns out the Judicial Games are set up to take place half way through the Late Autumn Festival. This means, they will start at the end of this week. To everyone's surprise I came in with a giantess and these annual games have not had a giant for a long time, much less a giantess to fight for them! Apparently female giants are very rare indeed and as such are likely to draw a very large crowd who will pay lots and lots of slev just to see her fight! So then, my proposal is this; if you can free my giantess from her obligation to the Judicial Games then I will gladly take another hundred weight of slev as payment for her; and I will then release her from the contract she has with me!"

"I will only consider half a hundred weight for a giantess that I have not yet investigated," I told her softly, "I mean, how do I know that she isn't ill or has the pox or is incapacitated!"

"Maybe you should talk to your giant and ask him what he is willing to pay! However I'll take the half a hundred weight of slev for the giantess you are offering. But, before you go rushing off and celebrating your victory in your bargaining skills over me, I am going to ask for another half a hundred weight for personally arranging the meeting between you and the captain of the games. Then maybe you can bargain with him to have her released from her contract as a judge for the games. After all, I sold her into his hands so that he can use her in his games as he so wishes!"

Again it was her reference to Böder which worried me the most, for she seemed to have a lot more information about us than we had on her. I was certainly perturbed by this chain of events, as I could see there was a very real danger to us all especially if we were we to make contact with the captain of these games personally. And yet I really couldn't go back to Böder without putting up some sort of a token investigation into the cost for Xalarlla.

"These Judicial Games what are they exactly and what do they mean?"

Traxxa had told me of what he had learnt about the games but I wanted to hear it from this Vixawman.

"The Judicial Games are a special event where those who have been found guilty of crimes are given the option of fighting in an arena as opposed to serving time in captivity. And believe me; serving time in the dungeons of M'Lenn-Fida is not a pleasant experience at all. Anyway, these criminals are given weapons and are promised that if they can beat their judges, then because of the entertainment they have given to the people of Regil-Ter, they will then be set free. They will of course be banished from M'Lenn-Fida forever, but set free nonetheless. The main attraction this year of course is the fighting of a giantess against the criminals – but only because this has never been seen before!

"As you have not yet made it known whether you will meet with the captain of the games to bargain for my giantess's release, I made a temporary agreement with him on your behalf. This means I have taken the unusual steps to vouch for you to the captain. So, if you wish to try and secure her freedom you will have to meet Kyrack the captain of the games at the main gate of the stadium tomorrow morning one hour before the first of the markets are due to open. To ensure that your negotiations will even be considered you must take your giant with you when you go to meet with Kyrack.

"If you do decide to meet with Kyrack then I expect to receive my payment from you as per our agreement. If, in bargaining with Kyrack, you reach an understanding where the giantess is released into your care then again I will take my payment as per our agreement over the matter of my freeing her from my personal contract with her.

"And if for some reason the agreements we have made materialise and you do 'not' send me my payments then be warned the contracts and agreements I have made with you are much stronger and more enforceable than anything you have ever known in your physical world of understanding! Because of this I am warning you now, as one who doesn't know me yet, please take our agreements very seriously!"

"Oh and one last thing, Kyrack is not a Buffaman (*half man half buffalo*) to be kept waiting or to be made a fool of! If you decide you do not wish to meet with him tomorrow, then decide quickly and send word to him today that you will not be there to meet with him and continue on your journey to wherever you are headed! But whatever you decide I recommend that you do not make an enemy of Kyrack but more importantly don't make an enemy out of me!"

And with these words of warning ringing in our ears we bade her a good day and left Zharlla's campsite with her standing at the top of the steps into her caravan. But as we walked away I found I was extremely puzzled, and I guess badly shaken. Reuniting with the others we went and had ourselves a meal and a drink at a tavern close by. It was here that I told them all of what Zharlla had said to me, at the end of which, it was Jareck who made a most thought provoking comment.

"Do you think Ribard might have come back to Zharlla and revealed the truth about the treasure, and our camp?"

"To what end?" I asked not discounting his theory completely.

"I don't know, maybe to get himself back into the witches 'good books'!" Jareck replied, struggling with his own idea.

"But why didn't she mention Böder by name instead of constantly referring to him as 'our giant'?" I asked.

"Perhaps Ribard did mention Böder by name, but she didn't want to reveal her source and by keeping Böders name to herself she has left us with some doubts!" Traxxa suggested.

"But remember," said Kaira adding to the conversation, "She also referred to Xalarlla as her giantess as well!"

Then Traxxa added another thought.

"Also, there is nothing to say that she didn't send someone to follow you back to our campsite after your first visit to her caravan. Remember I was staying in Regil-Ter that night and if I had been with you I might have noticed someone following us!"

"Are you suggesting that we're too trusting?" I asked.

"Something like that!" Traxxa responded evenly. "But I would also say that you have never been in this situation where you are possibly posing a real threat to someone else's world!"

"Okay, so she knows we have a giant. We have to assume that she probably knows where our campsite is also." I said.

"Yes but don't forget, she demanded nearly a year's wage just for buying Xalarlla's contract from her and implied that it would be ultimately Böders decision whether we do this or not." Traxxa said emphatically. "The meaning behind this of course is that she knows that it's his treasure and therefore his wealth, to do with as he pleases!"

"But if she knows about the treasure then surely she'll know its whereabouts as well." Put in Earlich sounding a little fearful.

"So then, what do we do now?" Jareck asked, as perturbed now as ever I had been.

"We move - tonight and secure the treasure in another place!" Said Traxxa "And we should also get the hundred weight of slev to the witch whether we secure Xalarlla's freedom or not, so at least we don't have to come back to her in case we have to leave quickly."

"Good idea!" I said.

There was a moment's pause as each of us digested our food and our thoughts. Finally Traxxa began outlining a plan of sorts and allocated jobs that needed to be done as we made preparations to meet with Kyrack and possibly become involved with the Judicial Games to a greater extent than we had at first intended.

"Jareck and Kaira you go down to the stadium and see if you can at least find out where Xalarlla is. If you can get to see her or even make contact, well and good. But don't count on it!

"We have to assume from the way Zharlla insisted we take Böder with us tomorrow that Kyrack has plans to take Böder against his will and make him part of the games. If not instead of Xalarlla, there is the very strong possibility they will want both giants, as a one off, to bring in the crowds and ask whatever they want as an entrance fee to the games!"

"And weapons?" I asked, "Surely they won't let Böder take a weapon in with him. The last thing they will want is to have an armed giant in the cages where the combatants and judges are being held!"

"But we've already worked out a way to get weapons to Böder and to Xalarlla if that's possible!" Replied Traxxa thoughtfully. "We talked about this last evening! Now it is up to us to ensure that they are in the stadium and available for him by tomorrow and let them take it from there!"

"Earlich," I spoke up as a thought came to me, "I want you to go down to the docks and secure for us a boat or a barge that we can use at a moment's notice. Then join up with Jareck and Kaira and see what can be done as to looking after Xalarlla!"

"Why? What do you mean?" He asked a little confused over the last instructions. "I mean, I understand the need for a boat but what was that about -- looking after Xalarlla?"

"Well in games like this," I spoke slowly and carefully to ensure they were all with me in my thoughts and words, "they use the women for spectacle gratification. This means they will either have her naked or at the very least with minimal clothing. Remember the games are a spectacle designed solely to bring in the crowds and what better way to do that than to have the novelty of a naked female giant fighting other naked female criminals!"

"So, how do we go about fixing this?" A shocked Kaira asked. "I mean, I am a seamstress, I work at making clothes. Perhaps I can help by getting some fabric together and maybe make a top for Xalarlla and try and get it to her somehow!"

"Now that's a good idea," I said.

"And I'm sure Jareck will help me!" She said smiling sweetly at the farmer's embarrassment.

"Fine." I said smiling despite myself. "I'm sure you can manage to do all these jobs between the three of you then. Make your way down to the stadium together and arrange where to meet once your jobs are finished. Just be back here by the late afternoon!"

Earlich ever the scribe recounted back the instructions.

"Organise transport, try and contact Xalarlla, and then begin to make arrangements for some clothing to help cover her up. Is that it?"

"Pretty much," I said. "Have I missed anything Traxxa?"

"I'll go and look for a new place to set up camp for tonight." He replied. "It should be alright today as I don't believe whoever knows where we are camped will try and take the treasure whilst a giant and a troll are guarding it. Which reminds me, I'll be taking Bartrow into the city with me tonight! I'd like to check out an escape route from the stadium and also I want to make sure the weapons are in place for when Böder or Xalarlla need them!"

"Alright! But why would you want to take Bartrow into the city with you?" I asked genuinely interested.

"Trolls are incredibly gifted at finding underground passages and ways into and out of dark and wet places. I think taking Bartrow into the city and under the stadium would be something not only that he would love to do, but that he would excel at doing. But just to be sure, you three," and here he turned to the others, "can also look for the quickest way from the stadium to the transport you are going into the city to organize for us. Then we can compare notes later tonight. Okay?"

Earlich, Jareck and Kaira all nodded in understanding of the newest expectations of them, as the elements to this interesting adventure continued to develop.

"Just remember," continued Traxxa, "whatever you plan, we may need to move fast with two giants and a troll, which means we will probably be travelling at night. Therefore it would be better if we have some knowledge of all the obstacles, if any at all, that are going to be along the route we hope to take! Also just to be on the safe side have a couple of alternative routes in mind as well! Is that understood?"

Again they nodded their heads in unison which was actually quite comical to watch.

"Well then I guess that just leaves me," I said almost as an afterthought, "I'll go and inform Böder of our plans and to put him on his guard in case there is an attempt to try and take the treasure! I'll also try and get Zharlla her slev by today and meet up with you three here later this afternoon!"

With that said the three set off into the city, as Traxxa and I went to pick up our horses before making our way back towards the camp. As we got close to our camp, Traxxa broke away from me to go in search of another suitable campsite.

Even before I reached the camp I knew that something was wrong. There was a deadly silence in the woods all around and the stillness was unnerving. I approached the small clearing silently, walking my horse and taking stock of the eerie quiet of the woods all around the glade. I could almost smell the blood and the fear it was so palpable.

But there appeared to be no-one around, when suddenly Böder stepped out from behind a tree directly in front of me. He was all bloodied and fearsome with his mace up raised and menacing and his manner extremely dangerous and threatening.

CHAPTER SIXTEEN

EARLICH

I'm beginning to like this adventure. It's taken me a little while mind, but I think I'm getting the hang of it.

After all I'm now running errands and keeping fit both physically and mentally. I've just been through Regil-Ter meeting up with some ships captains and trying to find Böders newest companion interest.

Sort of!

Anyway, I can hardly wait to pass on my exciting news to Tor Jellick and the others.

Captain Stemm of all people, how fortuitous is that?

JELLICK

"Welcome home is it?" I asked stepping back nervously in case he somehow didn't recognize me.

This seemed to break the spell he was under, for he suddenly smiled sheepishly at me and said, "We've been kinda busy whilst you were away today!"

'Busy' was definitely an understatement. I counted four bodies of Bidomen lying scattered around the camp in various forms of dismemberment and contorted limbs, which indicated to me that they had died quickly and violently. I was assured there were another two lying in the bushes a little way off, out of the vicinity of the camp and at least another three within the confines of the cave with Bartrow. I went in to have a look and to see that Bartrow was alright. He seemed a bit startled by my appearance but was otherwise unharmed and genuinely pleased with himself. There were two bodies lying about and I asked him if he wanted me to remove them from his cave.

But he was nonplussed and in fact recommended that the other bodies should be brought in and hidden in the depths of the cave to avoid difficult questions should any authority figures come passing by. This seemed like a good idea. So Böder and I set about retrieving the bodies that were strewn all around the camp and threw them in to Bartrow who insisted on moving them back into the depths himself. At one time, as I was lugging one of the bodies into the cave, I thought I saw the remnants of what appeared to be a half devoured Bidoman hidden in the shadows. Bartrow came out from the depths and darkness of the cave and seemed a little bit disturbed about what I might have seen. I handed over the body I was carrying and left the cave with troubled thoughts about this young troll. But then I remembered that he was exactly that – a troll! Untamed, operating on instincts and so far, showing all signs of being our friend and an extremely competent ally. With this in mind I was determined not to let this aspect of his character interfere with our relationship. I helped tidy up the rest of the camp and then as we sat in the shadow of the caves entrance, Böder and Bartrow told us of their encounter that morning.

The nine men had come rushing out of the surrounding forest thinking they had surprised the giant. Little did they know, he had smelled them coming when they were still a hundred meters away, and had heard them chattering when they were still hidden in the bushes. Bartrow had also noticed them, but being unable to venture into the sunlight was of no help to the giant. That is until four of them made the mistake of entering his cave. Once in the trolls' domain, he was then able to dispose of three of them before the last one broke free in fear and, trembling, ran back out to face the giant. But the five that had tried to tackle Böder out in the open were met with his mace and fury. The last one ran off and Böder was out to track him through the woods when he encountered the one rushing out of Bartrows cave. This one met with a quick and untimely end.

The last one was found hiding in the bushes about fifty meters from the camp, apparently he had been running around in circles before he realised that he was getting nowhere. Böder sniffed him out and despatched him to the afterlife, angry that they had tried to take him on without recognizing his capabilities. Bartrow was just happy to get some exercise and some extra eating material – that is if I didn't mind him taking these attackers on as food. He shrugged his shoulders, in a matter-of-fact way, when he said this. It was as if to say, '*Well you now know who I am and what I'm capable of, so I may as well tell it like it is!*'

I smiled grimly and thought, '*Yes of course; what the heck let him have his fun and food.*' Whilst we sat there I told them of our encounter with Zharlla and informed them that we would be moving just to make it harder for the next attack that might come. I also let Bartrow know that Traxxa wanted to take him into Regil-Ter that night through the waste tunnels and asked was he up for that?

This seemed to thrill him and he said that, despite the excitement of the day, he would try to get some rest before the night came on. I then outlined what Zharlla wanted and that it could mean Böder having to go into the games if Kyrack had his way, and what did he think of this?

To my surprise he was unperturbed about the cost of slev that the witch wanted. But, when I thought about it, why should he be upset? There was just so much treasure that had cost him relatively little -- aside from the battering the troll had given him in the fight to obtain it that is. He also talked about being happy to be going into the arena and meeting any obstacle that he might encounter there. But above all else, he just wanted to help Xalarlla the giantess he hadn't even met yet!

"But what if you aren't allowed to take a weapon into the arena with you?" I asked and then I thought how stupid that sounded and told him not to worry about answering that question. After all, as I looked around, he had just sent six men to their deaths here in the woods, without even breaking into a real sweat.

I told him of our plans then to get a weapon in to him before the games began and what we planned to do once he had battled his way out to freedom along with Xalarlla. I also told him of how Earlich, Jareck and Kaira were going down to try and make contact with Xalarlla as we were talking, and of what Kaira was hoping to do, as in making clothes for Xalarlla. When I told him this I could see a tear in his eye trickle out and onto his cheek, even though we were sitting in the shadows. Bartrow noticed this as well and moved off to do something or other at the back of the cave to allow his big friend a bit of time to himself. And it was just this one simple thoughtful act by Bartrow that confirmed to me that I had indeed been right about him all along.

Following Bartrows' lead, I too busied myself by putting the small chest of slev together to take back to Zharlla.

When I was ready to go I called out to Bartrow from the entrance to his cave. He came forward to meet me, and here I told him, "I think you've done a terrific job, Bartrow, and I am very pleased with you!" And here I clapped him heartily on the shoulder.

I moved off to reassure Böder that all was well and hopefully we would be heading south towards his island in two days' time. I then rode uneventfully with Zharlla's slev back to Regil-Ter, confident that we had probably the best security in all of Durogg guarding Böder's treasure back at the camp.

As I dropped off the chest of a hundred weight of slev, I tried to engage in mindless chit chat with Zharlla, which I think she seemed to enjoy (*possibly because there was no-one else around who seemed interested in taking the time to talk to her*). In any case she offered me some refreshment and a small repast. I was going to accept her invitation, but then I remembered how she had changed Ribard, so I politely declined and changed the subject by trying a tactic of discernment.

"Oh, by the way," I said, as casually as I could muster, "I thought I'd just mention in passing, that whilst we were here in the city earlier our camp had some unexpected visitors. You wouldn't happen to know anything about that would you?"

"An official visit from the city was it?" She asked, avoiding the answer.

"Not that I know of!"

"Mm-hmm! And?"

"Oh no, they were no trouble!"

As I had been talking about this, I was watching Zharlla closely to see if there was even the slightest register that she knew or was interested in this mindless event.

"Oh good!" She said quietly, with no discernible response and certainly no physical reaction.

"However they probably won't be returning!"

As I made this parting remark, whilst I couldn't be absolutely certain, I thought I saw a black shadow pass over her countenance if only for a moment. And then it had passed. I saluted her briefly with a cheerful wave, turned and without looking back I left her sitting as before, on the top of the steps into her caravan.

I returned to the tavern where I was to meet with the others and after ordering a small plate of food and a tankard of ale, I sat and I waited. I watched, with mild interest, the easy banter in trade between the merchants and the passing flow of people in the streets along the way. It was here I found myself savouring this small moment of time being on my own.

I saw them approaching a long way off, with Jareck leading them and carrying a large awkward parcel. After they had settled into their seats around the table, Earlich began and related in short precise sentences how he had come across Captain Stemm down by the fish markets.

"After a brief greeting we proceeded to negotiate for the hire of his boat and I believe I was successful! In essence we have the hire of the *Riverrock* once more as from tomorrow! He showed me where it was berthed. But more importantly, he told me that we can have access to it any time after noon tomorrow!"

This was good news indeed! We had dealt with Captain Stemm before, and I was confident that we could trust him. But I couldn't help wondering what he would say if he knew the full extent of the cargo that we were hoping to impose upon him! Probably give me a robust piece of his mind and then happily proceed regardless, especially if he was being well rewarded! I smiled at this last thought. And then I was brought back to where we were, as Kaira began telling me excitedly of her and Jarecks visit to the main stadium.

"We parted company from Earlich and made our way to the stadium. Whilst there were no shows on today still the main entrances were open to the public for general admittance. Of course there were a few stalls and some street marketeers who were using the sheltered colonnade and walkways of the stadium as a place to set up shop and catch the curious crowds coming to see the empty arena. It was much like it was yesterday when we were down there with you and Traxxa!"

Even though it was a simple description of what we already knew, her level of excitement as she relayed it to me was infectious and I just had to smile and wait patiently for her to get to the heart of her tale.

"We cautiously approached and tested every avenue and corridor enquiring where we could, observing when we couldn't. The first main thing of interest was the waiting area where the judges stand before they enter the arena. It's on the west side of the stadium and is distinct from where the criminals will come from. These will be released through a number of individual cage doors dotted around the arena wall. This just means that those who run the games will be able to release the exact number of criminals they want to enter the arena at any time and from any position in such a way as to ensure they will have the greatest affect upon the activities and battles in the arena.

"But anyway! From this waiting area we were able to follow the nearest walkway away from the arena which led us down into the corridors beneath the stadium floor. Here we found a number of different doors and barred walkways as well as a room full of resting guards. We backed out unobserved and went and got some jugs of wine and some choice morsels. This was Jarecks idea and we returned to offer the guards our bribes of food and drink. When it was accepted and received warmly, we then asked if we could see the giantess we had heard about that was imprisoned nearby for the games -- if only for a minute or two?

"We must have seemed inoffensive because they were happy to show off one of their prized exhibits. So we got to meet Xalarlla. Jellick she's lovely!" Kaira cooed. "And she seemed genuinely pleased to see us and talk with us. But there are just a couple of things about her that might be a problem for Böder!"

And it was here that Kaira started to stumble as she tried to figure out how best to tell me the things that might be a problem. Then Jareck spoke up, to put her out of her verbal misery!

"Xalarlla is not a young girl as Ribard made her out to be, in fact, if anything, I think she may even be older than Böder by at least five years."

"The other things are," interjected Kaira quickly, "Xalarlla needs a wash because she is very dirty and smells really bad and finally she is a black giantess!"

At which point Jareck regained the narrative stating confidently, "But knowing Böder, these things won't be the problem that Kaira thinks they will be!"

"But that's only because I've never seen a really black person before, much less a black giantess," said Kaira defensively.

"But what about me?" said Jareck with pain in his voice, "I'm black!"

"No you're not!" Kaira said, pouting just a little. "You're well-tanned!"

I smiled at the way her voice got higher as she strived harder to get her point across to me. But Jareck continued almost as if he hadn't heard her interruption.

"Anyway, be that as it may, I believe our biggest problem will be getting the clothes to Xalarlla and the weapons to Böder. That is assuming they put him in with her! After all, we only saw one cage beneath the stadium that was big enough to hold both giants and she was in it!"

"Oooohhh! The clothes!" Squealed Kaira and here she started to open the parcel that Jareck had been carrying, with the obvious intention of showing it to me. Being a merchant I was happy for her to show me her bargains and marvel at the material she had bought. But then Jareck brought us back to the problem at hand, that of planning our next move.

"There is something that might be of interest to us. When we were investigating the waiting area we saw cleaners and maintenance people going in and out of a room. We waited for an opportunity and then we checked the room out. It was unlocked and is huge. It was a vast storage room for all the tools and equipment needed to look after and maintain the stadium. Inside were the brooms, rakes and shovels that they use to look after the sand in the arena and keep the halls and walkways clean and well swept!"

"And all this is on the west side of the stadium near where the waiting area is?" I asked, just for clarification.

"Yes, it's just to one side of the walkway which leads down to where the judicial fighters or judges are being held -- or at least that's where they are holding Xalarlla!"

"And she appears fine and healthy to you?" I asked.

"Of course she's healthy Jellick," said Kaira indignantly. "She just needs a good wash and some clean clothes; I think she has Zharlla's disease! And it's just as you said before. The clothes on her were almost non-existent, positively indecent. I despair sometimes at the people -- mostly men I would wager -- who gain satisfaction at watching females fight with next to nothing on in the arena! I will never understand it's attractions I shouldn't wonder!"

I smiled quietly as I realized this little country girl was slowly becoming aware of the big bad city life.

"Come, come Kaira," I said reprovingly. "I take it you have never watched a mud wrestling match between women at any one of the many country fairs? Or how about catching the pig contest where groups of manimals, usually young girls try to catch a pig on the run for a prize?"

We all smiled as we watched Kaira struggling with these two prime examples of known country festival activities. Finally she just 'harrumphed' and we all laughed knowing that she had just been caught out!"

I stood up, put my arm around her and gave her a big hug.

"We love you Kaira, we think you're great. But now that we've finished our errands here in the city, I think it's time we returned to our camp and tell the others of our findings!"

And with that we paid the bill, left the tavern and reclaimed our horses to ride back to the camp.

We arrived just as the first grey hints of the coming night began revealing itself to the sky and forest around us. Böder and Traxxa had just begun to break camp. Traxxa had been waiting for the cover of darkness before making this move.

"I found a campsite three kilometers northeast of here." said Traxxa evenly. "It is closer to where the Dund and the Mirack rivers meet. I don't believe we need to move, but we will just to be on the safe side!"

We quickly set about reducing the camp while Bartrow and Böder carefully brought the cart of treasure out from the cavern. We hitched up the horses to both the carts and moved out. Traxxa gave Jareck and I directions on where he wanted us to go as he, Böder and Bartrow dropped back and vanished into the gloom of the coming night forest. He didn't need to tell me what he was up to! They were ensuring we would not be followed this time.

At the point where we were just beginning to flounder, Traxxa appeared quietly and suddenly just in front of us and took over the reins of directing us through the forest to the new camp. As we made our way through the forest I took the opportunity to tell Traxxa all that Jareck, Earlich and Kaira had found out about the stadium and Stemms' boat. He didn't say anything but in the descending gloom of the evening I felt sure I saw him smile and somehow I knew that whatever he was planning was falling into place for him. We arrived at the new camping spot, which I saw was a small sheltered glade with a brook running through it. The first thing we did was unhitch the horses and transferred all the treasure onto the largest cart before pushing it deep into the folds of a dense gorse bush.

"I'll leave you to set up camp." Traxxa said matter-of-factly. "Bartrow and I are going in to Regil-Ter to scout out the sewer ways and waterways of the main island beneath the stadium! Böder and Jareck can stand on guard until we return, though I don't think you'll have any trouble tonight!"

At this, Bartrow and Traxxa turned and left us standing in the silence of the forest around us. However, I did notice as they left, Bartrow was carrying Böders sheath and sword whilst Traxxa carried a pair of his more vicious looking shin guards. I stood quietly wondering what Traxxa could possibly be up to as they disappeared into the gloom of the night. I also found myself subconsciously trying desperately to hear the slightest sound they might have made as they left. But try as I might, and I thought I had very good hearing, I heard nothing of their departure.

We set up a simple camp and made a good strong fire to warm up some food for the evening meal and keep the chill of the forest night air at bay from our incidentals. Later on, I sat with Earlich watching and listening as we remained on guard after we encouraged the others to get some sleep. In particular I wanted Böder to be fresh and alert for tomorrow's encounter with Kyrack the captain of the Judicial Games.

It was well past midnight when, without warning we had Bartrow and Traxxa standing beside us warming themselves by our fire. It startled the minkle out of me and I almost dropped my mug of hot broth.

"Thanx for keeping me on my toes," I said as they both laughed at my obvious discomfort. "Well, would you like something to eat?" I asked as Earlich rallied to round up some hot food and drink.

They both nodded Then Traxxa went over to his gear and brought out some clean and dry clothes and changed. It was then that I noticed two things about them; the first was they were both soaking wet and the second thing was they were no longer carrying Böders sword or his shin guards.

"Been in the water?" I asked a little lamely.

"Yeah we swam out to the main island of Regil-Ter and back!" Traxxa said, pulling on the warm dry clothes near the fire.

"What about you Bartrow, don't you want to change your clothes?" I asked. "You must be freezing!"

"No I don't feel the cold like you manimals and besides being wet is just another sensation that I can enjoy by myself!"

It was a strange reply but I left it at that.

"And Böder's sword and guards, what happened to them?" I asked as offhandedly as I could muster.

"They are buried under the sand on the left hand side near the wall in the waiting area of the stadium." Traxxa said with a mischievous smile dancing around his lips. "So, whenever it is convenient for Böder, he can dig them up at a moment's notice and be properly prepared for any encounter he might meet in the arena!"

"So, should we tell Böder this before we meet Kyrack tomorrow morning", I asked smiling along with Traxxa. "What else have you found out?"

"We found the sewer way that leads under the stadium and Bartrow here found some interesting tunnels that could come in handy should we need to get in and out of the stadium undetected. I used one of the sewer holes to come out in the walkway under the waiting area and used the stairs that Kaira and Jareck told you about. I found the storeroom and grabbed a shovel and broom and was able to bury the sword and shin guards in the sand of the waiting area. When this was done, I simply swept it over and returned the way I had gotten in. The only thing is these entranceways into the sewers are not big enough for a giant to get down into or even travel through. That's the only drawback. But I'm sure, if we think about it, we may be able to use this knowledge to our advantage at a later stage as we make our plans to help free Xalarlla in the near future!"

With that I encouraged them to eat and recounted to them some of the things I had learned from our own adventures in Regil-Ter that day. It was only as I was telling Traxxa of my encounter with Zharlla in detail that I realized I hadn't told Böder about Xalarlla being a black giantess. I looked over to where the giant was sleeping comfortably under his large quilted blanket huddled around the fire. It was lovely to see Kaira curled up in the folds of his big arms; this had been her favourite place to sleep ever since the mountain meadow. I smiled and decided to let him continue sleeping because they looked so sweet and innocent together and I hardly dared to consider the consequences of waking him. I continued to smile as I thought more and more about them and then I noticed Bartrow was getting up.

"What are you up to?" I asked softly.

"This is my roam time -- remember! I'm off to go exploring. Don't worry! I won't go far. I'm going to be your guard for the rest of the night! So go, catch up on your sleep!"

He smiled and moved off noiselessly back into the comfortable folds of darkness of the surrounding forest. I smiled but the thought of the half eaten body I had seen in Bartrows cave earlier that day came back to haunt me and helped freeze the smile on my lips.

"Great!" I mumbled quietly to myself, "I'm gonna sleep well tonight – me!"

But Earlich responded positively by excusing himself. He grabbed his blanket and found a warm nook on the other side of the fire and lay down to grab some much needed sleep. He was snoring gently within minutes. In quiet desperation, I turned to Traxxa and talked in low tones about Bartrow and what I had seen of him earlier in the day.

Traxxa listened without interrupting and then he turned to me and still wearing his traditional half smile he said softly. "What did you expect Jellick? He's a troll after all. The question is though -- do you trust him?"

I didn't have to think about it I had already done that, so I answered. "It's funny but I have come to trust him even more over the last day or so. I just wanted to bring you up to speed with the latest revelations of our little group."

Traxxa's smile never wavered, he just reached over placed a hand on my shoulder and still whispering said. "Good night Tor Jellick. But, before I go, I want to let you know that you have a good crew around you. And should anything happen to change any of that, just remember I will be right here to make sure they stay good towards you." And with that, he too grabbed a blanket and nestled down where he had been sitting and promptly fell asleep.

I sat for a long time watching the fire, listening to the soft night sounds of the forest and thinking. Finally I went and got a few large pieces of wood to top up the fire. When that was done I grabbed a blanket and moved around the fire to find a suitable place to curl up and sleep.

The last thing I did before closing my own eyes in search of sleep was to look carefully around the fire checking to make sure that my companions were all still sleeping comfortably. They were and, somehow, this made me feel warm and peaceful and I fell asleep in complete contentment.

CHAPTER SEVENTEEN

JELLICK

Bartrow woke me with a gentle nudge about five minutes before I had planned to wake up in any case. He startled me with his leering grin staring down at me in the soft darkness of early morning as I suddenly remembered my last recollections of him from yesterday. But I steeled myself and smiled back up at him and asked how he was doing and thanked him for waking me.

"That's no problem, good Jellick," he said softly, "I'm letting you know that I'm going to ground. I'll be beneath the cart hidden in the bushes! I think it's safe enough from the sun. But I won't be able to move around much. Not like I could in the cave I was in yesterday. I don't think I'll be as good a guard over the treasure as I was before. Is that okay?"

"Sure Bartrow! I don't think we'll be having any problems from anyone today! In any case, Earlich, Jareck and Kaira will be here to help you survive the day without me!"

He smiled at my joke (*revealing his horrible sharp toothy smile*) and moved over to the gorse bush. Then incredibly, he seemed to burrow beneath the thorny branches, before disappearing into the shadows and shrubbery.

The others began stirring at the noise of our brief conversation and after a quick breakfast, we hitched up the cart carrying the weapons to one of the pack horses and deliberately placed a canvas tarpaulin over the weapons and the supplies as though to conceal them. When all was ready, Traxxa and I made to saddle up and ride into Regil-Ter leading the pack horse and cart. We didn't expect Kaira to ride with us today, but then she suddenly pleaded with me to take her along. I politely reminded her that she had said she was going to make a shirt of some kind for Xalarlla and that it would be safer for her to remain in the camp.

"But I could stitch it up in no time whilst riding in the cart!" She said petulantly.

"No!" I said firmly, "The cart is a decoy to distract any would be thieves who might be watching us as we make our way into Regil-Ter. You will just get in the way and your first duty today is to make the clothing for Xalarlla! Isn't it?"

"Yeeeessss!" She said slowly but then she perked up as a thought hit her, "But I don't have her measurements! I'll have to come in with you!"

"Take your measurements from Böder then. You saw her; I didn't! Is she that much different in size to Böder?"

Kaira did a quick mental comparison. "You're right! I can do this! I mean, I should do this properly! Can you wait for just a moment whilst I take some quick measurements of Böder before you leave?"

"Be quick," I said and smiled as I watched her scurry off to get some string, some parchment and a quill. Then with the help of Earlich and Jareck to hold the string in place and the aid of the cart to give her height and Böder laughing gently as he lay down, we watched Kaira measure his arms and torso and chest and waist. It was fascinating to watch our little Kaira working as the seamstress in our company. But then she whispered something into Böders ear and together they had a quick quiet conversation. When they were finished, Böder stood up brushed himself off and grabbing his mace, joined Traxxa and me and we headed off to the stadium in Regil-Ter.

On our journey towards the city, I talked with Böder about all of the plans that Traxxa and I had been working on. I also outlined many of the details concerning Xalarlla that had not yet been told to him -- in particular her age and the colour of her skin. As was expected, from what Jareck had told us, this did not alter Böder's intentions towards her one bit. Traxxa gave some final instructions as to what was the most likely scenario concerning the reception and treatment we might get from Kyrack and those in charge of the games. When all this had been told to Böder, I asked him again was he still prepared to go through with the plans that we had made in preparation for the coming events.

"Oh yeah, good Tor Jellick!" He said emphatically. "This is my opportunity to help someone who is of my kind. I definitely want to see this through -- just as long as I know that I have your support and that you will look after me and those close to me!"

"Of course you do! Absolutely! We are here for you!" I said firmly with Traxxa voicing similar sentiments at the same time. For greater emphasis I placed a firm hand on his wrist the only appropriate part of Böders body I could reach without asking Böder to stoop or lower himself.

With us on horseback and the lengthy stride of Böder we made good time into the city. This time we rode our steeds into Regil-Ter and followed the roads and bridges all the way up to the stadium. I saw a small group of people outside, as we approached the stadium. But at the time it didn't register to me as to why they might be there. I just thought they were part of the early morning festival crowd. We were a little way from the small crowd, feeding the horses and brushing them down when Kyrack and a unit of the city's militia came over and made themselves known to us. They were a unit made up solely of Buffamen, fierce, strong and known for their extreme loyalty. Kyrack was the biggest Buffaman of them all. His large prominent horns had been filed down and his tail either trimmed or remained permanently hidden as were the others in his unit. This was part of the custom of all manimals who wished to live within the respected social circles of all the larger cities. Kyrack was nearly three meters in height. He had a big strong build which was highlighted by his arms which were thicker than my thighs and yet his large barrel chest contrasted alarmingly with his relatively thin waist and long slender legs. He seemed pleasant enough though I could sense an underlying hostility in Böder towards him. So too could Traxxa, who instinctively turned Böder away to talk quietly to him and to keep him from confronting the captain of the games After the courtesy introductions between ourselves and the clasping of our wrists, I began the delicate negotiations for the release of Xalarlla.

"I believe you have our friend Xalarlla the giantess, held in captivity in the stadium. What will it take for you to release her into our care?" I asked politely.

"She has been pledged to me to act as a judge in the coming Judicial Games. What are you proposing to offer me in return for her release once she has completed her time as judge?"

"I can offer you a hundred weight of slev if she can be released to us right now!"

"My job here, as captain of the games, is worth a lot more than a hundred weight of slev!"

"But I'm not asking for your job! I'm asking for you to release my friend Xalarlla the giantess!"

"I know what you're asking me -- but I don't think you know what you're really asking of me. If I was to release her before her duty as judge was completed, then not only would I lose my post, but there is every chance I would lose my life and the lives of those in my family including my children and my wives. Now I'll ask again, what can you offer me for the release of your giant friend -- once her role as judge has been completed?

"I'm assuming that there is no monetary figure that I can offer you that would allow you to release her into my care right at this moment?"

"None! You see there is an oversight committee concerning the games. It is they who have entrusted me to ensure that the games have a giantess as a judge in the first bout of the games set to be played out tomorrow afternoon. And if you look around about, you can see some people have already started lining up to get good seats for the first of the games knowing there will be a female giant acting as one of the first judges!"

I looked to where he had pointed, and indeed, almost for the first time, I saw the people who were already lining up and camping out in the streets waiting for the first of the gates into the arena to open. In fact as I looked on I realized that most of them were looking at Böder in a way that I had never expected people to look at him before. It wasn't fear or loathing, it was more like awe and admiration, a bit like the way the people in the mountain community began looking at him after they had heard the tale about how he had fought and defeated Trow. But surely these people hadn't heard of Böder so far from the mountains. I turned back towards Kyrack and noticed that he too had seen the way the crowd were looking at our imposing friend.

"I tell you what." said Kyrack suddenly, almost magnanimously, as if he had only just thought of it right then! "Why don't you release your

192

giant friend over there into my care and he can ensure that your friend the female giant is looked after. It will only be for one night and a lot of things can be accomplished in just one night. *(Here he smiled an innocent almost sincere smile and not a leering obnoxious grin that one might associate with a comment like the one he had just made).*

"The games will commence tomorrow at lunch time. The first of the games will be for the female prisoners and criminals. She will be there to act as judge in those games. As soon as she has finished her role as judge, we can then release her into your care and we won't even charge you a fee for looking after her for you! How does that sound?"

"That sounds alright," I said almost by rote because this was the proposition that we had been expecting anyway. "But I best check with Böder, my giant friend first."

"Well you better hurry then. I have other duties that I have to attend to and I can only keep this offer open to you for say, the next five minutes!"

He was a shrewd business man! I'll give him that, I thought, as I went over to Böder and told him of the offer made to us by Kyrack. Böder nodded his head as he understood what was being offered to him and the price that was being asked of him. So he walked back with me over to meet with Kyrack. The Buffaman was big, but he was way too small for the likes of a giant and his respect was immediately noticeable from the moment he first spoke to Böder.

"So it is you, the mighty Böder, the killer of trolls and the returner of stolen treasures! It is my great honour to finally meet with you!" Kyrack said solemnly, as he extended his arm by way of greeting.

We were all at a loss for words at this greeting, none more so than Böder. However in automatic response mode he bent forward and presented three of his fingers and allowed Kyrack to clasp them as he would an arm. I think both Traxxa and I were pleasantly surprised to see Böder so easily won over.

"So the deal is this," Kyrack said evenly. "We will put you in the same quarters with Xalarlla for the night. The apartment has been specifically designed for your size and stature. She will serve as judge for the first of the games tomorrow and then I personally will see that she is released into Tor Jellicks care the moment her service has been completed! Are you alright with this?"

Böder nodded his head slowly, there was something missing from this verbal contract but he couldn't quite see it for what it was.

But I could, so I stepped forward and asked.

"And what about Böder? When Xalarlla is released, what will happen to Böder? Will he also be released?"

Kyrack answered slowly, sounding like he was a little aggrieved. "I thought you understood fully, the price for Xalarlla's freedom is that Böder must serve as a judge for the remainder of the Judicial Games. This will begin right after Xalarlla's service as the first judge! That was what I understood our deal to be!"

"How could we understand that?" I asked a little confused. "When were these terms that you've just now stated, to have been spelled out to us!?"

"I'm sorry!" It was Kyrack who sounded confused this time. "I was under the impression that you knew about and had agreed to the arrangement that had been struck between myself and Zharlla the witch. She made it plain to me that Böder would come forward willingly to act as a judge in the games on the condition that Xalarlla be released into your care once her part in the games were completed. Have I got this wrong? How else was I to know that you were coming to finalise the details here this morning?"

By this time Böder was spluttering and Traxxa was doing everything in his power just to keep the young giant under control and stop him from lashing out at Kyrack.

Realising that something was not quite right, Kyrack tried a new tack.

"Böder, I believe you might be a bit upset, but I'd like you to think of this as a service to the people of M'Lenn-Fida. You will take on the role of a giant judge within the arena and dispense with some very unsavoury criminals and extremely dangerous and bad manimals. This is a real privilege and a great honour, and I can think of no-one else I would like to hand this honour over to, other than yourself! And I mean that sincerely.

"At this very moment, Xalarlla is in our care as part of a deal made between her owner and ourselves. She is destined to provide a great service for this land and this city as she seeks to dispense proper justice as a judge in one of our long standing traditions that makes the Judicial Games so great. Think how you too could stand with her and help dispense this kind of justice within our games. After all this system has been in place for centuries!

"If you could look in on Xalarlla right now you would see that she is in a luxurious apartment with every conceivable whim being catered for. You can join her and once she has served her country she will be handed over to Jellick and once you have done your service, you too will be allowed to leave and know that you have served your land well!"

"Can I take my mace in with me?" asked Böder thawing to the idea of what was being requested of him.

"Sadly no, there are very strict rules concerning what the judges can use and a mace is not one of them. But you will be given a weapon when the time is ready for you to enter the arena. Now! What is your answer to be?"

After a lengthy thoughtful pause by Böder, Kyrack, sensing his moment continued, "come, my time is valuable, are you doing this and adhering to our agreement or will Xalarlla be returned to Zharlla once her service as a judge and the games are completed in a weeks' time?"

"Let me get this straight," I asked, "are you saying, that after her game tomorrow afternoon, you will be sending Xalarlla back to Zharlla."

"No!" Kyrack said sympathetically, "there are a great many games to be played after the women have been dealt with. Sadly for you, but good for us, Xalarlla would make a wonderful judge in a number of other events planned for the week and will make for great entertainment for the people of Regil-Ter. So once she has completed her contract with us, which may take her through the whole week of games, then of course she will be returned to Zharlla. But as I understand it, you will have to negotiate a fee to have her released into your care from there. However Böder, if you agree to replace Xalarlla in the arena, I will see to it that she is released into your friends care after just the one event with the female prisoners and that will be by tomorrow mid-afternoon!"

Böder and I turned to one another and I knew that he was not happy but it was what we had half expected in any event. Still, it was hard to accept even though it was confronting us up front. I suppose it's one thing to expect the worst but quite another to have it made real to us like it was being done right now.

"And what if we just smashed our way in and rescue Xalarlla with this mace against all your units of militia!" Böder said evenly, with not a trace of menace in his voice.

"I admire your spirit there Böder, but the games are much more important to us than your rampaging immaturity." Kyrack responded just as evenly. "Sure you may injure and perhaps even kill us out here in the street, but the moment it becomes known of your intentions to interfere with our giant, then we have a number of options available to us!

"You see we have bows and arrows and swords and guards and if we can't slow you down then we will most assuredly kill Xalarlla long before you could even get anywhere near her. So let me just say from the outset that all your efforts to free her will have been in vain, not to mention that you will have been responsible for having your friends killed here as well!

"But, here, let me help you. Why don't you be sensible and put that aggression into something worthwhile? Let Xalarlla serve her time as a judge in the first event with only the female prisoners, then you can take over and finish off the service that she has been pledged to serve. From there you will be able to vent your anger on real criminals and save your friend. And not only that but you will be able to spend time with her in private, encouraging and comforting her and preparing each other to face whatever is in the arena when it's your turn. So, come Böder, what do you say? Because it is time for me to go right now! What is your answer? I need a decision from you, right now!"

Böder looked towards me and then towards Traxxa for help or perhaps he was just hoping to hear the right words to continue, so I spoke up with as much conviction as I could muster.

"Whatever you decide Böder we will be right here waiting for you and ready to come to your aid should you need it!" And I grasped the two fingers he offered me as a goodbye gesture. Traxxa too grasped two of Böder fingers and shook them twice by way of his goodbye but before releasing them he spoke, soft and quiet but with just the hint of a strength and hidden power that a good trainer will always have for their student.

"Böder, you knew we came here specifically for this to happen. You can do this, and you know that we all believe in you!"

And with these last words of encouragement, Böder turned to Kyrack and said, "Okay let's do this thing! Take me to my friend and consider me

·

to have taken over her contract once she has finished serving her time as a judge in the first event!"

He then tossed the huge, ungainly, exceedingly heavy mace into the back of our cart as casually as one would toss aside a walking stick, but which severely tested the strength and structure of the cart.

As he moved towards the stadiums main archway, Kyrack suddenly paused and turning back he looked thoughtfully at Traxxa and said, "Traxxa you seem to be a confident warrior, would you consider being a judge in one of the game's events as well? But first, I must ask! Do you think you would be good enough as a judge? Remember the games are to the death, so don't say yes, if your fighting skills are less than exceptional. Also I will not think any less of you if you decline my invitation!"

I must say I was surprised as I truly hadn't expected an invitation of this kind. I looked quickly towards Traxxa to gauge his response. He was smiling but shook his head slowly.

"I was in your games for two years running some three years ago. This year however, they are not for me. But thanx for asking this of me, you honour me greatly for recognizing me as I know for certain that you have!"

And here we saw Kyrack smile in acknowledgement of the little subterfuge he had been playing with Traxxa and then he extended his arm to be grasped by Traxxa before he turned to me and offered me the same parting courtesy. As we broke contact he reached into his tunic and handed me four small metal discs.

"These are special passes to the games" he said before he continued encouragingly. "Please accept these and attend any of this week's events as my personal guests. From these allocated seats you will watch the Judicial Games with me and my family and no doubt begin to appreciate them for what they are!"

I thanked him before calling out a parting goodbye to Böder who waved, smiled and bending his head forward just a little bit he walked beneath the huge archway and entered the main walkway around the arena. He followed after Kyrack and together they disappeared around the natural curve of the stadiums architecture.

The moment they were gone I turned and looked at Traxxa with a renewed interest and a questioning look in my eye. He just smiled and began readying the horses for travel. A couple of seconds passed. He obviously sensed that my eyes were focussed on the back of his head, so, still smiling said. "I will tell you about it one day, probably when we've had a meal and a couple of tankards of ale".

"Okay you'll tell me about it one day! But first, why didn't you tell me -- any of us -- that you knew Kyrack?"

"That's because I don't 'know Kyrack', I'd never met him before this morning – or, if I had, I don't remember him. Kyrack was not the captain of the games during my time as a judge three years ago"!

I looked closely at Traxxa and knew what he had told me was the truth, but I also knew this conversation was closed for the moment so I helped him turn the horses. We walked the horses along by the side of the stadium and turned down a quiet out of the way alley. After ensuring there was no-one around to watch us we bent down and pulled up the main alleys sewer grate. We then unloaded all the weapons from the cart and dropped them one by one down into the depths of the sewer. The last to be dropped down was Böders favourite mace. We attached a rope to its handle and secured the other end of it to the sewers grate so that the mace would remain standing and not become lost in the muck and water moving about through the sewers beneath the road.

Next we walked down to the quay and, after a brief investigation we came across Captain Stemms boat. It seemed a lot smaller than what I remembered it to be but then I realized that was only because I hadn't imagined Böder sailing along with us before. I was reasonably sure it would take him and us without too much trouble, I was just not convinced that it would take the combined weight and size of two giants instead of just the one.

We announced ourselves to Eddron, Captain Stemms first mate, his cousin and the officer on duty that morning. He gave us a formal invitation to come aboard and, after greeting us as was the custom, he showed us into the captain's cabin.

I had decided to be honest with Captain Stemm even before we stepped aboard the *Riverrock*. I figured we would not be able to do the things we wanted without his knowledge, help or advice. Besides it would save us a lot of unwanted grief should he find out afterwards that we had been lying to him or at least not keeping him completely informed!

I told him that our cargo consisted of a great treasure, two giants and a young troll. I could see this was severely testing the bonds of our relationship, so I put a hundred weight of slev and another hundred weight of glemm onto his table and asked would this help him to understand our predicament and maximise his co-operation in helping us achieve our goals of getting out or Regil-Ter at a moment's notice and transport us safely back to the Black Island?

To Captain Stemm's credit, this, and the fact we had a bit of a history of service and trade between ourselves, brought him into alignment with our own plans. He then let me know how and when the best times would be to leave Regil-Ter. Further to this he described, in detail, how much time we would need to be successfully clear of the Regil-Ter authorities if they decided to pursue us. What we could expect if they did decide to pursue us and then he went on to explain where along the riverbank it was best that his boat could safely land and either load or unload the full contingent of our cargo.

We discussed at length what was needed to successfully storing and keep safe a youthful troll and what was required in order to transport two large giants out along the river.

When all these details were completed, we came to an arrangement and an understanding regarding the fee that was to be paid in full upon completion of our journey. He in return pledged himself to be on high alert and in a permanent state of standby with specific instructions to wait for my call but to be done preferably within the next three days. After which he said, he would have to meet with us to talk about any further costs that might be caused by unforseen developments.

From this, I gathered he was saying, if we hadn't sorted ourselves out in three days' time then he was going to renegotiate for a higher fee. This, he indicated, would be based on the amount of stress and tension we were going to help create between himself, his crew and the authorities of Regil-Ter.

When this was all finished we transferred the remaining cargo from the cart onto the *Riverrock* including Traxxa's two large mysterious bags. But these, Traxxa asked to have placed in such a way that he could access them swiftly and easily. He also gave instructions that they were to be left alone, but if handled out of necessity this was to be done very carefully.

Stemm was intrigued but was professional enough as a captain of his boat to recognize the intimate cargo of his passengers and after being reassured that the sacks were not illegal cargo and did not pose a threat to his boat or his crew, he had the sacks stored in a chest on the deck. Traxxa and I thanked him personally before we turned and left him standing musing silently on the deck of the *Riverrock*.

He smiled quietly to himself as he realized with dawning clarity that he was in the midst of a deal that if successful would cover him and the services of his vessel for the next three possibly even five years. We, too, were smiling because we had just confirmed the finding of a captain who was willing to risk all for us. But realistically, what was left of Böders treasure was more than enough to buy another twenty-five boats similar to that of Captain Stemm's for ourselves.

But then again -- it was only treasure! And Böders treasure at that!

* * *

It was mid-morning by the time we left the docks and Captain Stemm's boat. From there we battled the great throngs of people and decided the easiest way forward was to sell the cart and horse and proceed unencumbered. There was little left in the cart as it was. The weapons were hidden and all our stores were aboard the *Riverrock*. We got a fast price which is not always the best price but it was one less thing to carry around with us. After a brief discussion we decided we would pay Zharlla another visit before heading back to our camp. So we made our way slowly out of the city towards her caravan. There were a few things I wanted to talk to her about -- in particular what exactly she had told Kyrack about us for he seemed to have known a great deal about us before we had even met him. Plus I wanted to know a bit more about Ribard, in particular, what exactly her relationship was to him, and perhaps what were we likely to expect from this Lizarman in the future. Was it through him that she knew the things she did about our camp the people in it and in particular her knowledge of Böder. And then of course I wanted to know what she knew about the treasure.

I found, *(not surprising really)*, that Zharlla suddenly didn't wish to speak to us about anything anymore. This was exceedingly frustrating, but there was little I could do. I was only able to ask her a couple of questions before she dismissed us brusquely with a wave of her hand. She then turned and disappeared inside her caravan and closed the door on us leaving Traxxa and I standing looking up at the door and feeling belittled and very insulted.

Still there were better things to do in my life than to look at the angry caravan door of a witch that clearly didn't wish to talk with us, so we turned around, mounted our horses and headed slowly out of Regil-Ter.

Once we were clear of the crowds of the festival, I talked with Traxxa at length to bring to a close some of the things we thought we had extracted from this, as Ribard had called her, the 'beeatch of a weeatch'.

I believed Traxxa had unusually good skills in reading people who didn't wish to give things away -- possibly even better than mine -- but even he was a little perturbed by how little we both had gotten out of her. Our reading of her non-verbal cues in her looks and body language, and even the inflections caused by her reaction to some of the questions I had asked had, in fact, told us very little.

However, we had gotten a few things out of her, perhaps without her even realising it. The first of which was she still had some sort of relationship with Ribard. That had been obvious from the outset, but the extent and depth of that relationship had been harder to gauge. The fact she had passed information on to Kyrack was also obvious. But again, to what extent and for what purpose? From this we could only agree that both Zharlla and Kyrack were not to be trusted concerning the handling of Xalarlla. All else really, was of no further concern to us. We had paid our debt in full, and had Böder in with Xalarlla to protect her and comfort her during this difficult time. More importantly for us, we had our plans in place, which we could adapt and change at a moment's notice. We had a way out of the city and all we needed to do now was to prepare ourselves for any eventuality that might come our way.

Halfway back to our camp as we sat by a small stream for a quick repast and bit of a rest, Traxxa slipped away quietly before I had even realized he was going. About ten minutes later he returned openly. He was smiling grimly wiping blood off his swords and leading two new horses.

From this I knew that he had taken care of the two who had been tracking us from the city, after our short visit with Zharlla!

CHAPTER EIGHTEEN

EARLICH

When we finally caught up with Böder, after he had fulfilled his role of judge in the arena as part of the Judicial Games, he was able to relay the full account of his story to me in great detail. This was helped along of course, by input from Traxxa, Jareck and even the lovely new giantess, who also gave us some insights from her own account as well. This then is the story of Böder and his time in the arena.

BÖDER

"After I left Tor Jellick and Traxxa by the main entrance to the stadium, Kyrack led me along the outer archway of the arena. As we walked together he told me about the stadium - such things as how long it took to build, how many people it could hold and what its purpose was. At my request, I was taken into the arena. It was large and round and huge. My very breath was taken away as I looked up into the public stands. It all seemed so incredibly big and high and just so grand. It was marvellous and very awe-inspiring. I had never imagined such a place could exist. The ground -- or pitch, as Kyrack called it -- was largely covered in sand.

In the centre of the pitch was a fenced-off square. This looked very much like it was a large fireplace. The area was completely covered in sticks and wood and was ready to be fired up at a moment's notice. Dotted around, within the square, were at least five blackened stone posts. Kyrack told me this was used to secure offenders who were destined to be burned for the entertainment of the people. Dotted around the arena were eight stone obelisks, all around ten meters in height. These had chains attached to them and I was told they were to secure prisoners according to their crimes. The walls of the arena were made of sandstone all smoothed over. These too were easily ten meters high.

About seven meters up the wall there were inlaid terraces and alcoves looking out over the pitch. Kyrack told me these were to hold the archers and bowmen. The archers I found out were there to help keep the fighters in place and protect the judges as well as prevent the games from descending into chaos. Just below the bowmen's terraces were lengthy spikes facing down towards the arena and a guard rail. These he told me were designed to stop all attempts by any of the fighters from climbing out of the pitch and into the stands. At each of the main points of the compass in the audience stands, were four pavilions. I was told that these were for the games host, their families and honoured guests.

I was then taken into the waiting area, the one Traxxa had described to me earlier. I looked towards the sand at the base of the wall where he had told me was where my sword and equipment were buried. I could see it had been disturbed and raked over recently to hide Traxxa's handiwork. The bars of the gate between the waiting area and the arena closed behind me and we moved from there to a wall of bars on the other side of the waiting area. From here I could see across the far wall of the walkway we had used earlier. I was told to wait for just a moment. I was a little confused until Kyrack pulled a lever and the far wall broke apart and became two large hidden doors. These swung out on silent hinges and completely blocked off the walkway under the arena. This allowed me to walk upright across the walkway from the waiting area into the room beyond unobserved and unhindered.

Behind these doors was a large ledge or small hall much like another waiting area. On the far side of this area was another large gateway made of interwoven steel bars. Beyond this gateway was a ramp slanting down into the depths. To my left was a rock wall. I looked to my right and the ledge went for four meters up to a solid oak door which was as tall as a little over half my height. But the door was open just a little and through it I could see a room full of Buffamen guards and their equipment. The unit of Buffamen that had been with me up until then moved towards this guard's room as the doors into the arena walkway closed slowly behind me and sealed us in. Kyrack and two other Buffamen led me by torch light through the steel gate and down the ramp. With my little knowledge of things, I would swear the gateway, the doors and now this ramp were all made for giants or people of bigger size than most manimals. In any case, it was easy enough for me to walk down. At the bottom of the ramp, which took me five of my strides to complete, there was a large well-lit room.

The room was filled with tapestries to hide the rough stone walls and rugs to keep the cold rock floor in check. Plush settees and cushions were scattered about to provide comfort and ease. But more importantly, they were all overly large to hold even my big frame. On tables all about the room were many great plates and trays each covered with food and drink. Dotted around the walls were plenty of light crystals and in the centre of the room was a large hearth fire. These provided both light and warmth. The height of the room's ceiling allowed me to walk around easily enough without having to bend my head, even in the slightest. I suppose I could have touched it if I raised my hand but I didn't want to -- at least not just then!" I thought, smiling mischievously.

"Kyrack turned to me as I walked around marvelling at the beauty and size of this room. He pointed to two doors one on each side of the main room. They were so cleverly designed within the inlay of the walls and partly hidden by the tapestries that I would have easily missed seeing them, had I not been directed to look right at them.

He said to me, "these two rooms are sleeping quarters!" He then pointed to the far wall, opposite the ramp. "That room contains a bath and a place for your ablutions. Xalarlla could be in any one of these rooms. I will leave you to find her and meet with her in your own time. These are your quarters whilst you are a judge for the games. You may sleep where you want and eat or drink what you will. If you have need for anything, anything at all, you need only to pull this bell rope or call out and an attendant will come to you at once. Is that all clear?"

I nodded my head to indicate I understood what he had told me. He inclined himself to me with a slight bow then turned and with his two guards went back up the ramp. If I bent over I could just see their feet as they went through the steel gate. This was then closed and locked behind them. But by then I had lost interest in him as I began to think seriously about my meeting with Xalarlla. It was only then that I remembered it was barely dawn and perhaps she was still enjoying her sleep. The other thing I thought of was that she was due to go into the arena as a judge around noon the next day. From these thoughts I wondered about what I could do to help her prepare for the games.

Probably nothing and I smiled remembering some of the things that Kaira told me about females as I looked around the room. I saw the food and I suddenly realized just how hungry I was. So I sat on some cushions and grabbed a handful of food. I was pretty certain Xalarlla had been informed that I was coming down to be with her. So I thought if she wanted to see me she would come to me in her own time. Until then I decided I would enjoy the pleasant morsels which were set out before me.

I had been sitting and eating for only a little time when Xalarlla emerged from the bedroom on the right. The first thing I noticed about her was she was a lovely-looking giantess. I couldn't say that she was overly beautiful in the way that Kaira is. But to me she was very pleasing to the eye. I saw immediately that she was both a little bit shorter and perhaps a little bit older than me. At the same time, I also noticed she was dirty and unkempt, which Kaira had warned me about. Beneath the dirt, her skin was the same colour as Jareck's when he has been out in the sun for too long. Perhaps she was just a little bit darker. A dark tan! Yes that describes her colouring the best. Her face was more oval than moon shaped with a strong pronounced jaw, high cheekbones and a broad flattened forehead. Her nose is slightly flat but not overly wide. To me it is more like pert and lovely. But it was her mouth that caught my attention the most. Her full sensual lips had just the right hint of mystery, suggesting a lot more to me than concealing her full set of strong white teeth.

Yet, despite her loveliness, it was her clothes that really bothered me the most. They were filthy and smelled strongly of sweat, fear and grime, and, to be quite honest, they were almost nonexistent. I mean you really couldn't call what she had on as being clothes in the regular sense. She had a scrappy blue top hanging off her left shoulder whilst the right strap was torn and hanging loose. This helped reveal more of her full breasts than actually covering them up. She had another dirty slip of blue material hanging around her hips by the merest of threads. These two bits of raggedy cloth barely hid the fullness of her female form. But the most disturbing thing about this lovely woman, hidden by dirt and scraps of material, was her hair. At one time it had been straightened out but now it was bunched up and matted together in a lump on her head by dust and dirt and grease. It reminded me of how the witch Zharlla had been described to me.

In spite all that I saw, I tried to smile up at her, though I'm sure she just saw me grimacing. Then I remembered what my father Jarck had always told me, that it was polite for a male to stand for a female whenever she entered the room. Jareck and I had done this many times for my own mother when she would enter the room, whilst we were either sitting at the dinner table or before the fire. So I scrabbled up out of the cushions and brushed the crumbs of food from off my tunic and out of my hands. I then announced myself as 'Böder, a friend and her rescuer'!

I think she smiled more from the silly title I had given myself than from relief at being truly rescued. But this small smile was enough for me. To me, it was like the soft wings of a white butterfly flitting to rest on a flower. She came into the room and sat herself down unceremoniously on a couch near to where I had been sitting. She was so close I could smell her and it wasn't very pleasant, I must say.

"Please," She said indicating with her hand that I was to sit down with her. "My name is Xalarlla and I am here to be rescued." And here she started to giggle. My heart yielded itself at once to her charms and I was dumfounded.

I sat down and offered her a plate of food, which she looked at rather disdainfully. She looked up into my eyes and though I could tell they didn't trust me, they were still unable to hide her fears or her hunger. In the end she finally took some food and after a few mouthfuls of food and some drink which I also offered up to her, she finally spoke and asked. "So good Böder, what are you doing here in these chambers?"

There was no apology, nor any show of social restraint for the food she ate, nor for the juice and wine she drank. She was voracious and she threw her scraps without a thought for me into the fire or onto the floor in a heap. I was a little taken aback by her disgusting eating habits. But as I thought on this, I was mindful of what she must have gone through and how she might be feeling. Not only by how she had been treated by Zharlla *(as told to me by Ribard)*, but also in the fact that she may not have eaten anything whilst being held captive as a judge beneath the stadium in this ample and luxurious cell.

So I began tentatively to tell her how I had come to be there in the judge's apartment whilst she continued to eat and drink like a hungry animal. I also let her know that we had come to help her and how we had paid Zharlla. When I mentioned this, Xalarlla looked up sharply from her food. She looked real closely at me for a moment or two before returning to eat. I must say, her looking at me in the way she did unsettled me deeply.

But I continued regardless. I told her how I was to replace her in the Judicial Games once she had finished her role as a judge the next day. I also told her of our plans and where we were going to take her once everything had been completed. As I was talking to her about Kaira and Jareck, she suddenly perked up and actually stopped eating for a short time.

"A young Bidowman and her friend came to visit me yesterday and I talked briefly with them!" She said. "They told me that someone was coming down here to help me! Is that you they were talking about then?"

"Yes of course it's me! In fact, Kaira is making some clothes for you right at this very moment. And my other friends are preparing a safe place to take you once you have been freed from your service in the games!"

Xalarlla dismissed these platitudes with a wave of her hand and asked. "What about Zharlla then? She has been my captor since I was a child! Do you seriously think that she'll just let you take me away from her?"

"I'm not here to speculate what she will or won't do! All I know is that there are some very resourceful people waiting to help take you away with us back to my home on an island in the middle of the river Dund."

"And why would they want to do this for me?"

"Because you have captured my heart sweet Xalarlla and I wish to help you! Don't you want to be rescued?"

"And what exactly do you want from me Ser Böder?" Xalarlla said. And here she spread her legs embarrassingly so. My eyes were inextricably drawn to the thatch of curly black hair covering her pubic area which had only just been concealed by her skimpy skirt.

I had never seen anything like this before. I mean a woman's intimate parts. Of course I had seen my mother when I was younger and had even watched Kaira take a bath a couple of times in the fresh waters on our journey together. But she is a lot smaller and is just a young Bidowman to me. I have always thought of her as a sister, and watching her was more out of interest and curiosity than anything else. However, I had never been invited to look upon a female of any kind so close and so personally as I was at this time. But now there was this very attractive giantess with next to nothing on and here she was making it obvious that she wanted me to look at her!

And then I remembered just how dirty she was and I also remembered what Kaira had said about her needing a bath. So I stood up and went over to the bathroom door and reached out for it. I took a quick look behind me and I saw Xalarlla following my movements through eyes of puzzled amusement. She had obviously received a response from me that she just hadn't anticipated. And now she was trying to figure out what was going on in my befuddled but confronted mind. I opened the door to the bathroom and, after looking in, I saw something that staggered me. There was a huge pool in the middle of the room with soft wisps of steam hovering gently over the still water. I turned to see that Xalarlla had followed me over to the door. I saw in her face that it was as much out of curiosity to see what was in the room as to see what I was up to. Just as she came close to look through the door into the room, I could smell her strongly once more and it almost made me gag.

"Do you know what my friend Kaira told me when she tried to describe you to me?"

"No what! Said Xalarlla absently as she moved into the bathroom and began looking around the room with a renewed curiosity. It occurred to me then that she may not have even bothered to come into this room much less explore the full length of her cell beneath the stadium.

"She said that you need to take a bath, to wash your hair and also your clothes!"

Here Xalarlla stopped and looked closely at me. This time there was no smile in her eyes or anywhere else on her face or about her person. But by then it was too late. I had already made up my mind about what I was going to do. So before I thought about it and lost the moment, I just did it. I put my head down, held my breath and grabbing her around the waist, I lifted her up and off her feet and pushed her backwards so that together we both fell into the pool.

It was a bit of a shock to my system I must admit. Every single experience of washing in my entire life had always been in fresh water that was either cold, or nearly freezing. There had been the odd occasion where I had experienced warm water, especially in the hot summer days when the shallows of the lake had been warmed up by the long hot days of a full sun. However the warm water of the lake had barely come up to my knees, let alone been able to cover my whole body for a decent warm bath. So this was my first real experience of full immersion in what can only be described as a hot pool of water.

The water was hot but not scalding. Whilst initially it took our breaths away we sort of splashed around a bit just to get our heads above the water and tried to make sense of things. It took but another moment or two before we had fully recovered from the shock. It was then that we found neither of us wanted to move. The feeling of the warm wet water was delightfully luxuriating. This was something I had never known before and looking across at Xalarlla I knew this was new to her as well. So we both lay back and sighed together in a state of lovely warm bliss.

The pool must have been at least four meters deep because when I stood up in the water it came easily up to my midriff. Feeling that it was time to have a full on bath I took off my own clothes. As I chucked them out of the pool, I looked around the bath chamber and saw something that made me smile. There were bottles and jars and containers of a whole range of soaps and shampoos. I turned back to Xalarlla, who was looking at me speculatively. I couldn't tell if she wanted to continue being angry at me or to start being pleased with me for introducing her to this delightful new experience. I decided I had already taken the plunge with her so there really wasn't any sense in being coy about where we were or what we were doing. I made my way purposefully over to her and said. "Come on! Get your clothes off! You and I are going to enjoy this bath while we have the time to do so!"

At first, I sensed I was going to get some strong resistance from this lovely giantess. I tensed my body for a physical encounter. However, I had decided in my heart that whatever was to happen I was resolved to get this thing done. Then, suddenly, her beautiful white butterfly smile was there again. She placed her feet on the bottom of the pool and rose out of the water. Her dark tanned skin was dripping wet and the soggy material she called clothes were hugging her body tightly in a most pleasing manner. They were barely coping with the weight of the water but still refused to come easily away from her body. As I threw the two pieces of material out of the pool I grabbed a handful of the bottles of shampoos and made my way back to Xalarlla who had settled back in the water up to her neck. By this time I could tell she had become willing to accept whatever ministrations I was intending to give to her. It was as if the warmth of the water had helped warm her spirit to my attentions.

She saw me coming towards her with the shampoos so turned her back to me and waited as I began to pour the rich liquids into her hair. When there was enough I placed the bottles on the edge of the pool and began to massage my fingers through her greasy, grimy, dirty matted hair. As I massaged the shampoo in I released the pins and clips which were holding her hair in place and threw them away. When the lather had barely got going I rinsed her hair massaging and managing her hair all the while. I needed to apply the shampoo another four times before I began to get the results I believed were the appropriate ones that declared Xalarlla's hair was clean.

When she sensed that I had finished she turned around and embraced me. Her big beautiful wet breasts were flat against my sparsely covered hairy chest whilst her arms were long enough to circle around my neck and shoulders and hold me tight to her. Then, for the first time in my entire life I felt the kiss of a woman who was not my mother. It was not the long, lingering lovers' kiss I imagined one to be; it was a quick thank-you kiss of lips upon lips from a friend. But this was enough for me.

Before I knew it she had turned me around and had grabbed one of the badly depleted bottles of shampoo and began to pour it onto my scalp. From there it was a glorious feeling of her long strong fingers ministering such beautiful pleasure that, at one stage, I never wanted it to end. Then there were the soft gentle fingers full of water rinsing my hair over and over again. I knew my hair was not very dirty, but still I closed my eyes determined to enjoy the moment. I leant back into this delightful woman, allowing her to keep repeating the process until I believed I had died and gone to heaven. I could feel her breasts brushing up against my back and this also had a strange new effect on my being.

There was a pause and I felt Xalarlla move away from me. For a moment I was disappointed as I thought I had lost this woman to another distraction when I felt her hands come over my shoulders and her breasts come up to my back once more. My whole body shivered with the electric delight of her touch. It was then that I realized I was being soaped up as the wonderfully strong fingers of a working giantess began to lather up soap all over my body, but she didn't stop with just my chest and stomach. Her hands searched me out and together we discovered the true extent of just how much of an effect she was having on my body.

This was a first for me and I am simply unable to describe fully what I was going through at that very moment. However, I can say that I had never had such feelings before nor the kind of response from my body ever in my life either. But there was no real release in the first place. Just the pleasure of her touch was enough for me. She then went down on my legs, her strong fingers kneading and massaging my thighs. The pleasure continued to grow as Xalarlla did each leg down to and over my knees and then onto my shins. She massaged my calves so wonderfully that the strength of her fingers and her touch almost hurt my walk-weary and hardened muscles. Then, just when I thought it couldn't get any better she took my feet and began kneading them with her fingers and I thought I would truly die. My feet are very sensitive but I was determined not to struggle and so I allowed her to have her way with my feet as she deemed best.

I was now lying completely back in the water and felt a completely new sensation happening around my feet and toes. So I opened my eyes and raised my head as best I could and saw that she was licking my feet and sucking on my toes. I groaned softly and laid my head back into the water and enjoyed what this lovely woman was doing to me and my feet. And then I felt her leaving my feet and climbing slowly up my legs and this time she sucked but not on my toes and then I knew release in a way I had never known before. And all I could do was quiver and sigh and for this I nearly drowned. But then her strong hands came up and held my back and supported my head once more above the water.

I marvelled at the sensation as Xalarlla's large hard nipples and breasts traced along my body as she came up to my face. Just the feel and thought of her in this way was extremely comforting and exciting at both the same time. I felt her hands beneath my head and then she brought my head up and out of the water. I opened my eyes to find her face right up close to mine. Her eyes were bright and shining and every bit of her was smiling down lovingly at me. And then her lips were meeting with mine. This time our kisses were long and wet, and excitingly vibrant as only lovers' kisses can be.

After a time I took back the control I had lost and I began to administer a wonderfully long bout of soap and lathering all over the body of this beautiful giantess. And for the first time I too enjoyed the thrill of giving pleasure through my fingers and mouth to a woman in much the same way that she had done to me just previously. I discovered her body afresh and I could tell by her soft moaning and other physical responses that she was enjoying my touch probably as much as the pleasure I was receiving through stroking, tickling, lathering and massaging her wonderful body. I found her soft beautiful feminine parts very exciting indeed. But, unfortunately, I was a little bit unsure on how best to proceed. Xalarlla helped at this point by instructing me silently, gently tenderly with her own fingers. And then I remembered what she had done for me and I thought I'd reciprocate. This had an amazing physical response from her and which to this very day I can never recount with the most appropriate words. But, suffice it to say, her body was racked with a startling array of physical responses that were both very exciting and rewarding to know that I had actually done something right by her. Anyway, she was as obviously depleted in much the same way that I had been when she had brought release from me moments earlier.

I do remember that after this very physical and sexual experience I came to notice the state of her back in greater detail. At first I felt, rather than saw, the smallest of deep scars all over her lower back, her buttocks and thighs and the backs of her legs. I then looked at Xalarlla's body and back and saw that it had been marked and scarred in a way that I had never known or seen on anybody else ever in my life before. I realized of course that someone had whipped the scars into her and despite their size, had left a permanent mark on her lovely body that was ever there to remind her of the poor treatment she had received. It made me feel suddenly very sad and isolated and alone. So I caressed each individual scar very slowly and I believe with great tenderness. I remember asking her as gently as I could about them.

There was a very long pause and at one point I thought I might have asked too much too quickly. But then slowly she began talking. By this time I was sitting with my back against the wall of the pool and Xalarlla was sitting with her back against my chest. My left arm was around her waist and my right arm was over her shoulder with my right hand naturally cupping her left breast comfortingly. Without turning around she nestled back into my arms and began to tell me slowly all about her life.

"My mother had been a very dark giantess. She had been born and raised in the southern regions of Durogg -- in particular the land of Undoryck. One bleak day, my mother (*so she told me*) had ventured too far from her home village and had been trapped and caught and then sold into slavery. She was taken up the coast of the mainland of Durogg to eventually end up under the rulership of one of the feudal tordans in the land of Korgan. There she met my father, a white giant who was a major guard within the king's court. But their relationship was frowned upon and openly discouraged. But this didn't stop them from getting my mother pregnant with me.

"Shortly after the pregnancy was discovered by the officials in the court of Korgan, my father disappeared without a word of where he went to or what had happened to him. Apparently feeling very distressed and alone, but still a slave who was watched and guarded at all times, my mother continued to work diligently within the court but she now was determined to flee the courts of Korgan with me, her only child, at the very first opportunity. Finally she did escape with me. But by now I was all of 8 years of age. Desperately we headed to the Taka Mountains hoping to find refuge or a place of sanctuary in the harsh eastern wilds of Korgan. Unfortunately it was whilst we were travelling through the heart of the Taka Mountains that my mother and I were set upon by some ferocious rock creatures. With the help and sacrifice of my mother, I was barely able to escape from the mountains with just my life in place.

"It was whilst I was running scared from the rock creatures that I met up with Zharlla the witch and her caravan of circus freaks. They were travelling through the foothills of the northern most part of the Taka Mountains. With the promise of being kept safe from the courts of Korgan and being looked after, I made a commitment to stay with Zharlla. This became a verbal agreement between her and me, though I didn't know it at the time. The first thing she did was to give me a new name. But I realized soon enough that, just like my own mother, I had become a sort of slave to this witch. She forced me to work hard for her and if I didn't do it exactly the way she wanted me to or in the time she told me to do it then she would beat me or fail to feed me! And it has been like this ever since and going on now for me for nearly twenty years!"

As she was speaking about her time with Zharlla and the cruel way that she had been treated, Xalarlla suddenly stopped talking about herself and became very quiet. She then turned around and crushed me to her nestling her face into my neck just below my jaw and held onto me. I could feel the warmth and wet of her tears trickling down my neck and over my chest. And yet she seemed to draw strength and comfort from me by my just hugging and holding onto her.

A thought occurred to me at this time, so I asked her as gently as I could.

"You said that Zharlla gave you a new name. Do you remember what your real name is?"

Xalarlla stopped breathing and looked up into my eyes at this point. She pushed herself up and away from my chest and, for a terrible moment I thought that I had overstepped my right to intrude. After a couple of very tense moments, I saw her struggling deep inside through the conflict in her face.

Finally, she said to me. "You know, I have never given much thought to the name my mother gave me until just now. But as I've been lying here in your arms and recalling the warmth and wonderful touch from your fingers and hands and your tongue earlier." She smiled shyly as she said this. "I have suddenly remembered, quite vividly in fact, the name my mother gave me and called me so many long years ago!"

I waited another long minute before I was able to ask her, "Well what is it? I want to call you and know you by your real name and not the name the witch gave you!"

"Really?" She asked incredulously

"Yes of course really! Come on girl, names are very important! So then, what is your real name?"

"My name is Jevan!" Said Jevan exultantly, crying and laughing at the same time.

And though it might sound funny to you, just the act of calling out her own given name there in the warmth of that large pool there come a sudden breaking of a spiritual hold over Jevan which I am unable to express fully. But when she tried to talk about it, Jevan just simply said she seemed to become a new person at that very moment. We paused to think of this and what it could possibly mean for us both.

Then she returned to her position with her back to me and pulled my arm to hold onto her like I had earlier. After a short lull I began to tell her about my own life experiences. I must say, this was just a beautiful time of being together in the pool and talking about ourselves. It was pretty emotional and a lot of feelings and experiences were shared and at the end of which there was a tremendous feeling of intimacy and understanding between us. But then it came time for us to get out of the pool. By this time the skin or our fingers and toes were both so wrinkled we thought we would end up like this forever, and Böder smiled self consciously.

We found some towels and dried each other down. Then clothed in robes that were big enough for us, we went back into the main hall for some refreshments. All the while we were eating and drinking we were still talking about our lives, what we were up to and where we were hoping to get to.

After a lengthy time of talking and eating and now a healthy bout of drinking we were both pleasantly relaxed and very comfortable with one another. So the time came and we decided it was time for us to go to bed. This again was a whole new wonderful experience for me. Not just to be able to sleep in a bed that was pleasantly comfortable and delightfully big enough for me! It was the fact that I could share this bed and time with another person -- female or otherwise -- that was also as big as I was. This was just too nice a time for me and perhaps the most significant experience of all for me. To say that I was pleasantly and wholeheartedly surprised by this most tremendous of all experiences is an understatement.

I am unwilling to go into the finer details of my first night with Jevan at this time. Suffice it to say that as of that night I now consider myself to be both the husband and protector of Jevan. And as such I will do everything in my power to ensure that she is never mistreated ever again and looked after as only a woman should be by her man.

Chapter Nineteen

BÖDER

Jevan and I woke to the sound of knocking on the door to our sleeping quarters. I rolled out from under the many sheets on top of the huge divan where we had been sleeping. I quickly pulled on a robe and went over and opened the door. There to my surprise stood Kaira and Jareck. They were both staring up at me and smiling like they were running out of room on their faces for anything else.

I staggered out into the main welcoming room. All the plates and jugs had been replaced with fresh food and drink. I sat down where I had sat the first time when I was waiting for Jevan.

As Jevan came to the door naked, Kaira saw her and squealed, saying, "you can't come out like that!" She rushed over to bar her from coming out of the bedroom, which looked kind of funny as the young Bidowman was just about the same height as Jevan's knees. "Böder, please help me!" she cried out frantically. "I've bought her the clothes I've been working on, so help me get them onto her before she presents herself!"

I stood up quickly and introduced everyone. "Kaira, Jareck, this is Jevan. Jevan this is my friend Kaira and my brother Jareck. Jevan, Kaira has been making new clothes for you so you don't need to wear the rags you've been wearing

"Really clothes for me?" She squealed excitedly and I smiled because she reminded me so much of how Kaira sounded when she also got excited.

"What then do I do with my old clothes?"

And here she held up the two pieces of clothing I had found her wearing when we first met. They were clean and dry from our time in the pool together, but they were still tattered and worn.

Here, remarkably, Kaira began to take control. "Come with me Jevan! I have an idea of what we can do with those. Jareck can I have the bag of clothes please!"

Jareck who had been transfixed by the visual feast of this lovely giantess came slowly to his senses before rallying himself and handing Kaira the huge bag. She could barely hold it, much less carry it. I took it off her gently and handed it over to Jevan, who held it easily enough. I then directed her back into the bedroom saying, "You girls take care of this in the bedroom, Jevan would you like something to eat? I could bring in a tray of food for you if you like!"

She smiled at me and nodded, "thanx I'd like that Böder!"

Kaira and Jareck looked knowingly at one another before she followed after Jevan and disappeared behind the closing door into the bed chamber. I stopped for a moment and looked at Jareck. He had not stopped smiling broadly since I had first seen him earlier. He helped me load up a tray of meat and another tray of fresh fruit without saying a word. I took the trays over to the door and feeling like I was suddenly intruding into a female's world, I knocked on the door. As prompted by a voice from beyond the door, I went in. I placed the trays on top of the divan and then quickly turned and left without really looking at what Kaira and Jevan were doing.

Jareck and I sat down to eat our own breakfasts together. I must admit I felt there was a moment of awkwardness between us as we sat there quietly. After all, this was the first time in my life that I had experienced anything like what had happened to me over the last twenty-four or so hours. But beyond that it was also the first time that I had experienced something which was so personal and had not wished to include Jareck. These memories and feelings came forward and it somehow put up a barrier between Jareck and me. Although I wanted to tell him everything that had happened between me and Jevan, I felt I just couldn't. I was determined to keep our most secretive intimacies from ever coming out. Even between brothers. To his credit, Jareck seemed to understand this. After a short time of awkward eating he began to tell me all that had happened since I had been led away into the stadium. And then he became serious and spoke with a softer voice saying, "We have some work to do whilst the girls are preparing Jevan for the games. Is there a drain here in this apartment somewhere?"

I tried to think and was even looking around at the floor hoping to discover the grate that should be around here in this apartment somewhere.

"What about behind these other doors?" asked Jareck, pointing to the door at the far end of the hall.

"Of course" I said, "That's the hot pool room. There must surely be a drain in there!"

We went through the door and walked all around the large room. The pool looked warm and inviting and I smiled at the thought of what had taken place in there only a sweet memory ago. We found the grate soon enough. My first thought was there was no way I would even get my leg down there, much less use it as a means of escape. I told this to Jareck, who looked at me with a concerned, slightly bemused look.

"You're never going to escape down there through the sewers, you big lump, you'd never fit. No I am putting this down to show Bartrow where you are in order to send up some weapons for the games."

And here Jareck lifted his shirt and unwound a long, thick, brightly coloured rope from around his waist. He then tested the grate and we found that it came up easily enough in his hands.

"Good!" He said as he replaced the grate. He then tied an end of the rope to one of the bars and dropped the rest of the rope down through the grate. "This will tell Bartrow where you are when he finds the rope. You may need to check this grate every now and then in case he tries to get a message to you. "Do you understand all that?" he asked.

I nodded my head a little confused.

"Why are you talking to me like I'm a child?" I asked.

"Because by the look on your face you don't appear to be back here with me yet," he said smiling as he slapped me gently on my knee. "Come on, let's get back and see how Kaira is getting along with Jevan!"

We found them sitting in the hall eating, drinking and chatting quite comfortably with one another. I smiled warmly because this was what I had in my mind when I pictured Kaira and Jevan meeting. Jevan stood up and my breath suddenly refused to come in or out. She was beautiful. She was wearing a dark blue smock, which was just a little too short for a dress, but it did cover her body right down to the tops of her thighs, almost as far down as the reach of her flowing black hair.

"You look stunning!" I said without thinking and beginning to breathe once more. She smiled and this alone arrested my heart again. But then a thought occurred to me. I turned to Kaira and asked. "What happened to the bright material you showed me back at the camp the other day?'

"It's still here!" said Jevan smiling and grabbing the hem of the smock she lifted it up to reveal the underside of the material. Here I saw the brightly coloured print that Kaira had shown me when she had been excited about making the clothes for Jevan. As she showed me this, I caught a glimpse of the bright blue material covering Jevan's hips under the smock she was wearing. It was then that I realised what a clever girl Kaira really was. Jevan was wearing the smock of dark blue but it could also be turned inside out and be worn as a brightly coloured skirt. So, not only had she made Jevan two dresses from the one piece of material, she had also made her some undergarments from Jevan's drab bits of original clothing. I turned to Kaira and I must admit a tear came to my eye. I couldn't help it. I was just so overwhelmed to see Jevan so beautiful and happy and also pleased and proud to see that Kaira had been a part of this.

"Thank-you, Kaira!" I said quietly.

Jevan saw me and came over to me and gave me a big hug. But then of course Kaira hadn't done this for me, she had done this for Jevan. And Jevan was happy to tell me this in no uncertain terms, but I could see the glint of a smile in her eyes as she said this.

Kaira had been watching us hug from behind Jevan and I could literally see her mind working overtime as she looked up at us.

"Oh there is just one more thing we need to do before you go out into the games as a judge!" Kaira said, suddenly taking charge once more. "Come along, Jevan. We have some more female work to do and the two of them went back into the bed chamber. Once more, all Jareck and I could do was sit and talk and eat. We talked more about what was planned and what we might expect from the games. The women were gone for a much longer time than before and I was just beginning to worry when the door opened and Kaira entered followed by Jevan.

With a sweeping hand Kaira announced. "Gentle folk, meet the new Jevan!"

And the new Jevan was even more beautiful -- to me anyway -- if this was possible. Nothing much more had been done to Jevan other than her long, clean but unmanaged hair had been neatly cut back to shoulder length and placed in such a way as to accentuate the strong round features of Jevan's lovely face. However, even with just this minor adjustment, it seemed that Jevan had been given a whole new lease of life. She not only looked different, but there was something dynamically different about her. I can't explain it fully, because I have no real knowledge of these things, *(though we were to find out later what had really happened)*. Still the aura around her, that which I had seen from the moment we met, had changed completely somehow -- for the better I might add.

Just then we heard the gate at the top of the ramp opening. We all looked towards the ramp and watched as Kyrack came down with two of his guards. He stopped when he saw Jevan and was momentarily taken aback.

"Well," he said thoroughly impressed, "It's true what they say then! When females get together they can change the world. And you, young lady," he said looking at Kaira respectfully, "have most definitely changed Xalarlla's world for the better!"

Both Jevan and Kaira said nothing but the smiles on their faces said that this compliment from the head of the games was most welcome indeed. I was aware Kyrack didn't know of the complete change in Jevan but I was happy to assist in putting him on the right track."

"Her name is Jevan good Kyrack," I said in the most menacingly quiet voice I could muster. "And we would appreciate it if you would call her and announce her by her real name from here ever onwards!"

"Surely!" responded Kyrack generously. "Jevan the time has come for you to fulfil your duty as judge, if you would; please follow me!"

"Can I go with Jevan to the waiting area?" I asked, inching forward, hoping that I wasn't appearing to be too intimidating.

Kyrack stopped in his turn back towards the ramp and looked carefully at me, before responding. "If you promise not to interfere in the proceedings, then yes you may stay with our judge in the waiting area until she is called into the arena. Do you promise?"

"Absolutely," I said, most emphatically. Then, like a little child giddy with the fun of the fair before me, I walked with Jevan to the top of the ramp. We went through the open gates up the last little rise in the ramp to go through the doorway into the walkway beneath the stadium. The doors had opened to block the walkway so none of the crowd could see us enter the waiting area. But I also noticed that the opened doors stopped us from deviating from the path between the judge's apartment and the arena. I looked behind me and saw that Kaira and Jareck had followed us up the ramp without interference from the guards. But as we made our way across the walkway into the waiting area, Kyrack and the guards stepped aside and allowed Jevan and I to go through, but Kaira and Jareck were stopped from entering.

"This waiting area is for judges only." Kyrack said evenly. "But since you have played such an important part in preparing Jevan for the games you may sit with me in my own pavilion if you wish!"

"We would like that very much -- thank-you!" Kaira said, looking at Jareck as if for confirmation that this was the right thing to do. Jareck took his cue and simply nodded, yes; this was what they wanted to do.

Before the gate to the waiting area was closed, I asked Kyrack, "What about weapons? Isn't Jevan going to be given something to help administer justice on behalf of the people of M'Lenn-Fida?"

"All in good time Böder"! He replied. "Don't you worry. We always look after our judges as we see fit!" And with that he indicated that the gates to the waiting area be closed. It was only then that I noticed both gates on either side of the waiting area were covered over so none could see us from either the walkway beneath the stadium or from the arena. But we could hear the roar of the crowd. So it was obvious to us they were being entertained by some spectacle or other on the other side of the gate inside the arena.

The moment the gate to the walkway was closed, I moved over to where Jareck had told me the weapons were buried and quickly moved the sand away. It took me but a minute to unearth the shin guards and the sword, which were wrapped in a cloth. Jevan had been watching me a little bemused, so I called her over. Together we placed the guards around her shins and when they were on I asked her how they felt. They were a bit large for her but she said they were comfortable enough and didn't interfere with her movement. Without wasting any of our time together, I gave what little instruction in handling weapons I could think of that might help her prepare for her role as a judge.

"The only part of your body, any attacker can reach comfortably are your legs. I don't have the time to instruct you fully, but I just want you to use whatever weapon they give you in conjunction with this." I handed her the sword and took the sheath off showing her briefly how to hold it and swing it and use it to strike and to block. I was close to her with my hands on hers showing her how to hold and move. We were so close I could smell her hair and feel the warmth of her breath on my arms and it was driving me crazy. It took all of my self control just to focus on the job at hand. As she practised I stepped back a little and realized she must have handled a weapon of some sort before because she seemed to know how to hold it and use it. But we didn't have the time to talk about these things as the door to the arena could open at any time.

"The only thing I want to say to you, Jevan, at this moment, is to remember to use your strengths to your advantage. You will be bigger, stronger and heavier than anything you will meet in the arena. So use your height, your strength and your reach rather than let anyone or anything get close to you to inflict any kind of damage. But, if they should somehow get in close to you, with these guards helping to protect your shins, don't be afraid to kick out as well. Okay!"

Jevan nodded her head but I could tell she was scared. I couldn't help it! I just wanted to protect her so much. So I did the only thing I could think of; I hugged her and held her close. She smelled so nice. I remember whispering some words of encouragement and promised that if anything went wrong I would do my utmost to come and help her. I released her and for the next few moments I asked her to practise swinging the sword and showed her a few tricks that Traxxa had shown me in my many hours of training with him.

And then the gates into the arena suddenly parted rolling back into the stone settings on either side of the doorframe. We heard a muffled announcement about 'Jevan the Giantess' at which Jevan and I looked at one another and smiled knowingly. But then the volume of the roar from the crowd really hit us and, despite our size, it almost sent us staggering back it was so loud and forceful. Jevan took a deep breath and stepped boldly forward through the opening and the roar seemed to rise in crescendo. I remember thinking I was so very proud of her right then. But the moment she was through the gates they came out silently from their settings to lock together once more. It was then that I noticed the strong steel bars were covered with thin sheets of ply wood. I couldn't get through them but the coverings were not going to stop me from watching what was taking place in the arena. So, without thinking of the consequences I punched and ripped the wood off the bars until there was nothing left of them to restrict my view of Jevan in the arena. I watched as she made her way out into the middle of the pitch.

A stick was there for her to use! A feeble, termite ridden, stick! It was at best guess two meters in length. And when it was held in Jevan's huge hand there was barely any wood left sticking out. I failed to see how this could possibly be seen as a means of protection in the fight that was sure to be coming, moreover how was she supposed to mete out judgement of any lasting kind using such a weak instrument of justice?

And then they came out! There were six of them and they were forced out from the many grilled gates dotted around the arena walls and all at the same time. They were big females of various degrees of ugly and brutishness. They consisted of a Wolfawman (*half woman half wolf*), there were two Bearawmen (*half woman, half bear*), two Larcawmen (*half woman, half large cat*) and a very large Buffawman (*half woman, half buffalo*). Each was scantily clad revealing more of their human and feminine attributes than I would have thought possible. But then I remembered; whilst it was decently inappropriate they were part of the games and were there only for the entertainment of the lustful crowd. And yet they had been sent into the arena to fight for their lives as part of the Judicial Games. As a result, they were also partly covered in various forms of armour. Whilst they had remained in their human forms in order to carry the weapons and wear their armour they arrogantly and proudly displayed their beast parts. These included their snouts or jaws their tails, ears and claws whilst the Buffawman I saw had her set of horns at full length and swished her untouched tail proudly almost like a ribbon of honour. Each one was carrying a weapon of merit. Two had swords, two were with spears and one of the Bearawman and the Buffawman each had maces and all carried shields.

As they ventured out into the arena they automatically clustered together at one end of the pitch for mutual support especially when they saw how big Jevan was. These were vicious violent female criminals who had been condemned to a slow death in the dungeons of M'Lenn-Fida. Fighting in this arena, against a judge, was their only way out from a life in the foulest of conditions the prisons throughout the lands could hope to offer. But now when they saw who their judge was they were having a rush of doubt that maybe this wasn't their best way forward. Still there was the chance of freedom if only they could kill or at the very least defeat this giant. They looked at one another and knew without words they must work together if they wished to survive. But even as they moved about, the crowd hissed and booed and screamed and howled abuse at them with the intention of letting them know they were the bad girls and the giant was there to mete out some justice for everyone's amusement except their own.

As the female criminals rallied together, another four gates opened at the other end of the pitch and two lionesses a bear and a tigress entered the arena. Whilst these too were female manimals they had decided to reject all aspects of their humanity and so remained permanently in their animal form. Some even had the ragged remnants of human clothing still hanging loosely from around their bodies. Despite this, they somehow knew they had a common enemy in the giant in the middle of the pitch and began to stalk her immediately.

Jevan took all this in and decided she would restrict their access to her by dealing with one group at a time. So without warning she ran towards the six manimals. When they saw this they separated into two groups to isolate her attack on them. Jevan decided, at the last moment to deal with the largest of them first. She feinted to one side before dropping to one knee and swung the sword in her right hand towards the Buffawman. The swipe of her sword was so quick and strong that the Buffawman didn't have time to react as it separated her head from her body completely and she slumped over bleeding profusely into the arena's sand from the now gaping hole in her neck. The crowd roared its great pleasure at seeing some action and blood so quickly and stood as one to clap the efforts of the giant judge.

The Bearawman with the mace was on Jevan's left-hand side and stepped forward to try and take advantage of the giant as she was kneeling. She moved in quickly as she raised the mace in her hand to strike at Jevan's hip or thigh. Sensing the movement, Jevan merely poked the stick in her left hand into the unprotected chest of the attacking Bearawman. The stick became pulp with the impact, but it also stopped the Bearawman fully in her tracks and she bounced back slightly with the force, fell to the ground and didn't move. Jevan didn't know if she was dead or winded -- but she didn't care. What she did see though were both the maces from these over large females lying uselessly on the ground near their bodies. Sensing an aspect of vulnerability, the other female criminals all rushed in as one to try and get to the giantess before she stood up. Dropping the useless piece of wood as she reached out, Jevan picked up the mace of the Bearawman with her left hand. Without really aiming, Jevan simply flung it easily at the large target of several bodies moving together as one. The second Bearawman took the full brunt of the flying mace which bounced off her chest and smacked into the head of the Larcawman and both dropped to the ground severely injured.

The remaining Larcawman and the Wolfawman both lunged at Jevan at the same time. They were in the action of flying through the air in front and to the right of Jevan when she noticed them. The Larcawman with her sword held high, was dropping from the apex in her flight hoping to strike at Jevan's vulnerable thigh. The Wolfawman was coming down with the point of her spear aimed to inflict as much damage as she could on the giants exposed right knee. Jevan stood up and the spear hit the top end of her shin guard and the sword swung uselessly through empty air. But the Wolfawman had over extended herself and stumbled into the area of the pitch where Jevan's knee had been but a moment before. Without really thinking Jevan merely dropped her knee once more and using her weight effectively she squashed the stumbling Wolfawman into a bloodied pulp. At the same time, her sword came down on the Larcawman who was also slightly off balance and was struggling to regain her composure. It was then that Jevan's sword sliced through her shoulder guard and continued to separate her right arm and side from the rest of her. She screamed a most horrible full bloodied scream as the giants sword continued down to her right breast, where her armour finally played its part and halted its momentum. But it was too late to save the Larcawman as the scream stopped short in her fearful mouth at the same time that she died and began crumbling in a bloodied mess to the ground.

Jevan knew she had spent too much time focused on the six manimals and she had to stand and move to meet the four creatures behind her. As she began moving, she felt the claws of the she-bear striking at her unprotected left buttock! In quick reaction to the pain, Jevan stood up and turned all in the one movement. She then brought her right leg around and kicked out at where she believed the she-bear to be. Instantly, she felt and heard the satisfying crunch as her right leg and guard caught the bear and propelled the savage creature across the arena to hit one of the giant stone monoliths dotted around the arena. The she-bear hit the monolith bounced back off it and dropped down to the sandy pitch without moving again. The three large cats were suddenly cautious but continued to circle around the legs of the giant. When they saw just how big she was they snarled and spat at her and began to back slowly away from her.

Foolishly believing she had them on the run, Jevan threw caution to the wind and moved forward without really thinking. It was the tigress who reacted first. She stopped and, with but a few short strides she leapt through the air for nearly five meters to land on Jevan's left thigh. Here she sank her sharp claws and teeth all in the same movement into the toughened giant flesh breaking the skin and drawing blood. Jevan screamed in pain and this was enough to encourage the remaining two lionesses to begin rushing in as well. With her right hand she brought the sword round and slapped the tigress sharply with the flat of the blade. It was awkward and whilst it didn't kill the tigress it did however stun it so forcefully that she released her grip and fell the three meters to the sand covered pitch. Not bothering to bend down or stop her movement Jevan simply took a step forward and with her left foot she crushed the life out of the stunned big cat.

Taking another step with her right leg she knelt again by just dropping her right knee. At the same time she brought her right hand, which had been hovering around her left thigh after hitting the tigress, with the sword still in hand, around in an arc and with the flat of her sword she smacked the two rushing lionesses. They were thrown into a muddle in the middle of the pitch but it was not even enough to stun them. Hearing a growl Jevan looked around and saw the Bearawman. This was the one she had poked with the stick in the first bout and she was slowly beginning to rouse herself. She had obviously been only winded and it was only a matter of time before she would become part of the battle again. So with a quick step backwards Jevan reached round with her left hand and picked the Bearawman up under her arms and before the lionesses could rally themselves, they found a flying Bearawman smacking into them. This time there was damage. One of the lioness's legs was broken and the crushing weight of the flying Bearawman was enough to severely wind the second lioness. Jevan had not waited to see the end result of her throw; as she rushed forward the moment the bear had left her hand and, gripping her sword with both hands she brought it down point-first three times. The first was down into the heart of the winded lioness, the second was into the crippled lioness and the final blow was into the heart of the Bearawman.

At the first two strikes from Jevan's deathblows, the crowd just roared and screamed ferociously in unbridled bloodthirsty hysteria. But as the final blow was meted out the crowd simply went berserk. There was cheering, whistling, screaming and a myriad of horns and other instruments were sounded as well creating a cacophony of approval from the crowd. When Jevan looked about her she saw that even the vast crowds along the terraces high above and around the stadium were all cheering and shouting and whistling and applauding long and loud and steadily.

Sensing that all was not completed, Jevan walked over to the Bearawman beneath the monolith and for good measure she kicked it with great force back into the monolith. It never moved again and Jevan enjoyed the exhilarating moment of the applause and acclamation from the crowd. She lifted both her arms with the sword still in her right hand and the people in the stadium stood as one and the roar of all the watching people throughout Regil-Ter continued to rise in volume and strength.

As it continued without appearing to settle or diminish, Jevan turned and saluted the pavilion where Kaira and Jareck were both beaming and stood screaming her name whilst clapping wholeheartedly next to the smiling Kyrack.

Chapter Twenty

BÖDER

I hugged Jevan tightly when she came through into the waiting area. I didn't want to let her go I was just so pleased with what she had done in the arena. But the most important thing to me was that she was unharmed. That is until I felt and saw her wince when I patted her bottom playfully. It was then I remembered the rake of claws by the she-bear. The door to the waiting area was opened and Kyrack and the guards accompanied us back to the judge's apartment. As we went along, Jevan asked Kyrack to bring her some herbs and ointments (*which she named but I can't remember*) to deal with her scratches and wounds.

He nodded and, after he closed the gates to our apartment, he said to her.

"I will send them down to you as soon as I have them!"

We continued down the ramp into the apartment where to our surprise we saw not only Jareck and Kaira waiting for us but also Jellick and Traxxa as well.

JELLICK

Böder introduced us one by one to Jevan and I am pleased to say that Böder seemed positively buoyant and was beaming from ear to ear. He appeared to be thoroughly captivated by this dark skinned giant beauty and I was pleased for him

"Come," said Kaira, taking command of Jevan once more. "Let's get you washed and those wounds taken care of!" And the two women went off into the bathing room.

We had just started talking when Kyrack called out from the top of the ramp. Jareck went up to get the ointments and herbs and bandages that Jevan had asked for. We waited for him to take them through to the women next door whilst engaging Böder in some small talk. We were standing around and nibbling at the food on the trays in the room when the first to speak up was Traxxa.

"I've had a look around your cell and I hate to have to say this, but the hole from the pool room down to the sewer is just too small for the head of your mace Böder. So, even as we speak, Bartrow is chipping at the stone walls to make them larger or at least softer to allow you to rip the mace up and out of the manhole into your cell!

Apart from that, what else has been happening?"

Here Böder smiled coyly and said, "Would you like something to eat? Anyone for food or drink?"

And here, recognizing the beauty of his innocence lost during his night with Jevan, we all laughed and acknowledged the moment before continuing with the food and the drink and the incidental conversations. Then, when it was appropriate we each clapped him on his knee, thigh and hands -- or any other part of his body that the giant allowed us to touch as friends and companions.

Finally I began to direct the conversation towards the next step in the plans we had been making around securing Jevan's freedom.

"The first thing to do, Böder, is to get Jevan out of here as Kyrack promised we could!"

"I couldn't agree more!" he replied emphatically.

"But I don't want to go!" came a voice from behind us. We all turned to see the shining face of Jevan standing in the door to the bathing room. She looked lovely and fresh despite having just killed ten violent criminals in the arena! Her wounds had been washed and bound and she looked radiant like she had just had a quick bath to look good for her man. Kaira had helped her take off the shin guards and they had turned her dress around. She was now in a short dress comprising of a print of vibrant coloured flowers set against a dark blue background.

We all stood up and congratulated her on her role as a judge in the arena, and I asked, "Why don't you wish to come with us? You know we can't protect you if you stay here and there is every chance that Zharlla will try and retrieve you if you do!"

"Because I want to stay and be here with Böder," she replied. "He supported me when I needed it most and now it's my turn to support him!"

"Support him? How?" Traxxa asked quietly.

"I don't know! But, whatever I can do, I will!"

"And that's good enough for me," said Böder rallying to her side and taking the shin guards out of her hand and placing them by the ramp.

"Oh yes, Kaira and I heard some loud scratching sounds from the overflow grate by the pool when we were in there just now. Do you think they could be rats?"

"Minking big rats!" said Kaira with feeling and shivering slightly, "by the sounds of it!"

"Yeah a big rat, by the name of Bartrow!" I said smiling.

"Bartrow? What's a minking Bartrow?" Asked Jevan innocently confused and we all laughed. So I told her who and what a Bartrow was and what he was up to.

"But, about getting you out of here Jevan...," said Traxxa still using his quiet voice and steering us back to the problem at hand. "Seriously, when the time comes we may have to move quickly. Will you be up to running through the streets of Regil-Ter and escaping by boat along the river?"

"If Böder is with me, then I believe I will be up for anything. And also I'll have my little friend here to protect me," and here she brandished the sword still in her hand.

I must say I liked her spirit, not the kind of spirit that I expected from one who was under the control of Zharlla and this surprised me a little. I think Traxxa noticed this as well, for he asked in his usual tactless way. "Don't you have any sense of duty to Zharlla anymore?"

"No! No I don't!" She said emphatically, "at least not until I had my bath with Böder and Kaira cut my hair. Why do you ask?"

Traxxa and I looked at one another and the rest caught a glimpse of this underlying current of thought between us. But it was Kaira, *(who I was to find out is much more sensitive to these things than most people)*, saw it first and asked. "Why? What does this mean having a bath and cutting her hair? Have we violated some sort of giant lore or something?"

Traxxa looked at Kaira before turning towards Jevan and asked her to come down and look into his eyes. She brought her face down to his and, admirably, Böder stood up defensively, ready to protect her. But I placed a hand on his knee. He looked at me and when I shook my head at him, he stayed his hand from interfering.

"Jevan, you have light in your eyes. Böder," and here he looked at our young giant friend. "Have you noticed any significant changes in Jevan from when you first met her?"

"You mean apart from her being cleaner?" He asked.

To which Traxxa nodded yes.

"I sensed she lightened up a bit and also seems a bit freer from when I first met her. But then I just put that down to our time together!"

Here, he smiled shyly once more.

"Well; and I don't have any definitive knowledge of witches -- and especially not this Zharlla – but, generally speaking, the first thing those who wish to control others tend to do is change the name of their victims. I see that you've already changed your name back to your given name. Is that correct Jevan?"

"Yes, Böder asked me the name my mother had given me while we were in the bath. For some reason, I couldn't remember it at first but then, as I looked into Böder's face, it suddenly came to me. From then on he has been calling me Jevan and telling everyone we meet that that is my name! I guess that's kinda nice, isn't it?"

"Well, yes it is and that's where your initial break from Zharlla's control began. The next thing witches do is they like to mix their magic into the fabric of their victim or slave or whatever you want to call them. I remember hearing Kaira saying that you needed a bath and that you smelled. Well my understanding of witches is that they work with their hands. So Jevan, who did your hair and provide you with your clothes?"

Without hesitation Jevan said "Zharlla did my hair and instructed me never to wash my body or my hair, but the clothes I chose for myself -- at least the fabric. You see there are no clothes big enough for me to wear comfortably. But I never had the skill to make them properly like Kaira has!"

Traxxa nodded his head and I had to concur with him because I, too, had heard stories and knew a little about witch lore.

"The thing is Jevan," I said as gently as I could. "You had been placed under a spell of witchcraft by Zharlla almost from the moment you met with her when you were young. She began to take control of you right after renaming you and doing your hair for the very first time. After that there were other things she did that helped her take greater control of you, such as asking you not to wash, particularly your hair. That in itself simply confirms to me that the major control she had over you was in the hair and the cleaning of yourself."

"No!" said Jevan emphatically. "She's never had control over me!"

"Then why haven't you left her?" I asked

"Especially after she has beaten you and even sent you down here to be a judge against your will?" offered Böder, softly but with feeling.

"And you know, deep in your heart, that you could have left at any time you wanted, if you were able to choose to," said Traxxa. "We all saw what you did to those in the arena; do you think you couldn't have done that easily enough to one witch and a caravan of street performers?"

There was a pause and we could see the lovely giantess slowly processing this information. Finally she spoke. "You know, I did feel a sort of release and a little freer the moment I had the bath and washed my hair or rather when Böder washed my hair."

We all looked at our friend and we smiled at his slight embarrassment.

"Well done, Böder!" said Kaira comfortingly, "And don't worry. You're among friends!"

"But it was the moment that Kaira cut my hair, that I felt the most complete in years." And here she paused again as she realized the truth of what she was saying.

"I've been looking around," said Traxxa quietly and gently. "And this place is quite interesting, what can you tell us about this apartment, Jevan?"

Jevan was brought back to where she was with a start and replied, a little nervously. "Why do you ask me this?"

"Well this apartment or cell -- you can call it what you like -- was made specifically for a giant, or perhaps *giants*. If you have been with Zharlla since you were, what, 10 years old and she has been coming through here on an annual basis, then I would say that of all of us here you would know this apartment a lot better than we would!"

"What are you saying?" Böder asked suddenly very wary, suspecting there might be something more sinister in this line of questioning.

"Please Böder!" said Traxxa strongly but still with his soft voice. "This is all part of the healing and separation. Jevan needs to talk this through and realize for herself where she is and what she is about to do!"

"And what is she about to do – good Ser Traxxa?" Böder said with feeling and with emphasis on Traxxa's name. We could tell he was making an immense effort to try and restrain himself.

Traxxa turned towards Böder and said gently and with the smallest hint of a smile playing around the corners of his mouth. "Why -- good Ser Böder, she is going to run away with you to your island. But more importantly for us, she is running away from the witch that has been controlling her for well over fifteen years! And unfortunately Jevan needs to recognize this. Now please Jevan tell us about this apartment and why is it specifically designed to hold a giant?"

Jevan appeared very nervous. Again, Kaira spoke up as she placed her hand on Jevan's knee. "It's alright, Jevan. You, too, are amongst friends who want to help you!"

Jevan looked nervously towards Kaira and then at Böder before she finally spoke --slowly at first, but gaining momentum once she got going. "I have been with Zharlla since I was 8 years of age. For nearly ten of those years with her, we have been coming to Regil-Ter as part of Zharlla's annual pilgrimage to the south for the winter months. When we came here, Zharlla would lease me out for money to be the companion of the games resident giant judge."

Here she paused as we took in the impact that this information might have had upon us.

"His name was Muxtla and this apartment was apparently made specifically for him. Muxtla told me a little bit about this apartment. For instance I know the hot pool was fashioned and made for him after he was made a captive here. But I only ever used that room for my ablutions and only used the pool to douche but never to wash. Zharlla had instructed me never to wash but more specifically never to wash my hair.

"I hate to say this, but, I have always been proud of my smell. In point of fact, I felt that my being dirty has helped keep the unwanted affections of both manimals and giants at bay. But up until now, there was never any man for me quite like Muxtla, for the most obvious reason that he and I were both giants."

And here she looked at Böder nervously but she continued quickly all the same.

"But he never touched me!"

"And why is that?" asked Böder almost as nervously.

"Because, whilst he was held here for the games, he told me that one day they poisoned his food which put him to sleep. When he woke up he found that he had been castrated!"

And here she paused as we all took in the horror of what she had just told us. Böder, Jareck and Kaira weren't really sure what she meant until Traxxa showed them a quick movement in mime and then they too understood and Kaira moaned, "Oohh nooo!"

"Yes." Jevan said nodding her head in accordance with Kaira's feelings. "So when I came along, Muxtla's only interest in me was for the companionship of another giant. Just someone his own size to keep him company, to talk with and to listen to him as he voiced his fears and his pain, I guess. He was a very lonely old giant who had become sad and bitter with his lot. He had been abused much like I had been, but in a slightly different way. Apparently he had been a healthy young giant until they captured him and made him the resident giant here in Regil-Ter. It was here that they took his manhood from him and made him serve the people as a judge not only in the games but also as a guard for the elders of the city.

So I received no real intimacy from Muxtla. He didn't touch me nor did he ever ask me to lie with him even to help keep him warm during the night. This was just one of the many things he complained to me about. Personally, I think Muxtla was slightly disgusted with me, probably because I was dirty and smelled, but more so with himself for he wouldn't even let me touch him to comfort him in any way whatsoever. Although, I know he used to like me being around him.

"He was the resident giant here in Regil-Ter and he was used for ceremonial purposes and as a judge for the games, as I said. But he told me once that the only time he really felt free was when he was alone in the arena when it was empty. I knew Muxtla was very unhappy here, but this cell or cage is giant-proof even with your mace and sword, Böder, you will never get out of here without help. That's why I want to stay here with you until we leave together. I believe they have plans to keep Böder here as they did with Muxtla and will no doubt take away his manhood as well just to keep him in line, or subservient to their wishes. If I leave him here, I don't believe I will ever see him whole again!"

There was a long contemplative pause from all of us before Böder asked nervously as though he was almost afraid of hearing the answer. "And what happened to Muxtla?"

"Five years ago, it was during the games, Muxtla just gave up trying. I was watching him in the arena from the waiting area like you were watching me today. I knew something was up with him as he had been acting stranger than usual all day. By this I mean he was cold, impersonal, and more distant from me than I had ever known him to be. Then when he was in the arena he didn't even try to pick up any of the weapons they had left on the pitch for him. He simply lay down on the pitch and let the criminals he was supposed to judge kill him. They couldn't do any real damage even with their weapons he was just so big and his skin so leathery, but they did manage to slit his throat and the arteries in his legs and arms and everyone watched him bleed out before they could do anything at all about it. Needless to say, the stadium exploded into chaos and it took nearly twenty judges and many arrows from the archers just to bring everything back under control.

"When Muxtla died, the officials of Regil-Ter wanted me to take his place and keep me on as the resident giant. But Zharlla wouldn't release me. They tried to keep me here through force and wouldn't even let Zharlla visit me. Zharlla gave them a warning about what she would do, but they just laughed at her, that is until all the children of the elders of Regil-Ter came down with a strange illness. Zharlla told them if they didn't release me within one day, then their children would begin to die. Of course they didn't believe her! But when the two oldest ones died within the first day they immediately rushed to secure my release.

"I think they will want to keep Böder here to replace Muxtla and make another resident, giant, judge out of him. As Traxxa noticed, these rooms are a cell specifically designed for a giant or giants. So the only way that I will leave this cell is with Böder beside me and that I believe can only be done through the arena somehow!"

As she was speaking we could see the tears in her eyes. And we knew the truth of what she had been talking about. But I looked curiously over towards Traxxa and somehow I knew that he had known about Muxtla and possibly even about Jevan coming here to be a companion for Muxtla despite him being a judge in the games a year after Muxtla had died.

Just then Traxxa stood up and walked purposefully over to Böder and said strongly. "Come walk with me Böder, we should talk some about what you wish to do and what we can do to help you and Jevan get out of this stadium and cause some damage in the process!"

The rest of us sat in silence as Traxxa and Böder walked into the bathing room. Later Traxxa told me what he had talked to Böder about.

TRAXXA

"I have seen the arena Böder and there are two areas where you can focus on to provide first a distraction and then possibly a means of escape. The first area is the fire pit. Once this is lit this will provide fire and possibly smoke which may help reduce the chance of being seen from certain areas within the arena. Especially from the archers who will be your biggest problem. Remember we don't know what they have dipped their arrows into; this may well be poison or drugs. So don't be afraid to start throw flaming branches into the stands or at the archers themselves. This is a great way to gain a distraction and earn yourself some time. The big problem will be dealing with the bowmen in the arches. I may have to give them some special attention just to help you when you need it most.

"The second thing to do is to focus on the monoliths. If even one can be made to topple towards the wall then you might very well have for yourself a bridge in which to use in order to help you climb up into the stands. Once there you will have a very strong chance of getting out of the stadium. Whilst you are doing this, I on the other hand will try and get to the mechanism that releases the door to the waiting area and see if I can't open all the gates and provide you with another way out as well. In any case, I urge you to focus on just one monolith and this should be the one closest to the pavilion nearest the waiting area. That is where we will be sitting and is also where Kyrack and his family will be. If you can get amongst them then the archers will never dare to fire arrows at you whilst you are so close to their captain and his family."

Here I paused for a moment before continuing. "Perhaps we'll need a further distraction." I thought for a moment or two before I came up with an alternative plan and smiling I told Böder, "You know, I think I'll give instructions to Bartrow to come up out of the sewers. It might be interesting to see what kind of nonsense he can get himself into in some of the darker places in the rooms beneath the stadium. He's young, I know, but he is very strong and extremely quick in the dark. He's also fairly resourceful and who knows what kind of mischief he could get up to on his own in a place like this."

And here both Böder and I suddenly smiled knowingly.

"Bartrow, you can still hear him, is digging in the sewers to make a hole big enough for your mace to come up through. I want you to go into the arena with more than what they are going to give you. Perhaps we should go and give him a hand?"

JELLICK

When Traxxa and Böder emerged from the bathing room, Kaira was first to respond and went over to them. "Do you want me to braid Böder's hair to help keep it out of his eyes again?" She asked Traxxa.

Traxxa paused for just a moment and looked directly at her before shaking his head for no. "He needed to have his hair under control when he was facing the very real threat of Trow in the mountains in poor light! But now we need to have his hair flying about him to announce loudly who he is. The crowds of Regil-Ter will remember Böder as the great fiery giant fighter and his flying untamed hair will be a great banner for this. Also, in the arena, he won't need to keep the hair out of his eyes or off his face because it won't affect him in any way as he faces those before him, who, after all, will present themselves as no real threat to him. You will see what I mean in a very short while!"

He patted Kaira's shoulder comfortingly before saying. "But thanx for wanting to be of assistance in much the same way that you looked after Jevan. You have a lovely caring heart and we appreciate that very much!"

Kaira smiled weakly at this offhanded compliment as Traxxa made to move on. During this small interaction I had been watching Böder and noticed that he hadn't even looked down at Kaira which was most unlike him. He seemed distant and completely focused on the task that was fast approaching him. He was once more carrying his familiar mace with him and had a very formidable look in his eyes. It was the same kind of look he had had just before he began his battle with Trow in the mountains.

I looked quickly towards Jevan who I don't believe had ever seen Böder in this frame of mind before. Later she told me, when she saw him emerge from the pool room, she suddenly remembered how Böder had introduced himself as –

'The one who had come to rescue her'!

So upon seeing him as he was, as he emerged from the pool room with Traxxa, she realized for the first time ever and with a great warm smile that this was a very real possibility indeed!

CHAPTER TWENTY-ONE

JELLICK

When I had time to talk with him, Traxxa told me that he had told Bartrow to light some fires in the giant's room and wreak havoc wherever he could beneath the stadium. He also gave him specific instruction on what to do and where to go once he had created enough confusion and panic. But he warned him that if he met up with more trouble than he could handle, he was to slip back down into the sewers and meet up with us by the boats down at the docks.

Traxxa also instructed us that he wanted all the rooms of the giant's cell in complete darkness. This he told us would allow Bartrow to do what he liked best and was why Böder and Jevan turned off all the light crystals and doused the fire, before they left to go out into the arena.

All of us, except Kaira and Jevan, were taken out of the cell just before Böder was called out. So, when it finally came time for Böder to go out into the arena as a judge, we *(Traxxa, Jareck and I)* were in the western pavilion watching expectantly along with Kyrack and his family. We were there as Kyrack's invited guests. Kaira was with Jevan who was still holding onto her sword and they were watching Böder from within the waiting area. Somehow Kaira had been given extraordinary privileges of being able to remain with the giantess such was her influence over Kyrack who had fallen under the lovely mountain girls spell, *(very much like we all had)*!

It was early evening and darkness was settling slowly down over Regil-Ter. Meanwhile the whole stadium was abuzz and lit up with flaming torches and light crystals of every size. From when Jevan had completed her role as judge and vanquished all her prisoners, there had been a number of lesser battles handled by other competent judges. Whilst a couple of the judges had been injured none were in a serious condition and all the prisoners had been dispensed with as the games depicted they should be. This had taken place throughout the whole afternoon.

Most of the other judges had only one or two criminals to dispense with at any one time. Of course there were a few exceptional judges who could take on and kill three prisoners by themselves -- perhaps even more, if asked. Then there were two fights where two judges had taken on five prisoners. In all of these fights, where there was more than one criminal involved in any one game, there were always extra judges on standby or close at hand to help out should anything go wrong for the judge in the middle of the arena. In other words the games were designed so that no criminal would make it out of the stadium alive. Essentially you could say the games were rigged. The authorities knew it, the judges knew it, and even most of the audience knew it. Only the criminals were under the illusion they had a chance, which gave the games the edge it needed to be entertaining and enthralling. And that was what it was all about, disposing of unwanted criminals whilst providing entertainment for the crowds in the city of Regil-Ter.

The crowds, in this instance, were maintaining their buoyancy by singing rowdy songs and chanting and playing instruments they had brought in with them. Food and drink were being consumed and some people were even dancing where it was possible. But as the afternoon turned to evening they were becoming just a little restless and there was a palpable air of expectancy racing around the people in the stands which overflowed from the stadium and made its way up into the terraces.

Once the pitch had been cleared and cleaned and raked from the last encounter, there was a lull in the crowd as one by one the gates in the arena wall around the pitch opened and the criminals began to emerge. Here the booing and the whistles started and the lively chanting changed to hate songs. But even during this open display of hostility and involvement by the crowd they recognized that something was different. Usually it was the judges who were brought out first into the middle of the pitch. This was so the crowd could give applause, throw garments and flowers even money towards them as a kind of thanx for being part of the games. But this time the fierce, brutally ugly, heavily armed and extremely dangerous prisoners were being released first and the crowd let them know what they thought of them. Instead of flowers, rotten fruit and vegetables were thrown towards the most hated people of M'Lenn-Fida at that moment. But this didn't seem to intimidate the criminals in the middle of the arena it merely served as a focus upon which to summon up their most violent beings. They rallied together as one in the middle of the pitch pitting their screams and shouts and waving their weapons at the crowd who had come to watch them fight for their lives.

Finally, when they were all standing in the middle of the arena there was a criminal crowd of some twenty prisoners all with weapons and shields as well as another nine criminals who had remained in their animal state. Three prisoners had been tied to the stakes in the middle of the fire ring and two prisoners had been chained to the stone monoliths around the arena. These were quickly cut down and recruited into the ranks of the damned. It was really like the meeting Jevan had encountered when she had come out earlier in the day. A large number of criminals had been introduced after announcing Jevan as the one great judge. However, in this case, it was the criminals who had been introduced first to build tension as they waited for the next great judge to appear. When the people in the stands realized this, there came a sudden lull in the crowd and an expectant hush raced around the arena like a wildfire. It was as if the whole city had suddenly gone quiet. Then the whispers that the troll killing, treasure retrieving giant, Böder was about to act as judge for the final and major game of the day. The quiet and the whispers were more unnerving to the criminals in the middle of the pitch than all the shouting and open hostility that the crowd had recently been showing them. A sense of nervous energy began to mount within the ugly group of gangsters, thieves, murderers, rapists and vicious thugs waiting on the pitch.

Just as the hush began to break the announcer stood up and Böder's name and his exploits in the mountains were read out and he was finally announced as the next great judge.

The following applause and cheering was thunderous and deafening beyond belief such was the enthusiastic reception he received from the people in the stands and the terraces around the stadium. The gate to the waiting area slowly opened and as the cheering increased there came the most violently savage, brutally crazed, bloodthirsty roar that anyone had ever heard before or since and the crowd was shocked into silent submission. Then, before the roar had barely ceased, Böder rushed out of the waiting area and leapt thunderously high right into the middle of the pitch.

He was wielding his huge mace and before anyone knew what was happening he was amongst the crowd of criminals, sweeping them aside like dust before a broom. His beautiful boyish face had been replaced with that of an enraged and violent giant and this alone took our breath away. We could only look on in shocked awe as the sheer majesty of his power and energy was shown to us time and time again as he swiftly, brutally and callously dispensed judgement as only a giant of his strength and speed could do. The savage criminals in the middle of the pitch stood no chance whatsoever. In fact, you could have put another hundred manimals out into the arena to face Böder and they still wouldn't have stood any kind of a chance of survival at all.

I looked on in stunned awe at the giant in the middle of the arena and I have to say that at that moment I was so very proud to know he was my friend. I continued to watch in subdued shock as he violently annihilated all the lowlife creatures in the arena with such venom and fire. The sheer ferocity with which he moved and fought within the arena was just too terrifying to describe fully. Mangled limbs and lifeless bodies were constantly being thrown around the pitch, such was the force of the huge mace his fists and feet inflicted and all with such a speed that many times there were things that Böder did that we only registered in our minds seconds after the events had taken place. But, by then, our giant friend had gone on to administer other bouts of carnage and grief amongst the criminals in his care.

When he had rushed out into the arena, Böder was wearing a loincloth, his shin guards and a tunic that Kaira had made for him. He came out swinging violently at anything that got in its way with the mace in his right hand! He had been carrying a handful of spears in his left, which had come up to him through the sewers. All but one spear had been dropped in a bundle so that he could return to them whenever he wanted one. This allowed him to move quickly and with greater freedom. Each spear served its purpose well but, after a very short time, they were inevitably reduced to a handful of matchsticks. These were quickly discarded to be replaced by another as he passed by the bundle in his pursuit of his work as a judge.

When Kyrack and his men had come to escort us out of Böder's cell, I noted that they had seen the mace and bundle of spears. Whilst I'm sure they might have wanted to make mention that he was not allowed to carry these weapons into the arena, by the looks they gave one another, none said anything at all to the giant and certainly none were willing to try and take them off him. I also noticed, as we started up the ramp, that Kyrack despatched two of his guards to make a general inspection of the giants quarters just to make sure there was nothing else inside that should not be there. Presumably, he hoped to find out how these weapons came to be in the giant's possession here in his cell. In any case, I never saw those two guards again.

As Böder continued his unabated rampage in the middle of the arena, I looked quickly across to Traxxa. I wondered silently to myself what kind of instruction did this incredible warrior give to our quiet, likeable, young giant friend to turn him into this rampaging, mindless, low-life killing judge?

Later on, when I asked him this question, he looked at me and said.

"Just before we left the bathhouse, I turned to Böder and told him that he had nothing to fear from anyone here in Durogg. 'Remember,' I said, "you're a great minking giant, so be the giant you are deep down – in fact you're one of the finest of your race that I have ever had the privilege to meet and know! So when you go out into that arena tonight, you let everybody know that Böder is here and absolutely nothing is going to stop you from wreaking the greatest amount of damage Regil-Ter has ever seen in all the ages it has been a city and has held these Judicial Games! You got that?"

"And here he nodded once towards me. That is when I saw the look of who he was deep down come into his eyes as they turned dark brown and I knew he would definitely be a force to be reckoned with in the arena tonight."

Now, as I looked towards Traxxa, he stood up and quietly left the pavilion. As he left, he looked at me and nodded his head to indicate the time had come for us to start preparing to leave the stadium.

All the criminals were dead or dying with mangled bodies and limbs from one end of the pitch to the other. The sand was an ocean of deep red from blood and gore, but Böder was still restless and looking for more prisoners to deal with. At that moment a huge cage like door parted, one which we hadn't really noticed until then. It was on the opposite side of the arena to the giants waiting area, but now as this gate began opening we all focused on what might be coming out for it was much too big for an ordinary criminal. There came a huge roar from the dark depths behind the gate! It was that of a large hungry creature. Suddenly, to everyone's frightened disbelief, out rushed a drazil. It was much smaller than the one that had been killed on Böder's Island but it was still a drazil nonetheless.

I looked towards Kyrack who was smiling and obviously enjoying the show and I asked him. "Is this part of the judicial games? I didn't realize drazils committed criminal acts here in M'Lenn-Fida."

Kyrack paused just long enough to look at me, before replying. "This is entertainment for the people of Regil-Ter. This is a savage giant, who has acted as a judge and dispensed his judgement, but with weapons that weren't sanctioned by the games' authorities. So in a sense he has been found guilty of murder. In any case, it is all for the amusement and entertainment of the city of Regil-Ter and the people of M'Lenn-Fida."

"Oh I'll be sure and tell Böder that when he has finished dealing with this drazil judge."

Though the look I received from Kyrack gave no volume, I felt sure he was saying there was no way in Hadyes that Böder was ever going to be told about my last remark.

I looked back towards Böder in the middle of the arena to see how he was coping and I smiled broadly when I saw that Kyrack and his plans were being thwarted.

The drazil was about fourteen meters in length, with a further eight meters of tail. Its head and shoulders were just over three meters from the ground. But all this potential danger to our giant friend in the middle of the pitch was being lost, as this hungry scavenger made straight for the closest bits of dead criminal it could see. I looked quickly at Kyrack and the smug smile on his face had frozen and was being replaced by pursed lips of anger and frustrated rage. I saw him give a signal and almost immediately another loud roar came bellowing out from the same gate the first drazil had come out of. I watched in silent horror as a second, similar sized drazil as the first rushed out into the arena. When this drazil saw the first drazil it slowed down and moved carefully around and away from it. Then, much like the first drazil, this too went straight to the closest piece of carrion, lying in a bloodied mess on the pitch, and began devouring it.

At the first sight of the drazils, Böder had visibly flinched and paused as he readied himself for the fight of his life. But as the drazils made no attempt to attack him, he looked around a little confused. This was not getting him anywhere. He looked around the arena and made a decision to engage the drazils. They were obviously hungry scavengers who were bent on feeding but he knew they were also territorial and might perceive him as a threat to their territory. But of course they had to see him first and there was just too much food for them to worry about him at the moment, so he decided that he would have to change all that and make them aware of him.

During this time, the crowd had lost their voice as they had watched in frightened awe as the mighty drazils had emerged from their gate and gone straight to the bloody corpses lying nearby. Very few people had actually seen a live drazil and lived to tell the tale. But that was in the wilds. Here, in captivity, the people were the rulers and watching a pair of very dangerous creatures eating what had been a pack of violent criminals until recently could only hold their attention and keep them entertained for a very short period of time. Especially after seeing such a wondrous piece of violent mayhem inflicted on the scum of society only minutes before by their now favourite judge. But many in the audience also saw that this was an attempt by the authorities to destroy this giant judge. Whilst they did not understand the reasoning, nor all the facts concerning the matter, they were a volatile crowd who had become a little annoyed at the authorities for wanting to be rid of so tremendous a judge. So, soon after the drazils had been released, the crowd became restless and began booing those in charge and turning their disgruntled attentions towards those occupying the pavilions.

The crowd stopped booing as Böder moved to what was seen to be the closest monolith. Böder reached the rock monolith just in front and to the left of the pavilion where we were sitting. The monolith was three meters wide, a meter thick, and fifteen meters high. After readying himself Böder began smashing the back of it close to the ground with his mace. At each strike, great chunks of the monolith came away so that if anyone looked closely they would have said it was showing signs of being unbalanced. The crowd thought he was doing this to try and attract the attention of the drazils, because between each swing of his mace, Böder would call out to the drazils taunting them and cursing them. When this was obviously failing, Böder went and picked up a spear from the few left in the discarded pile nearby and threw it at the closest drazil to him.

It was one thing to try and attract the attention of a drazil by smashing into a monolith and making a loud distracting noise. But for most people who knew anything about drazils, the last thing anyone would think of doing, as far as the crowd were concerned, would be to try and antagonise a drazil by throwing a sharp object or spear at it and draw serious attention to oneself especially in an arena where escape is virtually impossible. So when Böder began throwing the first of his spears at the drazil the crowd stopped and held their collective breaths to see what might happen next.

At first the drazil did little more than just look at the giant as he came in closer twirling his mace in one hand and holding a spear up threateningly in the other. But when the second thrown spear pierced its hind leg after being hurled by this irritating giant the drazil knew that it had to deal with this threat to its territory quickly, so it turned and began to give chase.

When the drazil moved away from the carcass it was eating and started to pursue him, Böder turned and ran to the fire pit. He picked up a torch from the corner post as he went and halfway across the fenced off area he threw the torch into the wood behind him and hurtled over the fence on the other side away from the drazil. The wood was very dry and had been covered in oils so that it roared into flames the moment the flaming torch touched the wood. The drazil had just been about to clamber over the fence in pursuit of the giant when the pit leapt into flames. Staggering in its pursuit the drazil readjusted its run and made to go around the fire pit. The second drazil was still eating but was momentarily distracted by the fire and looked up from its meal. He saw the running drazil chasing the fleeing giant. It was then that it recognized a real threat to its territory and somehow knew that there would be no peace until this large creature had been dealt with as well. And so the second drazil left its meal also and moved slowly cautiously around the other side of the fire pit towards the giant.

Böder stepped to the left and just behind the monolith he had attacked earlier. Here he took a step back and using both hands he brought his mace raking down and across the back of the monolith. More great chunks of rock splintered and exploded out from the base of the monolith near where it disappeared into the ground of the arena. It now looked dangerously unstable, so Böder stepped purposefully in front of the monolith and waited for the drazil to get around the fire pit and make straight towards him. Böder picked up another of his spears and hurled it at the fast approaching drazil. The spear hit the head and glanced off without really making any visible sign of an impact. But it must have done something to the creature for it increased its speed and put its head down as though it intended to pummel the giant into the monolith and pin him there to be dealt with by tooth and claw at its pleasure.

Just as the drazil was on the giant it used its four powerful hind legs to propel it up and on towards its prey. At the last second, just before the drazils head went down to become a battering ram against him, Böder dropped and rolled to the side of the monolith. For his size he moved with the agility and speed of a close quarter combatant. But the drazil was unstoppable -- that is until its head, followed quickly by five tonnes of its own body and muscle, smacked with a resounding thud into the monolith. The sight of the drazil hitting the monolith with its head made even the toughest of the massive audience wince in empathy for its pain as they felt for the creature despite its savage nature and intention.

The solid impact of the drazils head and weight upon the stone monolith was extremely loud and rendered the large carnivorous lizard unconscious. Böder was up in a flash and quickly checked to see what kind of effect the drazil had made upon the large stone slab. Realizing it had not done what he had wanted, he moved to the back of the monolith and took another swing at the back and base of the monolith and then rushing around to the front of the monolith he prepared himself. He quickly looked to see what the second drazil was up to. He was relieved to see that whilst it was coming around the fire pit, it was still only stalking him, moving slowly, cautiously, warily. However he also recognized the signs that once this drazil had fully cleared the fire pit, it would undoubtedly prepare itself to run and attack. Without bothering to think on this, Böder turned back to the task at hand and ran and launched himself to have the full weight of his body hitting the large flat side of the monolith, as high up as he could. The moment he hit the monolith he heard the wonderful sound of the brittle stone snapping and breaking apart. He quickly assessed his work and with the damage done by his mace and the impact of himself and the still unconscious drazil the monolith was ready to fall. He did a quick check and the second drazil was just beginning to run towards him. Throwing his mace to the ground and bracing his feet wide and low he used his body to meet with the monolith and then with all the strength of his legs he pushed long and low and hard and felt the monolith tip ever so slowly towards the wall of the arena. Then, as the gap at the back broke down, the monolith tipped over and fell just as Böder felt he had given all that he had to give and there was no more.

He rolled exhausted off the large stone slab as it continued to fall. Halfway down it stopped suddenly as the top of the monolith hit the arena wall just below the balcony where the archers were waiting for the command to shoot the giant if he should try to escape or elude the drazils. Böder fell away from the monolith just as the second drazil was almost upon him. In fact it was even reaching out for the large giant when it suddenly realized there was a way of escape. It lost focus on the giant instantly and instead rushed straight ahead up the stone bridge of the monolith and on towards the audience in the stands. Many of the archers just stood and watched, so overwhelmed were they by the creature racing up the stone bridge towards them. A couple let off a few arrows but these only angered the drazil even more, and certainly did not slow it down at all. Instead it reached the wall and with its four powerful hind legs it launched itself off the stone monolith *(which was now a ramp)* and went up and over the parapet and into the convulsing screaming, scattering, crowd. This violent reacting crowd, who had, only moments before been mesmerized by the frantic actions of a doomed giant, were now considering themselves doomed instead and were taking whatever frantic and drastic actions necessary to ensure their own survival!

The next sequence of events happened very quickly and all at once. The first thing to happen was, as Böder rolled over and over out of the way of the drazil running up the fallen monolith towards its freedom, he retrieved his mace and another spear. The dazed drazil came back from it unconscious journey just in time to see the first drazil climbing out of the arena and into the stadium seats. Quickly realizing that here was an opportunity to gain its freedom as well, the second drazil simply stood up and scampered as fast as his recovering head and body would allow. This time the alert archers focussed on the threat and sent a flurry of arrows towards the dangerous lizard. With its snout and shoulders peppered with arrows, the angry drazil took a swipe at the archers in their alcoves and its hideously long claws pulled five archers out from the ledge to drop them mangled and bleeding onto the arena floor some seven meters below. And then it, too, was up the last few meters and clambering into the stands. Needless to say, the stand had become a seething chaotic mess with the audience, guards, dead and dying being scattered about like remnant leftovers from a banquet by the two drazils on the rampage.

At this very moment, another distraction began which caused the guards to be suddenly swept up in a rising sea of confusion and fear. Large billowing black smoke came up through the waiting area and made itself known by expanding as it reached the fresh air of the arena. This was the final straw in the seething stadium of half scared people, so what was left of the audience – those not directly affected by the drazils -- stood up and moved as one towards the stairs. They began screaming inconsolably and rushed headlong for the exits in a violent frenzy of escape and self-preservation.

In this confusion and fear, Böder was up and running as well, with his mace and last spear in hand, towards the gate of the giants waiting area. As he approached the gate he took a quick look up to the ledge where the archers were supposed to be watching and waiting and aiming. But he saw no-one was paying any attention to him or his rush towards freedom. He did however see us in the last section of the alcove waving frantically for him to come and help us get down and move with him towards freedom.

From the moment that Böder swung his mace at the monolith, Earlich, Jareck and I, without drawing attention to ourselves, had moved out of the pavilion as discreetly and unobtrusively as possible following after Traxxa. Traxxa had taken care of the two Buffamen guards outside the entranceway which was surprising in and of itself. Later I learned he had used his throwing stars which had an immediate effect on the guards and allowed us to move away from the pavilion without being stopped or challenged.

As planned we made our way down the circular stairway to the archer's walkway and into their specially designed alcoves. Here to our surprise and relief we found that all of the archers we were expecting to find had moved off. That is except for the three who lay dead in their own little alcove -- obviously more of Traxxa's handiwork. The others had either been called away or had followed the destructive path of the escaping drazils. In any case there were no archers to be seen.

We looked over the alcove wall and saw Böder directly beneath us making his way towards the gate and the waiting area. Jareck and I got his attention and asked to be helped down into the arena even as the gates to the waiting area clicked open and slowly began to part.

We were helped down quickly by Böder and we moved as one through the gates. Jevan rushed out to embrace Böder even before the gates had opened fully. Without stopping to recount all that had happened we moved quickly towards the walkway beneath the stadium. Here we found the doors from the waiting area that were supposed to be blocking the walkway had not been opened completely. This allowed both Böder and Jevan to move past them and into the walkway with us. Just as we emerged from out of the waiting area, Traxxa and a heavily disguised Bartrow (*who was struggling to carry a curiously rather large cumbersome sack of something or other*) emerged from the depths on the opposite side of the walkway amidst the fires and the smoke which was billowing profusely out from the giants' accommodation. Böder saw Bartrow struggling with his over large sack and quietly relieved him of his burden and gave him his last spear to carry instead.

So we moved as one with the flow of the frantically rushing people who suddenly parted and gave the giants, the troll and us a wide berth, allowing us to move quickly and unhindered out of the exits and into the streets of Regil-Ter.

Later, when we talked with Traxxa, we learned that once he had disappeared from the pavilion he had dropped down into the archers terrace and dispensed his own kind of justice. He had deliberately killed those archers who were most capable of harming Böder when he would try to escape through the waiting area. He then continued down to find the mechanisms which opened both sets of gates into the waiting area. This was what had allowed us to meet up with Kaira and Jevan and helped us continue our escape without a problem.

Looking back at the large billowing smoke I realized that most of the guards and servants of the stadium were completely focussed on saving the stadium from burning down completely and recapturing or killing the escaping marauding drazils. So I was quietly confident that little effort would be made to search for us or even try to interfere with Böder and Jevan's efforts at escaping. This no doubt would include Kyrack who would have had the most to lose, it would seem, if Böder was to leave without finishing his time as a judge in the games.

When we emerged from the stadium we followed after Traxxa who led us immediately into the shadows of the closest side-street away from the hustling milling crowd Böder suddenly realized he was carrying something but didn't know what it was.

"What have you got in here Bartrow?" He asked in a sudden bout of curiosity. He quickly looked inside and when he saw the robes and towels that he and Jevan and been using during their time in their cell he smiled down towards the ugly young troll, shook his head and said. "As if you didn't have enough to do? Thanx my good friend!"

Bartrow smiled a grimacing sort of a smile, nodded his head once as if to say you're welcome, then he sprinted ahead, spear in hand, readying himself to act as point guard with Traxxa.

CHAPTER TWENTY-TWO

JELLICK

We left the stadium behind us spewing forth its manimals and billowing plumes of smoke. Traxxa led us through a course of lanes and walkways which took us, more or less, straight toward the docks. We avoided a number of lanes because they were just too small to allow our two giant companions through with ease. At every corner and intersection we saw the streets and lanes on this large island alive with frantic, confused, manimals running scared and fleeing for their lives. In contrast, we moved quietly efficiently as a tight group. Böder was constantly twirling his mace with nervous energy whilst Jevan carried her sword safe in its sheath. They took short determined steps whilst Traxxa and Bartrow ran on ahead keeping lookout and directing us away from the slightest sign of danger or warning us to stay still and hidden till the problems ahead had passed us by. But these were rare and we really didn't need to worry about being intercepted by anyone at all before we reached the docks.

After what everyone had seen of Böder *(and Jevan come to think of it)* in the arena this day and with the people of Regil-Ter in a total panic, I'm sure the last thing anyone would want to do was to try and apprehend two supremely competent giants one armed with a mace and the other with a sword.

So it was that we reached the *Riverrock* without incident. Earlich was there to greet us warmly as he had been down on the docks all day with Captain Stemm. He had been organising the ordering and loading of supplies and ensuring the boat would be ready at a moment's notice! As we were about to rush aboard, Traxxa signalled to me to wait for a moment and told me that he, Böder and Bartrow were heading off to take care of the Regil-Ter fleet. Traxxa then raced up the gangway and after giving a quick salute to Stemm in recognition of his captaincy, he grabbed one of the bags which he had left aboard the *Riverrock* when we had first visited with captain Stemm the day before.

As Böder handed the bag that Bartrow had recovered from the cell to Jevan I looked around and remembered when we had first scouted out the docks. Traxxa and I had seen the two boats filled with armed guards and warriors at the far end of the furthest wharf. We knew they would pose a real problem for us if we tried to make an escape over water with Captain Stemm. Traxxa helped Böder unstrap his shin guards and dropped them onto the dock. He also encouraged the giant to leave his mace behind as well. Hopefully, he reasoned with him, he wouldn't need it and besides it would just slow the young giant down later when they were to swim out to meet with the *Riverrock* in mid-stream.

The three moved off as quietly as an eight meter giant, a troll and a seasoned warrior could do along the quiet and darkened docks of Regil-Ter. Traxxa was carrying one of his suspicious looking bags whilst Böder was taking short strides to accommodate his companions and Bartrow appeared eager and happy to be going into battle with his new spear and was prancing about like an eager child going towards a carnival.

Later Traxxa related to me all that had occurred during their encounter with the two war vessels.

Jareck, Earlich and I walked across the gangplank onto the *Riverrock* to make ourselves known to Captain Stemm who greeted me warmly and we embraced as good companions.

"Welcome aboard Tor Jellick." He said. "It looks like you've left this town in a bit of a fluster!"

"Now there's an understatement if ever I've heard one Captain!" I replied smiling. "Are we ready to cast off?"

"We are and can do as soon as we get Traxxa's signal!" He replied evenly, revealing a knowing smile in anticipation of the real excitement that lay ahead of us. "I'm assuming that he and Böder have gone off to deal with the two guard boats that we talked about the other day?"

I nodded a yes and said. "All we do now is wait and be ready to move quickly! You don't mind if we bring some more of our things aboard whilst we wait?"

"Good Tor Jellick, you're always so polite. It's always such a pleasure to talk with you. However, as of now, please consider this boat as your own until your journey is complete!"

I thanked him and went to attend to Jevan and to bring what little gear we had left ashore on board. Earlich and Jareck carried the shin guards and the mace aboard whilst I took Jevan over to where there were a number of empty warehouses and sheds along the dock. We had noticed these earlier during our scouting time and we now took advantage of them. I instructed Jevan to lie down on the docks in the shadows beneath the sheds and wait there until Traxxa and Böder gave us the signal to leave. Kaira and Jareck stayed with her to keep her company. She seemed happy enough with our plans and our intentions to leave Regil-Ter and was sensible enough to comply with our instructions without a word of complaint or fuss.

TRAXXA

We, my two warring companions and I, had gone as far as we could without being seen or drawing attention to ourselves. I cautioned Böder and Bartrow with a hand movement to stay in the shadows. Here I briefly recapped the next step in the overall plan which we had discussed at length several days earlier. However, now I told them exactly what was going to happen and what I expected of each of them. To their credit, both Böder and Bartrow nodded eagerly acknowledging they understood me and were still keen and prepared to go ahead.

"Alright then let's move. Böder you slip into the water and make your way in between the two boats. We will give you a couple of minutes until you're in position. When the first explosion happens you deal with the front boat first and then move as quickly and as quietly as you can to the back of the second boat. When the second explosion happens deal with the second boat and then start making your way out towards the middle of the river where we will meet with you there. Remember, the warriors should be occupied by our activities on the dock, but there may be one or two archers who will not have left their posts so just be conscious that you might still get an arrow in your head so stay out of sight and underwater for as long as you can. Do you understand what you are to do?"

Böder nodded his head.

"Good then off you go, and if anything goes wrong with us up here, we will call out for you. So don't be afraid to get up out of the water and join us in the battle which could be taking place anywhere on the dock or on one of the decks of the boats!"

Whilst I was grim faced as I said this, I saw there was a huge knowing smile on Böders baby face. Then without a word he moved off silently keeping as low down as he could towards the edge of the wharf. He saw a wooden tier lying uselessly on the dock and pointing to it he looked back towards me. He then made some quick hand signs which we had developed during our training together, to ask if he should take it with him.

"Perfect!" I mouthed, and gave a short rabbit punch into the air to indicate that every little bit at this moment would help.

Böder sat down on the edge of the wharf, grabbed the wooden tier and slipped quietly from the wharf into the water. He described it to me afterwards as, "it was cold and wet and it simply took my breath away!" But we heard nothing as he inhaled as best he could and moved slowly through the water towards the warrior vessels keeping to the shadows of the wharf and underneath it where he could.

As Böder moved off I divided my sack of items into two bags, then I looked around and grabbed a broken piece of wood and wrapped some cloth I had with me around it. I lit the cloth so that it became a small flaming torch, then Bartrow and I watched and waited until we were fairly certain that our giant friend had taken up his position in the water ahead of us. Together we made our way using the shadows and keeping out of sight as best we could up to the first boat. There were warriors everywhere, but mostly on the boats scouring the river for any sign of boating craft that was attempting to leave the city so late in the evening. I could see four but I suspected there were at least six guards on the docks by the gangplanks leading up to the war vessels.

They weren't really guards though; they were warriors who were bored watching the river for so long and for no apparent reason and were taking a measured break on the dock. So in respect to this, they were taken by complete surprise when a Wolfaman and a troll rushed out from the shadows and cut down three of their number before they even realized what was happening to them. After all who in their right minds was going to attack two fully loaded boats armed with warriors on the main dock of Regil-Ter? As Bartrow met with the remaining warriors on the docks with his wonderful new weapon, I lit another small piece of rag and placed it into one the two bags I was carrying. I then threw it high and long to land in the middle of the boat, where upon the jars inside the bag burst. Inside the jar was a mixture of oils and a rare powder which I had purchased from the fireworks master the other day. When the jars burst open the oil and the powder were released together which combined with the fire created a great explosion that made a very loud bang and which erupted into a large violent fireball shooting nearly ten meters into the air and sending burning hot oil all over the deck of the first boat. Those on the boat were thrown into sudden confusion. Some manimals were covered in burning oil and rags and started to scream with the pain before either jumping into the water or having the fire put out by those around them. The remaining three warriors on the dock were quickly despatched of by an over vigorous troll who simply loved killing. Once those on the dock had been dealt with, Bartrow and I moved on quickly to the front boat.

Böder later told me just before he heard the sound of fighting on the dock he was pleased to have found the rudder of the front boat under the water. Positioning himself carefully against the stern and using all his strength he pulled it apart feeling it crackle and break apart in his hands. At the sound of the explosion he stood up out of the water which was only waist deep for him and bringing back the wooden tier he smashed it into the base of the stern where the wood of the boat began to disappear into the water. His first attempt was too deep and he merely splashed water around him. Two more attempts and he succeeded in making a hole in the stern and immediately the river started to make its way into the large vessel. The moment he saw a hole big enough to start accepting water, Böder slipped again under the cover of the dock and made his way back to the stern of the first boat which was under fire and in pandemonium.

T.J.C.

JELLICK

When we heard and saw the first explosion and could see the rain of fire begin to climb up and spread out all over the boat at the wharf across from us, Captain Stemm and I knew that this was our signal to move out. He gave the orders to Eddron who was standing at the helm to cast off, whilst I called out to Jareck, Kaira and Jevan that it was time for us to leave. Jevan slipped into the water to swim alongside the boat. Here she gave a stifled squeal as the cold of the water caught her off guard. I looked to Captain Stemm and knew that this could present itself as a problem later on. She needed to be in the water for the moment though because she would have been too heavy and awkward for the *Riverrock*, at least not without proper ballast to compensate for her weight. In any case, she would not have been able to fit comfortably on the deck and would have disrupted the efficient running of the river craft where speed and departure were our primary concerns at the moment.

The ropes were released and to combat the cold of the water and build up some heat within herself, Jevan helped by holding onto the stern and began pushing the boat along with her legs. I noticed with concern that the water was up to her chest and rising. Kaira to her credit must have realized how difficult this all must be for Jevan. The first thing the lovely giantess had to do, upon her sudden release from the control of the witch for so many years was to help push a boat through a cold river to help us escape an angry city. And all for what? A chance to begin a new life with Böder, a giant she barely even knew.

I watched as Kaira went over to stand by the boats rail near to where Jevan's head was bobbing alongside the boat. From there she talked softly with Jevan comforting and reassuring her that all was well and possibly just to keep her company.

TRAXXA

Before the fire had taken a proper hold over the first boat, Bartrow and I had moved on to the front vessel which was our second boat. I could see the warriors on both boats were in confusion but there were still a few who recognized where the danger was coming from. Before those on the second boat could do anything though, Bartrow ran up and physically lifted the gangplank up and threw it into the water between the boat and the dock. Two warriors, who were on it, had been making their way down to the dock at the time. But they just fell into the water along with the plank.

As I ran down the dock to the second boat, I placed my makeshift torch into the second bag and before anyone could do anything I had lobbed it high up over into the second boat. I was careful to make sure it landed in a pile of sails, rope and rigging lying on the deck to ensure maximum damage and diversion. The following explosion was louder than the first and perhaps there was a greater resulting fiery form of chaos than had happened on the first boat but we didn't stick around to compare the damage.

At the back of the first boat, where those on board were still struggling to deal with the fire on their deck, Böder had found it easy enough to deal with this one's rudder in much the same way as the other boat. When this was done successfully he stood up in the water at its stern. He raised the broken tier once more and smashed it into the wooden stern three times maximising the greatest damage and watching the river find its way into the hull of the boat. Satisfied that he had done enough, he left the tier where it was and pushed himself out into the river and submerging his head he swam as far as he could before resurfacing.

Meanwhile, after the fiery bomb had left my hand, a couple of warriors had leapt from the second boat to meet with us on the dock. These few warriors were dealt with easily enough by the speed and agility of Bartrow who using his own weight simply pushed them backwards off the wharf and into the water before they could either use their weapons or regain their balance. I had to take up a solid sword attack to hold two other warriors at bay whilst Bartrow moved to catch up. I was just getting the better of the fight when Bartrow stabbed one of the swordsmen in the back and through the heart with his spear which allowed me to cripple the remaining warrior quickly and efficiently. I was just about finish him off when I saw plenty of reinforcements for them rushing along the dock from the first boat. I called out to Bartrow and we turned and ran down the wharf towards its end but not before I watched as Bartrow hurl the spear at an archer aboard the second vessel who was just lining up a shot at me.

The archer was taken out completely and the spear pushed him back several meters such was the strength and accuracy of the young troll's throw.

As we ran I sheathed my sword so that when we reached the end of the wharf, without thinking twice we leapt out into the river even as arrows and angry warriors came rushing down the dock after us.

Both Bartrow and I had known how cold the Mirack River was after having swum across it only two days earlier. Despite my familiarity with the cold it was still a shock to my system. But once in the water I knew how important it was for me to force myself to swim. This was all that was needed to get me going again. The first thing I did though was to check on Bartrow. But I needn't have bothered for the young troll was loving every minute of this short incursion on the dock and now the swim in the water. The cold and the wet didn't seem to bother him at all so together we made for the middle of the river. At one stage in our swim we heard the sound of a soft splash behind us. I looked back fearing pursuing warriors, so I was relieved to see Böder slowly making his way towards the middle of the river. I called out softly to gain his attention and directed him towards us.

"Now all we need is a boat to hang onto and we can get out of here!" He said smiling.

At this we all looked out to where we hoped we might see the shadow of a boat upon the river coming between us and the soft shine of the city lights. And the shadow of a craft was looming up on us very quickly. I saw the light of a crystal aboard being flashed towards us. I didn't think anything of it at the time. In fact I thought it was a late addition to our plans and a minking good idea it was to flash a light so we could identify the *Riverrock* in the darkness of the river on a cloudy night.

In response, I quickly pulled out my own small light crystal. I rubbed my hand over it to bring the soft glow of the crystal into life. But in the darkness of the middle of the river it was like a strong light beacon and those on board saw it immediately.

JELLICK

I was on watch on the port side when I saw Traxxa's light crystal and I quickly signalled to Captain Stemm that we had our naval attack team in our sights. I remember thinking at the time that Traxxa catching our attention by using a light crystal in the water was a good idea. And then I too thought nothing more on the subject as I leant over the side of the boat and asked.

"Is that you Traxxa or should we look further down the river for you!"

Then with some rope and strong willing hands, Traxxa and Bartrow were pulled up and out of the river and onto the deck of the *Riverrock*. Böder stayed in the water and with a cheerful hello across the boat to Jevan held on to the side and by using his strong young legs he kicked out which propelled us forward fast and smooth. This he did more to keep himself moving and warm than to increase the speed of our boat, I'm sure. In the meantime, we wrapped Traxxa and Bartrow up in some blankets to help keep them warm. Bartrow loved the attention but really didn't like the blankets around him much and let them slip to the deck of the boat at his first opportunity. When Traxxa had recovered sufficiently enough to be able to talk without his teeth chattering, he described their little adventure to us all.

Mindful of the cold of the water and the affect this might be having on our two giant friends, Captain Stemm put the boat into the riverbank on the southern side of the Mirack as soon as he thought it was safe to do so. The first thing our group did, along with Captain Stemm, was to build a sheltered fire that couldn't be seen from the river. Here we wrapped our two huge helpers as best we could in old sails and Böder's blanket to help them dry off and keep warm. As Böder and Jevan sat huddled together around the fire, Kaira and Jareck rallied around and warmed up some food for all of us whilst Captain Stemm produced a number of casks of very delicious beer and another two of mulled wine and together we ate and drank and chatted about the day's adventure.

The night was threatening to turn to morning by this time and though it was still very dark and there were a number of hours still away from dawn, Bartrow seemed nervous about where he was going to be staying during the day. After I had a quick talk with Stemm it was decided to wrap him up under some tarps and let him sleep in the storage rooms in the bottom of the boat. After hearing this, Bartrow seemed genuinely pleased with this arrangement and so settled down to enjoy our time as we sat around the campfire. I guess it was important for him to know that we were looking after him and making arrangements for his wellbeing.

Shortly after this Captain Stemm brought out a map and showed us where the Mirack and Dund Rivers met. He indicated on the map where we were and how much further we needed to travel before we reached the Dund River. He then showed us on the map the part on the Dund River where we had told him earlier we were wanting him to pull into the shore and so allow us time to recover the treasure we had still got hidden somewhere in the woods.

"As you can see, by the two rivers, the boat has to go down to the Dund and then turn back up against the current. Now I don't know where you've hidden your treasure, but it might be easier for Böder and Jevan to walk across this peninsula pick up the treasure and meet us on the Dund at the point where you indicated you wanted me to stop earlier. That way Böder and Jevan can keep warm and not have to swim in the cold waters of the Mirack and may even save us time as they collect the treasure. What do you say to that?"

Traxxa and I looked at the map and agreed with Stemm that what he said made sense. But we looked to Böder and asked if he was alright with this arrangement or did he and Jevan wish to stay with us paddling in the cold waters of the Mirack pushing the boat along to the Dund.

"Bear in mind," said Stemm, "the Dund River will be a lot warmer than the Mirack. For as you know the Mirack is coming straight down from the Tung Mountains and the Dund is the overflow from the inland Sea of Tamanette. But you would still have to put up with the Mirack for another couple of kilometers or so! What do you say to that?"

Böder looked at Jevan and asked, "What would you like to do Jevan, continue with the boat or go for a walk through the woods with me?"

"I won't go back in the Mirack River at this very moment for all the slev in Regil-Ter. I'm not even sure I want to swim with the boat up the Dund either!"

"Well we'll see how you're feeling by then when we get there. So that's decided then. Thank-you Captain Stemm for allowing us the option of walking or swimming! What you suggested makes a lot of sense to us so we've decided to walk across the peninsula and meet you at this point on the Dund. How long do you think it will take for you to reach this point?"

"I'd say it would take us about a day and a half, for us to get there." Captain Stemm said. "But it all depends on the winds of course! Still, do you think you will need this map?"

Traxxa spoke up at this time, "I don't wish to be a gooseberry to you both, but do you want me to come with you to help you find this treasure from here and then help you get to the rendezvous point on the Dund?"

Böder again looked to Jevan before answering. She just shook her head once which allowed Böder to answer as he wanted. "I think we would travel a lot quicker by ourselves and besides the treasure is still in the cart. So it shouldn't be too difficult for us to haul it to the Dund by ourselves. I'll have my mace and Jevan will have the sword so I don't think we should encounter many adversaries worthy of taking us on. If you don't mind though Captain Stemm, I would very much like to keep your map as it will help guide us along the way!"

"By all means," Stemm said handing over the map. "But before we part company Böder, would you be so kind as to give the *Riverrock* a little push back out into the river to get us going again. I grounded it pretty hard in an effort to get you in quickly in order to get a fire going and you both warmed up!"

"Not at all!" said Böder smiling comfortably now that his teeth had stopped chattering from the cold.

When all was settled, Traxxa and Böder walked off a little way and Traxxa asked Böder to show him on the map where he thought the treasure was hidden. He was pleased to see Böder remembered and knew how to get to where the treasure was.

"You should have no trouble on your journey Böder." Traxxa said comfortingly. "There are no towns or settlements in this area and probably only a few houses or farms if that. So you should be able to pass through these woods without even being seen much less troubled. I just wanted to be sure you knew where you were going!"

"I do, thanx Traxxa. Remember I'm a country boy! I know my north from south and my left from right, or is that right from left?" and he looked at his hands in confusion. And the two friends laughed at his little joke.

"Well then Böder, enjoy your walk with Jevan, and we'll see you in a day and a half all things being equal and they should be!" The two embraced as only a giant and his Wolfaman teacher and friend could and they returned to the fire.

We finished off the meal and the wine and all but one of the casks of beer by the roar of the fire until it was time for us to leave the company of our giant friends. Böder and Jevan waded out into the cold waters of the Mirack once more and together they pushed the *Riverrock* out of the mud and clear of the pebbly shore. As the current of the Mirack slowly tugged us away from the riverbank, we watched as Böder and Jevan standing by the water's edge, slowly merged into the shadows of the shoreline in the dark pre-dawn.

The only one who seemed truly glad to be aboard the *Riverrock* and moving was Bartrow. He quickly scrambled down into the hold and wrapped himself up in some smelly old tarpaulins and sails to hide from the coming of the dawn's golden sunlight and in but mere moments he was in a deep contented sleep.

CHAPTER TWENTY-THREE

EARLICH

Later on, when we were reunited once more, Böder told us of his and Jevans' travels across the land in order to pick up the treasure and to recover from their time in the cold river. They also told us of their adventures and how they had struggled to make their way to meet up with us again on the Dund.

BÖDER

I watched the *Riverrock* take my friends out onto the river and off into the gloom of the early morning darkness. Jevan and I stood quietly by the water's edge, with our arms around each other, till the boat was just a shadowy blur. We were just about to turn away and head back to our camp fire when I saw the flash of a light crystal. We paused to wonder what this could mean because neither Jevan nor I had a light crystal to answer back. But before I could dwell on this or even decide if I should wave or not, I watched in amazement as the light crystal flashed from the *Riverrock* three more times. Each flash differed in length and spacing than the others. I could only think that this might be something that boats had to do once they were on the open waters of the river. When the light crystal ceased flashing, Jevan and I turned and slowly made our way back towards our camp.

I was deeply puzzled by this strange occurrence. I looked at Jevan and, as if she could read my mind, she asked. "What do you think the flashing light crystal could mean?"

"I don't know. Do you think it could have something to do with the boat and the river?"

"Perhaps! But it worries me because I know that Zharlla has often used flashing light crystals to convey messages in the dark and sometimes even over great distances. I have never understood their structure nor meaning but now, I wish I did. Böder, I'm scared! Do you think she could be trying to follow us?"

"This I don't know but whether she is or she isn't, I'm here with you now and for always and I will not let her harm you again whatever the cost!"

She stopped walking and looked up at me and then turned into me and we hugged and held each other without saying anything. But I could sense the shuddering of her body as the tears came and felt them as they dropped onto my shoulder and wet my tunic.

When we were back at the camp I built up the fire and we sat down next to it. We continued to hold onto each other enjoying the warmth of the fire and our own bodies without saying anything. As we stared into the flickering, wavering, flames of the fire, slowly the soft and comfortable noises of the forest began to creep up on us and seemed to consume us. We sat quietly by the fire for a time that was immeasurable simply enjoying the feel of one another and loving the sense of companionship.

After a time as there was no-one else around we decide to strip down naked before the fire. We talked for a bit and when we were done talking we sat in silence once more in each other's arms. It was truly magical and a very precious time for us both. There was some wine left over and we drank till the cask was empty. Then, under the stars and the night sky we made love and lay cuddled together on top of an old silk sail given to us by Stemm and snuggled underneath my special blanket. It was delightful as I savoured the soft sweet smells of Jevan before we fell blissfully gloriously asleep together.

By my reckoning we slept for at least four hours before waking to the light and warmth of the mid-morning sun in a new day. We looked briefly at the map Captain Stemm had given us as we ate some breakfast. I tried to include Jevan, because I wanted her to feel that she was helping in the decision process, but in reality I knew exactly where we needed to go – I think she has guessed this already. *(She's a very smart woman).*

As Jevan indulged in her morning female ablutions and her finicky way of getting ready I ensured that the fire was out and was gonna stay out. I packed our things into two bags, the heavier one for me, obviously. I did my get going quick ablutions and after all this I still had to wait nearly half an hour before Jevan was finally ready to go. But I didn't say anything! I was just enjoying her company too much.

We followed a valley away from the Mirack River and headed southeast towards the Dund River. We soon discovered that it was not going to be a straight line as one obstacle after another got in our way. First there were some steep ravines and then there was thick underbrush which even our long legs and large strides made it difficult to get through. Luckily our thick skins, the sharp sword and my mace kept most of the violent vegetation at bay. I was just glad Traxxa wasn't with us or we would never have got through the way we went even as slowly as we did. We realized after a short while why no-one had ever tried to tame this land and live out this way. It was just too rough, uneven and inhospitable. It was then I remembered that Traxxa and Bartrow had made it into Regil-Ter and back in one night from where the treasure was hidden. So maybe it was me and I was just going the wrong way.

We stopped for something to eat after nearly three hours of walking. We were atop a small ridge and we could see the dark blue ribbon of the Mirack River way below us to the north and the muddy brown ribbon of the Dund River to the south and east. Both were a fair way off in the far distance. Captain Stemm thoughtfully had provided us with food and drinks -- enough for even our great appetites for three days. We had just finished our small repast and were in the process of tidying up and getting ready to go when we heard a scream.

It sounded like that of a girl and we looked to where the sound had come from. I couldn't see anything. Below us was a small window of a break in a hedge of thick trees. But all I could see through this was a little field between the trees. But Jevan wasn't waiting around to see if the scream would come to us again, she had drawn her sword and was running full flight down toward the field. I grabbed both bags and snatched up my

269

mace and was quickly after her. For a big woman, Jevan moved fast and freely and though I was a bit bigger than she was there was no way I was going to catch up to her before she could get to the field.

When I got to the field I saw Jevan trampling through the long grass as easily as though it was a well manicured lawn. She was heading straight towards what looked like a little Buffawgirl. The half horns on the head of this teenager told us her race. And though it is always hard to tell the age of Buffawmen she could not have been older than 15 years of age. Her dress was dirty and torn and hanging off her shoulders by the merest of threads and her elegant tail ribbon had unravelled and was trailing behind he. Her black blue arms and legs were all darkened from the blood coursing from her wounds inflicted upon herself after running frantically through the long grass. She was in the middle of the field and was surrounded by three, four-meter-tall, ugly dark green grasshopper like creatures. They were muttering something unintelligible to the Buffawgirl but she was shaking her head as though in fear or confusion or both.

Finally, in desperation, the creatures made ready to pounce upon the girl when Jevan let out a terrible giant female scream. This caused the creatures to stop for just a moment and look up towards where the scream had come from. They appeared to be nonplussed and were just returning their attentions to the girl, when the rock I had picked up and threw at them came hurtling in and struck the head and body of the closest grass hopper creature. The rock hit the skull and it exploded splattering his dark green blood all over his two companions. Their attention had been firmly grasped by now, but rather than face us and fight, they turned and fled back across the field heading due south. Chanting and mumbling their mantra as they hopped and jumped away, I changed the direction of my run to try and intercept them before they could reach the cover of the woods.

Jevan in the meantime was swiftly upon the child within three of her strides and bending down quickly caught the young waif as she collapsed to the ground.

I increased my stride but I realised soon enough that I was never going to stop them from reaching the wood. I dropped the bags and stretched out my left leg, grasped my mace with both hands and hurled it to where these two horrible green creatures would be in a matter of seconds. Together they landed from their awkward hopping stride on the very edge of the field. They must have heard my yell as I let go of the mace because they paused for just a moment to see how close the danger truly was. That's when the mace came hurtling in from the air and hit the first one fully in the head which exploded in a mass of green. The mace untroubled by the creatures head continued its traumatic journey, though the handle had swung around slightly. It was this part of the mallet which caught the second creature which was in the same line as the first and smashed into his chest. This creature was taken up off the ground with the force of the mace and was pushed through the air until they both came to rest a further three meters on. The creature just lay on the ground muttering confusedly to itself with my mace across its chest and I could see that he was in bad need of some massive TLC *(Tender Loving Care)*.

I knew they weren't going anywhere fast, so I turned back, picked up the bags and looked to see how the girl was doing and if Jevan was coping. Jevan had sheathed her sword and was carrying the young girl who was easily over two meters tall in her arms and moving slowly over to where I was. Realizing that Jevan had her under control, for the moment, I decided to go and see what these new creatures were up to, troubling a young girl like this.

I passed the first creature, or what was left of it, and went and knelt in the grass beside the second creature who was having trouble breathing. It was muttering something over and over but making no sound. I lifted my mace off its chest and held it menacingly in my hand. I looked at the creature which was far uglier up close than I had at first imagined and leaning in toward it I asked politely.

"Now why were you harassing that young Buffawgirl?"

To which the creature simply mumbled as softly as words could ever be said "giant Böder – giant, Xalarlla – giant!" It then gave a garbled answer and tried to spit great globs of gooey green blood at me. But there was no power in his spit and it simply came out of its lipless mouth and fell back onto its own ugly face. Realizing I was wasting my time, I let the weight of the spiked head of my mace succumb to gravity and let it drop down to smash the ugly creatures face into a dark green messy pulp.

I rose from my kneeling position and met Jevan at the side of the field near to where the line of the woods began. I got the flask of water in my bag out and handed it over to Jevan to try and help revive the young Buffawgirl.

When she opened her eyes and was able to regain her breath and finally speak, her first words were polite in the extreme. She introduced herself, which is always the sign of good breeding and then pleaded with us to help her and her family who were being attacked by these ugly hopper creatures.

"My name is Aiyisha *(pronounced eye-ee-sha)*" She said. "And I am from the house of Dourath. Quickly, please you must help my family. We have been trying to tame a large part of these over run woods which has been allocated to us when those hopper creatures decided that we were invading their territory and have tried to destroy our house and farm land.

"Okay, we'll do what we can to help. But first, where is your house?" I asked.

"Just over that hill," and here she pointed to the break in the woods where the other two creatures had been heading, before my mace had ended their hopes and dreams and of course their lives.

"Are you ready to go then?" and I looked down as tenderly as I believed I was able towards Aiyisha, but I was really asking Jevan if she wanted to do this thing.

Jevan nodded her head and Aiyisha was insistent. "Yes we must go! Right now -- please!" She implored us desperately. "Before it is too late and there is nothing for us to go there for!"

So we stood up and moved purposefully through the opening in the woods. Aiyisha despite her injuries and recent ordeal ran to try and encourage us to go faster. Her tail ribbon was in tatters and was trailing behind her. It looked kind of funny. But of course I wasn't laughing. In any case our strides were always going to out distance her, despite the speed of her running.

We walked a little way up a discernable hill and as we came to the top we looked down on a field of grain, half of which looked ravaged and depleted. The other half was slowly being devoured and torn apart by a line of the dark green hopper creatures. In the middle of the field, by a small river and a large pond we saw a magnificent double storey farmhouse. A little way away from the house was a large wooden shed. This was obviously housing livestock and chickens and such and next to that was another building used for storage. Both the shed and the barn were on fire and the slaughter of the farm animals was evident by the bodies of the cows, goats, horses and chickens that lay all around the grounds and yard. What struck us most though was the horde of the hopper creatures just beginning to surround the farm house. They had torches and were chanting a hardly discernible mantra as they danced whilst moving slowly towards the house intending either to invade it, besiege it, or burn it to the ground.

In any case this looked so much like what I had envisioned for my own farm on my island that I was incensed beyond reason. I dropped the bags to the ground and snatching up a thick branch of a tree lying nearby, gave an almighty roar and charged down towards the creatures invading the sovereignty of the farmers' house and land.

The roar caused the creatures singing their strange mantra in the field to recognize a real danger this time and so they stopped what they were doing. This unfortunately helped them to refocus their attention to the threat rushing down on them from the hill. They turned to face me and returned to singing their mantra which as I got closer to them with each stride became clearer and even more disturbing. They were singing in their horrible voice, "Böder – giant, Xalarlla – giant, Böder – giant...! Over and over again.

And then I was amongst them.

The first ones I smashed into were those in the field feasting on the hard work of the farmer. The continually chanting creatures came together as a bunch to try and overwhelm me with their numbers. Their leaps were nothing like anything I had ever seen in any other creature before. They could leap up to my shoulder from a standstill and from as far away as three meters. Their sharp claws were devastatingly effective for breaking into and holding onto my skin or ripping into my clothing and from this they were able to inflict countless wounds. They would hold on to whatever they caught and no matter how much I would shake or move about to try and get rid of them they just would not let go. And all the while they were attacking me or making their way towards me the whole number of them were chanting, "Böder – giant, Xalarlla – giant, Böder – giant...!

Their bodies were exceedingly light weight for their size. They were nearly four meters in height with slim shoulders and build with extremely powerful legs and claws for hands and feet. Despite this they still wouldn't have weighed more than Kaira on a full stomach. But this didn't stop me from battering a number of them at a time as they leapt towards me still chanting their horrible, name calling mantra.

Thankfully for me they disintegrated easily at the slightest touch of my mace or branch. Because they weighed so little they didn't seem to tax my strength, but there were just so many of them. From this, I determined in my spirit to fight till I could fight no more no matter what the outcome. So I continued to swing the mace and the branch through them all with such devastating effect. Heads and bodies were smashed and crushed, whilst limbs were mangled, broken or torn away from their bodies. Yet still they came towards me chanting as they came over and over again "Böder – giant, Xalarlla – giant, Böder – giant, Xalarlla – giant, Böder – giant, Xalarlla – giant, Böder – giant, Xalarlla – giant...!"

The number of them was enormous and far too many for me to count. At one time I must have had easily ten of the creatures clinging to my back, so without really thinking about it I just fell backwards onto my back and crushed them all. In doing so, twice as many leapt onto my front and tried to bite, through my tunic, with their pincer like tongues which came out of their lipless mouths, searching for my flesh. But this only angered me even more and I simply rolled onto my front and crushed all those that were there with my weight.

At one time as I was smashing away I caught a glimpse of Jevan who was battling valiantly against a dozen with her sword. Unfortunately this was not as effective as my mace, so I made my way slowly over to her kicking and stomping on the creatures as I went. I called out to her above the incessant sound of all these creatures chanting to take the branch to swing into them, but she refused saying she was just getting into it. I couldn't see Aiyisha and I hoped that she was staying well hidden. So I stood back to back with Jevan and together we continued to swing and stab and slice and kick and hit, doing as much damage to as many of these horrible green creatures as we possibly could.

But time seemed to be getting on and slowly the number of the creatures able to give us a fight began to diminish. But Jevan and I were tiring and I knew that it would only be a short while before we succumbed to the sheer numbers of these large insect-like men. I could hear Jevan breathing heavily and had noticed that her strikes and movements were slowing down with each mighty swing of her sword. This further inspired me to a greater effort to protect this marvellous giantess and I gave what I thought would be encouraging words to let her know that I was with her and that I would stand by her till my dying breath. Just as I thought there was no hope but to keep swatting these incessant chanting pests we heard the sound of a trumpet or a horn coming from the farmhouse.

All the hopper creatures paused and even ceased their chanting for just a moment to look towards this new sound. In this lull I took the opportunity to smack two of the creatures violently off Jevan's shoulder. They fell to the ground and I stomped on them with my foot. I then took a huge breath and looked toward the farm and saw five or six Buffamen all armed with weapons of some description rushing towards the back of the melee of the creatures that had been facing us. This heartened me and I swung my batons of death and destruction with a greater sense of urgency and force. I felt rather than saw Jevan slump to the ground at this time and I quickly stepped over her to stop any of the creatures from getting on top of her.

For the first time since engaging them in combat, the insect men in the field suddenly stopped chanting. They tried to turn and focus their attention on this new enemy. But by then it was too late as the Buffamen were amongst them and beside us, striking and killing and subduing the creatures ferociously, viciously and more violently than I have ever seen any other fighter do so before. So swift was their attack that in a relatively short space of time not one of the hideous insect beasts was left standing alive. When there was none left to fight, I quickly looked to Jevan to make sure that she was alright. She assured me that she was fine just a little tired and irritated by the huge number of bites she had received from these creatures. Then for the next half hour or so the Buffamen and I went through the mass of wounded and dying Hoppers to ensure they would never ravage another farm ever again.

When we were all finished, I turned to the largest of the Buffamen, who I took to be the head of the house, and introduced Jevan and myself to him and all the other Buffamen. I thought I saw an interesting moment and a curious look come into his eye and pass from one Buffaman to another, before he finally held out his arm and I took it as best as I could and he introduced himself.

"My name is Ozorkon and I am the head of the Dourath clan of the Buffamen. My daughter Aiyisha tells me that you rescued her from three of the Hoppers and at her request you came here willingly to help fight our battle for us!"

"We did!" I said feeling the exhaustion of the day's fight beginning to take its toll. I decided I needed to sit down beside Jevan for a moment or two.

Recognizing my distressed state, Ozorkon became apologetic.

"Of course, good Böder. Please take some rest. You must be exhausted!"

Here he turned to Aiyisha who was stumbling over and through the wreck of broken creatures lying strewn around the field.

"Aiyisha go and bring some food and drink for our two giant friends."

He then turned back towards Jevan and I and said, "We will continue to clean up and seeing as they have killed my stock we will get a fire going and we will cook you a meal like you have never had before. But before we move on, I just want to thank-you for looking out for my daughter as you did!"

Even as he said this, I saw a tear spring to his eyes and he was unable to stop them from cascading out onto his cheek. "She is my light and you have kept her shining for me and for that I cannot thank-you enough! My home, what's left of it, is yours please make yourself comfortable and we will attend to you as you so wish. Later, you can tell us how you came to be here and we will talk about how we came to have all these ugly creatures attack us in the way that they did! But perhaps the most important question I would like to have answered is why these insect men were chanting your name and a giant called Xalarlla incessantly from the moment they arrived on our land till they were destroyed!"

This was one question I could not answer. But I thought Jevan might know. But as I looked at her exhausted face I could not bring myself to ask it of her just at that moment. So we just sat quietly together and watched the family of Buffamen begin the massive job of cleaning up the dead and mangled bodies of the Hoppers. A short time later Aiyisha approached us with a tray full of some food and drink. She was wearing a shy smile on her lovely face as she told us her short story.

"I was playing in this field when these creatures came. I tried to yell and warn my family but they were too quick and too many of them and they cut me off from ever reaching the house. So I turned and ran away, but three of them came bounding after me. That's when you saw and rescued me in the next field. I want to thank-you for that. I didn't really thank-you at the time because I was so upset about my family being attacked!"

"That's alright dear." said Jevan gently. "We can only understand what you must have been going through at the time."

As the two girls began talking, I took the time to look a little closer at Aiyisha. She was a very beautiful Buffawgirl with large brown eyes that shone with intelligence and life. Her skin was a little darker than Jevans and she had a cute bunched up nose above a full mouth which hid just the slightest hint of an overbite. Her hair was long and black and curly and her young horns were already breaking through. This was probably why she had her hair up the way she did. I smiled knowingly. But the standout feature that drew most of my attention to her was her long black silky ears.

"You look awfully young to have been fighting three of those creatures all by yourself," I said smiling to let her know I wasn't serious, "How old are you Aiyisha?"

Jevan frowned in a protective female sort of a way.

"You don't ask young Buffawgirls that kind of question. You don't have to answer the brute if you don't wish to!" said Jevan half mocking, though half interested as well.

"That's alright I don't mind telling my rescuers how old I am. I shall be 12 next month." she said, all importantly. It was lovely just to see her smile the way she did. For an instant I understood what Ozorkon had meant when he had first described what Aiyisha meant to him.

When Jevan was ready, we got up and after retrieving the bags from the top of the hill, we made our way towards the farmhouse and the smouldering barn. Fortunately the wood used to build the barn was relatively new and as a result the fire hadn't really taken on. There was some damage to it, mostly smoke, but the structure itself was intact. The shed had been of older wood and was completely burnt to the ground. There were a number of fires lit throughout the farm. Most were in the field to burn off the carcasses of the Hoppers. But there was an open spit where the chickens, goats and two cows were being prepared for the feast that night.

"When you rushed down to meet with the Hoppers in the field," Aiyisha continued talking, "I ran home to let my father know that you were there fighting for us. He sent me up the way to get some of our neighbours and other members of our house to come and help us in the fight. Then my mother and father ran out with whatever they could find and started fighting the creatures around the house before they could set it on fire also. When I came back with friends and neighbours we finished off those closest to the house then I rallied them all together with a blow on my horn!"

And here Aiyisha showed us a hollowed out Buffaman's horn. It was finely polished and beautifully ornate the markings of a true craftsman.

"That's when we came to help you in the field. I'm sorry we took so long to get to you, but there were just so many Hoppers that we couldn't take them all on at once!"

I smiled, because she was so polite and innocent, and besides, it was all over now and Jevan and I were just really hungry and tired.

Eventually the rest of the family and friends came and introduced themselves to us. But the only names I seem to be able to remember was Aiyisha and her parents. I think she had a younger brother...!?

"Ordon is his name," put in Jevan, who seemed to be good with things like that. "And her mother's name is Merabeth in case you had forgotten!" she said with a smile.

"Anyway he was a bit smaller than her and I can't remember him all that much. Aiyisha's mother Merabeth made us feel very welcome indeed. She kept thanking us all throughout the evening as well as continually giving us food and drink and ensuring that we were well looked after.

Ozorkon came and sat with us after a time. He told us of the Hoppers and how they had suddenly appeared. "They have never been known to travel together in the way we have seen them today. My impression was they were migrating as a group travelling south and destroying everything and everyone in their path. They might have come down from Entarim or the Gloas and were making their way south through the lush belt of Gru-Nish-Dan and Bahaire and then on towards the southlands. In all my time I have only ever heard of them travelling like this once and that was over twenty years ago. But that was down through the Gloas and into Delgina and along the eastern coast of the Tamanette Sea towards the south that way."

Not knowing the geography of Durogg that well, I simply smiled and nodded my head in supposed understanding as Ozorkon continued.

"We tried to talk to the Hoppers but they wouldn't speak to us or didn't seem to understand Ucray (*the common tongue of Durogg*). Or perhaps they're not ones for communicating with those they attack and destroy. But the thing which disturbs me the most is the whole time they were destroying our crops and threatening my family and the farmhouse they kept chanting your name and the name of Xalarlla. Now, can you tell me why they would be doing this? And do you know who this Xalarlla is?"

He paused to let us answer.

"I don't know why they were travelling as they did." I said, "and it is true I have no idea whatsoever why they would be chanting our names. Unless..!"

"Unless?" prompted Ozorkon hoping there might just be an answer of some description hidden in the folds of our thoughts.

"Unless," put in Jevan, "they were summoned by a witch that up until recently was able to hold and control me. And I was known as Xalarlla by her. But that name is not mine; it was given to me by this witch, Zharlla by name. However since breaking free of her hold over me I have since reclaimed my real name and now I am known once more as Jevan."

"But Zharlla lost her ability to control me when Böder, this brave giant, rescued me. But be warned, for she is a most powerful witch and I have no doubt that it was she who summoned these insect men to search us out and destroy us. I can only think that these creatures of simple minds were distracted from their mission when they came across your fields and hunger for food got the better of them. But I don't know this for sure, however I do know that Zharlla, whilst most powerful, is also vicious and vengeful and someone you do not wish to cross swords with!"

Ozorkon looked long and hard at Jevan, almost to the point of being disrespectful. I was just about to say something and intervene on her behalf when he finally spoke up.

"Thank you for telling me this! I only wondered why they kept chanting your names and speaking none of the common tongue. But now that we have heard of this Zharlla, I will let you know this for nothing. My kin and I will do everything we can to see that she never again interferes in the affairs or estates of the house of Dourath the clan of my ancestors!"

Just at that moment Aiyisha came over and demanded that I pick her up and hold onto her. When I did this I saw out of the corner of my eye, the love of a father for his daughter shine through and Ozorkon just stood there and beamed up at us.

"For my daughter," he said, "I will always hold a special place of respect and love for you and Jevan!" And with that he stood up and walked over to get another drink for himself. He came back with a small cask of ale which he handed up to me and toasted his mug of ale with my cask, "to family and friends!"

"To family and friends!" Jevan and I responded as one.

After a while I had to appeal to Merabeth to come and take her daughter away from me and let me have a little peace before we all collapsed for the night. I think Merabeth was just so happy to have all her family safe after the ordeal of the day that she was allowing Aiyisha -- and also Ordon, to a lesser extent -- a little leeway with regards to the giants who had helped save their lives and home.

But finally we were allowed to find a place in the shelter of the blackened barn where Jevan and I slept on mats of straw and under a number of quilts and blankets.

Early the next day, Jevan and I were up with the farmers who had begun to rebuild their farm. I walked with Ozorkon and gave him a helping hand where I could. I also found it easy to talk to him about a number of topics, particularly about farming and growing crops -- stuff I felt I could use back on the island. He was very helpful and even gave me a number of different bags of seed and ideas about how to and when to plant certain crops and other useful information. I told him where I lived and gave him an open invitation to come and visit whenever he or his family were down our way on the Dund River. He thanked me for this and seemed genuinely pleased to receive this invitation.

But seriously, I didn't think he would ever take me up on this offer, so I felt comfortable enough making it. *(Though I'm sure I would be only too pleased to entertain him and his family if they ever did turn up on our shores).*

We returned to the farmhouse where Merabeth and Aiyisha had put together a healthy breakfast and prepared a beautifully packed lunch for our travels. After which we began to say our good-byes.

Ozorkon extended his arm and I extended my fingers and we parted as friends.

Aiyisha came and gave us all the hugging she could to giants who were just so big. So I lifted her up in my arms and gave her a quick peck of a kiss on her forehead and handed her over to Jevan who did the same, whereupon she placed her back on the ground between her proud and glowing parents.

For some reason, and fortunately for us, they never asked us what we were doing so near to them that Zharlla would have sent the insect creatures through their farm to reach us. But then again we never offered to talk about such matters either.

So Jevan and I waved good-bye to the family farmers of Buffamen and we headed off towards, I felt certain, was where we had hidden our cartload of treasure.

Chapter Twenty-Four

BÖDER

Without stopping, Jevan and I strode purposefully towards where the cart loaded with the treasure was hidden. We were conscious, all the while, that Captain Stemm and the others would probably be waiting for us long before we could get to the meeting point. We made good time and about half an hour after leaving Aiyisha and her family's farm we reached the familiar glade with its bubbling brook running through it. Without bothering to check to see if there was anyone around, Jevan and I hauled the cart out from under the thick gorse bush. After a quick double check of the map, we headed off towards where we thought the meeting point on the Dund was.

Going through the wood was much easier going down to the Dund than it was when we had been coming up from the Mirack River. In spite of the awkwardness of moving the cart through the forest and us having to lean over to push or pull it using the ropes Traxxa had left with the treasure, it still took us a little over two hours before we came to the top of a small rise overlooking the lush green of a rolling meadow before stopping abruptly at the muddy brown banks of the incredibly wide deep-flowing Dund River. The river was still a good kilometer away, (*a quarter of a league by the old standard*) so we sat down and rested for a moment having a drink and nibbling on some of the food that Merabeth had prepared for us, as we looked down over the peaceful scene before us to try and gain our bearings and take stock of where everything was.

It was as we rested atop this rise, that I saw Stemms boat slewing into a little bay further up the river, south of our position. They had passed our spot but were obviously pulling over to be out of the flow of the Dund and possibly waiting for us to appear. I was about to stand up and make myself known to them when I saw the three large skiffs riding just north and behind Stemms craft. They too were pulling out of the main flow of the river. The main one was just in front and the other two were on either side of the much larger *Riverrock*. My first thought was those fishermen will never catch much by hanging around the shoreline and in the sheltered bay like that.

But as we looked on, Jevan suddenly whispered frantically, "They look like pirates!"

"How can you tell from way up here?" I asked.

"I have seen pirates like that before. They have the colours of death on their pennants flying from the masts!"

I looked more closely at the three masts in turn and saw the strong telltale colours of red and black adorning the topmost pennants.

"Well now," I thought out loud. 'What do we do?'

Just then I sensed rather than heard something and reached for my mace. But I needn't have bothered because as I looked toward the sound, there running towards us came a big light brown female dog. It was Kaira in her animal form. She ran up to us wagging her tail and without thinking I swivelled my body around to meet her so that she could leap high and into my lap. As I cuddled my friend, a movement behind her caught my eye. I looked up and there standing in the shadows to our right and back of us was Traxxa.

"Jevan's right!" he said softly. "They are pirates! We thought you might come to this point." And then he motioned with his hands for us to stay low and to come to him away from the top of the rise. "I would rather they don't see you just at this time so come away from the open. Stay low and take the cart over there into the shadows of the bushes and trees on the far side of the clearing."

Carrying Kaira gently in my arms, we did as he asked and moved carefully away from the top of the rise. Once we were secure and out of sight of those on the river, Traxxa reached up and embraced Jevan first.

When I had handed Kaira over to Jevan we embraced as best a giant and his Wolfaman friend could do.

Traxxa handed a small bag up to Jevan and said, "Will you take Kaira over to the bushes and after she has changed into her human form help her to get dressed?"

He then turned to me. "How was your walk?" He asked, without his usual half smile, whilst his eyes moved back towards where the boats were upon the river.

Before replying, I sat down to meet his height.

"Perhaps we should talk about our journey a little later on! Right now, though, I think it is more important that you tell me what is happening to those on the river and why you are here in the woods with Kaira and not on the boat?"

"These are good questions." Traxxa said, taking his eyes off the river for a moment to look at me. "But I will tell you when Jevan returns with Kaira so that you both know what has been happening to us, at the same time. Aaaand, it will also save my tongue the effort of repeating my story!"

I remember smiling at this remark. Anyway a few minutes later Kaira and Jevan returned to sit with us. Kaira was smiling from ear to ear and looked fresh and vibrant and dressed as I have always known her. Elegantly fashionable and yet comfortable and practical like that of a country girl who knows how to dress. She had, as Jareck once described to me with a glint of humour in his eye as, having a 'pleasant look' about her.

"I am so happy to see you and Jevan again Böder." She said. "We were a little bit worried about you at one stage."

I smiled back at her and replied, "And I'm happy to see you too Kaira and yes we're alright -- thanx for asking!"

Traxxa acknowledged our safe arrival as well and then began his story.

"I saw those three pirate boats, the ones surrounding the *Riverrock* in the inlet below, drawing up to us early this morning, shortly after it was light. I recognized them as pirates straight away and went to warn Captain Stemm. But he had seen them at much the same time as I had. Stemm had been hugging the shoreline so as not to draw too much attention to ourselves, but those three boats seemed overly curious. We knew at once that it was going to be unfair to ask any of Stemms crew, who are just simple boat folk, to join with us and fight off the pirates. And it was too late in the day for Bartrow to be of any use as a fighter. Now normally Jellick has an accompaniment of soldiers and warriors with him whenever he travels, to meet with such encounters. But as you are no doubt aware, this has not been a normal trip for him or us!"

And here, Traxxa's half smile joined his face for the first time in the narration of his tale.

"Jellick, Stemm as well as the others and I discussed the options that were before us and we felt, the wisest and safest thing for us was for Captain Stemm to continue sailing up river and not to change course. This would show to the pirates that we were not attempting to avoid them or put into shore to try and escape or meet up with you. By doing this, we hoped the pirates would not consider us worthy of an attack as there was no visible prize to be had. After all there were no warriors aboard the *Riverrock* to protect any valuable cargo it might be carrying and we weren't trying to outrun them or avoid them. But we also felt it was sensible to have someone come ashore and find you to warn you not to show yourselves or your treasure to those on the river. At least not until the pirates had gone or had been dealt with completely.

As I was the strongest swimmer of all of us, I told them that I would slip over the side of the boat and swim to shore and hope that the pirates wouldn't spot me. It was Jareck who urged me to take Kaira into the water with me.

"I know she can't swim but surely we can't risk her being discovered aboard by the pirates!" He said. The debate stalled for a moment or two before he continued to plead with me, "You must know what the pirates will do with her if they find her!"

We looked toward where Kaira was hiding on the top deck and we knew what Jareck was saying was true. "Okay." I told him, probably a little brusquely. "She needs to enter the water naked. So put her clothes into this bag and give her a wide belt to wear. I will carry the bag for her in the river."

"Why naked?" asked Jareck a little defensive of Kaira.

Here Jevan and I looked at Kaira as she sat quietly by and I noticed that she had taken on a tinge of blush in her cheeks.

Traxxa filled in the details regarding these instructions. "The weight of her clothes will drag her down and slow her ability to save herself as she learns to swim the hard way. I will attach a short length of rope from my belt to the one she will have on so that if she loses her grip on me in the water I won't have to worry about losing her to the river. Also, the moment we reach the shoreline she and I are going to have to move very quickly if we wish to have any chance of meeting up with you and keeping up with the boat at the same time. In which case, once ashore she can simply change into her animal form and we will both be able to move swiftly through the tree line following the river. Also," and here, on the boat, I spoke directly to Kaira, "if once in the water, you start to struggle, simply change into your animal form and your natural instincts will kick in and you'll find that you won't struggle half as much."

"When they heard this part of my argument the others rallied to help Kaira prepare quickly so that we could slip into the water and follow after the *Riverrock* along the shoreline. As Kaira readied herself, Captain Stemm, to his credit, sailed us as close to the shore as he dared. At the moment we slipped into the water on the shore side of the boat, out of sight of the pirates, he then tacked away from the banks as though trying to catch the wind in his sail. If the pirates were watching, and I'm sure they would have been, hopefully they would have been distracted by this manoeuvre and not notice us leaving the boat and begin floundering in the water.

"I told Kaira to hold onto my belt and not let go and to take as deep a breath as she could and then together we pushed off from the hull of the *Riverrock*. I held my breath for as long as I could and swam with the current allowing it to take us as far downriver as I dared let it. When we got to the muddy bank I instructed Kaira to take on her animal form and undid the belt around her waist. We then made our way behind rocks and a fallen tree to help cover our exit from the water over the river bank and into the safety of the trees. The moment we reached land we raced along the shore keeping to the tree-line and trying desperately to keep the *Riverrock* in sight. At the same time, I was trying to figure out where you would most likely be waiting for us. My personal fear was because you didn't have all that far to travel, you should have been on the shore from early this morning looking out and waving to us at the pre-arranged meeting point. That is of course if you hadn't got lost and I somehow knew you wouldn't. But this obviously didn't happen as you are only just now reaching the river. This is very good for us, but it did worry Kaira and I just a little that something untoward had happened to you. Which is why I asked you how did you travel?

"Stemm reached this bay," Traxxa said and he pointed to the boats on the water, "about half an hour ago and the pirates have just pushed them into this inlet and now they are at a standstill. This was good because it allowed Kaira and me to catch up with them. Which we did, about ten minutes ago and we have been watching them ever since. I was trying to think of a plan on how best to move forward and I was just beginning to wonder where you were and what if anything had happened to you. It was then that Kaira heard you coming through the woods, lugging that great big cart along with you. She took off after you and I had a hard time keeping up with her to be honest. Our first and only thoughts at this time were to get to you quickly and warn you not to show yourselves to those on the river, and so here we are!

"So now tell us your story!"

"As we do that," said Jevan, ever the thoughtful one. "Why don't we have something to eat and watch what is happening to our friends out on the river!"

"Why don't we just rush down there and smash into those pirates and be on our way?" I said impatiently, angry that so many things were conspiring against me to stop me from continuing my journey back to my island.

"And that is the very reason why I came ashore," said Traxxa soothingly. "I am here to persuade you not to do that very thing. The moment you make a move towards the river, those pirates will see you and show you a friend and kill them right there on the spot before your very eyes to let you know they mean business. And there is nothing you would be able to do about it at all. Once the pirates have your attention in this way, they will then demand your treasure or they will continue to kill the rest of your friends on board the *Riverrock*. They will do this slowly to make an impact on you and to give you time to go and retrieve your treasure. Remember, that would include Jareck, Earlich and Jellick and, in the sunlight, even Bartrow would be at their mercy. And if we had not come ashore to warn you, the sheer number of the pirates would have ensured that Kaira and even I would probably not have come out alive either.

"We may even have been able to kill a great number of pirates in the process but we're talking of at least sixty pirates down there aboard those vessels and even my great skill wouldn't have been able to account for that many. No Böder, what Jevan suggests is a good thing. We should eat, you can tell us your tale and we can watch the boats and think of a way to get you, me and our friends on the *Riverrock* out of this situation without getting ourselves injured or killed in the process!"

And even as he had been talking, Jevan was rummaging around in the packs and with a little help from Kaira they brought out the food and drinks which had been given to us by Merabeth and Captain Stemm. We all ate and I started to tell Traxxa and Kaira our story as we continued to watch the boats by the shore.

"Hmmmm!" Traxxa said thoughtfully on two occasions during my tale. The first was when I told him of the light crystal aboard the *Riverrock* as they left us on the shore and the second was when I told him of the hoppers and their chanting of 'Böder – giant and Xalarlla – giant'.

"I have heard of such creatures before," he said thoughtfully when I had finished my tale. "But I have never known them to move about in the number you have described! Perhaps it is as you say, that they had been summoned by Zharlla to seek you out. Jevan, you know her best. Can she truly do such a thing?"

Jevan nodded her head. "I have seen her summon a swarm of bees and a plague of rats to deal out justice on villages and settlements that had treated her badly. If she can summon the likes of them then there is every likelihood that she is able to summon those insect men if she so wished! The fact that they were chanting the name Xalarlla tells me either she does not yet know that I have regained my birth name or she is simply refusing to recognize any name other than the one she gave me!"

"And now you are suggesting that there is someone on board the *Riverrock* who is passing messages by using light crystals." Traxxa said in reflective thought. "I recall now, seeing the light crystal that was used at the front of the *Riverrock* as we were leaving Regil-Ter during the night. Remember we were still in the water and I thought the light crystal was for us in the water to warn us of the *Riverrocks'* approach. But what if that was to inform whoever, perhaps Zharlla, that we were leaving and that you were almost aboard. And then later during the early morning telling whoever was watching that you and Jevan had got out of the water and were walking across the peninsula. That would account for the hoppers knowing roughly where to look for you!"

This last bit of information about a spy on the *Riverrock* was particularly infuriating. During the telling of my story, I had been slowly losing control because all I could think of was to go and help my friends on the *Riverrock*. But as Traxxa reflected his own insights on our story I soon realized how important it was to try and look at the bigger picture of exactly what was happening to us all. Still I was impatient now and just wanted to begin to do something about my friends on the water. Traxxa somehow sensed my growing unease and told me to calm down and listen to the plan he had been formulating whilst I had been talking.

When he said this, I stopped my thoughts in mid-flight and brought my eyes back from the boats and focussed on my mentor. What I saw in Traxxa's face made me smile broadly, eyes shining, teeth glinting and everything, because I knew that he had a plan which would see us moving forward.

JELLICK

We all held our breaths, along with Traxxa and Kaira, the moment they went over the side of the *Riverrock* and into the river. But none of us dared to try and catch sight of them in case the pirates were watching us as we knew they would be. Captain Stemm did a marvellous job tacking and weaving his boat back and forth as one would expect an experienced Ottarman to do upon the Dund. It was a lot harder this time 'round fighting the current of the Dund than when Stemm had taken us up river last time. But that was because of the strong warm summer breezes which had virtually pushed us along from start to finish. The pirates didn't break formation, as they continued to follow us. This was good as it told us they had not seen Traxxa or Kaira leave the *Riverrock* and swim to the shore. However, they began to move in soon after and we were pushed and nudged and made to enter the quiet waters of an inlet by the shore. We now sat and waited to find out what exactly they wanted from us

All three pirate boats were about two-thirds the size of Stemm's craft but, with approximately twenty men on each boat, they outnumbered us three to one. From the moment we saw the pirates we made a sort of a plan with Stemm. It was sort of comforting to know that if worse came to worst we could always run the boat into the riverbank and try and take our chances on solid ground rather than on the open waters of the river. However, as it happened, I think the pirates suspected this ploy because they put one of their boats as quickly as they could between us and the riverbank to stop us from doing that very thing. So now we were becalmed on this little bay -- more like an inlet really -- surrounded by three pirate vessels. The leader had already called out to us across the water demanding, "Where is your giant?"

Stemm answered as truthfully as he knew how; that we didn't know where 'our giant' was. It was after this first interaction, we decided amongst ourselves, from that moment on we would only answer the pirates as they talked to us. In this case it was how we would refer to Böder. Not by his name but as, 'our giant'!.

Shortly after this, the pirates drew up alongside us and they came aboard. Each of the three vessels unloaded ten of their men all with their swords drawn and ready for a fight. But upon prior instructions from Captain Stemm, they met no resistance from us at all! A number of the pirates went from bow to stern above and below deck and quickly returned to say there was nothing worth stealing from us as far as they could see.

I was very relieved that in their search they had not found Bartrow. Though I'm sure if they had found the troll there would have been a good number of dead pirates long before he would have come unwillingly to the deck of the boat and into the sunlight. Still I'm also very sure, once they realized he was a troll, the pirates would have simply opened up all the hatches and then engaged him in combat. From there it would have been but a matter of time before poor Bartrow, in his struggles, would have come into contact with some sunlight and then it would have been all over for our fearsome friend.

The pirate leader was one of the largest Bearamen *(half man/half bear)* that I have ever had the displeasure to meet. He was not unhandsome but his snout was more pronounced even in his human form than any other Bearaman I have ever known. His head was in a constant state of leaning forward almost as though he enjoyed being confrontational. His head, barrel chest and massive arms were covered in thick dark brown hair which was all matted down and looked all dark and slippery. This was probably as a result of the spray from the river rather than poor hygiene or excessive sweating.

He made himself known yelling, "I am 'Biargamouth" at us. "Now who among you is answering for this boat and its crew?"

Stemm stepped forward and spoke up, as was his right and custom of the day to speak on behalf of those on his boat. "I am Captain Stemm and the *Riverrock* is my boat,"

"I have been told there is a great treasure aboard this boat and that it is being protected by a giant. So unless you want me to start killing your men slowly, one by one, I will ask you only this one time. Where is your giant and why isn't he here with you on this boat?"

"Our giant, was simply too big to fit on this small vessel! He swam beside us when we came out of Regil-Ter. But the Mirack River was far too cold for him and he decided that he would much rather walk through the woods than catch his death of cold from waters of the mountain river!"

"And of the treasure that he brought down from the mountains, where is it?"

"I have not seen this treasure of which you speak. It is certainly not on my boat otherwise your men would have found it. All I have aboard are these merchants and stores to last until we get to Ibern."

"That's as may be, but I am led to believe that this giant is to be taken by you and your boat to the Black Island which he has made his own and is said to be near the town of Bernitz. What do you say to this?"

"That is true enough; we were instructed to wait for him in the town of Bernitz where for a huge fee we are expected to help him to swim beside our vessel over to his island. It may be that he has gone into the woods to retrieve his treasure and he will meet us in Bernitz carrying his treasure with him. But again, as I said before, I have not seen his treasure and I do not know where he is at this moment!"

Biargamouth believed he was a good judge of character and acted decisively according to his intuition. Probably because of this, he felt Captain Stemm was, for the large part, telling him the truth. But there was still something in Stemms story that didn't sit right with him. Perhaps it was the fact that the giant was to be walking in the woods to retrieve the treasure and then going on from there to meet with them in Bernitz. That was a full three day boat trip and nearly a week's travel overland through the woods. But more than that, why did Stemm refer to Ibern the capital city of Gru-Nish-Dan when he had clearly made arrangements to meet with the giant in Bernitz?

Biargamouth needed time to think.

He called his three generals over to himself and they moved towards the stern. They talked in low voices as they walked slowly around the deck. After a short time, one of the generals or captains set off and jumped back across the gunwales onto his boat. Shortly after this a small rowboat was dropped into the water and it set off with a crew of ten men and two rowers. They went ashore and the ten crewmen made their way up from the riverbank and into the woods. The two oarsmen stayed with the boat which had been pulled out of the river onto the shore.

As this was taking place Biargamouth turned back to us slowly and spoke with a soft menace in his voice. "There is something not quite right about your story Captain Stemm. So I am sending the best trackers I have to the shore. They will set off to see if they can't find this giant of yours that you say is walking with his treasure through the woods. If and when they do find your giant they will send word to me that what you have been saying is true. If it is true then my men will follow him down to the town of Bernitz and you will be allowed to leave unharmed. But at the same time, we too will sail alongside of you to Bernitz whereupon we will take over your contract of transporting this giant to his island by boat. Do I make myself clear?"

Captain Stemm nodded his head to say he understood. And yet at the same time I could swear I saw there was a glimmer of hope in his eyes.

"If however," continued Biargamouth arrogantly, "my men find even the slightest discrepancy between what you have told me just now and what they see in the woods, then I will surely kill you and all your men including your passengers. Then I will take your boat as payment for wasting my time. In any case, I will give you just one day and only one day for my men to verify your story and if it has not been proved in this time I will kill you all. Now do you understand me fully?"

Again Stemm nodded his head in understanding. But at this last ultimatum, I thought I saw a shadow of worry, for his crew and passengers, pass over his face.

But for me, the sixty pirates had just become fifty. And hopefully, Traxxa and Böder were also aware of this development as they would most probably be watching over us from amongst the trees on the bank. But I suppose there was still an element of doubt at the back of my mind. After all, we hadn't seen Böder or Jevan at our pre-arranged meeting point earlier that morning.

So what if something had happened to our giant friends?

It was unthinkable, but not to be ruled out fully.

Also we hadn't really seen Traxxa and Kaira make it safely to the riverbank?

What if they hadn't made it either?

After all the currents all along the length of the Dund are notoriously treacherous and there was every chance that it had claimed one, or even both their lives!

Still - what was I thinking?

Tsuhh *(I clicked my tongue subconsciously)*

Something bad happen to Böder!?!?

Not likely!

Besides, it just wasn't worth worrying over a couple of 'what if's', so I decided to hold my tongue and see how the game played out!"

Chapter Twenty-Five

Traxxa

We were just finishing off our small repast when I noticed one of the rowboats being readied to leave the cluster of boats upon the inlet. I nudged Böder and together we watched as the rowboat was dropped into the water and the twelve men aboard make their way towards the riverbank.

"Well now, this changes everything. And in our favour I might add!" I said half to myself and half to Böder and the girls. "Come, my friends, we have work to do!"

"Kaira," I said with urgency entering my voice, "watch the boat and don't lose sight of it at all. Tell us what they are doing and point out to us where and when they land!"

As Jevan quickly tidied up our picnic, Böder under my instructions grabbed the cart and pulled it out from the shadows and left it unattended under some trees. I got Jevan to throw all our bags together, around the cart, as though it was a hastily made camping place. It wasn't well hidden, but neither was it out in the open and hopefully not too obvious as our bait for the pirates. The clearing was just over the top of a steep but climbable bank and I quickly assessed that this was the most practical place where the pirates would come up from the river.

As he finished pushing the cart, Böder asked. "Why would they be coming ashore? Surely they have our friends and all the leverage they need on the boats?"

"I can only assume the pirates must know about your treasure and possibly that you have gone into the woods to get it. Perhaps as instructed by the light crystal the other morning, or, as told to them by our friends on board the *Riverrock*. In any case, that would explain to the pirates why you are not around and why your treasure is not yet on Stemms boat. This of course would be confirmed the moment the pirates completed their search of the *Riverrock*.

"Where Captain Stemm has told the pirates you are taking it, I can only guess. My bet, though, is they have told the pirates you are taking it down to Bernitz. Stemm most certainly would not have told them that you were bringing it to him to be taken to your island by his boat. That information would almost certainly doom him and all on his boat to a swift and immediate death. If their intelligence is as good as I think it is then the pirates will most probably know about your island already. I'm pretty sure Ribard would have told Zharlla as much about you as he could, that is if he was trying to get back in favour with her. This would include where you live and where we are heading. In any case, I am convinced that she is mixed up with these pirates in some way!"

And here I looked at Jevan, who nodded her head in agreement.

"From this it would be easy enough for them to guess that the Black Island is where you are ultimately heading. If I was to read the leader of the pirates correctly, especially as he has just lowered a rowing boat, I believe he is sending out some of his scouts ten to be exact by the number in the boat coming ashore. My guess is they have been sent to go and find you and your treasure in the woods!"

"But why would he do that? Why wouldn't he have just gone straight to my island and waited for us there?"

"I'm not sure, but I can only think the pirates would want to make certain that you really do have this mythical cart of treasure before sailing 500 kilometers south and back. So I can only imagine, in order to find your treasure all they would really need to do is find you first. After all you would be much easier to find than your treasure which you could have hidden almost anywhere. Once they have found you they would track you and of course send word back to the pirates on the water. When this information is confirmed I believe the pirates will either kill or release Captain Stemm and those aboard and concentrate on getting to you. After all, once they can work out a strategy and a plan to kill you, they will get their prize which, of course, is ultimately possession of your treasure!"

"Won't the pirates have killed our friends on Stemms boat already?" Böder asked.

"No! I can't see that happening just yet," I replied thoughtfully. "At the very least the leader of the pirates will want to know exactly what is happening here on the mainland. So my guess is he will wait until he has heard from his scouts before determining what to do with his hostages, and our friends. From this I'd say those on the *Riverrock* have perhaps another day at least as the pirates wait for word about where you are and what you're doing!"

We returned swiftly to where Kaira was hiding in the bushes watching those on the river.

"The pirates rowboat has landed on the riverbank just below us as we speak!" said Kaira taking the task she had been given very seriously. And here she pointed to where we could just see the ten scouts making their way carefully along the shoreline away from the beached rowboat.

"Well girls," I asked, "Are you up for some killing?"

Jevan looked at Böder and then back to me before saying with feeling. "I was a judge in the games two days ago, killing some female criminals I didn't even know. Therefore, I think I can kill a couple of pirates who are threatening the lives of my friends and the man I love!"

Hearing these words Böder looked up sharply at Jevan. He smiled, reached over and hugged her before giving her a quick kiss on the lips.

"Good," I said struggling to get my words out swiftly and yet remain concise and to the point, "because those ten pirates are coming up here to find Böder. Believe me when I tell you they will do whatever it takes to kill him and take his treasure. It is our job to ensure that not one of those pirates' lives to get back to the other pirates on the boats. The last thing we want is for anyone of them to warn those on the water that we are watching them from just over this first hill above the river bank. They must all die and we must do this quickly and quietly. But first, we must make sure they stay together, if they separate then the chances of one of them getting back to the boats will increase and you can be assured that all our friends on the *Riverrock* will die immediately.

To make sure they all stay together we are going to try and lure the pirates into this clearing with the sight of the cart and its treasure. I am assuming they will all come rallying across to the cart quickly in order to be the first to claim their share. That is the way of a pirate, fortunately for us. We will attack the moment they are in the field looking over the treasure. And remember not one of them must be allowed to escape or even yell out. Our friends' lives depend upon it!"

I sent Jevan to one end of the clearing where she hid amongst the trees with her sword out and ready. After telling Böder not to use his roar when the fighting began he went to the southern end of the clearing and lay down in a cutaway ravine. Meanwhile, Kaira and I stayed to keep the pirates below us under constant observation.

To my utter disappointment, three of their number began to follow the riverbank heading south.

"Quickly Kaira," I whispered desperately, "follow those three pirates and see if you can't lure them back up to this clearing using all your charms and feminine wiles. Remember the lives of our friends depend upon it. But above all else, don't get caught and try not to let yourself be seen by either those on the boats, or by those guarding the rowboat. Now quickly girl, go and keep your wits about you!"

When she had gone, I moved quickly over to a convenient place atop the hill where I hid myself from view. From here I planned to cut off any retreat the pirates might take once they realised the cartload of treasure was being used as bait to lure them to their deaths.

When the seven pirates topped the rise it took them a number of cautious steps out into the open of the clearing before the cart was discovered. Four of their number lost all caution and simply ran over to the cart to try and claim their portion of the treasure before anyone else could. But they had not even crossed half of the clearing, when both Böder and Jevan stood up at the same time and raced towards the greedy pirates with the speed and agility of lions protecting their cubs.

The moment the cart was seen, the three oldest scouting pirates drew their swords and became very wary. It was to these three that I began my own encounter. They saw the giants bearing down on their comrades and were in the process of calling out to warn them when I downed two of them with my throwing stars. As the third cautious pirate realized what was happening he turned to face me and died under the ministrations of my sword. I looked to see the other pirates in the middle of the clearing being easily dealt with quickly and savagely by two very angry giants.

I turned and raced to try and catch up to Kaira. I needed to know that she was alright. I was approaching at speed the break in the trees around the clearing where I had last seen her vanishing to follow after those three pirates, when Kaira came racing fearfully back into the clearing. Recognizing what was happening I dived to my left behind a thick leafy bush. Kaira saw me and to her credit she kept running toward the middle of the clearing where Böder was just turning to face her after ending the lives of the last of the four pirates. A mere five seconds later the three pirates burst into the clearing. They were in mindless pursuit of a pretty young Bidowman that had stumbled into them on her way down to the river. They were halfway between Kaira and the opening before they realized that there was a giant reaching for them with his mace. Two of the pirates never lived to regret their decision to follow Kaira because they were already dead and flying through the air into obscurity and some thick bushes. The third stopped and turned to flee the way he had come and once more my sword entered his chest and slicing his heart in two, ending any hope he might have had of escaping unhurt.

We regrouped and made our way cautiously over to the edge of the clearing where we could look down at the river bank. It was immediately obvious that the two oarsmen guarding the rowboat hadn't heard any sounds of the recent conflict in the clearing. I breathed a sigh of relief and congratulated Kaira and the giants on a job well done. After we had cleaned up the clearing of any and all signs of the ten scouts swift demise, we gathered together once more at the top of the riverbank. Hidden from view, we looked out over the river and down towards the four boats upon the inlet.

Here, in quiet conversation, we continued working on the next part of our plans to rescue our friends still held captive on Captain Stemm's boat, the *Riverrock*!

EARLICH

Four braziers had been set up on the deck of the *Riverrock* to form an invisible square. These gave off warmth and light and helped define the boundaries we were limited to whilst the pirates were in command of our boat. Captain Stemm, his crew and all the passengers, *(including myself)*, which was a total of sixteen manimals, had been placed in the square determined by the placement of the four little fires. The pirates from the three boats came and went, as they wished, whilst their boats remained tied up to the *Riverrock* which they then used as a common meeting ground. Besides the constant flow of pirates, there were eight armed guards on our boat standing or sitting just on the other side of the line of the braziers. In essence, there was always someone watching us. We had also been warned that if just one of those on board the boat escaped or even tried to escape then the rest of the captives would be tortured, killed and either eaten or thrown into the water whilst the escapee would be hunted down and could look forward to a long and tortuously slow dismemberment before being killed and finally eaten.

Despite these threats, this didn't stop us from watching what was happening on our boat or on the three pirate boats tied to ours, nor from observing with interest what was happening on the riverbank.

Also, it should be noted at this time, that the pirates still hadn't found Bartrow and it was only a couple of hours or so before it would start getting dark. In one sense, I pitied the pirates when the night-time came, because I had seen some of the damage that little troll could do. And so we waited patiently, in silence and expectation, for the darkness.

JELLICK

Watching from our imaginary prison in the middle of the deck of the *Riverrock*, we could see the two pirate oarsmen standing on guard beside the rowboat beached on the riverbank. They were obviously waiting for word from any one of the ten scouts who had gone in search of our giant. They were talking idly to one another, when they saw a young Bidowman making her way down to the riverside to get some water. They suddenly forgot their duty and slowly began to make a move toward the young female. The young Bidowman saw the two pirates and then in startled recognition of their lustful intentions, she turned and fled back up the way she had come down.

Realizing their intended victim was getting away from them far too easily they began to give chase. The Bidowman slipped in the mud, which gave the two guards the added incentive that perhaps they might even catch the young maiden and they increased their efforts to reach her. After all, that was half the fun of being a pirate and a thief, robbing people and taking what they wanted from those they could intimidate and pursue. But she got up all the same, looked back fearfully and took off running again, but they were slowly gaining on the young Bidowman as she topped the riverbank and disappeared through an arch of bushes and trees.

We couldn't see the clearing, nor what was happening, but Traxxa told us of all that occurred when we finally caught up with him.

TRAXXA

The two oarsmen broke quickly through and into the clearing laughing with the heady excitement of the chase of a young maiden. Here they quickly entered the afterlife just as my sword met one pirate and Böders mace met the other at roughly the same moment.

JELLICK

A short time later the two oarsmen returned to their posts down by the rowboat on the riverbank. That is to say, from the pirate boats in the middle of the inlet anyone looking toward the riverbank thought they saw the two oarsmen they knew as the ones who had rowed the ten scouts to the riverbank earlier that afternoon. It was getting late in the afternoon and the signal came from the pirate boat for the rowboat to return for a meal and to change the guards over. But instead of getting in the rowboat and heading towards the cluster of boats in the inlet, the two guards looked up the riverbank and after waving frantically towards the main body of pirates they turned and fled up the path away from the river and over the top of the bank and disappeared once more.

There was a sudden rush of activity by the pirates on the boat closest to the riverbank as they all became abuzz and another rowboat was quickly lowered into the water of the inlet. A further fifteen pirates jumped in and rowed as quickly as they could to the riverbank. Once ashore, four of the pirates became oarsmen -- two in each boat -- and paddled the two rowboats ashore back out to the pirate vessels moored in the inlet. The other eleven pirates, swords drawn and on high alert raced up the side of the riverbank following in the direction their comrades had gone only minutes before.

About half an hour passed and Biargamouth, his three captains and the rest of the pirates were all watching the riverbank expressing great signs of extreme keen interest. Then as if by magic the two sentries from before topped the ridge and made their way slowly down to the riverbank. They seemed to be looking for the rowboat and when they couldn't find it they waved to the boats upon the water to say they were back and to send another rowboat over to pick them up. By now, the gloom of early evening was such that their features were indiscernible and they could barely be recognized. And whilst they were wearing the clothes of their companions there was something about them that didn't quite make sense. I could tell from his manner and his words that there were clouds of doubt growing in Biargamouth's mind. He was obviously very unhappy and deeply unsure of what was happening to his men on the shore.

"I want to know what is happening on the mainland once and for all!" He shouted. "Ranka, load up all the rowboats *(which was one from each pirate boat)* go ashore and find out what has happened to my men!"

Ranka appeared to be Biargamouth's second-in-command. He too was a large Bearaman; though he was not quite as big as his leader. Still, we had heard he was reportedly very strong, very aggressive and exceedingly cruel but beyond that he was also exceptionally crafty. Biargamouth liked him because he was a very good tactician and had often helped plan a lot of their skirmishes both on the water and on the land. There were now thirty-seven manimals, consisting of six oarsmen and thirty fully armed and totally focussed pirates led by a very resourceful and dangerous Bearaman crossing the inlet towards the riverbank.

As the three rowboats got closer to the two guards standing on the riverbank suddenly they looked up as though being called or distracted. Then, before Ranka could call out for them to stop, they turned and ran up the now discernible path up the riverbank and disappeared once more over the top.

Ranka and his men got out of the rowboats. He divided his forces into three groups of ten men each. Ranka sent one group to the left and the other to the right along the riverbank. When they were about fifty meters to either side of his position, Ranka signalled and, together as one, the three groups began to climb slowly and carefully up the river embankment,. All three groups went over the top of the rise at the same time and all disappeared. They had been gone barely a minute when one of the original rowboat guards returned back along the riverbank coming in from the left. By now it was fairly dark and difficult to see exactly what was happening but it appeared that the six rowers left to guard the boats began talking with the lone returning guard and then they simply weren't there. It was as if a giant hand came up out of the water and all six guards suddenly disappeared. All I know is, as I watched the activity on the riverbank, one moment the seven dark shadows of guards were completely blacked out by a huge shadow of a creature which disappeared as quickly as it had arrived. And there on the shoreline was the lone figure of a pirate. But this one didn't seem upset or disturbed or even concerned about the other six pirates apparently not being there beside him. Then, just as suddenly, a second smaller dark shadow appeared from out of the bushes to the left and joined with the first shadowy pirate. Then together they got into one of the rowboats and began towing the other two boats out into the inlet back towards us.

BÖDER

After Traxxa, Jevan and I had destroyed the last group of eleven pirates, Traxxa gave instructions to take all the bodies and their weapons and throw them into a deep ravine. By now there were twenty-three bodies scattered in or around the clearing. When this was done, Traxxa gave us instructions on what he wanted us to do next.

Jevan and I were to take the cart of treasure as far south as we were able and then transport the treasure down to the shoreline but keeping well out of sight of the inlet. As we began to unload the cart, we were to replace the treasure with rocks and logs and anything else we could find that gave the cart some weight. When the treasure was hidden amongst rocks and bushes by the shore, we were to wheel the cart a bit further on and push it over the edge into another ravine. At the top of the ravine, we were to scrape the earth to deceive anyone who might be tracking the cart into believing that whoever was there had slipped and fallen over the edge and down into the ravine along with the treasure.

When this was done, Jevan was to return to be with Traxxa whilst I was to make for the water and watch what the pirates were doing from the safety of the point just south of the inlet. If nothing happened I was to stay in the shallows and wait for darkness when I was to start attacking the pirates on their boats one at a time starting with the boats on the river side of the *Riverrock*. If, however, a large contingent of pirates made their way to the shore, then Jevan was to keep low in the water and make her way along the shoreline once the pirates had disappeared inland. She would then keep pace with Traxxa and deal with whoever would be left guarding the rowboats.

Traxxa guessed correctly that the pirate leader wanted desperately to find out what was happening to his forces on the land and would probably send between twenty and thirty pirates hoping to deal with the problem decisively. From previous observations Traxxa reckoned there would be at least six pirates left on the shoreline to guard the rowboats. If this happened he would approach them and when he attacked he wanted Jevan to help in their destruction. At the same time I was to make my way to the two pirate boats on the river side of Stemms boat and start eliminating any pirates that would come within my reach. Traxxa told me that if a large number of pirates came ashore there would be at most fifteen pirates left to guard the prisoners and watch the boats. That meant at least eight to guard the prisoners and two pirates on each of the pirate boats. With this in mind, the moment I saw the three rowboats loaded to the gunwales with pirates heading towards the shore as Traxxa suggested they might, I began to make my way across the open stretch of water to deal with the pirates on the boats. By this time, however, the darkness was almost complete and we knew if we didn't make too much noise we could probably deal with the remaining pirates without any real threat being made to our friends aboard the *Riverrock*.

And that is what I did.

The water in the inlet was shallow and only came up to my thighs and waist. I didn't even need to use my mace. I simply moved up to the first of the pirate boats and saw that it was tied up securely to the *Riverrock*. There were two pirates upon this boat but they were completely absorbed in watching what was happening on the shore that my reaching into their boat and smacking their heads together rendered them both unconscious and no longer a threat. But just to be sure I picked one up at a time and snapped each of their necks before letting them slip quietly into the river to be food for the creatures in the Dund. I was moving to the second boat when out of the corner of my eye I saw a shadow pass by me over the deck of the first pirate boat. This shadow was moving with stealth and determination towards the same boat as I was. The shadow stopped and turned towards me. It smiled and waved and I had to stop myself from laughing and just waved back. Turning around, I re-focused my attention towards the pirates on the boat on the shore side of the *Riverrock*. This, I felt sure, would allow Bartrow his time of fun with the pirates on the second boat.

As I came around the stern of the *Riverrock* I froze, there coming back towards the boats were the darkened shadows of the rowboats. But then I saw the bulky shadow of Jevan bent over slightly to reduce her height and pulling the front rowboat which had both Traxxa and Kaira in it. This was the lead boat and it in turn was towing the other two empty boats behind them. I smiled as I now saw that Traxxa had tricked the pirates and now there were thirty odd armed pirates stranded on the shore and next to no guards on the boats in the inlet.

I looked around carefully and saw the last of the pirates on board the two remaining boats were peering desperately over the gunwales of either the *Riverrock* or the main pirate ship. They were obviously searching the dark of the inlet as best as their night eyes would allow to see what was happening before them.

Just as the rowboats drew up to the bow of the *Riverrock* behind the main pirate ship, Jevan and I stood up as one, grabbed two pirates each and pulled them from the boats and into the water. Jevan shoved her two pirates under the water and using her knees and her hands she kept them submerged until they no longer struggled. Meanwhile I let the second of my pirates flounder in the water as I twisted the neck of the first one. When he went limp, I grabbed the second pirate and snapped him in half and casually let them both drift off and away with the rivers flow. Before anyone even knew what was really happening I was already reaching into the boat to grab a third pirate before he could react and get out of my way.

Seeing Jevan and I tearing his crew of pirates apart before his very eyes, the leader of the pirates -- an incredibly big Bearaman -- roared like a frightened animal and stepped back from the ship's rail. He reached for his sword as he moved purposefully towards the defenceless prisoners. It was obvious he intended killing some of them before we could get to him when suddenly he was hit in the midriff by the incredibly strong shadow, who had smiled and waved at me earlier. Bartrow had somehow got a hold of Jarecks' vicious two headed axe and was already cutting up the winded pirate captain with fanatical precision. With two large gashes, one along his throat which the dying pirate tried desperately to hold and stop the flow of blood and one across his stomach where even as we watched his entrails began tumbling out. Then in a quick movement Bartrow brought the axe up and down and impaled the chest of the large pirate captain. Biargamouth was dead and falling to the deck of the *Riverrock* before he even really had time to grasp what it was that had destroyed him.

Then suddenly Traxxa and Kaira were on the *Riverrock*'s deck as well. Traxxa stood warily, swords in hand, ready to take on any pirate that made a move towards them or any one of the prisoners still remaining in the middle of Captain Stemm's deck.

CHAPTER TWENTY-SIX

JELLICK

We watched in amazement as Jevan and Böder emerged from the water to stand beside the boats at the same time. We also watched in horror as Jevan drowned the pirates she had grabbed and Böder killed three of the pirates by snapping their necks with ease before anyone could stop him or contend with him. In dismay I watched as Biargamouth turn savagely towards us whilst drawing out his sword at the same time. We knew he meant to kill as many of us before he encountered 'our giant' personally!

But then, in utter amazement, we watched as a shadow of muscle and speed step into the huge Bearaman and knock him backwards stopping him dead in his tracks with apparent ease. Then, with the savagery of thousands of troll years behind him we watched as Bartrow completely carved up and destroyed the huge pirate leader. Bartrow was not even half Biargamouth's size but he was faster, stronger and more determined to protect his friends than the pirate leader was to protect his own life. The anger of the pirate chief was never allowed to rise and help motivate his fighting skills as the troll was all over him before he even had a chance to call on his inner strength. This strength was what had helped make him a leader of murderers, thieves and cowards. Biargamouth died quickly by Jareck's twin-headed axe, wielded by the young Bartrow. I had not seen Bartrow move so fast or inflict such wounds with such devastating precision before and I must say I was both mesmerized and horrified at this bloody yet deeply satisfying result.

Then, as if realising their time had come, the three pirates, who were left still standing, swiftly dropped to their knees and pleaded for their lives. Because they were on Captain Stemms boat they were under his control and care and it was up to him to decide their fate. He took pity on them and instructed them to be tied up and made captive prisoners.

After embracing Traxxa and Kaira and shaking the fingers of Jevan and Böder in greeting, I asked the obvious question. "What now?"

To which Traxxa responded immediately. "We need to move off quickly and the sooner the better. Then we will be stopping off just around the southern point of this inlet where the treasure is hidden and waiting to be picked up. But, after that, we can continue on our journey south!"

The moment he realized the *Riverrock* was back in his control Captain Stemm gave Eddron orders to rally his men to ready the boat to continue its journey south. Eddron had been listening to what Traxxa had been saying and responded immediately by giving orders to cut the lines of the pirate boats when an idea came to me.

"Captain Stemm may I suggest you hold off on setting the pirate boats adrift -- at least until we have had a chance to explore them and search for anything of value. But the main reason I want you to keep the boats, or at least two of them, is I want to use them to transport our giant friends up the river. This will ease the pressure of them swimming across the Dund to their island. It will also take away the problem of waiting for them should they decide to walk to Bernitz. That is if they didn't wish to swim with us up river all the way to his island. Also I think we should keep two of the rowboats because we will need them to transport the treasure from the shore to the boat!"

When I put this to Stemm he took a long hard look at Jevan and Böder and then at the boats, which, until recently, had belonged to the pirates.

"This could work!" He said with a broad smile. So he changed the orders given to have some of his men check the boats for anything of value. A quick check was taken and there were five small chests with a number of interesting items of value within each. There were also a couple of large jars, but no-one seemed to know what the dark, syrupy looking liquid inside them was. Traxxa in particular was interested by this find. He sniffed them and said they smelled of rich almond paste. He allowed the smallest of a drop fall into a dish and touched the surface of it so there was the barest film of this liquid on the tip of his smallest fingers. He said it didn't burn but he could feel the warmth of the liquid. He touched it with his tongue and immediately his mouth went numb. He knew then what the syrup was and frowned. He spat the taste out of his mouth and washed his mouth out with some salt water.

He turned to Captain Stemm. "Do you mind if I keep these jars, Böder has a drazil problem on his island and I'd be interested to see what affect, if any, this liquid might have on them!"

"Why? What do you mean?" Stemm asked with a furrowed brow.

Traxxa replied, not exactly whispering but speaking low so that only Stemm and I could hear him. "The liquid inside these jars is a highly toxic poison. If anyone was to swallow the merest drop of this or it was to land on a scratch or get into an open wound it would render the person unconscious or may even kill them. If however a blade or an arrow head was dipped into this poison then whoever was cut or pierced by the point or blade, then again depending on how much is used, that person is likely to be knocked unconscious at best or at worst die within a very short time afterwards.

"When I watched the last group of pirates come ashore, late this afternoon, I noticed there were at least three archers within each of the teams that went up the riverbank. I think they were fearful of fighting Böder, even then. I believe the arrows they were going to fire and perhaps even their blades as well had most probably been dipped into this very poison. The wounds from their arrows or from their swords and blades on their own would have very little impact on Böder, but who's to say really what kind of effect this poison might have had upon him!"

Captain Stemm looked closely at the jars and then into Traxxa's face.

"You can keep these three jars of poison on the condition that you keep them safe and hidden away. But most importantly, no-one else but you must know about it. Is that understood?"

Traxxa smiled and thanked him and went off to do just that.

Once everything was in order and everything of value that was found on the pirate boats had been stowed aboard the *Riverrock*, Captain Stemm gave instructions to Eddron to have the crew cut the smallest of the pirate boats loose along with its rowboat and let it drift off towards the main river flow. As he was about to do this, I suggested to Captain Stemm that the four braziers be placed on the boat and that all lights on the *Riverrock* be extinguished at once.

"For why?" He asked with a frown.

"If any pirate is looking out from the shore they will have difficulty trying to determine what we are doing out here on the water. After all," I continued. "We have still yet to retrieve the treasure and it would be fruitless if Ranka and his pirates simply followed us up river to meet up with us on the shore near to where the treasure is hidden!"

Captain Stemm didn't need to think for long, he nodded his head and smiled grimly before waving his hand for Eddron to rally some hands to help him. Stemm had two of the braziers doused out whilst the other two glowing braziers were placed on the deck of the smallest of the pirate boats. He also left a few light crystals alive as well and cut it loose to have it float gently away on the slow inlet current.

As we watched the soft lights of the abandoned vessel leave us, Stemm, Traxxa, Böder and I talked softly about what we should do next. Realising the importance of speed, we began making every effort to set off immediately to recover the treasure and continue our journey south before the pirates on the riverbank realised what we were doing and followed us from the mainland. But from then on there were a myriad of little things that seemed to impede our progress at every turn throughout the night.

The first thing we discovered was that the ropes on the sail had been cut and tampered with and required attention to repair them and get them up and flapping in the wind once more. In the meantime Böder and Jevan put their shoulders to the stern of the *Riverrock* and began to push it swiftly out of the inlet towards the southern tip. The next thing we discovered was both pirate boats in tow had slipped their lines and were floating slowly away from us so Böder and Jevan had to stop what they were doing and go swiftly through the water of the inlet after the boats before they reached the fast flowing water of the main river. When both boats were reaffixed and a guard set over each of the lines our journey south began once more. Then in the darkness of the night Böder and Jevan were unable to find the exact location where they had hidden the treasure and they spent over two frustrating hours looking for their markers before finally stumbling upon their hidden treasure.

By this time the vicinity of the shoreline around the treasure had been thoroughly checked and there were no sign of any pirates. This was a relief so together we set about bringing the treasure from out of its hiding place and moving it agonizingly slowly down to the shoreline. Despite our best efforts it still took the two rowing boats three trips each to bring the remaining fifteen chests of treasure as well as Bartrows and my personal items from the shore to the boat. As Captain Stemm, Traxxa and I saw the last of the treasure being safely stowed into the hold of the *Riverrock*, we noticed, as if for the first time, that the soft light of pre-dawn was barely half an hour away and was threatening to reveal us to the world upon the river.

With this we realised we were running out of time so we quickly turned our attention to making the two pirate boats comfortable for our giant friends to be safely transported upriver. We looked at their size and believed they would be able to hold and transport both Böder and Jevan provided our friends remained lying down throughout the entire journey. The first thing we asked Böder to do was to break down the single sailing mast on each of the vessels with his mace. When this was done he then pulped the stumps of the two mast bases to make them nice and flat and comfortable. Böder did as he was instructed and was just testing to find out how comfortable their barge like vessels could be when word came down from the lookout that the pirate boat that had been set adrift earlier was coming up river fast. It was obvious that Ranka and his remaining thirty men had somehow retrieved the boat from the river and appeared intent on taking up arms against us once more.

Böder was for taking his mace and going out to meet the boat. But Traxxa put up his hand restraining him.

"No, don't go out to meet them in the water Böder." He said. "I have reason to believe they may have dipped their arrows in poison and just two or three hits from them and they might very well be able to kill even you or at the very least render you unconscious. We can't let them do that to you and even the *Riverrock* will be within arrow range in a couple of minutes! We need another plan and quickly. But please stay your hand for a moment or two whilst I give this new problem some thought!"

Stemm confirmed this and added. "Böder, there is simply no time for us to try and get out into the river and find the wind for the sails. You and

Jevan can't push us like you did in the inlet either. There the water was shallow, but the Dund gets very deep very quickly and it has a turbulent current. The way the pirates are moving they will be upon us in no time and they would find all of us easy prey whilst you would be floundering in the water!"

"Is there nothing I can do? Maybe throw something at them!?"

"The masts," said Traxxa quickly. "You throw the first one to gauge the distance and weight and balance, whilst I pour oil over the second one so that when you throw it, it will have a greater impact with raining fire of wood and sails!" He then turned to Jareck and told him to ready some flaming arrows.

As Böder lifted the mast, he jostled himself around to the stern of the boats being towed behind the *Riverrock* to see exactly where the pirates were. He saw they were much closer than he imagined, so he hefted the mast once, twice, leaned back and threw it high and long like he would with a spear or a javelin. The mast came down at the back of the pirate boat and there were angry screams, oaths thrown out and a number of arrows fired but they all fell wide or short. As he was doing this Traxxa, Stemm and Jevan prepared the second mast with oil for a quick fire.

The second mast was handed to Böder by Jevan and once more he tested it once twice and then hurled it towards the pirate ship much like the first. The moment the mast was launched with its sails tightly bound to the wood and covered in oil, then Jareck shot three flaming arrows one after the other in quick succession and each hitting the flying mast. By the time this mast hit the pirate's boat it was well alight and as a result had a much greater affect upon it than the first. The pirates screamed in fright and pain as they were hit by fiery debris as the mast smashed into the deck of the boat. But it didn't hit anything of importance and it didn't slow the boat down in any way. Another round of arrows were fired at them and, this time, Böder and Jevan had to move back out of the way as a couple of arrows got very close.

"That's it!" said Böder angrily, and he reached over and brought one of the rowboats over to him. "Here help me Jevan!"

Together they lifted the boat up out of the water and, as she held it steady it for him, he placed his feet wide and his hands in strategic positions under its hull. Traxxa gave some last-second instructions to Jevan to help

Böder's aim and intended trajectory. Then he suddenly remembered there was still a whole bag of his oil and powder jar bombs. Traxxa quickly grabbed one of them and signalled to Jareck to ready himself with some more fiery arrows. He gave the sack of bombs to Jevan reminding her to be careful with it and had her drop it gently into the boat without breaking it just as Böder stepped forward and launched the rowboat into the air towards the pirate's boat which was now less than twenty meters away from them.

The rowboat descended quickly, now fully alight from Jareck's fiery arrows and smashed into the bow of the pirate's boat. Then, as if by magic, both boats suddenly exploded in a violent flame and black smoke of fiery oil and burning wood. The front of the pirate's boat disintegrated at once in a shower of splinters and it lurched alarmingly into the oncoming river and the water from the Dund rushed in to fill the massive hole in the bow. Within seconds the pirates were screaming and leaping into the water to escape their sinking craft.

At the same time as Böder hurled the rowboat, the archers on the pirate vessel sent off a final volley of arrows, the majority of which were stopped by the flying rowboat. However three of their arrows found their way into Böder's left arm. Seeing the devastating effect of his missile, Böder was all for going out into the river and making certain none of the pirates ever made it alive to shore, but Jevan stopped him and brought his attention to the arrows sticking out of his arm.

"Quickly!" Traxxa cried out. "Jevan help him get aboard his boat so that we can tow him back to his island home.

When he heard the word 'home', Böder turned to his friends and smiled his lovely boyish smile, before stumbling sideways in the river. Jevan had already been reaching for him and with the little help they could give, Traxxa, Jareck, Stemm, Earlich and half the crew of the *Riverrock* helped Böder collapse onto the closest pirate vessel.

Eddron, at the helm, carefully steered the *Riverrock* close to the shore to allow Jevan all the footing she needed to ensure Böder was safely aboard his vessel. Only when she saw that he was safe and resting soundly did she slump aboard the other pirate vessel totally exhausted and near to collapse. Traxxa, Jareck, Kaira, Earlich and I stayed with Böder on his boat to ensure no harm would come to him as he struggled in unconsciousness as the poison from the arrows coursed through his system.

Traxxa only had eyes for Böder such was his concern, but he did manage to take a quick glance back towards the pirates to see they were all but gone. The majority of the pirates had drowned or were being slowly pulled under the water one by one until there was only a handful of half drowned thugs and thieves who were able to make it safely to the shore. Ranka was one of the first that made it to shore and he looked, with hateful fury, at the disappearing giants, his two boats, a treasure that was almost his and the boat and crew of a master sailor.

The only thing left of the pirates boat was its mast sticking up out of the river and this was floating rapidly downstream where within minutes it would be out of sight completely. It was then that Traxxa saw the slim line of another dark boat hovering on the very edge of the distant horizon in the soft light of the early morning predawn and he was careful to drew only my attention to it.

On the fourth day of our journey upon the rivers, two things happened in quick succession which were clearly disturbing and confirmed to me that all was not well on board the *Riverrock*. The first of these to happen came about mid-morning when all aboard heard the howls of sheer terror coming from Bartrow below deck. Upon an immediate and fearful investigation, we found someone had accidentally *(or on purpose)* opened all the hatches on deck. This had flooded the lower deck with sunlight and threatened to take poor Bartrows life. Fortunately for Bartrow he had been sleeping at this time and was hidden beneath a copious supply of smelly tarps and old sails. Order was quickly restored and it was made clear that upon pain of severe physical reprimand or even death that no hatch on the top deck was ever to be left open at any time during the daylight hours. Furthermore Bartrow was reassured that he could continue sleeping during the day undisturbed as we were out to protect him fully.

The second thing to happen, about the same time we were dealing with the problem of keeping Bartrow safe, we heard a sudden fearful cry of help from Jevan. We raced to the stern of the *Riverrock* to find Jevan holding grimly onto the handrails of the pirate boat floating beside her own, wherein Böder was lying still in a state of unconsciousness. Traxxa and Jareck, both of whom had been up all night accompanying their injured friend, had only just fallen asleep and were lying beside him on his boat. At the first howl by Bartrow, Traxxa had woken briefly but found it difficult to find his senses believing the howl was just part of a disturbing dream. But as soon as Jevan began crying out for help he came quickly out of his sleep and roused himself to rally to Jevans cry. Even as we looked on, he was racing to the handrail of his boat with a length of rope. He had grabbed it on the way, and with Jarecks help they looped it around the handrails to secure the two vessels together. Traxxa then went to the bow of his boat where another rope was thrown over to him and he was quickly able to reconnect Böders' boat to the rail of the *Riverrock* once more.

Traxxa pulled the broken connecting rope which was still attached to the handrail on the stern of his boat up out of the river and had a quick look at it. He and Jareck examined it and they saw that it had frayed, disintegrated and broke, which was why their boat had been set adrift. But there was something that bothered Traxxa about this and he went over to Jevan to ask her what she saw and what had happened.

JEVAN

"I was looking fondly over toward Böder who looked so peaceful as he lay there unconscious, at the very moment the rope snapped. I reached over without thinking and grabbed the rail of your boat, to stop it from floating away with the river current. I was just about to call out for help when something caught my eye and I looked towards the back end of the *Riverrock*. It was then that I saw a hand with a knife coming through the rails and it was attempting to cut the rope which was attached to my boat as well. That's when I started calling out. As soon as I screamed out for help, the hand with the knife disappeared and you began to wake up!"

After a reflective thought, Traxxa asked me, "Was there anything about the hand that might identify the one using the knife?"

"Yes," I said after thinking about it for a second or two. "He was using his right hand and it had a tattoo between his thumb and his first finger. I couldn't tell what the tattoo was of but it appeared to be blue and his hand was tanned brown!"

Jellick

With this information, Traxxa looked at the rope in his hand again before making his way laboriously back onto the *Riverrock*. Once back aboard he looked closely at the rope connected to Jevans boat. He saw it had indeed been frayed from the affects of a knife. Traxxa called Stemm and me over to where he was standing and showed us the two lengths of rope. Sensing something out of the ordinary, Captain Stemm immediately turned and sent his crew and everyone else away from the area. This left just the three of us looking with renewed concern at this obvious act of sabotage.

Traxxa then proceeded to tell us about seeing the light crystals on the bow of the *Riverrock* when it was leaving Regil-Ter, and also from its stern when it was leaving Böder and Jevan on the Mirack riverbank. The story of the hoppers was told to us and how they had been chanting 'Böder' and 'Xalarlla's name during the attack at the farmhouse. He also brought our attention back to the recent events such as the fouling of the sail ropes and the two pirate boats which had gone adrift whilst being pushed by Böder and Jevan. He then finished off by telling Stemm about the dark boat on the horizon, beyond where the pirate's boat had sunk after Böder had sent the rowboat smashing into it.

"Sers," he concluded, "we have a spy on this boat and a dangerous one at that. I believe he has been in constant contact with either Zharlla or the pirates or both. He probably let them know of your intended cargo, of Böders treasure and that we would be helping Jevan to escape from Regil-Ter even before we left. I'm also willing to wager that this spy let Zharlla know about Böder and Jevan being dropped off on the peninsula when they went to retrieve the treasure. From this information, Zharlla has somehow managed to summon a horde of insect men to try and find and destroy them. But fortunately for us she didn't count on these creatures being distracted by a farm full of a late crop of grain for food. This spy has tried everything he can to try and slow us down and now he has tried to kill Bartrow by opening the hatches on the top deck...!"

"But surely that was an accident or an oversight!" Stemm said. The concern in his voice, betrayed the fact that he really didn't believe this.

"Ordinarily on its own, I would probably have agreed with you. But with the sail ropes, the setting the pirate boats adrift, the flash of the light crystals and now the cutting of the rope to Böders boat and attempting to cut the rope to Jevans boat, I would say this person, after trying to kill Bartrow, wanted to separate the giants and myself from the *Riverrock*!"

"This is greatly concerning." Said Captain Stemm sombrely.

"I agree with Traxxa about there being a spy on board." I added, in support of Traxxa. "And even as I think about it now it all makes sense. For instance, I remember some of the things Biargamouth said when asking about Böder he kept referring to him as 'our giant'. Now who does that remind you of?" I asked looking at Traxxa.

Who answered immediately, "Why Zharlla of course!"

"That is my thinking as well, especially in light of these other disturbing incidents!" I added.

"But there is more!" Put in Stemm slowly resigning himself to the facts as they presented themselves to him. "Remember, the pirates asked the whereabouts of this wonderful treasure. Well, no-one on the *Riverrock* but myself and a few of my most trusted men knew this treasure was due to come aboard and even less knew that it belonged to Böder. But it's hardly surprising that these important pieces of information haven't been joined together, when you consider that the treasure returning giant has been the star attraction at this year's Judicial Games! That and of course the rumours of his exploits and his treasure have been racing all around Regil-Ter like a raging forest fire!"

"So then, what are we going to do, now that we know there is a spy aboard my boat?" Stemm asked with great feeling.

"Oh, I forgot to mention," said Traxxa looking directly at Stemm. "Jevan said she saw a blue tattoo between the thumb and forefinger on the tanned right hand of the perpetrator as he was trying to cut through her rope. Do you know who this might be?"

"You mean like this?" Said Stemm presenting his right hand which had a blue butterfly on it between his thumb and forefinger, which when the thumb moved it looked like the butterfly was trying to fly away.

"Yes, exactly like that!" Traxxa said evenly. "Does anyone else in your crew or on this boat have a tattoo similar to yours?"

Chapter Twenty-Seven

Earlich

Apart from Böder being shot with three poisoned arrows and falling into a deep sleep, after the treasure had been picked up and Böder had spectacularly destroyed the pirate's boat, I thought we had little else to worry about on the journey on towards Böders Island. However, something about the way Traxxa, Tor Jellick and Captain Stemm were acting before we had even begun our final voyage with Böder told me that I had missed a significant piece of information about what was really happening around me. So I did some investigating of my own, which uncovered the very real fact that there was a spy aboard the *Riverrock*. I must say, this had a strange effect upon everyone, including me.

Jellick

Captain Stemm waited a long time, as his face betrayed the fact that he was considering his next words very carefully. He obviously knew something but was struggling either with the information he had or how best to tell us exactly what it was that was bothering him. Finally he turned slowly away from us as and reached out for the closest heavy thing he could wield which was a turning pin and whispered almost despairingly,   "Eddron!"

Sensing we needed -- or rather *deserved* -- more information, he paused and turned back to us saying. "He was at the bow of the *Riverrock* searching the Mirack for you -- Traxxa, Bartrow and Böder -- when we left Regil-Ter. He was also at the stern somewhere near the helmsman at the time after dropping Böder and Jevan off on the riverbank. And finally he and I have the same tattoo which we got together as a sign of the bond we share here on the *Riverrock*. You see, he's my cousin and we've been together ever since we got this boat, but now, I think I'll kill him!"

As he said this, the knuckles of his hand whitened as he tightened the grip on the hard wooden pin before looking directly at me and saying with a deep sadness in his voice. "I'm sorry that he has done this! But I will fix this terrible betrayal right now!"

And he made a move to go and do what he had just said he would. Traxxa quickly reached out and put his hand on the arm holding the pin.

"No don't," he said softly, "I have a better idea!"

Stemm stopped and looked closely at Traxxa.

We turned and approached the crew, who had been watching us talking softly to one another and waiting for us, a little nervously, beneath the main mast in the middle of the *Riverrock's* deck. As we began mixing with the crew, suddenly Captain Stemm lashed out with his right hand which had become a balled up fist and smashed it into Eddron's chin who then promptly collapsed in a heap where he had been standing.

"Pick him up and throw him in the hold close to Bartrow!" Captain Stemm spat out, angrier than I have ever seen him before or since, whilst pointing to two of his crew.

When Eddron came round, Traxxa and I were standing over him. Bartrow was lurking in the darker recesses of the hold watching carefully and listening intently to all that we were doing and saying. Traxxa squatted on his haunches and looked down into the fearful eyes of the *Riverrock's* first mate as he turned to try and find out where he was.

Traxxa spoke softly and slowly with a menace in his voice that I had rarely ever heard from him before. "I am going to ask you a couple of questions right now. I am only going to ask each question just the once. If the answer you give me is either a lie or not complete, or even if I am unsatisfied with the way you respond to me I am going to cut off one of your fingers and feed it to Bartrow." Here, he pointed to the troll. "And he will be only too pleased to eat the one who tried to kill him earlier. Do you understand me?"

We could see the fear intensify in Eddron's eyes by the light of the large light crystal attached to the support beam just behind and above Traxxa.

But he didn't answer, he just nodded his head. Traxxa reached out for his left hand and brought out Jareck's vicious-looking axe. Eddron flinched and tried to pull his hand away, but couldn't under the firm ministrations of the Timber Wolfaman.

Traxxa whispered ever so softly, "I can't hear you!"

"Yes, yes I understand! You'll cut off my fingers one by one if I don't answer your questions correctly and fully!"

"Good, good! First question then, how long have you been communicating with Zharlla the witch?"

At this question Eddron appeared visibly shaken but had the good sense to answer without a seconds delay, "It was nearly a week ago. Anyway, it was shortly after you came to the *Riverrock* to discuss hiring us to get you out of Regil-Ter. Her men stopped me in the marketplace and gave me some slev to go and meet with her. I took it from them because I thought it was easy money and it required nothing of me as far as I could see. But then when I met with her she began to ask questions about you and our contract together. At first I was reluctant to answer any of her questions about you, but I found that I was unable to keep anything she asked of me without wanting to tell her. It was as though I was being compelled through no will of my own!"

Traxxa looked up at me and we nodded together as we suddenly understood what had happened. Eddron had accepted money from her, which, if it was covered in a curse, meant that he had unwittingly entered into a binding contract with her without him even knowing about it. If he had accepted anything of value from her without stipulating the parameters of the contract, then the contract was hers to determine what it would comprise of and ultimately what it would mean for both parties. Traxxa turned back towards the cowering Eddron and continued.

"So, from what you have just said, you have unwittingly entered into a contract with Zharlla, whether you know it or not! So now tell me, how have you been contacting her whilst on the *Riverrock*?"

Eddron looked at his hand fearfully and then over to where he knew Bartrow was lurking before he finally answered. "It was through the flashing of a light crystal!"

"Did you have any contact with the pirates?"

"No, they came upon us too quickly and were a complete surprise to me!"

Traxxa looked long and hard at Eddron before deciding he had been told the truth.

"So what was it that Zharlla wanted you to tell her?" He asked.

"Just to let her know about the giants and the treasure, that was all!"

"Where is Zharlla at the moment?"

"I think she is on a dark ship, just beyond the horizon behind us! I saw it first thing this morning, though it disappeared as the sun began to rise. Don't ask me how I know, but I sense it is behind and just out of our sight. What I do know though is it will stay with us and follow us all the way up the river."

"What was your last message and when did you send it?"

"I haven't been able to send any message to her, not since the message in the Mirack River." He said, cringing, "But only because there was nothing to report!" Eddron ended lamely

"And when were you going to contact her next?"

"Possibly tonight, once it got dark!"

"Does she ever contact you? And if so, how?"

"No never! All she told me to do was just to keep her informed of what was taking place on board the *Riverrock*. But she also told me from the outset that I was to do whatever it takes to help return her giant back to her and to send your giant to her also -- if it was at all possible!"

"So tell me, why did you try and kill our friend Bartrow over there in the dark?"

Eddron stopped himself from giving a quick answer. He first peered with utter fear into the dark towards where we knew Bartrow was sitting patiently, watching and waiting.

Finally, Eddron dropped his head and said slowly, fearfully, despondently. "The troll frightens me! I thought if I could just get rid of him or at the very least create a distraction by disturbing him, I could then cut the ropes of the giants boats and perhaps in the confusion create a situation where I might be able to take control of the *Riverrock*!"

"What? Are you saying there other crew members who were going to help you in this mutiny?"

"No, no," said Eddron quickly, a little too quickly thought Traxxa and his eyebrows knitted together and his eyes went as hard as steel. But he said nothing; he waited for Eddron to continue.

"I was going to release the three pirates on board and try and wrestle control from Stemm. Once this was done I was planning to motivate the rest of the crew by presenting them with the promise of a greater share in the treasure!"

"So you're saying that Captain Stemm and all of the other crew members of the *Riverrock* know nothing of your plans or anything else particularly that of Zharlla?"

Eddron nodded his head. Traxxa ripped Eddron's left hand towards him and stopped the axe blade just as it broke the skin of his littlest finger drawing blood and as Eddron screamed out.

"NO!! No-one knows anything about my plans or intentions."

"*What*?!? Were you just going to kill us and your cousin Stemm for all the treasure, is that it?"

Eddron's head had dropped again and he began to nod but then quickly raised his head saying, "Yes, yes that's what I was planning to do! But not kill Stemm! I was hoping to persuade him to join us. Otherwise I would have imprisoned him for a time and hoped to change his mind later. But not kill him! No, not my cousin! Not if I didn't have to!"

Traxxa looked long and hard once more at Eddron, before he asked his next question.

"And the treasure? What did Zharlla ask you to do about the treasure?"

"She told me not to concern myself with the treasure that I could keep as much of it as I wanted but that she would take care of it!"

Traxxa turned and said softly to me before turning back to Eddron.

"This means, she was obviously calling on the pirates to get it for her. That is, if her heart was after it at all! In any case she probably didn't trust this little minkle! Mind you, the pirates wouldn't have been any better at sharing the treasure with her, eh!"

And then to Eddron he asked. "So now Eddron, show me exactly how do you make words and send messages using the light crystal?"

Eddron, sensing a reprieve, became suddenly more than willing to show Traxxa how he had been instructed to pass messages to Zharlla. It took just over an hour to master the simple enough structure of sending messages via the light crystal. As Traxxa was being shown how to use the light crystal, I went over to Captain Stemm and told him all that we had learned from Eddron. As I talked with Stemm, I could see the pain in his eyes and I felt terribly sorry for him. He was a proud Ottarman and he was still coming to terms with the fact that he had family, like Eddron, who would willingly turn on him for the reasons I had just given him.

I concluded by saying as gently as I could. "Don't be too hard on him Captain. He has been manipulated and cursed, which means he has had his mind altered and, to a large degree, been controlled by a very powerful witch. This is why he was contacting her by the use of the light crystal. At this very moment Eddron is teaching Traxxa how to use the crystal in order to send messages to Zharlla. Apart from that of course, we do know there is evil in Eddron's heart because he told us he was planning to harm Bartrow, Böder, Jevan and the rest of my party in order to take control of our treasure."

"And, what of the treasure?" Captain Stemm asked tiredly.

"Oh yes, of course, the treasure! Well, we have all now recognized the power of greed in Eddron! However, upon saying that, I'm sure he would have kept you and your crew alive so that they could have taken a share in the treasure. But I guess we will never really know for sure, will we? I'm just sorry that our treasure has caused so many problems for you and your crew and revealed the true intentions of your cousin's heart!"

"I guess," said Stemm reflectively and with a certain amount of private philosophy, "I am grateful to you and your treasure because it has revealed to me the true nature of Eddron, whom, until now, I believed was totally trustworthy and an Ottarman of honour and integrity. I guess you don't know a person until great temptation is put before them!"

I nodded my head solemnly in agreement before saying politely, "And now, good Captain Stemm, I think I will go and check to see how our friend Böder is doing and see if there isn't some more assistance I can give him!"

"Go good Tor Jellick and let me know if there is anything I can do to help in any way!"

I nodded my head and then went to check with Jareck and Jevan to see how Böder was doing and they informed me that there had been no change in the peacefully sleeping giant. I told them to try and force some water and liquids down his throat and to keep him safe from the sun using some tarps and sails. I then met with Traxxa who told me that communicating using the light crystal was simple enough and that he would show me how to use it when we had some free time together. We then left Eddron with Bartrow and told the troll that if he had any trouble with him that he could take some of him for food. This, we knew, would keep Eddron in a heightened state of fear and capitulation.

When that day of fighting the currents of the River Dund was finished and darkness settled down over the river we brought Eddron up from out of the depths of the *Riverrock*. Once on the stern, Traxxa and I told him exactly what message we wanted him to send to Zharlla. I believed he was stalling as he told us the message needed to be sent at a particular time. I didn't trust Eddron at all, but Traxxa seemed to want to give him the benefit of the doubt. He told me privately that this would fit in with the thinking of the witch who might need to operate with moon and stars and clouds being in the right place and other such mystical stuff we had no knowledge of.

"And why don't we just send the message ourselves and be done with Eddron altogether?" Captain Stemm asked as we waited impatiently at the stern of the *Riverrock*.

"Because," I told him quietly, "It needs to be Eddron who sends the message. This way, if Zharlla can somehow sense the one flashing the light crystal she won't find anyone else behind the message but Eddron's...I don't know -- his spirit, or some other such rubbish! After all, we don't know the full extent of Zharlla's control over him, nor if she can sense any foreign influence over the message other than from the one she expects."

Captain Stemm nodded his head as though he understood, but his eyes told me he was very sceptical of all these wonderful powers we assumed this witch could possess. But he bowed to our better knowledge and experience of Zharlla and let us have our way on the matter.

So we watched and waited until Eddron told us the time had come for him to send the message. The light crystal was given to Eddron, who flashed out the message we wanted to give the witch, under the close watch of Traxxa. It was framed in the language and signs that could only have come from him and was to be understood by no-one but Zharlla

> *'Both giants killed by poisoned arrows from pirates.*
> *'Treasure not recovered - lost in the Dund!'*

The moment the message had been sent, Eddron with head down in humiliation and despair handed the light crystal over to Traxxa. He then turned slowly to go back to his post waiting in the dark depths of the *Riverrock* with Bartrow as his guard. That was when Captain Stemm, with one of Traxxa's swords, pierced Eddron's heart and he collapsed towards the deck of the *Riverrock* dead. Stemm with tears in his eyes and dribbling down his cheeks caught his cousin and held him close in his arms for a long time. With respect for their relationship, we left Captain Stemm alone for a time to be with this his dead relative.

Later that night, in a subdued banquet of wine and other assorted refreshments, we celebrated Eddron's death by burning the flesh of the dead first mate and eating him.

(*Eating the dead of those they had known and loved was the custom of all manimals in the land of Durogg. But it is always done in reverence and honour as part of their belief in rejuvenation and is a ceremony of sharing and remembrance.*)

Stemm took the customary first bite and then handed the majority of his portion over to Bartrow, before going and standing by the boat's handrail in quiet meditation. The only ones who were not given a portion of Eddron's remains were Böder who was still asleep, and Jevan. As a giant, Jevan didn't adhere to this particular manimal practise of sharing in the funeral celebration of an associate, a friend or a relative, by eating them. She found that even in this case she was unable to take part in this eating ceremony and just couldn't bring herself to do it, not even out of respect or sympathy to those who were a part of the ceremony. Also the three pirate prisoners were not invited to take part in this death ceremony as they neither knew Eddron nor had they been familiar with him.

Shortly thereafter, under the watchful eye of a quarter moon and in the darkness of the night, we pulled towards the shore of the Dund and waited for the coming of the dawn. This was because it could only be by the light of day that we dared to continue sailing safely against the currents of the mighty Dund River towards Böder's Island!

CHAPTER TWENTY-EIGHT

EARLICH

It is now our fifth day on the *Riverrock* with Captain Stemm and his crew. After the spy had been successfully dealt with, we began to focus our attention on continuing our journey towards Böder's Island. As it was fast becoming a real possibility that we could arrive there within the next three days or so, I fear this may be my last record of this first account of our ally and great friend Böder the giant!

JELLICK

Quite suddenly there was an almighty cheer and a great show of mid-morning exuberance when Jareck and Traxxa called out to us that Böder was stirring. This was followed closely by an overwhelming show of relief and emotion from everyone on board the *Riverrock*, especially once we learned from Jevan and Kaira that he was asking for some food and drink. This alone was a very good sign indeed.

Earlich, Captain Stemm and I made our way down to the boat on which Böder was being towed just to embrace and share this special moment with him as he struggled to come out of his poisoned sleep. We looked at his left arm and we saw, where the three arrows had been. In their place were three dark blue stains which were in the shape of three large tridents. These blemishes were to remain visible on Böder's arm for the rest of his life and so became a permanent reminder of just how close to death our giant friend had been.

It was only when Böder had eaten a little something and drunk his fill did we tell him where we were, and what had happened since he had fallen into unconsciousness after receiving the wounds from the arrows. Very soon after eating he seemed to have regained his indomitable boyish sense of humour and adventure, and showed no obvious signs of any side effects from the poison. Despite all this, we still continued to watch Böder closely over the next couple of hours and to our amazement he appeared to have recovered quickly and fully.

The rest of the day on the river was lost, for as soon as we were able to, Captain Stemm steered us into the first convenient place of shallow and calm waters where Böder and Jevan could stand up and stretch. There was a lot of embracing and kissing and playing in the water between our two giant friends. Indeed they inspired everyone, including the whole crew of the *Riverrock*, to take some time out to stretch and swim, wash and play and simply relax doing nothing at all atop a small rise overlooking the riverbank where we could share a proper meal and some good stout drinking with our awakening giant. This appeared to be just what was needed, for very soon afterwards we were all laughing and talking, eating and drinking end enjoying each other's company, which was just great. Especially when you consider what had happened to us over the last couple of harrowing days.

The only friend who missed out on this simple form of celebration was Bartrow who was left on board the *Riverrock* to watch over and guard the three pirate prisoners. Though we did hear him scream out a jubilant "Hurrah!" in his gruff, guttural, troll tongue, when word got through to him that Böder was alive and up and about and eating and playing around.

Led by Traxxa, members of the crew, including Captain Stemm, went off to go on a hunt to get some fresh meat. The rest of us, meanwhile, just sat on the riverbank or in the shallows of the water and spent some time talking and catching up on all of our stories. For me personally it was simply wonderful to watch as my friend Böder, in an apparent show of health and vitality, spent time with Jevan and us in friendly banter and easy conversation.

Somehow, it seemed, this poison induced sleep had done Böder a lot of good, helping him to rest and recuperate. In any case, Jevan seemed to be enjoying his recovery more than any one of us could ever have done.

And, after all, who could blame her? She seemed to loathe letting him go, for she was forever wanting to hold his hand and embrace him whenever he came close to her. Which, to be fair, was quite a lot of the time and he showed willing signs that he was enjoying her attentions. But it only lasted a short while as she slowly let him be after a time, recognizing that she was perhaps being a little too clingy and he needed to have his own space at times as well. And this too was a good thing.

We were having a brief nap on the shore when Traxxa and Stemm disturbed our calm by running back into our little encampment. Traxxa made straight for the *Riverrock*, whilst Captain Stemm stopped and told us. "We've seen a black boat moored a little ways down the river!"

Traxxa returned shortly afterwards carrying the last two mysterious bags of exploding jars of oil and powder.

Sensing that all was not well we rallied to him when he stepped ashore.

"Böder," he asked seriously, "are you up for a little confrontation with a persistent witch?"

"Ooooohhhh Yeah!" he said and asked, "Will I be needing my mace?"

"Probably not, but it won't hurt to bring it!"

"It might hurt someone!" Said Böder chuckling to himself as he went to get his weapon.

"Can I come with you?" Jevan asked

Traxxa looked up at her and said. "Of course Jevan, you are always welcome with us in a fight!"

So as Jevan and Böder rallied to get their weapons from the boats, I asked. "Do you want us to come along as well?"

"Yes of course, anyone can come, but you gotta be prepared to keep up, 'cause we'll be travelling swiftly!"

"Why? What are we up against?"

"Stemm and I were on a rise just north of here when we noticed the same dark boat I saw yesterday which had been sailing on the horizon behind the sinking pirate ship. The same one I suspect Zharlla is on. She's lurking about three kilometers down river and I think it is time we met her witchcraft with some sheer brute force. So if you want to watch, come let us go!"

With his swords and bag of explosives strapped to his back, Traxxa transformed into his wolf form. When this was completed he raced off quickly without bothering to see who was following after him. He headed north along the ridge above the river. Böder and Jevan soon caught up to him as Kaira, Jareck and I took on our animal forms *(that of two big dogs and a badger)* and raced after them. Kaira and Jareck were much faster than I, but I did my best to keep up and follow after them.

As we left, Captain Stemm called out to reassure us, saying the *Riverrock* would stay where they were until we returned. He also gave us an open offer to call on him for any assistance, should we need it.

Traxxa had reformed to his human state and was just finishing off giving final instructions to Böder when Jareck, Kaira and I finally caught up to them. We were just behind a rise, about hundred meters up from the riverbank of the Dund. I must say I was out of breath and in desperate need of a thoughtful collapse into a field of flowers. But I was determined to stay with it and watch the battle that was soon to take shape.

Böder stood up and moved forward carefully, trying hard to keep the trees' dense foliage between himself and the black boat moored in a sheltered bay out of the main flow of the Dund. Then, with Jevan and Traxxa's help, they fired up the first bag of the two jars of oil and powder and Böder flung it out over the bay and onto the deck of the black boat. Even as the first bag landed near the main mast and exploded in a huge ball of flame and smoke the second bag was flying across the bay to land just meters to the left of where the first bag had landed. Then it too exploded into a huge fire ball of orange and black and the flames on the boat increased rapidly setting fire to everything aboard where it burnt quickly and violently.

From our position high above the rivers bay, we could hear the screams and cries of those on board struggling to come to terms with this rapid attack.

"If you see the witch," I heard Traxxa telling both Böder and Jevan, "Then I want you to rush down and kill her as swiftly and as violently as you wish!"

But we saw no-one even closely resembling the witch, though we saw a number of pirates leaping around trying to fight a losing battle with the flames aboard the black boat. Finally, in desperation, many of the crew abandoned the boat and began jumping into the water to slowly make their way to the shore. The anchor ropes boat burnt through releasing the craft to drift away out into the flow of the Dund.

"Come!" said Traxxa quietly, "It's time for us to get up close and intimate. Kaira you can stay here with Jellick and watch. Jareck! Are you with us?"

"Mmmm hhmmm! Yes I am Traxxa!" Said Jareck hefting a short sword in one hand and his brutish axe in the other and followed rapidly after the Wolfaman. Jevan had already taken a step or two and together with Böder they emerged from the trees just as we lost sight completely of the black boat. Whilst I didn't see exactly what became of it, I am certain it began to sink beneath the surface of the water even as it merged with the Dund River before disappearing around the northern point of the bay.

In the bay however, I watched as fifteen crew members and twelve pirates (*those I recognized*) struggling in the water as they made their way to the shore. Just as they began to find their footing on the shoreline the two giants broke through the tree line and began attacking them with all the vengeance of ones who had been hounded, attacked and harassed. Traxxa was soon by their side, followed closely by Jareck, and together they killed in quick succession all of the pirates and thirteen of the crew. But neither Ranka nor Zharlla were seen in the water, on the boat, or among the dead.

Traxxa stopped the giants and Jareck from killing the last two crew members who were struggling just to stand up in the shallows of the river. From what I understood of it, he wanted to ask them questions about Zharlla the witch and what had become of her.

They seemed eager to give information to us about Zharlla, but every time either one of them opened their mouths to speak of her, no words would come out. They tried again and again but no word, no breath, no sound, no utterances; nothing came forth concerning the witch. Instead they told us willingly why they were where they were, that they had been instructed to follow the *Riverrock* but not to engage with her. They even told us they had followed us out of Regil-Ter and were associated with, but were not pirates themselves. But not a word did they utter about Zharlla the witch.

In silent, frustration, Traxxa bound their hands and marched them back to where the crew of the *Riverrock* were waiting patiently for us. It was late afternoon before we were able to place the two black boat

331

crew members into the hold alongside the three pirates. We now had five unwanted guests aboard the *Riverrock*. But we were not yet ready to resume our journey southwards. Traxxa, Captain Stemm and I talked together about why we were unable to leave just yet.

"Böder's Island needs replenishing!" I explained to Stemm. "Over the years there has been a constant poaching and illegal hunting of the boar and deer on his island. So much so that Böder's stock of deer and boar are dangerously low and the quality of these animals is desperately inferior to what they used to be. As part of our agreement with Böder, Traxxa and I are going off to try and capture a couple of stags and some deer and a similar number of boars and at least two sows whilst we are here on the mainland. So we thought we would begin by setting out to track and capture them when the *Riverrock* moors to rest over the next three nights.

"Yes!" Put in Traxxa at this point, "we thought we would begin tracking and capturing these animals tonight. As we seem to have vanquished the pirates and driven off those on the dark boat we thought we would begin to honour one of our pledges to Böder. What do you think of this?"

Captain Stemm was quick to voice his thoughts by saying. "As you are paying me for my time I am more than willing to allow you all the time you wish in order to help fulfil your part of the bargain that was originally agreed between you and Böder. My only request is that you ask some of my men to go with you as I am sure they would relish the opportunity of going hunting with you and Böder. After all, our own hunt for fresh meat didn't go too well this afternoon what with the discovery and destruction of the black boat. So by all means take all the time you want and we will accommodate you in whatever way we can!"

So when the day turned to night, Bartrow came out from his place in the hold and went promptly over to embrace Böder before the two of them led us on a wonderful chase throughout the land for both boar and deer. This continued to happen over the following three nights. During the day we would sail up river toward Böder's Island and during the night we would moor the *Riverrock* and go hunting and trapping for some good strong stock. Bartrow turned out to be an excellent hunter in the dark of the night, despite his age and temperament, and Böder was thrilled to be in fresh pursuit of good strong stock and excellent hunting game. Word quickly spread throughout the crew and even Captain Stemm joined the hunt on two of the nights such was the excitement and invigorating challenge. Each morning well before the first hint of dawn, the hunting party would return to the *Riverrock* and whatever stock had been caught alive was placed in care and the fresh meat was hung to be eaten the next day at the usual daily feast.

By the time Böder's Island finally came into view we had captured three young deer, two stags, four sows and two young boars as well as one mature boar. The mature boar I was told had been the hardest to track and capture alive. But Böder and now the budding hunter Jevan had done a marvellous job of not only capturing them but doing so without harming them in any way. And the lovely giantess had told me how much she had loved every minute of the hunt and the capture. Even Kaira had gone out on the last of the nightly hunts. She told me that she had enjoyed herself so much that she was sad to realize the trip was coming to a close and there were to be no more hunts for livestock on the mainland.

The prisoners were constantly watched and their bindings safely secured throughout their journey south. Only on one occasion, in all this time, did they try and attack and overwhelm Bartrow. This was done during the daylight hours but, to their regret, they sadly underestimated this sleeping troll. Before they even knew what had happened to them, in the dark confines of the hull, two of the prisoners -- both of them pirates -- were killed and the others subdued easily and quickly. Then, as was his due, Bartrow insulted the other prisoners by eating those he had killed in front of them without even bothering to cook the dead pirates. Funnily enough, Bartrow never had a problem with any of the prisoners ever again after that.

Midway through the fourth day, since destroying the black boat, we came around the last bend in the Dund River and there before us lay the dark formidable cliffs of Böder's Island. Captain Stemm sailed past the length of the island towing the boats where Böder and Jevan were still reclining. As we slowly passed the island, Böder was getting more and more excited. He would describe and point out to Jevan all the many wonderful features he believed his island had to offer. Frustratingly Captain Stemm sailed us about a kilometer and a half past the southernmost point of the island. He told me when I asked, he needed a good distance to successfully navigate the *Riverrock* and the two boats in tow across the dangerous currents of the Dund to the only place he knew of where the *Riverrock* could safely travel down into the heart of the island.

With unerring accuracy, Captain Stemm steered the *Riverrock* down the much smaller river that flowed from the Dund into the island. I remembered this river from my first time coming to the Dark Island in the middle of the night, what was it now? Just over four months earlier! I gasped slightly at the realization of the amount of time we had taken on this particular adventure. I turned to Traxxa by my side and told him of my personal revelation. He just smiled and said.

"You of all people should know that all good adventures need plenty of time to ferment before being brought to full maturity!"

Böder was getting more and more excited about finally getting home. So much so, the moment he found himself floating down his own river, he couldn't contain himself any longer. All of us aboard the *Riverrock* could only look on and smile as this overly large kid jumped out of his boat upsetting it badly and almost sinking it. He then helped Jevan off her boat and the two of them raced off disappearing almost immediately through the thick trees, bushes and shrubs along the riverbank.

But they were there with Barill and the islands cart on the open sandbank when the *Riverrock* came down the final stretch of river. Here Stemm dropped anchor midstream and we began the slow process of transferring all the passengers, stock and supplies from the *Riverrock* to the islands shore. The livestock were the first to come ashore. Böder and Jevan took each one gently and placed them in the pens until they were ready to be released into the wilds of the island as and when it was convenient.

Barill welcomed us all back with kind words and embraces. Kaira, Captain Stemm and the entire crew were introduced to this gentle retainer and he never ceased smiling for the rest of the day as he took in this sudden large entourage of guests, returning family and friends.

Jareck was also excited to be home, and took what can only be described as great personal delight in showing Kaira all that their island farm had to offer her. He, Kaira and Barill began preparing a great feast for everyone including the crew and the prisoners of the *Riverrock* in the field by the large lake.

By the first hint of the greying over in the sky with the coming of evening, the bulk of Böder's treasure had been transported to the rivers shore. As the last remaining chests of treasure were yet to be unloaded Böder approached the hand rail of the *Riverrock* and called out to Captain Stemm.

When the captain approached the side where the young giant was standing in the river, Böder said, with great feeling. "Those last three chests by the main mast yet to be taken ashore are to remain aboard and are to be divided between you and your crew as you see fit."

When Stemm started to protest that this was way too much for what they had done, Böder waved his hand to silence him.

"The first chest is to compensate you for getting us safely out of Regil-Ter, and the ordeal you and your crew suffered at the hands of the pirates and Zharlla on me and my friends' behalf. Consider the second chest a payment for the services rendered unto me and my friends which includes the hire of the *Riverrock*. And the third chest is my way of providing an insufficient apology for the loss of your first mate, your friend and cousin Eddron. Please pass what you wish from out of these chests onto his family on my behalf."

To make sure they understood fully what he was saying he pointed to the three chests he had deliberately set apart from the rest of his treasure.

There was an audible sound of silence as the captain and his entire crew, who had been watching and listening all this time, suddenly became gobstruck as they struggled to comprehend what they had just been told. And then as one they all cheered and screamed and embraced one another before dancing a little jig on the deck and thanking their big giant friend over and over again for his tremendous generosity. When they had settled down a little they recommenced offloading the remaining stores to the accompaniment of songs in praise of the generous giant to the tune of some of their own boating shanties.

Böder seemed to be almost overwhelmed by this sudden show of gratitude and the response he received from the crew of the *Riverrock*. But he returned to the shore and placed two chests of treasure at my feet and two more at the feet of Traxxa and one chest at Earlich's feet then kneeling before us said. "These chests are for you Jellick and one for you Earlich for leading me on the adventure of a lifetime. And of course, these two are for you my friend Traxxa for your help and support and training. I thank each of you deeply, with all my heart!"

I'm sure I saw an emotional tear budding from his eye, but I didn't care as Earlich, Traxxa and I moved in to embrace him as his size and conditions allowed.

When all the stores and treasure bound for the island were off the *Riverrock* some of the crew moved to pick up our personal chests of treasure and take them back to the boat. But as they moved to return Traxxa's chest to the boat, he stopped it and whispering to me and Stemm he said "I feel that my treasure would be much safer staying here with Böder on his island. What do you think?"

Captain Stemm, Earlich and I looked at each other and immediately we saw the logic of his reasoning. For myself, I saw that until I had specific plans to do with my portion of the treasure, the safest and best place to keep it would indeed be here with Böder on his island.

"Well then I suggest we ask Böder if he wants to take on the responsibility of holding onto and securing this vast amount of wealth on our behalf!" Traxxa said, "cause at the moment that is what I am intending to ask of him for myself."

In silent agreement, we called Böder down to us once more and each of us asked him if we could leave our chests of treasure in his care. As spokesmen for our party I told him. "We feel these would be safer here on your island than if we took them with us!"

"But that would mean if you wanted to access any part of your chests of treasure then you will have to come back here to pick it up?!

"Is there a problem with that happening?" Traxxa asked on our behalf.

"Why no, but that would mean we will be seeing each other again and again and I would really like that," Böder said with another of his huge boyish grins.

With this question resolved the rest of the day was spent unpacking the remaining goods and stock and taken up to Böder's cavern. When the sun finally disappeared altogether from the sky and darkness descended over the island, Bartrow came out onto the top deck of the *Riverrock* and looked around at his new home. Böder and Jareck and Jevan and Kaira were there to welcome him ashore and together they walked with him up to Böder's cavern beneath the mountain.

"This, Bartrow, is now your new home!" Böder said proudly.

"Take your time exploring it, but, for now, won't you come and join with us in celebrating our arriving home safely?" Jareck asked.

Bartrow nodded his head without answering, but I'm sure, by the soft light of the moon, I was sure I saw his ugly dark eyes glistening if that was possible. During our walk up to the cavern which was to be his place called home, Bartrow's possessions were carried by Böder personally.

We could all see that Bartrow was almost completely overwhelmed but he said nothing, just grinned. We left him to look around the cavern, checking out the chimney and Barill's workshop. That was when Barill made himself known to and also welcomed the young troll into his world. Immediately there was a connection between this master smithy and the son of a skilled troll. Böder and I were pleased to hear the old smith telling Bartrow that everything that was there was his to use as he so wished.

Then Böder, Jareck, Kaira, Jevan, Barill, Bartrow and I made our way back down towards where the huge campfire at the bottom of the farm near the lake was alight. Here we found Captain Stemm, Traxxa, Earlich and all the crew from the *Riverrock*, including the prisoners, eating drinking and celebrating the good fortunes of our first major adventure together with Böder.

EARLICH

As I sit and pen my last thoughts about our first time with Böder. I am pleased to announce that Böder and Jevan became a wonderful giant couple.

Jareck and Kaira also eventually teamed up as husband and wife, but that was to be expected.

The first thing Jevan and Kaira did, I was told and as I saw for myself, on our subsequent visits back to the island with my master Tor Jellick, was to add a female touch to the caverns. This was done in conjunction with moving the pig sty away from the front door and replacing it with a large and extensive herb and spice garden instead. In fact both front doors were replaced as well.

But we were more amazed to see how much Bartrow developed as he grew and how over time under the careful tutelage of Barill, he showed us the extent of his great skills in digging, designing and building tunnels and rooms. This included extending Böder and Jevan's cavern beneath the mountain

I was told he became the night sentinel on the island as well. Then he would roam free, killing and eating any would be intruders, thieves or hunters that were foolish enough to come stealthily to the island.

But all these and other stories about life on the island and many of their other adventures have yet to be penned about Bartrow the troll, Barill the smith, Jareck and Kaira the Bidomen and of course Jevan and Böder – 'the giants'!'

INDEX - DICTIONARY

A

AIYISHA: (Buffawman (*Half woman/half buffalo*) 11yr old rescued by Böder.

B

BARILL: (Larcoman (*Half man /half large cat*) Resident island smithy.

BARTROW: (Male Troll) Young troll rescued from Trow by Böder.

BERNITZ: Large river town on the Dund River.

BIARGAMOUTH: (Bearaman (*Half man/half bear*) Pirate tordan.

BLACK ISLAND: Island in the Dund to which Böder was exiled.

BöDER: (Giant (*Pronounced – bow-der as in bow-tie*) The hero of this tale.

BRAN-OCK: Seaway far to the north of the mainland of Durogg.

C

CALENDAR: (*or CALENDS*) Times and dates that this story is set within.

CAPTAIN STEMM: (*SEE STEMM*).

CENTRAL COUNTRIES: Group of countries within the central region of Durogg.

CONAGGER: (Name) The family name for a reputable line of merchants of which Jellick is the Tor and master of.

D

DAR: Another name of father or dad.

DARK/MOUNTAINS: Mountain range to the far east of the mainland of Durogg.

DATYIA: (Bidowman (*Half woman/half big dog*) Kaira's younger sister.

DOURATH: Name of a famous Buffaman family and house.

DRAGONS: As in the 'Time of the Dragons'.

DRAZIL: Large reptile that is both aggressive and carnivorous.

DRIKSAD: (Giant) Böders real father and first husband of Sheralie.

DUROGG: Continent on which these stories take place.

DUND: (River) Extending from the Tamanette Sea to the Bran-Ock Seaway.

E

EARLICH: (Weasalman (*Half man/half weasel*) Scribe recording Böder's adventure.

EDDRON: (Ottarman (*Half man/half otter*) 2nd in command of the Riverrock and Captain Stemms cousin.

ENTARIM: Country to the East and just North of M'Lenn-Fida.

F

FLOOK: River which runs from the mountains by Tungston to feed the Mirack River.

FRAHQ: (KING)

FRAHQ: (LAND/PEOPLE)

FRISHA: (Ottarman (*Half man/half otter*) Old boatman on the Dund out of Bernitz.

FROWASH: Country to the far East and North of M'Lenn-Fida.

G

GAROG: (Troll) Bridge troll, guardian into Trows territory.

GLEMM: (Money) The name of the gold standard used in Durogg.

GLOAS: A desert wasteland to the East of M'Lenn-Fida across the river Dund.

GORDESH: House of Scribes to which Earlich is the last known son of.

GRONTIC: (Animal) Large furry rodent like creatures.

GRU-NISH-DAN: Country south of M'Lenn-Fida

H

HADYES: Durogg mythology depicts that Hadyes is 1 of 7 hells.

HALLAS: (Expression (*Soft swear word*) Meaning the end of it.

HECKILTY BACK: A mountain chicken much like a roadrunner.

HOPPERMEN: (Half man/half grasshopper) or 'Hoppers'.

I

IBERN: City on the Dund half way between Regil-Ter and Katra.

J

JACK THE GIANT KILLER: The legendary story attributed to Jareck.

JARECK: (Bidoman (*Half man/Half big dog*) Dark skinned Bidoman.

JARCK: (Bidoman (*Half man/Half big dog*) Bidoman father of Jareck.

JEION: (Country) North of M'Lenn-Fida and its capital city is Ardoin.

JELLICK: (Badgarman (*Half man/half badger*) Merchant and author of these tales.

JEVAN: (Giantess) Mother is black and Father is a white giant. She is born in Korgan.

JUDICIAL GAMES: The games set up to entertain the masses of M'Lenn-Fida.

JUDGEMENT GAMES: (*SEE - JUDICIAL GAMES*).

K

KAEL: (Ottarman (*Half man/half otter*) Old fisherman who helps Böder.

KAIRA: (Bidowman (*Half woman/half big dog*) Seamstress and Böder's friend.

KATRA: (City) Known as the 'City of Islands'.

KAYLA: (Bidowman (*Half woman/half big dog*) Is the older sister of Kaira.

KHEDD: (Swear word) Meaning unclear but it is a fairly disgusting swear word.

KORGAN: (Country) To the west of M'Lenn-Fida and the Taka Mountains.

KYRACK: (Buffaman (*Half man/half buffalo*) Captain of the Judicial Games.

L

LEAGUE: Distance of some 3 miles or 5kms.

LEVIATH: Large mythical 2 headed water serpent.

LIGHT CRYSTAL: Elemental light/lamp charged and controlled by hand.

M

MANIMALS: Rulers and main inhabitants of Durogg. Half human half animal.

MAR: Another name for mother or mom.

MERABETH: (Buffawman (Half woman/half buffalo) Mother of Aiyisha.

MINK: (Swear word) Short form of minkle.

MINKA: (Swear word) Alternate form of minkle.

MINKLE: (Swear word) Soft form of a swear word in Durogg.

MIRACK: (River) Runs east from the Taka Mountains down to the Dund.

MIRNAULTE: (Sea).

M'LENN-FIDA: The main country in which the first story of Böder takes place.

MUXTLA: (Male Giant) 1st known resident giant at the judicial games of Regil-Ter.

N

NYANG: Country to the North and West of M'Lenn-Fida.

O

ORDON: (Buffaman (Half man/half buffalo) Brother of Aiyisha.

OZORKON: (Buffaman (Half man/half buffalo) Father of Aiyisha. Head of the house of Dourath.

P

PIROSTELLOSTIC: The name of the age in which these stories take place.

PLEBIARY: (Class) To do with the introduction of the Codes to Durogg.

R

RANKA: (Bearaman *(Half man/half bear)* Second in command to Biargamouth of the pirates.

REGIL-TER: (City) Capital city of M'Lenn-Fida.

RIBARD: (Lizarman *(half man, half lizard)* Cursed and changed into a toad but revealed to be a Lizarman.

RIBBET: *(SEE RIBARD)*

RIVERROCK: Name of Captain Stemms boat.

ROD: Length *(measurement)* - One rod equalling five feet.

RUGILAS: Nomadic warlike people living in the Gloas Wastelands.

S

SCINTAIRE: Mountain range which lies between Stengh and Entarim.

SEHOLD: Mountain range which lies between Stengh and the Gloas.

SHAYLA: (Bidowman *(Half female/half big dog)*. Kaira's older sister.

SLEV: Money. The name given to the standard measure of silver in Durogg.

SNIGGLE: Cross between a snigger and a giggle.

SNOT ROCK: Rocks formed from the expelled snot from trolls.

STEMM: (Ottarman *(Half man/half otter)* Ships Captain of the Riverrock.

STENGH: Country to the far north and East of M'Lenn-Fida.

SUCCOTH: Serpent god worshipped as a cult.

T

TAKA: Large mountain range extending from Nyang in the north down to Gushtaka.

TAMANETTE: (Inland Sea) Massive fresh water sea to the south of M'Lenn-Fida.

TERRON: (Bidoman (*Half man/half big dog*) Kaira's father.

TOR: (Title) Another name for Lord, master or head of the family.

TORDAN: (Title) Means over lord or another name for king, emperor, shah or ruler.

TRAXXA: (Wolfaman (*Half man/half wolf*) From the family of the timber wolf. Head of Jellick's security and becomes Böder's personal trainer.

TROW: Mountain Troll living in the first mountains of the Taka Mountains.

TUNGSTON: Village on the edge of the Taka Mountains in west M'Lenn-Fida.

U

UCRAY: Language. Common language of the people in all the lands of Durogg.

UNDORYCK: (Country) To the far south and west of M'Lenn-Fida.

W

WIZARDS: Magic makers and with the help of the giants helped rid the land of the dragons.

WOODLORE: It is a type of knowledge or form.

WURKE: Village near where Böder and Jareck were born.

X

XALARLLA: (*Pronounced Shalarlla*) Name given to Jevan by Zharlla when she was first captured and imprisoned.

Z

ZELAKS: Village in the country of Frowash.

ZHARLLA: (Vixawman (*Half female/half fox*) - Mysterious witch

WRITERS DEVELOPMENT

In 1980 I began writing the epic tales of 'Hergon' and 'Andoiz'. To facilitate these heroic characters I drew up a land which I called Durogg. This land was largely inspired by the map/land that Robert E. Howard drew up for his creation '*Conan the Barbarian*' and is loosely modelled on Europe (*well my Durogg is anyway*), the Mediterranean and North Africa.

During the early 1990's, after reading the BFG by Roald Dahl, I began planning a story about a giant. My reasoning at the time and up to its publication was that no-one has really written a story that is solely about the struggles that a giant might have in the days when people lived by the sword nor the adventures which they might have had to contend with at this time. Since then of course there have been a number of films and stories that have come out about lands where giants may have played a part. However, the character of a giant has still to be presented as the central figures in any of these stories.

My premise for writing about Böder was initially to find out for myself what kind of adventures, challenges, and hardships one might encounter should it be experienced through the character of a giant. Add to this the advantage of height and strength and discover a whole new kind of interaction a giant might have with the people within his environment, as well as the difficulties of coping with the incidents of a world where strength, violence and abnormal creatures and abilities are an everyday part of life.

But more than just the difficulties in all this, I also wanted to explore the fun things that a giant might encounter that we as humans don't even have to think about or consider. This, of course, is because everything around us has been designed to meet our needs, with particular reference to our size. For instance what are the considerations and planning needed just to meet the everyday items and requirements for someone who is perhaps 4-5 times bigger than we are. Such items as clothes, shoes, tools, (*including personal grooming and eating implements*) then of course there are the essentials such as sleeping on a bed, sitting down in a chair, and how would you plan travelling or simply moving about. To consider many or all of these things required some thought to detailing which I am able to do through the character of Böder.

Then there are some of the daily considerations that we wouldn't give a second thought to because everything in our lives has been designed to meet our present-size needs. Things such as the regular consumption of food, what and how does one observe personal ablutions, such as wash oneself, clean your teeth, or even brush your hair! Then there is the consideration of how to deal with such things as what would a giant do if you got drunk or sick including what type and doses of medicines would be effective. Then there are some things that we might never even have considered, such as what would a giant do to relax, train to keep fit, plan a working day and even down to how to dispose of your own giant waste.

Then I began to consider what kind of people would want to interact or even enjoy being around a giant, such as friends, workmates, hunters/ fishermen, salespeople? Then there is the consideration of what type of work would a giant do.

(Don't you get so annoyed with the creators of 'superheroes' who, when they write them into a working environment, never allow their characters to use their super powers in the working world. The best example I can think of is Superman – a reporter?

Really is that the best they can come up with.

Superman would be so much better working in the construction/ mining industry lifting and moving heavy and awkward equipment and products. Or, what about the transport industry? He could move containers and freight around so much faster and much more expediently than anyone or thing could ever do! But the best work ever would be in environmental areas. For instance disposing of harmful radioactive materials by taking them to another planet such as Mercury or Venus! – Something no-one else could do but be useful to the community or the world as a whole for goodness sake!

Spiderman!!! Really - is a pizza delivery guy followed by a photographer the best they could come up with? Give me a break!)

Anyway!!!)

Following on from there, I was wondering what a giant would need to do or be able to do to raise funds or even make for themselves a successful living. How would he be able to continually pay for the over-large and giant things he needs/wants/desires such as food clothing and other essential items. And how would he go about having everything made to meet his own special height, size, weight, strength and daily needs?

And finally, if I've created a giant I need to put him in a place that would best suit their special skills and be able to fit comfortably in with their surroundings. Furthermore, I need to place my giant in a world that would be acceptable to the reader. So I decided to place my giant in this land that I had made up for my heroic characters 15 years earlier.

One of the main attributes of the stories around Durogg was that all the characters revolved around the introduction of codes and the Codemasters. This structure and aspect of Durogg has little or no impact on the character of my giant, as that story is for another time and for another set of characters and incidents. However, in the early 2000's I added to the general make-up of Durogg the concept of having all the characters operating as manimals. This means all the main characters of Durogg are both half-human and half-animal. There was the intention, on my part, to develop the idea of evolution as part of the makeup of the manimals. This also falls neatly into place with the structure and story of the codes and their masters that I will introduce at a later stage in the development of the beings and characters associated with Durogg. The concept of the manimals has, however, added a whole other dimension to all my stories associated with this land and I am still working out the full implications of this as I apply these structures and principles to each of my stories and watch how they develop.

However, my giant story didn't need to work with the codes and the Codemasters, as I mentioned earlier, mainly because these things happened after the time allocated to the giant. However the concept of the manimals was an interesting addition and might well add to the flavour and intricacies of the giant and at present I can't see how it would detract from him at all. Though, to be fair, to the story of Böder I have not overplayed the manimal aspect which will be taken up more thoroughly in my other stories concerning Durogg in the form of the characters Hergon and, in particular, Andoiz.

But still, I felt comfortable enough in placing my giant(s) in this land of Durogg and more importantly amongst a land of creatures that had yet to be fully described but one in which they would quite easily fit in and have room for later development.

In considering the story of a giant, the first thing I needed was a name. My first thoughts regarding a giant were of a Norseman with their myths of giants, trolls and ogres and other gigantic creatures. One day as I sat thinking on this giant character from northern Europe I envisioned a giant chasing down some hapless hunters who were stealing/poaching his stock. From this the name of Böder simply ran off the tip of my tongue and together with him being hungry and wanting to frighten those he was chasing the words continued and I came up with...

'Böder hungry, he wants his deanah! Heh heh deanah! Böder is hungry and he's coming after you - heh heh heh heh!!!!'

I mean, how scary would that be? Imagine being in a game park in Africa and a huge male lion walks up to you, whilst you are sitting, where you believe you are safe, in your vehicle or on a tour bus and it stands upright on its back legs and speaks to you saying

'I'm hungry and I want to eat you - heh heh heh!

And then begins to climb into what you thought was your safe haven.

With the name of my giant chosen, the next thing about Böder was to give him his statistics. That is how big he is? I continually need to reference his size, not only on how big he is physically, but proportionally such as his arms, head, his appearance, his fingers and especially his appetite. But then there were other incidental things to consider, such as his clothes even down to the length of his legs to make up for the average length of his stride. After all, wouldn't you like to know as well as I what would he eat in a day, what would he wear, that kind of thing. So I have in my mind a giant that is 4 times the size of a normal man with the intent of taking him to maybe 5 or even 6 times the size of a man as he ages and grows.

Whilst going through this thought process, I began to realize that Böder would have to have come from a family. What then would he have been like when he was younger and smaller? How would he have been treated, how did he come about to be in the situation that he finds himself and general thoughts along that line.

I realized, whilst I could have a giant at say 20 years of age or so, where did he come from and how did he come to be where he was. So I began to plan and write his history and how he came to be friends with whomever was with him. I didn't want him alone, simply because it is much harder to learn things as quickly and develop in the direction I want to take him if he's on his own.

Originally I had Böder being rescued by an old man who taught him how to look after himself. But where did I want to put Böder? I thought about this and then thought about what I would do if I was part of a community and had to deal with the problem of an unwanted giant. I couldn't simply kill him because then there would of course be no story about a giant. So I came up with the idea of an island and later a sound reason why the local communities wanted to keep him out there alive.

So now I had the island idea. However, the crucial thing for this story is; why would this giant want/have to stay there and furthermore, why wouldn't the local communities have killed him in the first place?

But even this presented itself with a number of problems of their own, such as what would this giant do to survive ie food, shelter things like that. So I needed to make the island big enough with food and personal challenges on it and someone (*an older person perhaps*) instructing and showing him how not to consume everything on the island at once and preserving enough to live comfortably for a long time as well.

The next thought process was how do I get this giant onto the island and I came up with 'Jack the giant killer' who was there to help rid the communities of the troublesome giant(s) in the first place. As I was working out the complexities of Jacks character, his motives for wanting to rid the world of giants and his involvement with Böder I came up with the history of Jack and how it was intertwined with Böder.

At this point, to break from the name association, I changed the name of Jack to Jarck and tied it in with the relationship he had with his son. Then finally to tidy up the history process I needed to show how this related to how the community felt towards this giant. I needed to make this a 'strong feeling', for, in fact, it was this nebulous feeling of the community rather than the individual which really helped to fashion or define the 'giant killer' image that Jack/Jarck had in this instance and was to become known for.

As I looked at how to develop Böder further, I fashioned his history and the structure to keep him in check and where I wanted him to grow up and mature. It was at this point that I decided to make Jareck (*Jarcks son*) emotionally tied to Böder through his own involvement as to how Böder had become an outcast. There were problems that had to be overcome such as how Jareck got Böder to the island and why this island in particular became so important. I also needed to expound on the different skills they would need to ensure they could survive for as long as they did.

Once Böder's history and relational attachments had been established, I then, of course, to make the story interesting and exciting, still needed special adversaries that would seriously challenge both Böder's size and strength as well as his intellect and personality. And this is where the interaction between the manimals and the giant(s) began to merge. For if he has such adversaries that are his equal then what kind of training would he need before he was to meet with them and how would he best deal with them. From this came, what kind of skills do I want him to learn, and then of course, who would I get to teach him and why? Then there is how do I enable him to come out victoriously and also what kind of weapons if any would he use or need? But more importantly where would he get these weapons? Who would make them and how would he maintain them ie clean, fix/repair, upgrade them and how would he learn to use them properly. I mean just because he has a sword or a club doesn't make him a swordsman or a warrior or even a barbarian.

And so the story of my giant in this land grew and evolved.

In the final development of Böder and working out how to write his story, I was wondering how to present this giant to the world. It was from this that I began thinking about who would a. Have the resources or capabilities to tell Böder's story particularly in the time frame and b. Why would anyone want to write about him (*apart from me that is*) and from this came the idea of who would have the greatest interest in presenting Böders story and still be able to do it effectively?

I needed to create an interesting author, one that would not only want to write about the life of a giant but, more importantly, within this setting have the resources to do so properly and with some skill. I had a number of different individuals who could or would want to write Böders story at this time but I decided I wanted to have a merchant of some description pen his story. My reason for this is because a merchant is someone who could not only see the potential in befriending a giant but could actually make something out of him and perhaps use him for his own personal objectives. To this end this merchant would then have a reason to help this giant to reach his full potential – if only for his own selfish reasons.

It was then that I remembered, in some of my stories from the land of Durogg, I had created a character who was a master merchant who went by the name of Jellick. The structure of these stories was slightly different from what I had envisioned for Böder but nothing so dramatic that they couldn't be interwoven somehow. So if Jellick was to interact with Böder then I would have to put Böder in a place where Jellick would actually have the opportunity to meet up with him.

First off I had Böders history, and those he had relationships with around him. He had his own house (*well cave*) and land, a few trifling adversaries, and a sound reason for wanting him alive. And now I had someone who was willing and interested in writing Böders story. But the most important thing is, (because I was putting Böder into Durogg, and the writer was an intricate character from Durogg,) I had unwittingly placed Böder in an established well-documented land.

This may not mean much to many people, but to me this included a calendar which placed the story both in time and also in a cultural and a social environment. But more than this, it was the character of Böder who helped me to paint a fuller more colourful picture of Jellick who through these stories was also developing into both the manimal and the merchant I wanted him to be. Surprisingly enough, Jellick can now slip quite naturally back into his own story at a later stage in the development of Durogg. But above and beyond all that, because of Böder and the introduction of his history, I have also added a whole new dimension to my other stories that are related to the lands of Durogg.

Through Böder, I have been able to expound and consolidate the concept of the manimals living in the lands of Durogg, and introduced stories around the giants, the dragons, trolls, and formulated plans concerning wizards and witches which I hadn't, *(as yet)* introduced into any of my other stories concerning Durogg.

As I began writing about Böder and Jareck and how they were brought back into the community, through their stories brought to life by a merchant, I wanted to give a specific reason why the merchant would become so involved with this giant. After much thought on the matter, I came up with a number of reasons why a merchant would want to interact with Böder. The first and most obvious is what a merchant could sell with a specific market in mind. But the most compelling story would be to use him to regain a personal loss that would involve danger and a real threat to life. From this I came up with Traxxa who would become Böders private mentor and trainer. This also gave me a reason and someone who would help me to develop the character of Böder into the fighter and warrior, tracker, hunter and general tough guy I wanted to turn him into. By introducing Traxxa I would also be able to direct Böder towards a greater sense of independence and growth, both as a fighter and as an individual whilst still maintaining his relationship with Jareck and without compromising the integrity of Böder's character.

One day my daughter Jane came to me to see if I would help her develop a story about a princess overcoming adversity for a school project. So together we came up with Sasha and her involvement with a bridge troll. It was only supposed to be a single page story and she departed from the story with her own name and predicament and eventually a whole new story. But the story of Sasha had come about and whilst the majority of the story was very silly I decided to take some of the core ideas and change it to become a small story in its own right. So I changed her name from Sasha to Keira and *(after hearing someone already had the name Keira I changed it to Kaira)* eventually Kaira and gave her a bit of a background and I ended up with her story complete in its own way.

As I was developing Jellick's involvement in Böders life and trying to get him to act on his behalf by confronting a mountain troll I saw an excellent opportunity where the story of Kaira might interact with Böder. It was only afterwards that I saw how the character of Kaira might become a permanent fixture in the stories of Böder. From this I gave her skills which would help make her useful and interesting to both Böder and Jareck.

The story of Ribbard was essentially a dangling loose end. In the story of Sasha she was supposed to kiss the toad, (*despite him being toxic*) whereupon she was to fall asleep and when she awoke Ribbet was to have become a prince and takes her away to live happily ever after in his castle - wherever. But, in Böders story, this scenario didn't seem to work. So when I tried to tidy Ribbet up, it somehow began to take on a life of its own and the character evolved to Ribbard and eventually the story that has been presented. And now it seems the character of Ribbard and his association with Zharlla and interplay with Böders crew has become an entity in its own right. Now that this character has developed to where it is, I can see where Ribbard might play a much greater role, perhaps in later tales of Böder and possibly in other stories from Durogg, than I had at first imagined.

Zharlla is another character that I have taken from the chronicles and stories of Durogg. She was an interesting enough character in her own right but has since gained a bit of colour and depth because of Böder. Initially, I had only intended that she appear so she could take responsibility for and deal with Ribbard to get him out of the story. However Zharlla helped provide me with a bit of background for Ribbard and she may or may not have anything more to do with Böder. But if I was to include her in any more of Böder's stories I can see that it would give me the opportunity to outline some of my own views on witches and warlocks and their role in my land of Durogg. But for now I can't see how she will have very much more to do with any of Böders other stories. But I could be wrong, look how wrong I was about Ribbet/Ribbard!

And then I came up with Jevan. I have known and loved the female name 'Jevan' for a long time ever since I actually met a real life Jevan in the early 1980's when I was living in York England. I needed to give Jevan a reason to leave her environment and want to be with Böder. So I saw where she could be more involved with Zharlla. From this I had to come up with her history and this, of itself, added a whole new dimension to the stories associated with Böder's stories including that of a love interest and a compatible companion for Böder. But even more than that, it also allows me to introduce the concept of a handsome giant and a beautiful giantess having sex or at the very least intimate relationships! After all - why can't giants have and enjoy sex as well? *(If this really did happen I could see where the earth could move for them!)*

As with any super or unrivalled hero it is important to have an equally impressive adversary or at the very least one who is both challenging, threatening and exciting. We've had that in our first picture of the drazil *(lizard backwards in case you're wondering)*, the troll and now we have the hint of a witch with powers to ascend and confront even so formidable a hero as a giant. The trick is to come up with adversaries who are not so much as big or as strong but more subtle, more dangerous and more devious presenting Böder with challenges both intellectually as well as in strength and cunning. Not only this but that Böder might come to terms with his shortcomings despite his size and strength and still have to rely on others including friends and family.

When I first came up with the concept of a giant I had often thought how fantastic a spectacle it would be to have him/her fighting in the arena as in the style of the gladiators. I was planning on putting that scenario into my second story about Böder, however with the introduction of both Jevan and also Zharlla; I saw an opportunity to bring this scenario forward. Whilst initially I had a couple of adversaries that were equal to, or perhaps even stronger, than our giant.(ie a troll and a drazil), there was still the concept of Böder protecting himself. This changed to encompass his friends and family and now it has changed again where he now feels he is responsible for or the protector of a the love interest in his life.

But this is not, as we shall see, the giant being restricted because of his love, but rather a whole new dimension of giant aggression. And this may not only come from Böder! After all, who knows what the character of Jevan will bring to any of our follow up stories. We see glimpses of where these two will take us, as together they deal with a whole range of inferior enemies, such as those from within the gladiatorial games, the hoppers in the fields, and the pirates on the water. Each has their own kind of threat such as overwhelming numbers, to the complexities of threats to loved ones and the intentions and poisons from unseen adversaries.

All these and more will constantly challenge and help develop the character and skills of our friend 'Böder the giant'.

I guess at this point I should outline or at least go into greater detail of my use of the manimals in my story about Böder.

Manimals is, for my part, the level of evolutionary development that exists in my world on Durogg. They are the largest number of inhabitants on the continent of Durogg. A manimal is basically a person who is 1 half a human and the other half an animal of some description. A manimal can and will move around freely as a normal human but in moments of stress or as one chooses they will expand into the animal half as best suits their needs at the time. A manimal in general will look like a human for the most part but will have strong animal overtones or traits that will help make up their background. This may be in the skin coloring, eyes, ears, hair, or even some particular physical attributes such as horns, snout, mouth and tails or claws. Some may even be determined by their build such as wide shoulders or a particular gait or movement. Pigs, dogs and cats are destined to remain the last of the domesticated animals to retain their basic human qualities.

Some of the reasons horses, cows, sheep and all types of fowl never developed beyond their animal state can be attributed to either being too proud ie the horse and the deer, too dumb, sheep and cows or too pig headed such as the boar the elephants, hippos and the larger lizards. These animals will choose to remain in their animal form and will be very rarely seen to evolve into their manimal state. The only birds known to develop human qualities are the eagle, vulture/condor, and the Larwans *(large swans)* and of course the dragons. No fish of course - though it is said that some dragons and a few drazils or large reptiles including crocodiles/alligators have been known to possess the human element *(remember Ribbard)*. Then of course there are Leviaths which have yet to be introduced, at least in this story about Durogg.

Most manimals are restricted by size. For instance small rodents such as mice and rats never became manimals though grontics were thought to be rats trying to evolve. Still, the smallest creatures to retain their manimal characteristics are the Badgarmen, Ottarmen, Weasalmen and Wolvarmarines. Very few Skunkamen or Porkapiemen exist, instead they developed a whole other set of survival skills in their genetic makeup. And then finally there are those manimals that have been made into myths and legends such as the Centaur, the Minotaur, the Satyr, and some of the other

357

ancient Egyptian gods. But we shall see in time whether I will employ the use of any of these creatures or if they will actually help in developing any of my other stories concerning the land of Durogg.

So there you have in these few pages the working structure and developmental strategies I have given time and effort to in creating this particular story about 'Böder the giant'.

Please enjoy!

Thanx everyone for reading my story - Yours eternally grateful – T.J.C.

PS: I'm thinking of writing an extensive version of the story concerning 'Trow - the mountain troll'. That in my mind would be fascinating story to tell. Please let me know if anyone would be interested in reading about a psychopathic, underground or night time only killing creature. And why does he dress so well for a troll and keep his lair and his weapons so well maintained and why does he enjoy killing manimals?

You can contact me through email – tjcboder@gmail.com

Printed in the United States
By Bookmasters